New Yor

Vivian Arend

"If you've never read a Vivian Arend book you are missing out on one of the best contemporary authors writing today."

~ *Book Reading Gals*

"The bitter cold of Alberta, Canada, is made toasty warm by the super-sexy Coleman brothers of Six Pack Ranch."

~ *Publishers Weekly*

"Brilliant, raw, imaginative, irresistible!!"

~ *Avon Romance*

"This story will keep you reading from the first page to the last one. There is never a dull moment…"

~ *Landy Jimenez*

"I definitely recommend to fans of contemporaries with hot cowboys and strong family ties.."

~ *SmexyBooks*

"This was my first Vivian Arend story, and I know I want more! "

~ *Red Hot Plus Blue Reads*

"In this steamy new episode in the "Six Pack Ranch" series, Trevor is a true cowboy hero and will make any reader's heart beat a little faster as he and Becky discover what being a couple is all about."

~ *Library Journal Starred Review*

Rocky Mountain Devil

Vivian Arend

This is a work of fiction. Names, characters, places, and incidents either are the product of the author's imagination or are used fictitiously, and any resemblance to any persons, living or dead, business establishments, event, or locales is entirely coincidental.

Rocky Mountain Home
Copyright 2017 by Vivian Arend
ISBN: 978-1544130040
Edited by Anne Scott
Cover by Angela Waters
Proofed by Sharon Muha

Prologue

February, somewhere in rural Alberta

Jesse Coleman was lost.

He cursed as he spread the old-fashioned road map in front of him on the dash, the dim light from the overhead lamp not helping as he peered at the thin lines representing secondary roads. He'd grown up driving the back roads of rural Alberta, but mostly in the central parts. He was far enough out of familiar territory that with the snow falling like a thick curtain, he could barely find his own ass.

GPS was no help, and he gave up. No way he was making it any farther tonight. He needed a place to get off the road and out of the snow.

He was shoving the map back in the glove box when, miracle of miracles, headlights appeared behind him, coming over the rise. At least it meant he wasn't completely screwed. The truck slowed as it passed him, people with unfamiliar faces offering a friendly wave as they sent a swirl of fresh fallen snow flying skyward.

Jesse threw his truck into gear and hauled ass, horse trailer and all, following the red taillights like a beacon.

Fifteen minutes later the snow slowed enough to let the lights of a motel sign shine the first hope on his

1

miserable evening. It wasn't going to be pretty, but it was better than sleeping in his truck.

A small shelter with a fenced paddock stood behind the main office, so he got his horse settled, then slipped into the room he'd been given at the end of the motel row.

A single glance was enough to confirm what he'd already suspected. "Jeez. End of the fucking world, and I've found it."

Puke-green bedspread. A black velvet painting screwed to the wall over the bed — *classy*. The wood paneling on the lower half of the walls was so bashed up it looked as if someone had taken a hammer to it. One shelf hung on the wall with a two-foot-long bar under it, a few metal coat hangers tangled in a mess. The carpet — threadbare and stained.

He didn't dare look in the bathroom.

Still, one night was all he needed.

"I've slept in worse," he told Morgan.

His dog didn't seem to believe him as the animal worked his way around the entire room before picking a spot by the door to curl up. As if to say *he* was ready to leave anytime Jesse came to his senses and said the word.

Jesse patted Morgan on the head, rubbing the golden retriever behind the ears affectionately. "I hear you, but I need a drink. No, I need a couple of drinks," he told the dog. "Stay, and be good. Tomorrow we'll figure out how to get to our new home."

Morgan thumped his tail once then put his head down and closed his eyes.

End of the world, all right, but even in the boonies there was bound to be liquor.

The rooms stretched in a long arm west of the motel

office. On the other side was a small café and bar. Jesse paced past the *closed* sign in the café door, headed for where music was spilling from behind the neon-lit *saloon* sign.

The words he'd said to his dog haunted him as he pushed through the door. *Home*. They didn't have one right now, and this bar just made it all the clearer they weren't in familiar territory.

The place was not much more than three stools at a high counter, a couple of tables with hard wooden chairs and a dartboard on the wall. A large-screen TV hung over the bar, a hockey game in progress, but Jesse's attention shot straight to the redhead at the counter, glasses lined up in front of her as if she was settling in for a long, intense bout of drinking.

Sounded like a fucking great idea.

The wind caught the bar door, slamming it shut behind him, and all eyes turned in Jesse's direction. Two old-timers nursing drinks in the corner. The bartender behind the counter.

Her…

The woman's gaze brushed him, lingering on the bruise beside his eye before slipping down his body then back up, her lips twisting into a smile. He offered one in return.

Buxom redheads were his favourite.

Her hair was braided back, the long length of it pulled forward to rest over her plaid-covered breast. Tight faded jeans, working leather belt. Light brown leather half-boots that looked worn and comfy.

She must have felt his gaze lingering because she glanced up to offer him a glimpse into grey-green eyes, a smattering of freckles over her nose and cheeks.

Then she ignored him, motioning at the bartender as he brought forward yet another glass.

Jesse was intrigued. He made his way next to her. "Looks like a party in the making. Want a little company?"

"Knock yourself out," she offered.

He settled onto the barstool and waved at the bartender. "I'll have what she's having."

The grey-haired man stepped forward and held out a hand. "Then you'll be giving me your car keys."

Sounded as if some serious drinking was about to happen. Fine by him.

"I'm staying." Jesse showed his room key.

Bartender didn't move. "That decreases your chances of freezing in a snow bank, but I still want your keys. You can pick them up at the front desk in the morning."

Whatever. He tossed them over before leaning closer to the redhead to offer his hand. "Jesse."

"Dare." She shook his hand, her grip strong, and her palms rough enough to prove she wasn't wearing the cowboy gear as a costume.

"A working woman. I like that."

Dare took a sip from the lone glass of water in front of her, amusement rising. "You look the type who likes a lot of things about women."

Jesse shrugged. "What can I say? I'm a happy guy."

This time she looked him over for longer, her gaze lingering on what was soon to be a spectacular blue-purple bruise by his eye. "You like getting in fights?"

"Sometimes, but this?" He stroked a finger down the side of his face. "Farewell present from my cousin. Disagreement."

She met his gaze. Judging. Weighing him. "Oh. That thing guys do."

"Express our opinions with our fists? Yeah. It's a pretty natural form of communication for most men." Her gaze dropped and she stared at his lips. "You fighting over a woman?"

He honestly didn't know how to answer that. "Not a fight, but there was definitely a woman involved."

She snorted. "I bet. There's *always* a woman involved."

Jesse took the opportunity to admire her in more detail. Her hair shone in the lights above the bar, the deep auburn highlights flashing as she moved. A slight indent showed on the crown where she'd been wearing a cowboy hat, and his interest grew even stronger. "So, Dare, why're we having a party?"

"It's a wake," she corrected him. "Ten years they've been gone, and five since I started the tradition. But you don't need the details."

"Whatever you say." He eyed the drinks lining up in front of them. "I'm not going anywhere tonight."

He might have been curious, but he didn't need to know what she was commemorating. He knew what he was saying goodbye to, and he could finish most of the alcohol on the shelf without putting a dent in his pain.

Jesse lifted the first glass of amber liquid, three full fingers in the tumbler. Raised it in a salute to Dare. "Here's to forgetting everything except the pretty lady by my side."

Her lips curled at the corners, but she touched glasses with him before tipping the drink back and finishing it in a few swallows. Her throat moved smoothly, and he stared, mesmerized, until she lowered the glass to the counter with a solid crash.

She wiped her mouth with the back of her hand before pointing at his glass. "You drinking or watching?"

The whiskey was smooth — far too smooth to be tossed back like a dirty shot. He took a little more time and let the liquid linger on his tongue, looking her over with appreciation. "We're not going anywhere tonight," he pointed out. "There's no need to rush."

Dare nodded once. "I usually do this by myself. I forgot there's conventions involved with social drinking." She picked up the second glass. "To the guy who reminded me it's okay to slow down and taste the whiskey."

Another toast. Another touch of their glasses together. This time she rolled the liquid over her tongue before she swallowed, eyes closing as she lifted the glass in an additional silent, internal toast.

As for Jesse, this one was for his twin brother, Joel. His other half — although that hadn't been true for a good long while. Their separation, his own damn fault.

He finished the drink and lowered the glass to the counter a little harder than he should have, the bartender keeping a careful eye on them.

Two more whiskeys sat on the counter. Dare motioned toward them. "I'll pay. I like the company so far, and it'll be no fun if you have to stop before we're finished."

"I have no problems lasting. I'll take you to the finish line."

When she smiled, her eyes lit up, a dimple denting her right cheek. By the time they'd finished their third glass of whiskey, Jesse was tempted to lean over to take a taste of her.

"Your local bar?" he asked.

"Hell, no." She stared into her glass. "I tried drinking too close to home the first year, and my brothers showed up. Where's the fun in that?"

6

Jesse took note of the information. She had family somewhere. "Good to know you've got someone looking after you."

She raised a brow. "Do I look as if I need a babysitter, sweetheart? Last time I checked I was a big girl. I can make my own damn mistakes."

He rested his arm along the back of her chair as they tipped the next drink, the liquid tingling against his throat and gums as he took the hit. Dare turned toward him, half laughing, her eyes bright as she met his gaze, and for a second Jesse couldn't breathe.

Right then he could have sworn he was twelve feet tall and invincible.

They put their glasses on the counter at the exact same moment, and a sudden *crack* echoed. Dare cursed, lifting her fingers to her mouth, her glass lying broken in pieces on the counter.

"You okay?" Jesse asked as the bartender slipped over to clean up the shards.

Dare pulled back her hand and examined it as she wrinkled her nose. "I'll live."

"Not your fault," the bartender consoled her. "Looks as if we got a bad batch of glassware — next drink is on the house, okay?"

"No worries."

Jesse slipped his hand off the backrest and onto her shoulder. "You need a Band-Aid?"

She held up her hand, the minute cut barely visible. "It's fine. Unless you wanna kiss it better?"

Oh, that he could do. He slid his fingers into the heavy weight of her auburn hair. Her mouth opened slightly, her tongue slipping over her lips as she stared. There wasn't a single sign of retreat anywhere about her.

7

VIVIAN AREND

Jesse leaned in to brush their lips together for a split second. Teasing, taunting. Just to prime her senses.

She caught him in a full-on hug, wrapping her arms around his neck and keeping him close as her lips parted and let him in.

Instead of a brief taste he got the equivalent of chugging a full twenty-sixer of the essence of Dare. Instantly higher than a kite, his mind reeled as he slid his tongue against hers, upper bodies close enough the soft curve of her breasts pressed against his chest.

When they pulled back, they were both breathing hard. Staring at each other, hunger and desire rising. He was rarely tongue-tied, but right then for the life of him he couldn't think of a thing to say.

The bartender saved him, the clink of glasses against the tile countertop jerking their gazes apart as they turned toward the noise.

"This round your liver gets a reprieve," the man joked. "Either of you want anything from the kitchen? They're closing down soon."

The only thing Jesse wanted was to take Dare back to his room and strip her. He'd be happy feasting on *her* all night long, but it was too soon — far too soon — to make that kind of comment without sending her running.

"Just the drinks." Dare waited until the man walked away before grabbing the skewer from her drink, the one that held three maraschino cherries.

Jesse glanced at his own drink, horror sliding up his spine. Some god-awful fruity concoction sat there instead of the whiskey they'd been consuming like water.

Time to make the best of a bad situation. He ignored the drink, wrapping his fingers around hers and lifting the cherry-laden stick to his lips. He made eye contact

8

as he tugged the first red-bomb off with his teeth then bit into it.

Her smile widened, heat flaring between them.

"You stole my cherry. Now you gotta marry me," she warned.

Jesse damn near choked in mid-swallow, checking quickly to see if she was serious.

She offered a cheeky grin then pulled the second cherry off the stick, rolling it against her teeth with her tongue in the lewdest way as she looked him over. His body went tight, and he decided right then and there the party was not ending in the bar.

"If I took your cherry, of course I'll marry you," he promised.

Everything about Dare was lush and sensual, and she proceeded to drive him wild. They clinked glasses then shot back the drinks, sticky sweetness filling his mouth. Pressure rose as the sugar hit his bloodstream.

She moved quickly to the next drink, which didn't look quite as mind-numbingly sweet.

He'd had just enough alcohol for his mind to start rambling. No way was she a virgin. Not with how she'd laid her hand on his thigh, rubbing in taunting circles. Never quite all the way to where he needed her, but bold enough to state she had more than drinking on her mind.

The sugar rush from the last drink sent his system skipping into overdrive, and he caught her by the hand and pulled her with him toward the tiny open space by the jukebox masquerading as a dance floor.

Bartender shouted after them. "Machine's broken. Just hit the numbers you want."

They leaned against the glass front to pick their favourites. Jesse slipped his arms on either side of her as

9

she pointed to the playlist. Dare responded by pressing her hips back into his, and happily, his cock got harder.

She turned on the spot and slid into his arms, her body warm against his. Garth Brooks crooned in the background, but Jesse was fixated on the woman in front of him.

"There's another glass on the counter," he warned.

"Three more to go, but I don't mind a moment to stretch my legs." She slipped her hands around his neck and pressed their bodies together. "So, Jesse. Can you handle your liquor? Or should we cut you off now so you've got enough *get up and go* for later?"

Nice. Blunt and to the point. "You coming back to my room?"

She shrugged, easing closer, one leg on either side of his so she was damn near riding him. "Your place or mine. We're probably next door to each other."

"Good. Then we won't have to worry about our neighbour complaining about how much noise we're making."

"You think we're going to make a lot of noise, do you?"

"Oh, darlin', I'm quiet as a mouse, but I have a feeling it's the kind of night you need to do a little screaming."

Jesse twirled her, raising her off the floor before resettling her on his thigh. A throaty purr escaped her, and he damn near stumbled.

"Screaming orgasms are fun." She stroked a finger down his cheek, eyeing the bruises. "Maybe you'll be the one screaming, though, and not me."

His cock took the challenge personally, hard pressed to the front of his jeans. Jesse rubbed her against him again, loving how her lashes fluttered as pleasure washed over her features. "Let's go find out, right now."

Dare lifted her chin. "We can't leave until we're done our drinks. That's the rule. But in case you get some idea of being noble, or some such bullshit, and don't think you should take me to bed later because I'm drunk, let's make it clear. I'm damn happy to have you join me tonight. Ten years means it's time to move on, and you're part of it."

One night to put aside everything that had come before. He could understand the sentiment. He might be running, but he was also headed to a new start. That's what this was all about. Transition.

"Trust me. You want me to take you to bed, I guarantee you'll get what you want."

That finger of hers kept moving southward, now tracing his shirt placard as she slow danced with him. "I've got condoms, or we can use yours, but you get suited up, got it?"

"Always do."

"Hmm. You're nice and warm." She rested her head on his chest and rubbed them together teasingly. "I sure hope you don't suck in bed."

Jesse laughed. "I don't. Except the good kind of sucking. You?"

She tilted her head back and licked her lips. "You'll have to wait and see."

He woke face down on the lumpy mattress, Morgan whining softly to get his attention.

Jesse jerked up a few inches before the anvil hit his head. "Fucking hell."

Hangover. Big, nasty, *wild* hangover.

He moved slower the second time, opening his eyes carefully as he looked around at the trashed motel room. The bed sheets and quilt were on the floor, towels draped over the tattered furniture, and for some reason his boots were on the shelf. One toe pointed east, the other was upside down entirely with the sole to the ceiling and the boot tip pointing west.

Whatever the hell happened last night, it appeared his boots had a good time.

"Dare?"

No answer.

He didn't really expect one, but there was that small part of him that wished their one-night stand was more. She'd been so sad, yet so full of life. Lush and sweet under his hands —

God, he was getting hard again.

He made it to a sitting position, gazing around at the chaos in amusement until it registered that his jeans and wallet were nowhere to be found.

"Jeez — where the hell...?"

Dare's room. They'd gone there first after they'd finished their drinks. Naked had happened fast, and sex even faster, and he smiled as he teetered to vertical and headed to the shower to soak his head.

The sex had *not* sucked. Not one bit. Not in her room, or in his, although he couldn't remember why they'd switched rooms. He did remember walking buck-ass naked through the billowing snow, with nothing but their room card keys in hand and boots on their feet.

Dare looked good naked. So fucking good he'd had her tossed on the mattress within seconds of entering the room.

Condoms. That's right. They'd come to his room and proceeded to dip into his stash because she'd only had one, to her shock. Her digging frantically through her purse looking for more had sent them both off into laughter before doing the naked shuffle through the snowy outdoors.

Jesse stuck his face under the water in the hopes it would sober him up as he drifted back over the awesome memories of the night before. She'd been wild in bed, and his body tightened all over just thinking of it. The alcohol he was feeling hard this morning hadn't put a damper on either of them.

He closed his eyes, pressing a hand to the wall to hold himself steady so he wouldn't fall over.

Something clicked against the shower tile, and he paused in confusion, pulling his hand back and wondering what the hell was on his pinkie finger.

A...*ring?*

He turned off the water and still dripping walked into the room to find the driest towel.

Jesse peered at his hand closer. Not a class ring, but something Dare had worn. He'd...

Okay, he remembered the sex, most of it. He remembered laughing a lot, but there seemed to be gaps in the rest of his night, including what the hell he was wearing her ring for.

A keycard lay on the floor just inside his door, and he picked it up, standing slowly to stop his head from spinning as he opened the note he found next to it.

You might need this to grab your stuff. Thanks for the night — be happy and safe travels.
Dare.

He wrapped the towel around his waist and slipped his own key into his fist before poking his head outside. An icy blast of wind set Morgan whimpering, and Jesse hushed him before hurrying into the storm and swiping the card to get into Dare's room.

She was long gone, but his jeans and T-shirt lay on the bed, and he grabbed them up in one hand and...

There was blood on the sheets.

Not a lot, as in something-had-been-killed-in-a-midnight-ritual kind of blood, but enough to make him stare and wonder...

You take my cherry, you gotta marry me.

He shook his head to get rid of the cobwebs. But she *hadn't* been a virgin. He could've sworn to that.

Jesse stared at the ring on his finger in horror.

What had they done?

Chapter One

Heart Falls, Alberta, four months later

"You're daydreaming again."

A teasing voice brought Dare's focus back to earth, and she twisted toward her best friend to offer a smile. "It's a dreamy kind of morning."

Ginny Stone took the stairs onto the porch with her usual enthusiasm. Dressed for working the ranch in jeans, boots and a couple layers of shirts, her dark brown hair settled over her shoulders as she held a ceramic mug toward Dare. "I made a new batch of that fruity herbal mix you like, and I've time to sit if you want company."

The railing she'd been leaning on creaked as Dare straightened, turning from where she'd been staring over Big Sky Lake and the rest of the Silver Stone ranch. "I would *kill* for a coffee right now, but thank you for bringing the next best thing."

"My company makes it all the sweeter, right?"

Dare settled into the rocking chair while her friend curled up in the pillow-filled wicker chair beside her. "Please. It's not that long since I've stopped being nauseous every morning. Do you really want to send me back there?"

Her friend tried to cover it up, but it was clear her gaze lingered a little longer than usual on Dare's stomach.

She laid a hand over the growing bump, and Ginny's gaze darted upward guiltily.

"Sorry. Didn't mean to stare." She gestured toward Dare's belly. "It's just...you're starting to show."

"Yeah. Not too much longer before everybody in town and their dog knows I'm pregnant out of wedlock. Oh, woe is me."

Her friend peered over the edge of her mug, her startling green eyes dancing with mischief. "As if you give two hoots what the town gossips think."

Dare shrugged. "You're right, but while *I* don't think I'm a fallen harlot, I wish things had gone differently. It's got to be hard on your brothers, especially Caleb. I never meant — "

"Stop right now." Ginny's amusement vanished and her eyes snapped with anger. "My brothers are *your* brothers, or as good as. They love you, and they would never let anyone say or do anything to hurt you."

"It's not as if people have to go out of their way to make up shit. I *am* pregnant." Dare wiggled her hand in the air. "Oh, and look! No ring. Ergo, I am an unwed mom."

"In this day and age, who cares?"

Dare sighed. "We've had this conversation before. I'm fully on board with taking care of Buckaroo Banzai on my own. Still wish I could find his daddy — that's the only part that makes me uncomfortable."

Ginny leaned forward. "Any luck tracking down the sperm donor?"

Dare shook her head. "Short of hiring a private investigator — as if — the only way is if we run into each other at some point. What are the chances?"

"Who knows? Maybe it will happen."

Dare wasn't quite sure what to wish for. The night she and Jesse had spent burning up the sheets had been spectacular. But when she'd missed her period a month later and gone back to try and track him down — because she figured letting a guy know he was going to be a daddy was the decent thing to do — she'd come up with a total blank. He'd paid cash for his room same as she had, and the night clerk hadn't got a license plate or anything she could use.

And this was old news, and it was time to change the topic. "What're you working on this week?" she asked her closest friend.

Ginny gestured toward the oversized garden and greenhouse outside the main ranch house where she lived with her oldest brother and his kids. "Garden boxes and farmers' market, same as usual. What about you? You need help with any of your upcoming posts?"

She could always use more material. "I should come out and take extra shots this week at the Farmers' Market. You've got some new items in the Community Supported Agriculture boxes, right?"

"Yeah. I've already printed the descriptions and recipes you gave me to slip into the deliveries."

"I bet you're not the only CSA passing out things customers don't know how to cook. I thought I'd post pictures and recipes. Hopefully others out there will be grateful. Plus, I should start stockpiling a bunch of posts for when Buckaroo puts in an appearance."

"Smart." Ginny looked her over, smiling harder. "You need to start a new section to your blog. *Ranching with Buckaroo.*"

It was like lightning stuck. Dare hauled her jaw back into position and offered up thanks for her best friend. "You're brilliant. You're right — I do need to add a section."

"Anytime you need fabulous ideas, you know who to call." Ginny winked. "You coming up to the house for dinner tonight?"

"If I can bring dessert."

"Strawberry shortcake?"

"The girls' favourite — of course."

"We'll eat at five, but if you can come over for three, I'd appreciate it. Caleb said Uncle Frank's sending a group of new hands from the south, and he's not sure when he'll be done the ranch tour. I promised to be around when the girls get off the bus in case he's not done."

She was Auntie Dare in name only, but she didn't mind one bit. Those two little girls of Caleb's were the cutest things. "Sure, I can come help with the rug rats. It's good practice."

Ginny got to her feet, giving her a hug before stealing the mug back and heading to the main house. "You don't need practice. You're going to be a great mom."

Dare didn't say anything — it was one thing to have a baby on the way, but it was another to imagine successfully raising the kid all the way to adulthood when she had no mom to turn to for help.

Panic is not an option, she told herself for the millionth time.

She waved goodbye then headed inside the small two-bedroom cottage that had been her home forever. Growing up, she'd shared a room with her sister, then after the accident she'd eventually returned to make the place her own, the ghosts of her past slowly fading into memories.

Her childhood room was now her office, twinned

computer screens set up over the desk, a small single bed pushed against the opposite wall.

Not that she had many visitors. Everyone she liked enough to have over lived right there on the Silver Stone ranch. Family by choice if not family by blood.

Dare forced herself to move. She'd been staring out the window again, which wasn't a terrible thing, except daydreaming was for daydreaming hours, not for when she had work to get done.

While she'd made light of it to Ginny, the morning sickness had been spectacularly rough. She was just starting to feel human on a regular basis, so keeping ahead of the game with prescheduled blog posts was important.

She closed the blinds to block out the distraction of the sun sparkling on the lake, and turned back to the computer and her list of upcoming features.

Little Ranch on the Prairie. Her recovery journal turned online diary turned blog.

Drove the Stone boys up the wall that she made money from sitting behind a computer, but at least they didn't deny the amount of work she put in. Even when morning sickness had hit, she'd managed to post once a day, although she'd scrambled at times to make it more than "Ugh, I feel shitty. Here, have an LOLcat."

She laid a hand over the slowly growing bump in her belly. "One good thing, Buckaroo. Mommy's going to be able to stay at home with you. I need to get my butt in gear, though. Think I should start that kid's section. What should we call it?"

No response yet. She didn't expect there to be — although according to the baby books she and Ginny had peeked at, it could be anytime now she'd feel the baby move. "Buckaroo Roundup. My Little Buckaroo? Ranching With Buckaroo? They're all so cheesy, but then again, I don't mind cheesy — it makes good copy."

She punched the ideas into a search engine to see how many other blogs out there dealt with the topic.

She'd put her own slant on it, of course, but raising kids on a ranch was common enough for a portion of the population to get a kick out of her everyday comments, and just fantasy enough for others that she could possibly make this work.

Dare rested her hand on her belly, then laughed. "I know my first post, because I *never* used to touch my stomach, and now I can't seem to let go."

Her rising baby bump *would* be noticed in town, and she was pretty much ready for it. With her foster brothers looking after her, she wouldn't have to put up with too many in-her-face comments, but they'd still be there.

Single moms might be a lot more common these days, but being daddy-less in a small town was enough to make tongues wag.

She jotted down a couple of ideas for an extended section for raising kids on the ranch then opened her email.

The daily analytics from her blog opened, and Dare's heart rate jumped a notch. "Holy moly. That's not normal."

She hurried to her blog to double-check. Views had skyrocketed, and she traced it back to a post she'd popped up in a daze while sick as a dog, when Buckaroo was just making his presence known in her life.

Cowboy Back-bacon Biscuits. An innocent enough recipe.

She clicked through to the blog post and grinned. "Well, hello, Mr. Sexy Cowboy."

Okay, she didn't remember specifically picking that picture. It wasn't one of her paid stock photos, but an off-the-cuff shot she'd taken with her phone of the one responsible for putting Buckaroo in her belly. Normally she would never have used the picture, but obviously nausea-brain made for less-than-stellar choices.

"I hope you're doing great wherever you are, Jesse. If I could track you down, I would."

Posts going viral were good for her hit and advertising count, though, and hey — if it brought her cowboy out of the woodwork, so much the better. He'd been a decent guy, even though he'd obviously had something to drink about that night as well.

The anniversary of her family's death was a drinking event. The sex and the baby were bonuses.

Dare eyed Jesse's picture again. She'd taken it between bouts of really hot sex — and after a shower break.

That's why he had a towel barely clinging to his fine, firm ass, his backside slightly twisted toward her as he hammed it up. His cowboy hat was pulled down over most of his face, so the main event of the show were abdominal muscles that wouldn't quit, and those long muscular V lines angling toward his groin.

She sighed happily. He hadn't sucked in the sack, not one bit. She tingled when she thought back to that night. Which was good, because the memories of how much fun they'd had might have to last her a long time.

Which was very sad because she liked sex. And she'd *really* liked sex with Jesse, but going forward, the well was probably going to get a little dry.

She figured single moms-to-be weren't setting the sexual world on fire on a regular basis.

Her second sigh wasn't as happy.

Dare returned to her email and worked through them, a timer set to go off at thirty-minute intervals so she'd get up and move around.

She was just about done when a new email came through from her website.

Question re: model for post

Oops. Made sense if the post got a lot of attention, she'd get some feedback — of what variety, though? Readers and their comments on her blog were her bread and butter, but direct messages through her contact button were a potshot.

For a pretty PG site, she still got complaints about her content. The morality cops swinging through and deciding her blog had too much sex and skin — and it really didn't, although she posted bluntly about a lot of ideas.

Okay, the shot of Jesse was borderline. She glanced at it again and couldn't stop from grinning. Forget borderline, it was straight-up "print this off and use as fantasy material", and she wasn't even one bit embarrassed.

Where people got off telling her what she could and couldn't discuss burned her britches. She'd started opening the emails with a kind of BINGO card in mind.

Reference to burning in hell, one point.

Reference to having no shame, one point.

Offers of prayers for her soul, two points.

Her amusement faded as she read the actual comment, and her heart rate picked up.

I'm curious if you know where I could find the model from your March twenty-fourth picture. No worries — only he's family, and I'm trying to track him down. I thought I'd try you in case you had any current information.

If not — sorry to bother you.

If you do know where Jesse is, and you don't mind passing on a message, tell the ass to get in touch with us. When I find him, I'm going to tan his hide. (Okay, maybe don't mention that last bit. The boy gets on my last nerve far too easily.)

Your blog looks great, by the way. I look forward to going through your stuff. Ranch life is definitely up my alley.

Jaxi Coleman (Six Pack ranch, Rocky Mountain House)

Huh. Dare read the message over again, confusion stirring. It was a connection to her missing man, but if his...*sister?*...didn't know where Jesse was —

Did she contact them to say, *Hey, if he does show up, tell him I need to talk?* Potentially awkward, and she wasn't letting anyone else know about the baby before he found out.

If he found out.

Drat, this was impossible.

She pushed the email aside to think about it a little longer before responding. Worrying about her missing baby daddy wasn't going to keep her blog running, and in the end, that was the most important thing.

She'd do whatever it took to remain standing on her own two feet. If there was one thing she'd learned over the years, no matter that others had good intentions, if it needed to be done, in the end she really needed to rely on herself.

She finished by lunch, then spent needed time on cleanup tasks she'd been putting off. About two o'clock she wandered over to the main house to find her friend arguing on the phone.

"It's not rocket science. Are you sure you can't — ?"

Dare hid her grin best she could.

Ginny huffed into the phone a few more times, rolling her eyes in an exaggerated manner before muttering *fine* and hanging up.

"Trouble in paradise?" Dare teased.

Ginny flipped her the finger. "I have to go. They're having trouble sorting this week's orders and can't figure it out without my help."

Dare slipped past her into the living room. "No worries. I'll look after the girls when they get home if you're not back yet."

"Thanks." Ginny eyed her. "Ummm…is there something you're not telling me? Like, you're auditioning for the part of a homeless person?"

Oops. Dare glanced down at her outfit. "It's comfy, okay?"

"If you're comfy being half-naked, whatever. I should be back in thirty minutes, and I've already got the crockpots going."

"I'll get the cake in the oven before I start my yoga."

She was talking to empty air — her friend was already gone.

Dare didn't mind the time to herself. She headed into the big old-fashioned kitchen, and ten minutes later she had her cake in the oven. Time enough left to pull her yoga mat from where she'd stashed it behind the couch in the sunroom.

The big ranch house was as familiar as her own. She'd

spent hours and hours here growing up, her parents and Ginny's sharing meals on a regular basis.

They'd shared everything, including — morbidly — their untimely deaths.

She moved into position on the yoga mat and began her practice. As huge and life-changing as her family's deaths had been, after ten years it was more of an echo than a constant buzz.

There were times that brought to mind what they'd all lost — her and the Stone family — but usually life went on.

Including the *unexpected* bits of life…

Dare glanced down at her ratty outfit, the leggings so full of holes and the fabric worn so thin it was barely there. Definitely time to buy a new set, but she'd been trying to hold off until her expanding waistline made it impossible to wear her old things.

She had her butt in the air and feet tangled over her head when the door opened and Caleb's oldest daughter let out a shout. "Auntie G, Auntie D."

Dare slowly worked to untangle herself. "I'm here, honey. Auntie Ginny had to go into town. She'll be home soon."

"Emma's hurt." Sasha seemed more excited than worried.

A loud, exaggerated sniffle accompanied the announcement, and Dare shot to her feet, teetering for a moment as she turned to face the door to discover the little girl cradled in the arms of her missing cowboy.

25

Chapter Two

He'd come looking for Dare, but after months apart, Jesse hadn't expected the first thing he spotted to be her spectacular ass.

Her all-too-memorable ass, wiggling in his direction as his wild child untwisted herself to stand before him. Her red hair was barely tamed back into a ponytail. Threadbare leggings caressed her legs, and her faded sports bra hugged every curve while leaving a lot of skin uncovered.

He pulled his jaw back into place, suddenly thankful the little girl in his arms and her talkative sister stole the spotlight.

"Auntie Dare, Emma fell down and she was crying, but Jesse said you'd make it all better."

Jesse met Dare in the middle of the room. She checked the faint scrape on the little girl's knee, clicking her tongue soothingly. "Wow. Were you riding the bucking broncos again?"

Emma shook her head, teeth digging into her bottom lip.

"She was chasing Demon, and she tripped," Sasha announced. "There was a *big* rock."

"She was pretty brave," Jesse offered. "But Sasha said it hurt too much for Emma to walk on, and I didn't think she should hop all the way to the house, so I offered to help."

"Because you just happened to be hanging out on my front lawn?"

"*Little Ranch on the Prairie?* Yeah, I was *hanging out* pretty hard."

Dare pressed her lips together, but she smiled. "So… Hey. You found me."

"Hey. I did." Emma squirmed in his arms, and he lowered her to the floor. "You okay, cowgirl?"

She nodded, one hand drifting to her mouth. She chewed on the side of her fingers as Dare dropped to her knees so they could talk face-to-face.

"Does your knee hurt lots?"

The little girl shook her head.

"She needs a Band-Aid, though." Sasha's suggestion. "Maybe two."

"Hmmm." Dare looked over the teeny cut again. "Let's see after we get it cleaned up. No use putting anything on that's going to fall off right away."

Emma dipped her chin.

"Okay, I've got an idea. How about a bath before supper instead of after? That way your scrape will get clean, and we'll knock all the road dust off at the same time."

"I want a bath too. Emma wants me to help her. And she wants to wear her new pyjamas, right, Emma?" Sasha had her sister by the hand as they walked backward toward the hallway. "And I want to wear my pyjamas too. Only we don't want to go to bed early. Emma wants to watch movies."

"Bath, yes. Pyjamas, yes. Movies — not until after your homework is done. I'll come help get the water started."

VIVIAN AREND

Dare pointed down the hallway. "Hurry up. I'll be there in a minute."

"Is Jesse staying for supper? Emma wants to sit beside him," Sasha tossed over her shoulder.

"*Bathtub.*"

The one word quickened the girls' steps, and Jesse chuckled as they vanished around a corner. "Well done, Auntie Dare."

"They'll take every advantage they can get." She glanced at him. "Give me a minute to get them in the water?"

"I'm not going anywhere," he promised.

Jesse strolled around the room after she left, a million questions darting through his brain. Emma hadn't made a sound since he'd seen her fall, not even to cry. She'd defaulted to her big sister speaking for her — there had to be a reason for that.

In the meantime, though, he looked for clues to his mysterious woman, glancing at the pictures scattered everywhere. There were a few with a redheaded little girl, maybe Dare, but far more of Emma and Sasha. It was a comfortable room, like in any ranch house. Could have been the one he grew up in, although his mom kept things a little more spit and polished.

Then again, he had no idea what it had been like when he and Joel were little and his mom had been wrangling a houseful of boys.

He glanced out the window toward the lake and the outbuildings neatly arranged east to west. Arenas, paddocks — the Silver Stone ranch was impressive. Something extra was going on today. A whole lot of trucks were parked over toward the barns, and a group of men had gathered beside one of the split-rail fences.

Jesse double-checked to the west, but his truck was far enough to the side of the main drive to be out of the way. He'd seen the little girl fall, and he'd been out from behind the wheel before he'd thought it through. He figured carrying her to the house would cause less trouble than loading her into his truck.

"Hey."

He turned to face Dare as she reentered the room. "All settled?"

She wiggled her fingers. "For now." She broke her gaze from his to stare past him. "We need to talk."

"We do. Plus, I have something of yours."

Her nose wrinkled. "Yeah, I have something you left behind too." She pointed him toward the side of the house. "We can sit on the porch."

"Hello? Dare?" A new voice.

"There. There, see?" The helpful and talkative Sasha burst into the hallway leading another woman into the room.

Dark-haired, her brilliant green eyes were filled with a great deal of curiosity. "I see him."

"I *told* you he was a cowboy." Sasha pointed straight at Jesse's waist. "He even has a buckle. Not as big as Uncle Walker's, though."

The woman pushed the child's fingers down. "Be polite, please."

"He's strong, Aunt Ginny. Maybe as strong as Daddy," Sasha piped up, waving at Jesse as she offered a gap-toothed grin.

Ginny made some noncommittal noise as she all but stripped him with her gaze before turning to Dare. "This him?"

"Yeah."

"Niiiiiiiice."

Jesse grinned. They'd obviously talked about him at some point. "Thanks."

Dare gave Sasha a pointed look. "I thought you were having a bath and doing your homework."

Sasha's eyes widened, then she twirled and ran from the room.

Dare caught his hand in hers and tugged, speaking to Ginny as they moved. "Since you're home, we're going to my place to talk."

"I've got dinner. And the kids. Oh, and I'll set an extra place at the table."

His wild child took a deep breath. "Ginny, I don't think — "

"I'm taking Dare out," Jesse cut in. Family dinners with little tykes were okay, but his main agenda for the evening involved adult-only entertainment.

Ginny shrugged. "Text me if you change your mind."

Dare guided him outside. He figured she would drop his hand the instant they left the porch, but she kept a firm grip, leading him away from the main house and the barns.

He whistled for his dog who came running from where Jesse had told him to stay in the shade on the other side of the house. "Remember him?" Jesse asked Dare.

She glanced at the golden retriever, a smile sneaking out. "Morgan, right? Hey, boy. Good to see you again."

She held her free hand to Morgan without slowing her pace. The dog sniffed her fingers then put on a burst of speed to race ahead of them to the next field to sniff and explore.

"He'll behave," Jesse assured her.

"Our dogs are good too. There's about a half dozen

all told. If they spot Morgan, they might do a little jostling to figure out who's most dominant, but if you're comfortable with bringing him, I'm good with it."

The gathering by the barn was still there, a few horses being put through their paces in the arena. "Nice-size spread."

"Silver Stone? It's… Yeah, it's okay." She gestured to the group. "Family from Lethbridge area sent up a group of new hands, and they're getting the welcome spiel."

A big enough operation to need extra hands — Jesse slowed to try and get a better look while Dare all but hauled him across the lawn toward a small cottage with a porch.

Their rapid-fire trip across the yard didn't go unnoticed. A sturdy young man separated himself from the group and headed their direction, jogging at first, then picking up speed as he set what was obviously a line to intercept.

"Expecting company?" Jesse asked.

Dare swore and jerked on his hand, damn near making them run. "I'll explain in a second, but we need to get inside, stat."

It went against Jesse's instincts to hide, but they were already up the steps and into the house. She pulled the door shut on his heels.

The banging started a moment later.

"Dare?" A youthful, masculine voice.

"Go away."

"Who's that with you? Open the door, Dare, or I'll break it down."

Jesse bristled on her behalf. "You need me to take care of him?"

Dare blinked, then rolled her eyes. "Oh, jeez. I forgot

the whole *express opinions with our fists* bullshit is genetically built into all males. I can deal with him."

She stood to one side of the door, blocking the bottom with her foot before undoing the lock so the wooden frame could only open an inch. "Dustin. Is there a reason you want me to rearrange your face?"

"There's a man in there with you."

"Really? Gee, I never would have known without you telling me."

"Who is he?"

"None of your business."

"Dare, I'm going to count to ten, and — "

She cracked the door open farther but spoke softer, her voice dripping icicles. "Seriously? You want to try *that* bullshit? Forget it. I was going to be polite, but you blew it. Go away, or I will tell Tansy at Buns and Roses you have a crush on her again."

The blustering outside the door came to an immediate stop. "You're nasty, Dare. I'm just trying to — "

" — be bossy and overbearing? You nearly succeeded, only I care enough to nip bad behaviour in the bud. I will rip you a new one if you so much as touch my door again."

Barely visible through the narrow sliver Dare held open, the young man glared daggers in Jesse's direction, dark brown eyes flashing in frustration. "Bring him to the house when you're done. If he leaves without seeing us, I'll track him down and peel the skin from his body to make a rope."

Jesse held his tongue until the door was closed, taking a deep breath as she turned toward him. "That was interesting."

"He's a jackass, but he means well."

Jesse paused. "Old boyfriend?"

She gagged. "Hell, no."

"Protective."

"You have no idea."

He ignored the comment because waiting wasn't making this any easier. It'd been ages since they'd been together. There really wasn't a proper way to restart something after a memorable one-night stand, let alone ask some awkward questions.

Tracking her down — that was a good place to begin. "Thanks for putting up my picture. I had no idea how to find you until the guys at the bunkhouse spotted that damn meme."

Dare frowned. "Sorry for the whole posting without your permission, but...meme? I just noticed today my blog post had a lot of hits."

"Yeah, because someone found the picture about a week ago and slapped *Prime Alberta Beef* across my backside. It's been making the rounds on social media. It took me until yesterday to track it back to your blog."

She shook her head. "Sorry about the invasion-of-privacy issue. I'm usually a lot more careful about that."

"Like I said, no problem. It was the breadcrumb trail I'd been looking for."

Dare shifted farther into the little house, pointing toward the living room couch. "You were trying to find me?"

He offered a grin. "Is that so surprising?"

"We both said it was only one night."

She looked uncomfortable, and he kicked his own ass for assuming just because he wanted another ride that she'd be available. "You seeing someone? Because I don't want to get in your way, or anything."

"No — I'm not seeing anyone." Her eyes widened. "You?"

"Hell no." Although he wasn't sure why. Lack of time? Lack of privacy in his new digs in the bunkhouse?

He'd hooked up plenty before, even with those kind of deterrents, but for the last couple of months every woman he'd looked at paled when he thought back to Dare. Fucking around to fuck around had begun to leave him cold — and that's when he'd begun searching for her in earnest.

He wasn't such a shit as to keep seeing random women when he was picturing them with Dare's face. Now that he'd found her, he was ready for a second serving.

Which would never happen if he didn't get them past the tough issues.

"I'm glad I tracked you down, and first up, I'm sorry if I was too...*enthusiastic*...last time."

She looked lost. "What?"

Damn, there was no way to say this delicately. "Back in February. There was blood on the sheets."

She thought for a moment before holding up her hand, a smile teasing her lips. "The glass broke, remember? We were kind of distracted and didn't notice that the cut reopened." Her amusement slipped to distress. "Oh my God, *no*. I wasn't a virgin. You didn't..." She kept rambling while he enjoyed the relief rushing his system. "I mean, your enthusiasm was *very* much appreciated."

"I was thinking of the whole cherry thing, and it got me confused. Oh, and there's something else. I have this. I don't remember why." He pulled the chain around his neck from under his shirt to show her the ring.

"You're kidding. I thought I'd lost that. I'm so glad..."

She reached toward him, then stopped. "Wait, this isn't what we need to talk about. I mean, I'm glad you have my ring, but I need to tell you something important."

Jesse stepped closer, the scent of her teasing his senses. He tugged a strand of hair that had fallen loose from her ponytail. "Want to tell me over dinner? I hear there's a great steakhouse in the area."

"There is, but we're not going anywhere right now. You need to sit down. And…maybe you should put your head between your knees."

He laughed. "Isn't that what they tell you when a crash is imminent?"

Guilt flashed over her face. "Can't you hear the sirens in the distance?"

She hadn't struck him as the melodramatic type, but hey — they'd only had the one night, well-lubricated at that. "Come on, it can't be that bad."

"I'm four months pregnant."

As if a shock wave had struck out of nowhere, a sudden ringing made Jesse's ears seem stuffed with cotton. "*What?*"

"I'm pregnant."

She'd said the words again, but they still made no sense, mostly because stars were forming in front of his eyes, and there was no oxygen in the room.

Months and numbers danced in his brain. "Four months, eh?"

She nodded.

He wasn't going to insult her by asking if it was his. She didn't know a thing about him except he liked dirty sex and strong whiskey. No reason on earth for her to tell some potentially dirt-poor cowboy he was going to be a father in the hopes of getting anything from him.

It might have made him the biggest loser around, but it was this or fall over. "I need a second."

Jesse took the chair she'd offered a moment earlier, cradling his head in his hands as he concentrated on breathing and on not passing out — not passing out would be good too.

Dare snickered before clearing her throat. "Sorry, but I did warn you. Don't feel in any rush to move. When the test came back positive, I stayed curled up in a fetal position for nearly a week before my brain came back online."

He wasn't sure if he was freaking out because she was pregnant or because *she* wasn't freaking out.

His brain wasn't functioning at full capacity.

"I'm not sure I can...talk right now."

She offered a sympathetic pat on the back. "Not judging you one bit. No way can you say the perfect thing unless you were in a sitcom and somebody was feeding you lines."

"Is there a perfect thing?"

"Actually, that's the problem. Other than there's a whole bunch of things you *shouldn't* say, the right one, right now?" She squeezed his shoulder then stepped away, her feet moving out of his line of vision. "No, sweetheart, I can't think of a single phrase I absolutely want to hear out of your mouth."

It took a while until the room stopped spinning enough Jesse figured it was safe to look up. He found Dare leaning against the wall next to him, sympathy written all over her expression.

He rose to his feet. "At the risk of being one of the dozen things I shouldn't say, I'm damn sorry you've had to deal with this by yourself."

She paused. Made a face. "Huh. I need to add that to the list of stuff I *didn't* expect."

"I mean it, Dare. That must've thrown you for a loop when you found out. I hope you've had support from your friends, and your brothers…" Oh shit, he was in a hell of a lot of trouble. "Let me guess. That was one of your brothers pounding on the door a few minutes ago."

She wrinkled her nose. "Okay, we need to sit down and have a good long talk, because that's another one of those yes/no answers that would be a lot simpler once you hear some history. Only I'm not blaming you for not knowing. I'm the one who said you didn't need details of why I was drinking my ass off."

Now that he was stable again, Jesse moved in closer. "Then let's talk."

"Right now?"

"Why not?"

Dare glanced at her watch. "I guess. What's your time like? Where're you working?"

"Down near Pincher Creek. I've got tomorrow morning off."

She examined him for a second before that oh-so-expressive face of hers changed. "You were hoping to hook up tonight, weren't you?"

"When there's a sell-out performance, an encore is always appreciated." Shit, maybe he shouldn't act so cocky, all things considered. "I guess I shouldn't joke about that night."

"Oh, don't go getting serious on me. Memories of how much fun I had was the only thing that got me through multiple bouts of puking."

He caught her hand in his, guilt overtaking his panic. "Again, sorry you were all alone."

37

"It's fine. I didn't need anybody to hold my hair back." But she shouldn't have had to deal with it on her own. That was the point. She shouldn't have to deal with any of this on her own.

For the first time something stronger than panic hit. He'd been around his brothers when they'd announced they had a kid on the way. They'd damn near glowed. Something inside him twisted, and a strange, uneasy sensation settled in his gut.

Jesse sure the hell didn't feel proud. The panic might be natural, but he wasn't going to let that show again. Other than that first moment of weakness, which Dare had taken amazingly in stride, he was done messing around. There was no use waiting even another minute.

He knew what his parents would say. What his brothers would say, and he knew without a single doubt if any of the Coleman clan were in that room, they'd be waiting for him to man up and deal.

So he did.

Jesse squeezed her fingers tighter and offered as reassuring a smile as he could manage.

"Okay, then. We'll get married."

Chapter Three

It was funny to consider how long she'd spent plotting ways to tell her cowboy the news if she ever found him. There were a couple scripts she'd expected the conversation to follow, and she'd planned appropriate responses.

Worst-case scenario he'd say, "hell, no, it's not mine". She'd get that in writing, just in case, ask about his family health history on a "hypothetical" basis, and happily never see him again.

Best case she'd come up with was he'd say "oh, shit", she'd say "right?" and they'd figure out something that involved him sending her a bit of childcare money every now and then until he forgot.

The sex had been fantastic, but you couldn't judge the strength of a man's character by the way he used his dick.

Not even with her vivid imagination had she expected the proposal, which meant she was currently running without a script. Which, okay, meant he got blunt.

She freed her fingers from his grasp and stepped away to put some physical distance between them. "I assume that was shock speaking. You don't know a thing about me, and you want to get married?"

"I know you're having my baby. Isn't that enough?"

"Hardly. I don't love you."

"What's that got to do with it?"

Dare glared. "Everything. I'm not marrying a man I don't love."

"You're having my baby."

"That doesn't mean I love you. It means we had sex. Good sex, but that's not love."

"Really *great* sex. And of course you're going to marry me."

"Slow your roll, asshole. I don't *know* you. The list of things I know about you I could count on one hand, maybe two, without needing to go to my toes."

"I know you make this noise when you come that gives me shivers."

All the air sucked out of the room, and annoyingly, Dare felt her face heating. "You didn't just say that, and I do *not*."

Jesse flashed a grin that made her knees tremble. "It's not a bad place to start, and you totally do."

Dare pressed her fists to her temples and counted to ten. Okay, so he didn't fit either of her main scenarios, which meant she had to come up with an alternative solution, fast, because no way in hell was she agreeing to get married as if there were a shotgun to both their heads.

Just a baby in my belly.

She took a deep breath then faced him. "What about we compromise for now? I mean, you're right. It's your baby too, so you get to be in their life if you want, but I don't think we should consider something as drastic as getting married when we don't even know each other."

The poor man was getting a workout today, his handsome face tugging into a scowl. "You want to *date*?"

"Well, that would be one way to find out more about each other than just our first names."

40

Jesse shook his head. "I agree we need to get to know each other better because, yeah, it will make raising our kid easier, but I don't see why we shouldn't just do it."

It was horrible that the only thing that registered out of his entire statement was *do it*, and her thoughts had nothing to do with dating, or marriage, or even babies, and everything to do with sex.

Jesse had the moves, and she knew it. Intimately.

It was totally unfair he'd missed the entire too-sick-to-consider-herself-a-sexual-being months, and instead had arrived when all her hormones seemed to be percolating at higher than usual.

She might have had more resistance to his sex appeal when she'd been feeling green. Now all she could think about was how he'd made her tingle so hard she'd been seeing stars after her third — or was it fourth? — orgasm. A hard pulse hit between her legs...

...and great. She'd been daydreaming about sex while staring into space.

Or staring at him.

Dammit, she'd been staring at his package, and as she jerked her gaze up to meet his, there was a faintly mocking expression in his eyes.

She powered her way forward. "Excuse me, what did you just say? I'm not being a smartass. I really need you to repeat what you said two seconds ago."

His smile escaped, and another shiver of desire slipped over her body. Slamming up stop signs on her aching libido hurt.

He held up a finger as if he had an idea. "Let's meet in the middle. Let's get engaged, because that commitment will be enough to stop most people from talking." Jesse grimaced. "I know small towns, and small minds, and

41

I hope nobody's been giving you grief."

Dare shook her head. "Not many people know yet. Basically just family, although the Buckaroo bump is going to give me away pretty soon."

He nodded thoughtfully. "What you think? We're engaged now, and we can get married" — he counted on his fingers — "early October."

"Good Lord, is that really necessary? Like are you telling me you don't want to have *an illegitimate child*, so we need to rush things?"

"No. But this is about...what did you call him? Buckaroo. Whatever he'll have to deal with down the road, I figure we should do everything we can to make his life easier, right?"

Smooth bastard. "I can't argue with that."

"So it's settled. We're engaged, and we'll — "

"It's *not* settled," she snapped, feeling a little stupid about complaining, but all control seemed to be tipping rapidly out of her hands. "Other than spending one night together, I know nothing about you. My family knows nothing about you."

"So, let's go meet your family. I'll convince them that I'm not an axe murderer, and you'll tell them we're engaged."

She eyed him. "The guy I met at the bar that night had a lot of smarts and charm. Either you're not really him, or you hit your head hard sometime between then and now."

"What am I being stupid about? Tell me." He offered another of those seductive smiles. "I can be charming, darling."

"Obviously, since you charmed your way into my panties easily enough — " Dare cut herself off and shook her head. "I'm sorry, that's not fair. This is *not* your fault, and I was totally on board with the panty charming. I just need a minute to get my head on straight. Okay? Today's held a few shocks for both of us, in different ways."

He eased back and his body language went soft, like the guys did when they were around horses that spooked easily.

That she caught what he was doing was balanced by the fact he knew how to do it.

Jesse spoke quieter. "How about this? I should move my truck. I kind of abandoned it when Emma did her header. Come with me to get it. Heck, if you feel up to it, you can take me on a tour of the ranch then we'll grab some burgers. Nothing fancy, nothing involving a big outing in public — "

" — safe from my brothers coming and giving you the third degree before we've even found out each other's last names?"

"That too." He held out his hand.

It took a moment before she realized he was pretending to meet her for the first time. His grip was firm, but careful, his far greater strength held in reserve.

"Jesse *Coleman*."

"Darilyn Hayes, but everybody calls me Dare."

One of his brows arched higher. "Darilyn? Pretty. I was wondering if it was a nickname or something."

"And now you know."

"Now I know." Jesse released her fingers and gestured to the door. "Show me your home."

What the hell was *wrong* with him?

*Dare was right. Jesse knew how to be charming, and yet he'd gone and barreled forward without paying one bit of attention — which was the exact opposite of how he usually treated the ladies. No wonder she'd shoved walls up right away.

She'd dashed off to pull on different clothes, giving him time to start pondering, and now the self-recrimination continued as they walked in silence down the gravel drive to where his truck was parked.

He didn't blame her one bit for not wanting to marry him. *He* wouldn't want to marry him, either — cocky, arrogant bastard. If this had any chance of working, he needed to up his game big time.

Although, he was struggling to put together everything that meant.

A kid.

Married…

It was as if his brain was happier if he just ignored thinking what those words actually added up to. If he looked at them through a hazy glass as if they were far in a future that didn't involve "soon" and "the right thing" and "brothers ready to kick his ass into tomorrow".

She'd been walking and watching the action by the barns where a few men were working with the bay and chestnut horses.

Okay. *Get to know you* time. That much he could deal with. "You have a horse?"

Dare flashed him a quick smile. "Yeah, Baby."

Jesse opened his mouth, then shut it. "Seriously?"

"He's a sorrel gelding, and nearly ready for retirement. He was my mom's, and when she passed on, I took him as my own."

Oh man. "I'm sorry to hear about your mom."

She nodded. "Hey, I did have a hint at your last name."

Obviously changing the topic. He went with it for now. "Was it tattooed on my ass?"

"Your sister emailed my blog today. Wanted to know the current whereabouts of my March model."

Sister?

"That picture just keeps giving and giving. Who was it that emailed?" He led her to the driver's side, holding the door open for her.

She frowned.

"You know the territory. You may as well drive."

Without another word Dare climbed in, adjusting the wheel angle to place herself comfortably on the wide bench seat. She waited until he settled on the passenger side before answering his question. "Someone named Jaxi. She said you got on her last nerve."

"The feeling is mutual at times. She's my sister-in-law. Married to Blake, my oldest brother." How much did he share? Man the torpedoes, full steam ahead. "I had a wicked crush on her at one point, but she and Blake are perfect together. Disgustingly in love."

She drove to the end of the driveway and headed west. "Typical younger brother in love with the forbidden older woman?"

Jesse snorted. "Forbidden, because Blake would have ripped me apart once he stopped being stupid and denying he was in love with her. But she's barely a year older than me. She just bosses the hell out of everyone because she kind of grew up with the family."

"Sounds a little like Caleb — the bossy part."

"He your oldest brother?"

"Sort of?" She turned onto a gravel road and drove

45

them up a steep section of road, following the sweeping curve of the foothills. In the near distance the Rocky Mountains rose majestically, sharp grey granite peaks and dark shadows. The mountains were closer than the section of Rockies the Colemans saw at home, the landscape changes here in central Alberta sharper and more intense.

Dare took them counterclockwise, the road changing to angle northward as they rose. They were now tucked against the hillside, the mountains to the west hidden from view, but the land to the east was laid out like on a map. Thin roads stretched in straight lines all the way to the horizon. Between them lay acre after acre of grazing land, tiny dark dots of cattle and horses peppering the land.

She parked at a wide turn out on a corner. Jesse got out and shut the truck door behind him, waiting until she came around to join him. His gaze drifted over the land. They didn't have this kind of viewpoint back home.

"That is a gorgeous sight. We have a few rises where you can see for miles, but this is incredible."

Dare paused. "It is. I find it humbling. We're just a speck in the middle of something so much bigger than we are."

"Cowboy philosophy 101. There's always something bigger than you are."

"Seems that way." She touched his arm briefly. "Follow me."

She led him to a path at the side of the lookout where a narrow trail meandered horizontally toward a patch of tall pine. Tucked into the trees was a bench, and Dare settled on one side, leaning forward to rest her elbows on her knees. She stared over the land, and he paused to admire the closer view. With worn jeans, a pale blue shirt and a dark cowboy hat, she made the prettiest picture, and the panic that had seized him eased slightly.

He didn't know her yet but she seemed a decent person. They could do this.

They had to.

He joined her on the bench, taking a cue from her and checking the land.

She pointed toward the base of the hill where the sunlight was turning the lake surface into a shimmering mirror in the midst of a green setting. "Silver Stone ranch. Boundary to the west is behind us, up against the wilderness area. You can see the south border parallel to the highway, but the north is out of our sight. That's Big Sky Lake, and the smaller one is Little Sky." She pointed farther north. "We're lucky to have two water sources and the river running through the ranch. You can't see it from here, but if you keep walking this path you end up at Heart Falls, the source of the river."

"The town's named after it?"

"Yeah. This bench where we're sitting and the waterfall don't belong to the ranch anymore. About an acre got donated to the municipality so everyone could enjoy it." She glanced over at him. "My dad, Joseph Hayes, who was known as Silver, and his best friend Walter Stone bought the ranch together — thus the Silver Stone ranch."

Interesting. "I love hearing where names come from. I mean, sometimes it's obvious, but that's one with a lot of character."

"Jaxi mentioned she lived on the Six Pack ranch. Big drinkers?"

"Ha, not really. Six boys, two generations in a row."

"Damn."

"Means there's a bunch of Coleman around. Four of the original six settled in the area, so we've got Six Pack, Angel, Whiskey Creek — that one's simple enough to explain — and Moonshine."

"You'll have to tell any child-appropriate stories to Sasha. She loves to know that kind of stuff. Have to be careful, though. She'll talk your ear off if you let her."

"Sasha seems like the type to want to tell a lot of stories." Jesse paused. "Because she talks for Emma as well as herself?"

Dare turned toward him, pulling her feet up on the bench. "There's a million things to say to you. So much history, and yet I can't find a place to start. It's not like a simple 'what I did on my summer vacation' essay."

Jesse chuckled. "Don't start on the school memories. I already feel a little as if there's going to be a flash test sometime in the next half hour. Let's start simple. How old are you?"

"Twenty-six."

"Me too."

Dare's lips twisted. "Gee, we have so much in common. We should get married."

Jesse laughed. "Smartass. We do have a lot in common. Sounds as if you've got a lot of brothers.

She made a face. "I do, and I don't. It's complicated and it's not something I enjoy talking about, so I should probably just get it out of the way before things get too awkward."

"Snapshot is fine," Jesse insisted. "We'll have plenty of time to get to know details later."

Dare nodded. "So — my parents and their best friends bought the ranch."

"Joe and Walter?"

"Best friends, like I said, and they did everything together. Got married around the same time, moved to Alberta, bought the ranch, started having kids. Only ten years ago there was an accident, and all four of them and my little sister died."

Oh my God. "Jesus, I'm so sorry."

"Thanks. It was hell, as you can expect, but Caleb was twenty-four and old enough to take over the ranch and be guardian to us all. I'm not legally their sister, but in all the ways that count, I am. Make sense?"

She'd said it clearly, and pretty much straight-up unemotional, but he was floored. "You told me in February you were holding a wake."

"Yup. Ten-year anniversary of the accident."

Jesse couldn't stand it any longer. He slid closer to her and lifted her into his lap. She seemed almost not to notice because she didn't protest. Just sat there, frigid and cold.

He curled an arm around her and pressed her close to his chest. "I'm sorry that they're gone."

"Me too."

They sat in silence, Jesse rubbing her back as he considered how much pain that must have been for a sixteen-year-old to face. Just sharing the story had turned her brittle, her body stiff and nearly frozen, and minutes passed before she took a deep enough breath to supply her body with what had to be much-needed oxygen.

She softened slightly, leaning into him and resting her head on his shoulder. Her eyes were dry, but so, so sad, and something inside him snapped.

Jesse wanted to fix this. He wanted to be there for

her. Not sexually — hell, he was attracted to her, but this was completely different. It wasn't about jumping her bones, but man did he want to lighten her load. He wanted to turn this around...

And there was nothing he could do. He was helpless in a way he'd never been before.

A moment later Dare patted him on the shoulder and straightened up. "Sorry. I don't usually lose it like that. It's not as if I spend every minute of the day and night thinking about it. Not anymore."

Jesse shook his head. "You didn't overreact one bit."

"But it's in the past," she said. "Ginny and I were sixteen when Caleb took over the ranch, and he did his best. The other boys helped as much as they could. We kind of all worked through hell that next year. Caleb, Luke, Walker, Ginny, me and Dustin. They're not really my brothers, but they are. Anyone else who asks I simply say they're family, but you and I — well, our relationship is a bit more complicated than the average pair of strangers."

Way more complicated, she was right about that.

"They're family," he agreed. "It makes perfect sense."

She nodded, climbing off his lap and brushing her hands on her thighs. "Come on. I'll show you the falls."

As if she wanted to walk away from the memories.

Jesse followed her down the path. The dirt trail was wide enough to walk side-by-side, but they strode in silence, Dare staring ahead determinedly, Jesse considering what she'd shared.

Hell of a thing for everyone involved. Heck, Caleb had taken over running the ranch at twenty-four? A momentary twinge struck Jesse, considering he was older than that and barely responsible for himself.

50

"Do you all work on the ranch? I mean other than I know you've got the blog."

"The guys do. Walker is on the road a bit these days — he's riding the circuit — but Caleb, Luke and Dustin are always around. And Ginny, of course. Plus, I've always done my share of chores but I have less time and energy now, and the blog brings in money. Well, it's not enough to live on. Close, though."

"Your blog looks great. You definitely post awesome photos."

She snorted. "Thank you for being photogenic." She glanced over and swore lightly. "I'm sorry, do you want me to take the picture down? I should've asked right away."

"No reason. The horses are out of the barn, so to speak, and there's no getting the pictures off the internet, so you may as well get as much mileage on your blog as possible."

She rubbed the side of her nose. "I'm so glad you aren't an asshole."

He was pretty sure there were mixed opinions on that assessment, but he'd take the compliment at face value. "That's good, because one of my biggest life goals is to be considered not an asshole."

Her sad expression brightened a little, and he counted it as a win.

They stepped out of the trees into a clearing and the falls burst into view, and the next while it was all about the scenery.

But something inside Jesse turned inexorably forward, like a set of old-fashioned wind-up gears that couldn't be stopped until they'd reached their destination. The bright wild child who he'd played with for what he thought would be a brief moment in time was far more complicated than he'd expected.

The future was full of questions, and they'd barely even scratched the surface.

Chapter Four

What a twisted, mixed-up day. The Merriam-Webster definition of an emotional rollercoaster — Dare was nearing exhaustion.

They'd grabbed dinner-to-go from the local bar then she'd taken him around the back way to sit by the shores of Little Sky Lake for a picnic supper.

Somehow they'd gotten on to the topic of school and their favourite subjects. A random discussion, and low-key after the intense sharing she'd had to do right off the start. The storytelling was exactly what she needed to settle her soul.

Only the entire time they'd talked, there'd been this buzz of sexual awareness growing between them that she needed to fight.

Didn't she?

The right and wrong of sexual attraction to this man was too much to consider while sitting beside him, his sleeves rolled up to reveal strong forearms, muscles flexing as he twisted the lid off a pop and handed it over.

Their fingers touched, and his gaze darted up to meet hers, a sensual smirk on his lips. "You got something on your mind, darlin'?"

"Just considering how I can take advantage of your mathematical genius," she lied. "I barely made it through Math 30, and don't ask me to explain my work."

Jesse leaned back on an elbow, long legs stretched in front of him. "I'm game to help you, any way I can."

He wasn't talking about arithmetic, damn him anyway.

Dare ignored the innuendo best she could. "Tell me something about your family."

His expression lost a little of the shine, and she wondered if they were treading into dangerous territory. The email from his sister-in-law had seemed good-natured enough, but sometimes it was hard to tell what was at the root of family problems.

Jesse rallied, taking a swig of his pop before answering her. "Lots of brothers, just like you. In fact, I beat you by one."

"Ginny would tell you she's as tough as any guy."

He grinned. "I like her already."

Dare poked him with her foot. "Five brothers. Let me guess. You're the youngest."

He frowned. "What's that mean? I'm not the youngest."

She shrugged. "The fact you're here and not there makes me think you've got more freedom than some of the others, that's all. I mean Caleb would cut off his arm before he'd leave Silver Stone, but Luke went on the rodeo circuit for a few years. Walker is there now, and I figure Dustin will head out at some point for a while."

He nodded slowly. "I guess that makes sense. Maybe there's something about being the oldest that hits them harder about home and hearth. My brother Blake is like that — I told you about him. He's the one married to Jaxi. They took over the house I grew up in. They've got four kids and another on the way."

Dare swore. "Ambitious woman."

"Coleman are a fertile lot."

Great to know. "Thanks for warning me ahead of time, asshole."

But she patted his hand to let him know she was teasing before urging him to go on.

"Next oldest is Matt. His wife owns a quilt shop, and they had their first kid last November. Middle brother is Daniel, and he married a woman with three older kids he's adopted."

"Middle?" She was going to need to write this down to remember it, but that made no sense. "You said there are six of you — "

"You'll understand in a minute," he promised. "Travis comes next, and he is a bit of — Hell, a wild card?"

"Black-sheep-of-the-family kind of thing?"

Jesse shook his head. "A Travis kind of thing. He lives with his boyfriend and girlfriend, and they're expecting a kid this summer."

Curiouser and curiouser.

"Whoa, that's — " She was struck by something, counting on her fingers. "Six brothers, and three babies on the way, counting ours? You weren't kidding about the fertile thing."

"I'm glad to know it's the baby thing that snagged you, not the fact my brother is in a permanent threesome."

"Hey, whatever turns his crank, but damn — the *babies*..."

"There's at least one set of twins every generation," he informed her. "I'm a twin, and the firstborn, therefore *not* the youngest."

Panic gripped her. "You're kidding. You've got a twin?"

"Identical."

Awesome, just what she didn't need — two of Jesse messing with her hormones. They had to be devastating standing side by side, but even that image was rapidly overlapped by a bigger, more vital concern. "Is it catching?"

Jesse laughed. "Is what catching? Being a twin?"

"You said there's a set in every generation. Oh my God, what if I'm having twins?" She collapsed dramatically onto her back and stared up at the sky.

Jesse stretched out beside her, obviously trying to temper his amusement. "You don't know?"

"Haven't gone to my first prenatal yet," she confessed. "It's a week away."

His expression changed. "That's late, isn't it? I could have sworn my sisters-in-law were dragging my brothers to the doctor the day they suspected."

She curled up and nodded guiltily. "I was in denial for a while, and then I wanted to figure out for sure what I wanted to do. I tried to find you, as well — "

Jesse paused. "You want to keep the baby, don't you?"

That was one question Dare could answer now without hesitation. "Yes. It might be crazy, but I think it's the right thing to do."

He nodded, and she was glad to see relief on his face. The baby was a shock, but he wasn't going to try to change her mind about keeping it.

Not that proposing made her suspect he would.

Lordy. He'd proposed…

They cleaned up the picnic and headed back to her cottage, another stretch of silence between them. This time it wasn't quite as comfortable, but that was more because Dare was thinking hard about what would happen when they got home.

They'd talked, they'd eaten. Was it wrong that images of fooling around kept flashing into her brain?

Sex got you into this mess, the angel on her shoulder reminded her.

Really hot, body-shaking sex that had not sucked? I remember, the devil on the other side retorted.

Jesse held the door open for her then followed her inside. It was bright daylight, and would be for a long time, so she debated asking him if he wanted to sit on the porch.

The alternative was asking him to strip and make her evening.

Dare ignored him for a moment and filled a glass at the kitchen sink, drinking the water as she gazed out the window and tried to slow her racing libido. There were cattle in the field on the far side of the lake, and she watched them graze. Peaceful and calm, completely different than the wild thoughts racing through her brain.

He stepped behind her, a hand landing on either side of her hips on the counter. Far enough back he wasn't pinning her in place, but she was definitely in his arms.

Dare took a deep breath then pivoted.

Her gaze met heat and desire, and she swallowed hard to stop herself from too willingly accepting his unspoken invitation.

"I don't know if we should do this."

He caressed his knuckles over her cheek. "Are we doing something?"

Jerk. He was going to make her say it. "We could be. I just don't know if we should."

His fingers brushed lower, slipping down her neck. "I don't seem to remember us having any problems *doing it*. I had fun, you had fun — or at least I'm pretty sure you had fun. Four or five times. Maybe six?"

"You're playing dirty." Every nerve in her body was

tingling. Dare managed to get out the words, but her voice had gone low with lust. "The sex was awesome, and you know it."

His cocky grin was back in place. "A guy likes to hear it, though."

Amusement and desire warred, and she couldn't decide what to do.

Jesse didn't have the same hesitation. "Let's put this into perspective. We met one night, and had a good time. If there weren't consequences to that evening, and I tracked you down, what would you have been thinking right now?"

"I would have jumped you," she admitted, the confession bursting free. "Three hours ago. The instant you arrived I would have hauled you into my bedroom, and we probably wouldn't have come up for air yet."

It was his turn to hesitate, the hand on her hip tightening as he fought for control. "Now who's playing dirty?"

She let her hands roam up his chest. "But there were consequences, Jesse. That changes things."

He shifted his position, and their hips bumped, the heat from his torso slipping over her.

"There's a lot we've got to figure out over the next while that's complicated. This?" His gaze roamed her body, a heated expression back in his eyes. "Sweetheart, this is the simplest thing in the world. It's also the biggest thing we've got going for us, so we may as well take advantage of it and enjoy the ride."

Forcing her brain to function was damn difficult when all her hormones were percolating like a soda machine set on high. "Wait. You're right. If we'd found each other again, fooling around would be logical and fun, but there is something because of that night." She looked him in the eye. "This isn't just our lives we're messing with. You clean, Jesse? Because I'm going to assume you've been with other women since me, and I'm not about to trust a condom, since they obviously work oh-so-well for us."

He made a face. "I enjoyed our night together, a lot, but you're right. It was only one night."

Dare lifted her hands to his shoulders, easing them apart as the sexual tension slipped off potential-now-screwing-around into future-screwing-around, which was not great for her current aching hormones, but still something to look forward to.

"Then get proof and we'll talk."

"Oh hell, we'll do more than talk."

Jesse unbuttoned his shirt and stripped it off in record time before catching her against him. Once more she was trapped by strong arms, this time with the full-on furnace heat of his body melting her resistance.

He'd pinned her arms between them, and her palms were pressed to bare skin. She traced the muscular chest under her fingers. "You have a strange way of slowing down, cowboy."

"You said no sex, which makes sense. I'm glad you're going to be a stickler for keeping Buckaroo safe." He lowered his voice, and a challenge came into his eyes. "Nothing to say I can't get you off without sex."

Something was wrong with her that she wasn't nixing the idea immediately. "You're not going to end up walking around with blue balls?"

"I have no intention of keeping the pressure so high they turn blue. I can get us both off in a way that keeps you safe."

He nibbled his way along her neck, hands cupping her ass to pull her tighter to where his erection bulged the front of his jeans.

Distracting. Very distracting. Dare struggled to focus. "I still want to — "

" — fuck? Me too."

She laughed. It was impossible not to. "Stop interrupting, asshole."

He sucked lightly on her neck, pressing his advantage when she quivered involuntary. "You do want to fuck, don't you?"

"Yes, eventually. Papers, yada, yada, but I also want to date you. I'm serious about that too."

He untucked her shirt and his talented fingers made short work of her buttons. "We'll date for a while. Have lots of talk time. I'll find my baby books so you can admire all the shots of my bare butt."

He ran his hands delicately up the sides of her body, hands on bare skin under the open tails of her shirt. He undid her bra with rapid skill before sweeping forward under the fabric to cover her breasts with his palms.

An electric storm shot through her. "Careful."

"Jeez, Dare. This is the baby thing, isn't it?" He peeled off her shirt, tossing away her bra. "*Fuck*."

"No. No fucking, but yes — " She gave up and gave in, a long moan of pleasure escaping her lips. It was too good to not let him have his way with her. "God, do that again. Like that."

He'd lifted her breast with one hand as he leaned in and swiped his tongue over her nipple. It beaded tight under his touch and a tingling sensation washed over her. "That's so good."

She gasped as he picked her up and carried her to

the kitchen table, dragging out a chair with one foot to arrange her in his lap. "I'll be busy for a few hours. I hope you don't mind."

He shoved her back up to overdrive immediately, this time wrapping his lips around one peak and sucking. His tongue flicked rapidly as pleasure tore through her system, faster and faster, as if she were a pot of water, and once she'd reached the boiling point she could just stay there for a good long time.

He murmured happily, switching sides, her breasts hot and heavy against his mouth. His big palms supported the weight as if he were her own personal servant, and even through the haze of pleasure, the image made her snicker.

Jesse pulled back far enough to offer up a smile. "What're you giggling about?"

"Just picturing you walking around with your hands over my boobs for the next five months."

"Jeez, is that an option? Because hell, yeah." He flashed a grin full of pure lust and happiness. "Close your eyes and relax. I'm serious. This is a little bit of heaven, and I'm in no rush."

"Breast man?" she teased.

A contented hum was all she got in return as he slid his tongue wickedly over her nipple followed by a brief caress of his lips. He pinched lightly, then swung to the other side, and she gave in and closed her eyes like he'd suggested.

It was all sorts of amazing, and it had been a long time since anyone had touched her, other than herself…

She glanced down to discover he was smiling in that way that made her shiver. "Stop looking at me as if I'm on the menu."

"Darlin', you're not only on the menu. You *are* the menu. I'm on a Dare diet, and I'm planning on enjoying as much all-you-can-eat buffet as possible."

He was too cheesy to be real, but that *tongue* —

Damn, she loved his tongue, and she knew well enough from their previous interaction his talents in using it involved a lot more than her breasts.

She could hardly wait.

"Stop talking and keep doing the other things," she ordered to stop from giving in to temptation and telling him to go for it.

"Yes, ma'am."

Seconds later another moan escaped her. She wondered if it was possible to come from just him playing with her breasts. Jesse was completely dedicated to his task, focused on what he was doing, so intent as he grabbed her hips and placed her on the tabletop, reaching for the top button of her jeans.

The strangest sound echoed through the house. One Dare hadn't heard for simply ages.

Jesse cursed softly, his fingers stilling on her waistline. "You expecting company?"

Oh, damn, that sound was the doorbell, and here they were both naked from the waist up.

"Give me my shirt," she whispered in a panic.

She grabbed what he offered, which was *his* shirt, not hers, but the doorbell was going off again and she had no choice but to pull the fabric on as Jesse pushed the chair away and kicked her bra and shirt out of sight under the table.

"How do I look?" she asked frantically doing up buttons.

"Edible."

Of course he would be completely unhelpful.

"Awesome." She hurried to the door, eye to the peephole to discover her nieces on the other side.

"Drat."

"Need me to climb out a window?"

Before she could answer, the door opened and Dare stepped back as Sasha and Emma poured in. The little girls were clad in their pyjamas, travel mugs in one hand and DVDs in the other.

Neither of them focused on Jesse, more intent on storming across her living room to throw themselves onto the couch.

"We didn't know which movie you wanted to watch, Auntie Dare, so I brought *The Jungle Book*, and Emma brought the movie about pixies, and Jesse gets to decide."

The gentleman in question was standing with his back to the door, a wide grin on his face. Other than his bare chest, she never would've guessed they'd just been interrupted from a highly charged sexual situation.

Dare sucked in a quick breath and worked to sound as casual as possible instead of wracked by lust. "We're not having a movie night, girls."

Sasha looked confused. She glanced at her sister before turning back. "But Daddy's out tonight, and we always watch a movie when Daddy goes away."

Heaven save her from little girls. "You can watch a movie, but to make it extra special you should watch it in Auntie Ginny's room."

There was another knock, obviously just for show because the door swung open an instant later and Ginny nonchalantly stepped into the room, an oversized plate in her hands.

"I wondered where you little turkeys had taken off

to. I told you we could drop off some dessert, but that's it." She eyed Jesse appreciatively before passing over the plate. "Hello, again."

He took the offering before offering Dare a rueful smile. "It's gotten a little chilly in here. I'll just go grab a shirt."

"Don't bother on my account," Ginny deadpanned.

Dare wondered that he didn't take off and run for the hills at the lack of privacy caused by the revolving door on her house.

He didn't seem upset, though. Just walked to the table by the front door to dig around in a bag she hadn't noticed he'd left there. He found a dark T-shirt, pulling it over his head then tucking it into the jeans clinging to his lean hips while she watched with far too much fascination. Not even the distinct sound of Disney theme music starting up in the background could interrupt the sexual buzz jolting through her.

She wasn't sure how it happened, but she ended up being corralled onto the couch with Jesse on one side of her, and a little girl on either side of them. More specifically, Sasha had settled beside Jesse and was intently watching the opening credits of the movie while Emma leaned past her to stare at him with wide eyes.

Ginny took the open seat in the recliner, peering over the top of her glasses. "I guess I need to mention to Caleb that the furnace in here needs adjusting. Since you're having trouble regulating the heat and all."

"Shut up," Dare muttered with affection.

Her cheeks had to be beet red, and she wasn't usually a blusher.

Then again, she rarely had the opposite sex over, and even less often got caught in compromising situations.

She'd had a steady boyfriend in their final year of high school before he'd gone away to college, but if anything she'd spent more time hanging out with the Stone family than in a long-term boy-girl relationship.

It seemed whatever she'd been lacking before, she had it now. The long-term business.

She glanced across the room at her friend, trying to put a world of meaning into her pleading expression.

Ginny blinked innocently, exaggeratedly so.

"You will regret this," Dare warned.

"Nice shirt," Ginny returned. "Is that the latest style?"

Dare glanced down to discover she'd buttoned Jesse's top up so frantically she'd missed a notch, and the shirt front was out of kilter left and right.

She let her head fall back on the couch with a thud, attempting to ignore Jesse's firm thigh muscles pressed against her leg and the echo of lust ricocheting through her veins.

The wolves howling on the screen had nothing on the howling going on inside her belly.

Dare dragged her head back to vertical so she could glare at Ginny again, extra hard. The look usually reserved for moments of *I will never forgive you for teasing me like this…*

Her friend let out a long-suffering sigh before winking, then leaping to her feet. "My goodness, you guys, I totally forgot that Auntie Dare's out of popcorn. I simply can't watch a movie without popcorn."

Sasha jumped off the couch, gaze pinned to the screen. "I can get some."

Dare moved quickly and turned her niece to face her, placing her hands on Sasha's shoulders to give a firm squeeze. "You are such an amazing girl, but you know

65

what? You brought cake for me and Jesse, and I don't think we can eat cake *and* popcorn, so you and Emma go ahead with Auntie Ginny, and enjoy your movie."

Sasha looked as if she was about to argue, but Ginny saved the day, adding in a low whisper aimed straight at the girls. "Maybe they can't eat cake and popcorn, but I'm pretty sure we could sneak another piece."

Ginny pressed a finger against her lips as if she hadn't said that in public, and miraculously little people were rising off the couch, nabbing the DVD and heading for the door.

Which meant her and Jesse's plans were back on track.

Dare wasn't sure if this was good news, or terrible news, but at this point she was pretty much willing to go where the adventure took her.

———————⌒◦⌒———————

The girls were out the door and across the space between the houses, their arms held out like fairy wings as Sasha howled loud enough for two.

Ginny stepped to the threshold. "Don't stay up too late, kids."

Dare miraculously waited until her friend was completely outside before sliding the door shut. Jesse would have slammed it on Ginny's heels, but then she wasn't his best friend. Especially not after her horrible timing dropping in.

Blame it on the girls — *ha*. That had been all Ginny's fault.

"Let me get that for you." He moved in tight behind her, reaching to lock the deadbolt. "Should have locked this earlier."

Maybe there *was* something wrong with the system in the house because he was suddenly on fire.

She twisted toward him, body pressed to his. Meeting his challenge head on. "You are trouble."

Jesse rested his hand on the door, his arms on either side of her head. "I thought by now that would be pretty apparent."

"Maybe I'm on a trouble-free diet."

He inched in closer. "You don't have to eat if you're not hungry."

Damn, he wanted to kiss her. He wanted to throw her over his shoulder and march off to the bedroom so he could make her scream. But he had to follow the rules —

He hated following the rules. It was more fun to bend or break them.

Inspiration hit. He caught hold of her fingers and tugged her with him to the bathroom. "Come on. Two locked doors are better than one."

He paused in the hallway, though, not sure there was enough room for both of them in the limited space of the bathroom.

He popped open the button on his jeans, lifting his gaze to offer Dare a challenge.

"Did you get cake down your pants?" Dare demanded, but he heard it. An appreciative hum as he shoved his jeans and briefs to the floor, kicking his way out of everything else to stand naked in front of her.

She shook her head, moving closer to touch the bruise on his hip. "Another fight?"

"Argument with a horse."

Her brows rose. "How did you lose an argument with a horse?"

He reached for the buttons on his shirt, the one

she was currently wearing. Slowly stripping her as he spoke. "Who said I lost? That was a friendly love tap after I stayed in the saddle long enough to prove my point."

"We're not having sex," she reminded him as he tossed the shirt to the floor. "How did he bruise you?"

"Shoved me into the corral fencing. Just an affectionate nudge before I left."

He kept working as he spoke, and suddenly she was once again naked from the waist up and he was back in heaven.

"You need a shower," he announced. "We both need a shower really badly."

She opened her mouth, probably to protest, but screw that. He'd had enough of waiting around, and the hardness in his cock wasn't going away. He caught the waistband of her jeans and pulled them down, grinning when instead of panties he found bare skin and soft curls. "I like the way you dress."

She threaded her fingers through his hair as he knelt by her feet. Body heating up immediately as he tugged her pants free.

"I like the way you undress me," she confessed. "No sex, remember?"

Right then he wasn't sure what his own name was, so the reminder was appreciated.

"You're driving me crazy."

He picked her up, and she wrapped her legs around him, their bodies pressed together. Warm, naked skin, strong thighs, and those *breasts* —

Everything about this woman was lush and perfect. He squeezed her ass, resisting the urge to stop and press her against the nearest wall. Temptation told him to drive himself deep and rut on her like a wild man.

Civility told him to follow the fucking rules. Right now Dare was trusting him to keep his word, so as much as his balls were begging him to do one thing, he let his mind take control and brought her into the tub enclosure with him.

He turned the taps on full, waiting until the water splashing at their feet was a decent temperature. That gave him time to press his front to her back and allow his hands to drift over her, caressing and teasing, drifting back to cup her breasts, the heavy weight of them heaven in his palms.

She wiggled, her body warm — no, more than warm. She was a fiery furnace that set his need soaring.

"The first time I can have you I'm taking you in the shower," Jesse warned her. "Or, maybe not the first time, because I won't be able to keep my hands off you long enough to get you in here. Maybe the second time, because you dripping wet for me, body slippery — fucking *works*."

Dare let out a soft moan, reaching up to hook a hand around his neck.

He caught her earlobe between his teeth and worried it for a moment before whispering in her ear, "I want to look into your eyes when you get close. I want to see you lose control and tip over the edge like an out-of-control explosion, like before."

She rocked against him, and Jesse slid his fingers between the lips of her pussy and stroked, slow enough to tease, hard enough to drive her wild. Over and over as he nibbled on the back of her neck between telling her every dirty thing he had on his list.

"I'm going to fuck you from behind, and up against

the wall. I'm going to lick every inch of you and then take you from one end to the other."

A shudder rocked her, and her hips pulsed forward.

He turned and pulled on the tab to send the water up to the showerhead, standing protectively so the cold in the line hit him first. The instant the water went warm he twisted them, water driving between his fingers where he cupped her breast. Moisture dripped from her nipple, and Dare laid her head back on his shoulder and groaned, the sound driving into him and sending a pulse straight to his balls.

No sex, no sex. Keep your fucking cock away from her.

He listened to himself, mostly. The shower made things even more slick, and he increased the pressure on her clit. His other hand he curled around to tease between her butt cheeks as he fastened his teeth on her shoulder and nipped.

Her hips pulsed helplessly against his hand, and he increased the tempo, fingers working her like a concert pianist while he stroked over the tight hole of her ass.

"So close," she offered, her voice tight. Her fingers were wrapped around his wrist with a death grip, pulling him closer, not pushing him away.

He adjusted position, pressing his cock into the hollow of her back. Rubbing to ease his cock even as he worked to bring her pleasure. His hands worked independently, multitasking like a mofo, one intent on getting her off, the other needing to soak in the lushness of her breasts.

"Oh. Oh, *Jesse*…"

Her grip tightened, fingernails digging into his forearm. Jesse kept up the demanding pace on her clit, rocking his hips and fucking against her in a desperate race to completion.

One earthmoving pulse later, she came apart in his arms. A long, low moan escaped her, and the noise triggered his release. He set his teeth together and his release exploded, seed spraying over her back and rubbing between them. He slowed his fingers as aftershocks rocked her.

He forced himself to stay vertical, the beat of the water around them dull in his ears as blood raced so hard the roar drowned out everything else.

He fought for air.

She relaxed in his arms, turning to catch his face in her hands then dragging their lips together to kiss him deeply. The same fire he'd experienced that night in February scalded him.

He pressed on her shoulders and inched them apart. "You shouldn't kiss me," he warned.

She threaded her fingers through his hair, chest rocking with her heavy breaths. "I know, but maybe I'm not as smart as I should be."

He wasn't about to insist he was safe, even though he really thought he was.

She rested her head on his shoulder, curling against him, and he held her, the moment strangely intimate —

More intimate than seconds earlier while giving her pleasure. Right then there was nothing but them, naked and unguarded. Nothing between them but a fine sheen of water.

Nothing but them...*and a baby*.

Jesse's heart rate kicked into overdrive all over again.

Chapter Five

They'd had sex and crawled into bed before, albeit drunk as skunks, so getting into bed wasn't an issue. It was after, as they lay in the dark for a while until it was clear neither of them was sleepy yet.

"I should talk to your brothers," Jesse murmured against her neck as he spooned behind her. "Who's going to be my biggest trouble?"

She didn't hesitate. "I'm your biggest trouble."

He smiled into the dark. "Of course you are, darlin', but I don't want one of them to get the wrong idea and grab the castrator."

Dare considered for a moment. "He's not your biggest trouble, but you should talk to Caleb first."

"The oldest, right?"

She nodded. "Sasha and Emma's daddy. You can find him in the barns in the morning. Now go to sleep. I'm tired."

"Good tired, I hope," he teased.

"Shut up," she whispered.

Silence fell again, but while she stayed quiet, Dare wiggled and squirmed and jerked far more than he remembered.

She finally rolled over, shoving his arm away. "I don't mean to be rude, and thank you for my orgasm and all, but I can't sleep with you right now. It's too hot, and my skin twitches every time we touch, and normally I'd just get over it but I'm really, really tired..."

"Say no more." Jesse kissed her nose then tucked her in again. "I saw a bed in your office, right?"

"Uh-huh."

He paused in the door — she gave one enormous sigh then slipped right into dreamland.

Rest didn't come as easily for him.

Every time he tried to close his eyes, her voice poked him awake. Just repeating one word, over and over.

Pregnant.

Which meant a baby. Which meant his life path had altered.

It had been simple to push that detail aside as they talked, as huge and life changing as it was. Like a single note hit off key during a song, the idea had slapped him upside the head and he'd reeled for a moment, but then it passed, and the things he'd been dwelling on drowned out the reality —

Not for long, but for long enough that every time the phrase *pregnant* hit his consciousness, his heart pounded and his breathing kicked up a notch all over.

It didn't help that Dare was so matter of fact about it. Hell, if she'd been panicking, he would have an easier time dealing. Calming her down, offering his assurances. Lying through his teeth that everything was going to be okay.

He'd missed that stage, he guessed. The thought left him floundering.

He must've fallen asleep at some point, but come four a.m. he was wide awake like usual. No use lying in the postage-stamp-sized bed any longer, so he got dressed and headed outside.

Morgan joined him instantly, tail wagging hard enough that his hindquarters quivered.

Jesse petted Morgan's head for a moment as he sat on the porch, feet on the stairs to put on his boots, looking around the ranch. The faintest pink light etched the distant horizon to the east.

A long, hard walk helped, the familiar scents of the ranch enough to set some of his panic aside. Okay, so this wasn't what he had planned, but it was the hand he'd been dealt and he'd have to do the best he could. He felt like crap Dare had already dealt with months of this on her own.

That was the central thing on his mind as he wandered into the biggest of the barns after exploring for nearly an hour.

A dozen heads all turned in his direction. No, make that a baker's dozen. The horses examined him briefly in the hopes he was going to offer them food.

A calico cat balanced daintily along the ridge of a railing, making its way along the length to a post where it sat to greet him with a good morning *meow*.

"Morgan, stay."

His dog sat, hindquarters plopping into the dirt as Jesse moved confidently toward the cat to offer it a quick scratch under the chin.

The animal graced him with its presence for a moment before stretching regally. Then it jumped to the ground and, after offering Morgan a disdainful sniff, walked away with tail upright, the very tip flicking back and forth as she headed off hunting.

Comfortable. Familiar.

Not home.

Regret swamped him much in the same way

the shock of that life-changing statement *pregnant* kept intruding.

As much as he wanted to go home, he couldn't.

As much as he wished Dare had greeted him with different news, there was no going back.

Noise travelled in the quiet of the barn, and Jesse made his way toward the distinctive scrape of a rake at work. The barn was warm, the scent of horses and hay a rich, earthy wash in his nostrils. Silver Stone had a lot of quality animals, and Jesse took his time walking past the stalls, pausing to brush a nape and pet a nose.

"Are you lost?"

Jesse turned slowly, even though he'd been surprised, making sure not to spook the animal he stood next to. "Morning."

The man stepped forward into view, and Jesse recognized him as one of the Stone family. There was enough of a resemblance to Ginny, although this man had to be in his early thirties, and his face held nowhere near the laughter and impulsive mischief painted on every inch of Dare's best friend.

Dark hair, dark eyes. He was as solidly built as any of the Coleman clan, perhaps a little shorter than Jesse, but obviously a man of the land.

Also someone who was probably prepared to take off Jesse's head.

No getting around it. Jesse held out his hand. "We haven't been introduced. Jesse Coleman."

"Caleb Stone." He stared at Jesse's hand for a moment as if it were smeared with shit. "You the one who got Dare pregnant?"

It was a little awkward with his arm just hanging there, so Jesse let it fall to his side. "I am."

75

"Ginny told me you were here." The man eyed Morgan.

"He won't make trouble," Jesse promised.

Caleb squatted low and offered a treat he'd pulled from his pocket. Morgan didn't move until Jesse gave him leave, then took the treat and head-butted Caleb as thanks before returning to Jesse's side.

The other man nodded in approval at the dog, then grabbed a second rake off the wall and held it out to Jesse.

Thank God.

Not only did it give Jesse a familiar task for his hands, it was also a pretty good indicator he wasn't about to be shot or hogtied, since both were tough to accomplish if Caleb's hands were full.

He followed Caleb to a section where the horses had been moved, stepping into an empty stall and willingly getting to work. Over the years he'd had an awful lot of conversations through wooden walls like this. Jesse wondered briefly if it was one of those things that cowboys did because men talking about emotional shit —

Walls were a damn good metaphor *and* made some of these tough talks a hell of a lot easier.

He'd taken a half-dozen drags with the rake when Caleb spoke, his deep voice clear in the otherwise quiet of the barn.

"You didn't expect to hear Dare's news." It wasn't phrased as a question.

The man would want honesty. "Could have knocked me over with a feather, yeah. Bit of a shocker, but I'll do right by her."

"Can you?" Noises in the stall one over paused. "She's family. I'm not going to let her ruin her life by hooking up with someone who needs babying. The last thing she needs right now is another person to take care of."

Jesse held back a flash of anger, knowing it wasn't a personal attack. This was a man looking out for someone under his protection. "I'm not a slacker. It wasn't my fault she's had to manage things by herself until now."

Caleb grunted. "Dare made it clear she didn't blame you when I offered to hunt you down, which is why you're not lying in a ditch, bleeding. Nothing you could've done, other than protect her a little harder in the first place, but that boat's sailed."

"It wasn't from a lack of trying," Jesse protested.

An awkward pause from the other side of the wall. "I don't want details."

Right. Dare was like a sister. No sex discussions with the man. "I wasn't an asshole then, or an asshole now. I offered to marry her."

"Did you now? What did Dare have to say about that?"

Jesse played it up as best he could. "She didn't say *yes*, but we'll get there."

"Is this something you do on a regular basis? Treat a woman's *no* like it's a *yes*?"

Well, that sounded slimy. "Hell, no. I didn't mean that at all. I just meant... Well, you know how it is. Sometimes women change their minds."

If anything the disapproval in Caleb's voice grew stronger. "You've got a high opinion of women."

Jesse thought he had the highest opinion of women. They were a hell of a lot more complicated than guys while being soft and smelling fantastic. He *worshiped* women, but he figured there was no way he was getting out of the barn that morning without physical damage. Better to get the anger in the open.

He leaned his rake on the stall wall then stepped

into Caleb's line of vision, hands hanging by his sides. "Go ahead."

Caleb stared back, iron-cold.

Jesse shrugged. "Everyone in my family has laid me out at some point, and I usually deserved it. I feel like shit that Dare had to deal with things without me, but if you want to put me on the floor — "

The man's poker face was deadly. Jesse wasn't sure if his offer was going to be taken up or not.

After the longest time, an exasperated sigh escaped Caleb. "Already told you Dare's opinion on the matter. Until she wants you beat up, you're in the clear."

Huh.

Jesse stood silently until Caleb resumed raking, then he went back to his side of the wall, the practical exchange a little anticlimactic.

"You plan on sticking around?" Caleb asked.

"I'll have to do some juggling for a while, but I'll be there for her."

"Job?"

At least he could answer this one with something positive. "Bar M, outside of Pincher Creek."

"That's a high-class operation. They've got some quality animals."

"I'm planning breeding programs for them."

"Really?" A touch more interest lit Caleb's voice at that bit of info.

Jesse grinned. He wasn't just a hayseed cowboy. He loved working with his hands, and had no objection to being in the field with the men, but he had more to offer. "Got a diploma in genetics with a minor in computer programming. Considered going for a degree, but I figured some hands-on experience with the programming was worth more to the family than another piece of paper."

Another *oh* from Caleb, his curiosity continuing to rise as the rake-motion sounds slowed. "Got any samples of your work?"

Most of it was planning he'd done for the Six Pack ranch. He'd been trying to not exploit the connection, but considering this man was a potential brother-in-law… "For you, sure."

Nothing more was said, but Jesse hoped the gears were already turning. He wasn't going to bail on Dare, and if he kept his word, Caleb might offer him a job at Silver Stone before the dust settled.

They worked in silence. Caleb showed him where the fresh pellets were, then glanced into the stall when Jesse was done.

There'd be no qualms over his work. He'd been cleaning stalls since he was barely able to lift the rake, him and his brother working together to try to impress their father.

A far-too-familiar twinge hit his gut. He hated how long it'd been since he'd seen the man.

Seen his brother.

"You got any other kids?"

The glib answer that would normally hit his lips — *not that I know of* — stuck in his throat, and now Jesse had another rock in his belly.

Had there ever been another accident somewhere over the years? He didn't think so — at least not with anybody in the Rocky area, but he'd flirted and fucked his way through a lot of Alberta, and the thought he might unknowingly have more kids left him a little shaky.

Instead he answered the implied part of the question.

"No one special in my life. I wasn't with anyone back home, and I've been trying to..." What did he say? He'd hadn't felt like joining the debauchery he'd normally thrived on? "There's no one."

"And your family?"

There was the million-dollar question.

"My family is fine, but I'm going to talk to Dare more before you and I start exchanging life histories. I just wanted you to know I'm in the picture. I'm not running."

Because running doesn't solve anything. His cousin's parting shot before Jesse had gone and done exactly that.

He looked up to find Caleb standing less than a foot away.

"You sound like a decent guy." Dare's brother by choice looked him over, the lazy, half-hooded gaze hardening as a steely edge came into his eyes. "Don't screw up with Dare."

"I won't."

Caleb grunted and turned away.

Jesse walked the opposite direction, lost in thought. What he did had to be up to Dare as well, but if he was going to give up his position at Bar M to be close to her, he needed a way to make money. He'd have a family to support —

Another hard rock slid into his belly.

He wandered around a corner, jerking to a halt as he came face to face with a tall youth, obviously a younger brother of Caleb's. His features were familiar — and when a hard gleam of anger swept across the young man's expression, Jesse identified him as the irate door-banger from the day before.

"Dustin?"

The young man narrowed his eyes. *"You."*

Jesse held out his hand. "Jesse Coleman. I want — "

Pain splintered his concentration. His eye throbbed and his cheek suddenly lit on fire.

What he *wanted* was for people to stop punching him in the face.

Dustin had moved without any warning, and while Jesse was usually more alert, it was because he hadn't expected to get whaled on. Talking so reasonably with Caleb had set him off his guard, although he should have anticipated Dustin would go off half-cocked and use his fists instead of laying out a welcome mat.

Jesse backed away, raising his hands to a protective position even as he warned Morgan off from where he'd slid between them, teeth bared in warning at the newcomer. "You think I'm going to stand here and let you beat on me?"

Dustin bounced closer, fists at the ready. "You made Dare cry."

"I didn't know, but now that I do, I'm going to take care of her."

"You don't get to march in and do that. *We'll* take care of her, like we always have. Go on and get the hell out of here."

Dustin took another swing. This time Jesse dodged to the side, the kid's fist sweeping past with a hell of a lot of force. "You've got some nice power behind that mitt, but if you do that again, I'm taking off the gloves and giving you some of your own medicine."

"I'd like to see you try."

A soothing quiet settled over Jesse as he stepped back and pulled off his shirt. In a way, this was what he needed. A hard, fast brawl would fix a lot of what was currently ailing him.

He and his brothers had done this many times. Frustrated? Upset? Find a reason to mix it up it and scrap until you got it out of your system.

He slammed a fist into Dustin's gut before the kid had a chance to anticipate the blow, then reveled in the sound of his pained exhale.

The next moments were a blur of hands and elbows, curses flying as fast as their fists. The swearing was all on Dustin's side. Jesse didn't waste energy talking — it was more satisfying to figure out where and how to land another punch then watch Dustin reel backward.

"What the hell is going on?"

Someone ripped them apart, and Jesse braced himself in case it ended up two against one.

Only the dark-haired newcomer shoved them back hard enough Dustin stumbled and fell. Jesse kept his feet with a great deal of difficulty.

"Dusty? You were warned about fighting with the hired hands."

"He's not — "

"Shut up." The man turned his attention to Jesse. "I don't remember you from the orientation. What's your name?"

"Jesse Coleman, and I don't work here." Yet, and it seemed his chances were going down instead of up.

"He's the bastard who knocked up Dare." Dustin used the stable wall to help get to his feet, disgust in his tone.

Maybe the attitude was all about Jesse's actions, but it sounded a lot like a diss on Dare, and *fuck that*. Anger rolled through Jesse at high speed.

He rushed forward, slamming Dustin into the wall and shoving an arm across his chest. Pinning the youth in place, Jesse moved in until their noses were almost touching. "Darilyn is not knocked up. She's expecting a child, hers and mine, and if you talk about her in that tone of voice again, I will make you sing soprano."

A heavy shoulder hit the wall next to Dustin as the newcomer leaned on it, glancing between the two of them. Amused judgment on his face as he checked out Jesse.

Jesse ignored him. The baby with the attitude had all his attention.

Dustin slammed his mouth shut, but kept jerking unsuccessfully to try and break Jesse's hold.

Damn if the stranger didn't chuckle before straightening up and offering some advice. "You might want to ask him to ease back a bit, Dusty. It's hard to rope with broken ribs, and I don't think this one — Jesse, was it?"

"Yeah."

" — I don't think he's in the mood for you."

"Fuck you, Luke. He hurt Dare."

"Dare is a big girl, and unless you want her even more pissed at you than usual for getting up in her business, back off. You deserved the slam into the boards for that *knocked-up* crack."

Dustin stopped writhing. Jesse stepped back so suddenly the kid lost his footing again. He slammed himself upright and gave Jesse one final dirty look before storming off, wiping blood from his mouth.

Derogatory comments about Jesse's ancestry and his personal habits slowly faded into the distance.

Jesse took in his new companion more closely. "One of the Stone boys, I take it?"

He nodded. "Luke Stone. I'm the sound, rational one in the family."

"I thought Caleb was pretty sane."

Luke grinned. "Yeah, but I'm level-headed without acting like I have a stick up my ass." He looked Jesse up and down once quickly then sighed heavily. "You're trouble. I can see why Dare would like you."

"Thanks?"

The other man chuckled then tilted his head toward the open yard. "I'm headed to a meeting. Walk with me."

Jesse pulled on his shirt then ran a hand through his hair to straighten himself up as much as possible before joining Luke. "Appreciate you not killing me, and all."

"No problem. It's not off the books yet, by the way. Killing you. But Dare told us what happened — her version, no details. I'm actually shocked to see you show up. How'd you find her?"

"Her blog."

"Huh." Luke pulled a face. "You didn't know she was pregnant."

"You're quick."

"Yup. Going to be blunt with you. If you're not planning on doing the decent thing and being around long term, do the next decent thing and leave sooner than later. Dare deserves more than some guy who's maybe there. You're in, or you're out."

"We're getting engaged," Jesse snapped.

Luke's feet tangled for a moment before he hit a smooth stride again. "You are a brave man."

"It's the right thing to do."

"It is," Luke agreed. "Course, it's nice to actually know the woman you're marrying, or so my fiancée says."

"You're getting married?"

"Yup. Penny Talisman. You'll meet her sometime if you're sticking around."

"She work for the ranch?" They were narrowing in on a group of cowboys — and a cowgirl or two.

"Nah, but her family breeds horses too, so she likes to hit the barns when she comes to visit." Luke jerked to a stop a good twenty feet from the gathering. "Look, it comes down to this. Dare is very special to me, and if you fuck up, I will hurt you, then I'll kill you and hide your body so thoroughly it'll be as if you never existed."

A man after his own heart. "We're good."

Luke touched his fingers to the brim of his hat then turned, leaving Jesse grinning until he thought of something.

"Hey," he shouted after Luke. "There's one more of you around somewhere. Should I expect death threats from him as well?"

Luke pivoted on a heel and walked backward as he kept moving. "Nah. Walker's not around right now — just make sure Ginny doesn't get it in her head to poison you. She's the one with the creative mind, and she holds a grudge."

"Good to know."

Luke left, and Jesse strolled slowly, rambling along the edge of the lake. The Stone place was familiar and new all at the same time. It was also somewhere he might be spending a lot of time in the future. That changed things. A lot.

How the hell had this happened? He'd been looking for another roll in the hay, not defending a woman's honour and playing *get to know you* with her family. Control had been swept out his hands.

He needed a little more air.

85

D are was putting the finishing touches on her next four scheduled posts when the door to the cottage opened and Ginny strolled in.

"Hello, the house. Is it safe? Jesse, don't bother dressing for my sake — it's always clothing optional for non-family cowboys around the Silver Stone ranch."

"You're a regular comedian," Dare drawled. "I'm in the office."

"You're out of bed."

"Master of the obvious, too. What do you do for an encore, lady? Pretend to read my future in the dirty sink water?" Dare spun her chair toward where Ginny had thrown herself on the guest bed.

Her friend eyed her closely. "Hmmm."

"What?"

Ginny wrinkled her nose, then tipped over and buried her face in the pillow, sniffing loudly.

Dare flushed. "You are *not* sniffing the sheets to try to figure out if we slept together."

"I'm not? I could have sworn I was. I like his soap, by the way. Ivory? Irish Spring?"

God. The only thing worse than a best friend was a best friend who was close enough to be family. "He slept in here, and I slept in my bed. Now go away and stop doing your bloodhound imitation."

"Why'd he sleep way over here, Dare? It's not like you could get pregnant, or anything." Her friend wiggled off the bed and pressed a hand to Dare's forehead. "You're not feverish, are you?"

"He proposed."

The words slipped out, and instantly Dare wished she could take them back, although she wasn't sure why. This was *Ginny* — of course she was going to tell her everything.

Only when her friend sat back down on the bed without offering a teasing joke, Dare was glad. It seemed too big of a thing to joke about.

"That's...good, isn't it?" Ginny asked.

"We can't get married," Dare snapped. "We don't know each other."

"Biblically speaking, you do."

Dare resisted rolling her eyes. "Well, that moment of seriousness lasted all of three seconds."

"Carnal knowledge is very serious business," Ginny insisted, "but I mean it. I'm glad to hear the dude's got more going for him than a magic penis."

"Magic — *ha*. Super-powered sperm is all we know for sure. Able to power through condoms like kryptonite." Although it had been a very nice penis, Dare reflected, and she was kind of counting the days until she got to make a more thorough reacquaintance with it.

With him. Attached to said penis, and all.

A loud clatter drew her gaze upward.

Ginny was clapping her hands to get her attention. "You're welcome for the awesome daydreams, but on to other matters. Since you avoided meeting everyone at dinner last night, you two coming over for lunch?"

"I don't think so. That's too much family, too soon."

"They have to get to know him. He proposed, and he's too yummy to ignore."

Oh brother. "Lunch with the hoard can wait, and a relationship isn't built on yummy, Ginny."

"Don't knock the yum factor, that's all I'm saying." Ginny slipped across and hugged her tight before whispering in her ear. "You know I'm here for you. Truth or dare, forever."

Dare's throat tightened at the quick reminder of their childish slogan. "Truth or dare, forever."

They linked little fingers for a moment, sharing a smile.

Boot falls on the outside deck warned them of a cowboy's approach, and they were in the living room when the door swung open.

Jesse peeked in. His eyes lit up when he spotted Dare, some of his enthusiasm fading as he noticed Ginny was also in the room.

Still he came in the rest of the way and sauntered over to Dare's side. "Morning."

Fully focused on her, he ignored the extra person in the room and leaned toward her, his intent clear.

Dare held up a hand before he could kiss her, touching the side of his face. "That's what was missing. I don't know how I recognized you without your war paint."

"Your brothers were kind enough to help me reapply it. *Brother* — Dustin isn't a fan. Caleb and Luke don't seem too put out."

"They're just biding their time," Ginny warned, bouncing down on the couch. She glanced back and forth between them, anticipation in her expression.

Dare folded her arms and glared at her friend. "You have things to do."

"Isn't that supposed to be a question?"

"No."

Jesse laughed softly. "I can tell you two have been together for a long time."

"Besties," Ginny informed him. "Which is why if I ever find out you do anything — "

" — to hurt Dare, you'll poison me?" Jesse offered.

Ginny looked affronted. "Damn that Luke.

I accidentally give the man one little bout of food poisoning, and I'm never going to live it down."

Dare bit her lip to stop from laughing out loud.

Jesse stood next to her, slipping his fingers over her nape and playing with her hair as he answered Ginny. "Very unfair. I'm sure you're a great cook."

"I totally am. But I'm an even better shot, so…"

She stood and marched closer, peeking up at Jesse with deadly intent. "Hurt Dare and you'll end up with buckshot where the sun don't shine. Then while you're picking lead out of your nether regions I'll — "

Jesse turned away from Ginny to focus on Dare again. "And on that note, breakfast? Want me to cook?"

Dare motioned toward the kitchen. "Be my guest."

"I like my eggs scrambled," Ginny announced as she slipped into the kitchen ahead of them, like an annoying mosquito they had no chance of removing from the room before it drew blood.

"I bet you do." Jesse turned to Dare. "Your house, your rules, but I was hoping for talk time before I leave. Alone talking."

"Goodbye, Ginny," Dare announced.

Her friend sighed good-naturedly before turning for the door. "Next time come for dinner. I mean it."

"Awesome." He sounded sincere. "I look forward to it, and you can go now."

"I need to see you kiss her," Ginny announced.

"You do not — "

The rest of Dare's words were lost under Jesse's lips as she found herself pressed against his long, hard body and kissed senseless. Every inch of her was tingling before he let her up for air.

His grin was both cocky and satisfied.

VIVIAN AREND

"I heard your toes curl from here," Ginny announced.

"Shut up."

Ginny finally left, and Jesse proved his expertise in making fried eggs and toast. It was tasty, but she was distracted by the abuse her family had inflicted on him.

"I'm sorry you got hit. I told the guys not to go off half-cocked."

Jesse smirked. "Half-cocked is the defining characteristic of all teenage guys. Dustin's what, eighteen?"

She nodded. "Old enough to know better."

"Give them time." Jesse pushed his eggs around on the plate for a moment before offering a wry smile. "I'm wrapping my brain around it myself, so I hardly expect them to be thrilled with me."

They finished the meal, Dare considering his words. The fact he hadn't run the instant he'd heard her news impressed her.

She still wasn't marrying the man.

"I should hit the road," Jesse said finally. "Where's your calendar? I'll do some juggling so I can be here for your doctor's appointment, but if I catch my foreman before he sets the schedule for the week, it'll be easier."

She scrambled on the computer for the details, and he added it to his phone along with her number.

Which reminded her. "I should send a response to Jaxi. Or did you want to get in touch with her?"

He made a face. "Can I get back to you on that one? I mean, I'm just not sure..."

She wasn't about to push, since she didn't really know his family history. "No problem."

Jesse met her gaze full on. "I'll be back in a few days. We'll figure it out then, okay?"

Dare nodded her agreement, even though the email was going to burn a hole in her account until she responded. "I can wait."

He touched her cheek gently, gaze drifting over her face as if he were considering hard, but then he turned and left without another word.

Morgan unfolded himself from where he'd been curled up on the porch. He bumped her legs then headed out after Jesse.

The two of them left as silently as they had arrived, but with their coming, her world had totally changed again.

Or had it?

Dare stared after his truck until it vanished in the distance. People left. They always left.

She turned and went inside the cottage, suddenly cold.

Chapter Six

Blog post: A Day in the Life

It's definitely the start of summer here on Little Ranch on the Prairie. We get the four seasons with a vengeance in this territory, which I love. Means I appreciate the green growing things that keep popping up all over after the icy cold days of winter let go. By the time I don't appreciate them anymore (weeds!) the fall days have arrived and temperatures drop.

Right now in our latitude, the sun is up early, and sets late, and we're not quite at the longest day of the year. After feeling as if I hibernated for a lot of the winter, the bright mornings are a nice change to wake up to. Early chores are a lot easier when they're done with the sun watching. Also, going out after dinner means you can visit with friends for hours and drive home while it's light.

Those of you who get sunup and sunset around the same time every day, all year — what's that like? Do you still feel as if summer is a fresh, bright experience?

⸻

It was nearly eight in the evening four days later when Jesse dropped his bag outside the door to Dare's cottage. He'd called to let her know he was going to be late, but now he hurried as he slipped back to his truck to grab Morgan's dog bed and bowls.

He tucked the flannel blanket into the corner of the porch where it would be out of the weather. He filled the water bowl from the outdoor tap then whistled for his dog who was exploring the flowerbed beside the house.

Morgan came running, and Jesse knelt to pat him on the head, pointing to all his necessities, including filled food bowl. "There you go, boy. Home sweet home while we're here."

Morgan took an opportunist lick at Jesse's hand before examining both bowls then dropping into the bed. His tail thumped a couple of times before he settled his nose on his paws.

"Guard."

Satisfied that Morgan would stick within his allotted distance, Jesse slid into the cottage.

Dare was in the tiny kitchen, mucking about with some pots. He watched her for a moment before clearing his throat.

She glanced up. "Oh. You're here."

"I am." He was suddenly aware of the dirt he'd dragged into her clean house. "I'll grab a shower."

"Of course. Go ahead."

She got busy, as if something was waving from the bottom of the pot.

He slipped into the second bedroom/her office, stripping to nothing but his underwear. She kept her back firmly toward him as he marched the short hallway to the bathroom, glancing around the tiny space.

The entire room was filled with her presence. Her robe hung on the back of the door. A pale orange towel was arranged neatly on the towel rack to dry, but she'd put out a dark brown facecloth and towels for him.

Stepping into the shower was like being surrounded

by her as the scent of her shampoo and soap got stronger. He unwrapped a new bar of his own soap, attempting to combat the lingering fragrance filling his nostrils and sending all sorts of urgent messages to his body.

Demands he couldn't answer right now, although, *damn*, he wanted to.

By the time he got out of the shower, he was more determined than ever to make her remember how good they'd been together. Yes, he'd put into play what he needed to get the medical proof she'd asked for, but while he was suffering, maybe it wouldn't be a bad thing for her to be itching for him as well.

Going without sex was rough on a guy —

Okay, fine, he was sure it was equally tough on a woman. Heck, for a woman in her condition there had to be some sort of positive hormones released during orgasm that would help deal with the whole creature growing inside her.

Of course, he should try to find a way to phrase that more diplomatically than suggesting she was possessed by aliens or parasites, and wouldn't she'd like to come?

He joined her in the kitchen. "What can I do?"

"How are you at cooking green things? We could use a salad."

"Salads. Oh, those things you don't put ketchup on?"

Her lips curled. "I've seen one of the old-timers down at the Copper Kettle douse his entire plate, lettuce and all."

"A man only does that if he's desperate," Jesse assured her. "I can make a salad."

They ended up at the dinner table with a surprising array of food. Fried pork chops, a green-bean casserole, mashed potatoes that Dare made him do the honours and smash thoroughly, and the salad.

His mouth watered as he scooped food onto his plate. "You like to cook."

"I like to eat. Cooking seemed a logical step in putting food on the table that wasn't grilled or ready to serve out of the box." She tugged the mashed potato bowl from him, serving herself a hefty amount. "My mom was a good cook, and I used to help, so it wasn't as if I was starting from scratch. Between me and Ginny, we kept the table full enough to satisfy the guys."

He thought back to the little girls. "What about Caleb's wife? Didn't she help?"

Dare made a face. "Wendy and Caleb didn't get married until I was twenty. Neither Ginny nor I enjoyed the idea of an extended diet of the bachelor cooking my brothers considered acceptable."

Jesse wanted to ask about Wendy. Why she wasn't in the picture anymore, but like Dare had said during that first visit to the falls, it wasn't as if they had to know everything about each other this instant.

Instead they talked about TV shows and movies. Music and their favourite sports teams. Small talk, yes, but slowly filling in empty gaps in information.

When Dare yawned on for the third time, though, Jesse rose to his feet. "I've been up since four a.m., and you're ready to hit the hay too."

She nodded, moving to place her empty teacup in the dishwasher before taking his as well. "I have much more energy now than I did before."

When she would've slipped away, Jesse caught her by the wrist and pulled her back into his arms. It might be too soon for him to have her the way he wanted, but damn if he was going to let her leave without at least holding her in his arms for a moment.

She was warm against him, her spine stiff and body tight for about fifteen seconds before she softened. Pressing herself closer and accepting his embrace. He didn't try to notch up the tension, just held her and rubbed her back as what felt like a genuine connection grew.

When he let her go, her smile was a whole lot more real than it'd been all night.

"I'll see you in the morning," she said.

That should've been that.

Jesse waited until she was done with the bathroom then got himself settled for the night, shaking his head at the teeny width of the bed. "It's better than sleeping on the ground."

Yet he couldn't get comfortable. For the next thirty minutes he rolled from position to position, his entire body aching.

Fuck this. The truth was he didn't want to be sleeping alone on this tiny mattress. He didn't want to be on this side of the wall, he wanted to be on the *other* side of it, no more than five feet from where he currently lay. That would put him on the same mattress as Dare. Hell, it might even put him directly on top of her, which hello, even better.

Thoughts of covering her body with his turned into a full-fledged fantasy. Imagining the lush swells of her breasts and generous curves of her hips nestled under him was enough to make him hard.

He shoved back the covers and laid an arm over his eyes, praying for sleep to come.

Instead, in the silence, he heard a low-pitched buzz.

No fucking way.

Jesse listened harder, sure he must've made a mistake, but no, it was definitely there. A low-pitched sound that sent a million more dirty images springing into his brain. Dare with a vibrator in her hands, her naked body spread on the mattress as she played with herself.

What type of vibrator did she have?

And why the hell was he even trying to picture it when he had a perfectly good cock for her to use?

He hadn't been invited in, though, which was probably why she felt the need for some battery-operated-boyfriend time. Well, screw that. He didn't fucking care what she had other than it was currently replacing him, and he was not going to stand for it.

If she wanted to get off, he'd be her real-life vibrator, thank you very much.

He made his way silently out of his room, padding down the hall to stop outside her door to be certain he hadn't imagined the entire thing.

The sound was there. A steady buzz, followed by her swearing, soft and heated, and Jesse lost it. He shoved the door open to find Dare on the bed, her head snapping up to meet his accusing gaze.

She had a plastic object in her hand, all right, but it wasn't shaped like any vibrator he'd ever seen. Moreover, she wasn't naked. She had on a pale pink cotton pyjamas top and shorts, the fabric so thin it was nearly see-through. On top of the quilt she'd placed a towel, and her legs were twisted in front of her.

"What the hell are you doing?" she demanded.

He stepped closer. "What's in your hand?"

"This?" She held it up, confusion on her face. "A razor."

His bluster faded like she'd punctured a balloon. "Oh."

An annoyed growl escaped her. "What're you doing busting in here uninvited? Go away. It's hard enough to get at some spots, I don't need an audience."

Jesse was trying to knock the images of her using a vibrator out of his head. "I thought…I mean, there was this noise…"

She rested her hands on her hips. "Jesse, get out of my bedroom."

Fuck it. He'd stepped in it, but meekly walking out of the room wasn't in the cards, either.

There was no turning off his erection, so he ignored it and headed toward her. "Shove over," he ordered.

Dare dragged her gaze off his body and up to his eyes, and he appreciated that it took some effort.

"What're you doing?" she demanded again as he dropped onto the edge of her bed.

"I'm helping my fiancée shave her legs."

"I don't need help."

Screw that. He climbed straight over her, forcing her back to the mattress. His knees rested on either side of her thighs, and with his hands planted by her head, he hovered over her. The temptation to drop lower and press their bodies together was strong, but he ignored the evil lure.

"There's no reason for you to be stubborn, Dare. Pretend I'm a high-end consultant at one of those ritzy spas. Deliver yourself into my capable hands."

She grunted. "That's not a selling feature. The only time I've gone to a spa is when I won a coupon, and Ginny made me use it. They put this hot sticky wax on my leg, and I swear they ripped an inch of skin off with the hair. Once I stopped screaming, I left."

"Smart."

"It did."

Jesse had never understood how women could put up with the torture, but he sure appreciated the results.

"I promise I won't rip anything off." *Except maybe her underwear.* He told his brain to shut the fuck up then stole the razor from her fingers. "Close your eyes and relax."

"And think of England?"

He eased into position beside her, pulling her leg over his lap. "Hardly. Think about how good it is to have someone take care of you."

If he hadn't been watching, he would have missed her brief grimace.

"What?"

She glanced at him. "Nothing, just... Okay, fine, you win. But if you do a good job, I hope you realize you're stuck doing this for the next five months, because it's only going to get more awkward as Buckaroo gets bigger."

Jesse teased his fingers down her leg to see where she'd already finished. "God, it's probably a sexist thing, but damn I like it that you shave your legs. Don't know why it just seems right for you to be all smooth and lickable."

She snickered. "Yeah, sexist, but I agree with you. I had a friend in high school who went all Earth Mother and decided to stop shaving. It was fine during the winter, but come the springtime I swear she could've braided her arm hair into a bikini top. "

Jesse's fingers jerked, and he dropped her leg. "That's one I didn't need to know."

He checked out the shaver, but it was no different than his electric razor, so he used gentle strokes over the few spots she'd missed. He took advantage of the situation, letting the razor touch her, but then sliding his fingers after it down her long legs. Teasing with his fingertips as he stroked. Long motions that reignited his cock as the images he'd thought up earlier were replaced by ones even better because they were real.

"Did I mention that I like your hair? Glorious colour — and very you."

"I like it too. It's real, you know."

"Oh, I got to tell pretty quick that the curtains and the rug matched. It's this glorious shade that makes me think of trees in the autumn with the sun beaming down on them."

She leaned up on her elbows, smirking a little. "Compliments will not get you sex any earlier, but thanks."

A laugh burst free. "Woman, shut up and relax, or I'll make you."

Dare settled back on the pillows with a smile. "Really? Threatening the pregnant woman?"

Jesse stroked her leg again. "Did you ever think about going away to university?"

She hesitated. "Think about it? Of course. Plan on it? No. We weren't in a position those days to deal with the expense, and it wouldn't have been worth it."

Her words were clipped and a bit more hostile than he'd expected. Jesse put aside the razor and slid his thumbs over the arch of her foot in a firm massage, urging her to lie back again. "Why wouldn't it have been worth it?"

Dare sighed. "I couldn't decide what to focus on. Too many subjects interested me, but none of them to the extent I could say — *that* one. That's what I should spend four to five years of my life learning so I can spend the rest of my life paying off student loans."

"That's more cynical than I expected," Jesse admitted.

She threw an arm over her face even as she shoved her foot at him harder, silently asking for more. "Those were my cynical years. Now I'm rolling in peace and contentment. My life one hundred percent planned out — *not*."

He laughed softly. "Yeah. I hear you on plans changing. I guess my dad would call that quote, unquote *life*."

"Your dad still around? You didn't mention your folks."

A knot threatened to form in his throat, and Jesse shoved his discomfort aside to answer as lightly as possible. "My parents are alive and kicking. Mike and Marion. Dad works the ranch, and my mom is enjoying being a grandma far too much."

Guilt struck. He'd sent one email to his parents since he'd left. A terribly un-explanatory note to the effect of wanderlust and wide-open skies beckoning.

I.e. he'd lied his ass off.

No way could he explain why he'd left in a letter. So he hadn't, and his guilt was lighter now because he wasn't reminded every day of what he'd done. Yet while he could go whole weeks without thinking of the rift he'd caused in his family, it was still there.

Jesse pulled himself out of his musings to discover Dare had gone silent as well, lost in her own world.

Screw this. "You ever had sex in this room?"

The out-of-the-blue topic change dragged Dare back from the hole she'd stumbled into. His brief mention of his mom as a doting grandma had started a chain reaction inside of all sorts of thoughts and emotions she wasn't sure she was ready to face.

She'd decided to keep Buckaroo — that part she was completely on board with. Jesse seemed determined to stick around, and while she wouldn't count on it, she had to admit she was enjoying getting to know him better.

But she must have watched too many Hallmark movies over the years. The ones where grandmas held out their arms to pudgy-cheeked cherubs had done a number on her, probably because it was a scenario she had never envisioned in her world.

But Buckaroo *did* have a Gramma. The realization was enough to shake her very foundation.

Jesse's sudden change of topic offered a welcome respite from things she didn't want to think about right now.

She poked him gently. "Jeez, where'd that come from?"

"Curiosity. I lost my virginity in the back bed of my truck. You?"

Blunt talk usually didn't get her this flustered, but there was something about discussing it with Jesse when they couldn't have sex that sent her cheeks heating. "I should tell you it was in a seedy hotel room one February when I had a one-night stand."

Jesse grinned. "Hey, I will admit I stole your cherry, but neither of us were virgins that night."

She gave him that much. "Fine. It was on a floating swimming platform at camp with my camp boyfriend the summer I was sixteen. We snuck out of our cabins after curfew and went skinny dipping."

"Daring."

"Stupid, but fun," she admitted.

"Was it any good?"

Dare tilted her hand. "It was exciting because it was forbidden, and I think I got off more on that than his technique." She wiggled upright. "Most forbidden thing you've ever done, since you took us down this bunny trail."

He looked uncomfortable for a moment, which shocked the hell out of her. The man who had blown her mind so many ways that night in February didn't seem the type to ever hesitate while discussing sex.

"I don't know what you consider forbidden. You'd better clarify before I confess to the most vanilla of adventures."

Recklessly Dare went on. "I had sex with a camp counselor — not the same summer, but the following. That's only slightly forbidden because he was nineteen to my seventeen, but it counts."

"Wild child. Sounds as if I should've gone to camp."

She made a face, remembering back to the chaos of those days. "It was Caleb's solution to getting us younger ones out of the way for a month every summer. I don't blame him, and it was actually a good thing because being surrounded by organized activities pushed me out of my funk."

"My brothers pushed me when I got into asshole mode," Jesse admitted. "Especially Joel."

Dare pulled her legs up and wrapped her arms around them, gazing at Jesse comfortably now as they talked. "Do you miss him? I've heard stories about how close twins can be."

His poker face failed for a moment. It was clear there was some hurt involved in this topic.

She was going to apologize for the question then change the topic when he finally answered.

"I miss him like crazy, but this is what I'm doing right now."

She nodded. "*Move on, do the next thing.* That was my

mantra — still is, I guess." She wanted to get rid of the sudden awkwardness, so she took a cue from him and went for shocking. "You're holding out on me. Ever have sex with a guy?"

"Nope. Not my thing. You?"

She grinned. "Yeah, I've had sex with guys."

"Tease." Jesse's gaze trickled over her, his admiration clear. "Tell me about your pillow fights, darlin'."

"I don't kiss and tell." She drew herself up haughtily before offering a dirty grin. "Well, just this time. Tried it once. We both got off, but I spent more time giggling than riding that edge of excitement, if you know what I mean. I think if there'd been a guy with us, it would've been awesome."

Jesse raised a brow. "A threesome?"

He didn't look as shocked as she'd expected, and then she remembered his brother lived with two other people. "To be blunt, I like cock. But man, did she ever know how to go down. Blew my mind."

"I've heard that."

She eyed him. "You? Threesomes?

His cocky nonchalance seemed to be teetering on the edge of discomfort as he confessed, "Yeah. For a while it was a thing with me."

Huh. "A thing? Like more than once in a blue moon?"

He pulled back slightly, leaning his body away as if he were putting up a bit of a barrier in case she reacted poorly to his words. "We used to pick up one woman between the two of us, then Joel and I would make sure they had a very good time."

Dare wrapped her brain around his confession. "Okay. That's…"

He was waiting, trying for a *don't give a shit* expression, but it wasn't working.

She went for blunt. "I'm torn between this rush of *oh my God* at the thought of two guys built like you doing nasty things to me and how good that would feel, and a rush of negative *oh my God* that you and your brother — "

"Nothing ever happened between me and Joel," Jesse drawled. "It was always about the woman, but yeah, it was a kink. We haven't done that for years."

Which was good, and bad.

Dare shook her head to knock out the images of being worked over by two Jesses before offering a grin. "Well, I'm not going to be a hypocrite and condemn you when my first reaction was to think how hot that would be."

"Thanks. I'll totally be a hypocrite and say no way in hell is another guy going near you when I'm around."

He looked so serious Dare reached out and laid a hand against his cheek. "I'm not looking for any extreme fun and games these days."

"Me neither, although I can't wait to touch you again."

A mass of information was swirling and twirling in her brain, but that blunt edge of sleepiness had finally returned. She fought to hide her yawn, but it was no use.

Jesse smiled knowingly. "I think that's the real cue it's bedtime."

Dare nodded. "I'll see you in the morning?"

"I'll be here."

He slid to vertical, and she looked him over hungrily one more time, admiring the flexing muscles and tousled hair. He stood in the doorway for long enough she got a lovely mental snapshot that hovered in front of her eyes even as she closed them.

Chapter Seven

He'd followed her directions simply enough, which put them sitting in his truck, behind a three-storey building on Main Street, with five minutes to get to her prenatal appointment.

He was already on the sidewalk opening her door before he realized she hadn't moved. Her fingers wrapped in a death grip around the seat belt crossing her chest, Dare turned her face to him but didn't say a word.

He stepped back a little and waited.

She took a deep breath that rocked her shoulders up then down, but still didn't move.

"Need a hand, darling?"

"Couple of shots of whiskey would go down fine right now," she suggested.

Jesse hummed thoughtfully as he reached in to undo her belt so he could tug her unwilling body out the door. "That's kind of what got us into this state in the first place."

"I know." She was staring at the building as if it held something putrid. "Tell me I have to do this."

"You do have to do this. Buckaroo requires it of his mom, and he's requesting you might want to shake those mama hen tail feathers a little quicker if he's going to be on time for the show."

Jesse wrapped his arms around her, lips pressed to her temple briefly. She shook in his embrace before pressing against him, a return squeeze like a rah-rah endorsement.

Dare pushed herself free and accepted the hand he held out. "Sorry about that. Momentary panic as I thought back to all the other times I've been in this place."

"No prob. Makes sense — family doctor?" Why had he not thought to ask before?

"We've gone from childish illnesses to the disasters of teenage life, to post-accident mental health recovery, to grownup discussions on what I should use for birth control — which in spite of our current situation, I did have planned out. Yet this is the first trip that feels like a particularly adult thing to do."

They were in the elevator, rising to the third floor, when his nerves jagged out of kilter. He was headed to a prenatal checkup with the woman he'd spend the rest of his life seeing in some shape or form, and they were about to talk about a baby who was definitely going to be in his life forever.

Too damn grownup — he knew exactly what Dare was talking about.

The elevator doors slid open, and he followed her down the hall, pausing when she did.

Dare wrinkled her nose. "I…um…need to take a pit stop. If the doc's going to push on my bladder, I need to be prepared."

"I can see why."

She eyed him, as if wondering if he was teasing, but she jerked a thumb over her shoulder down a narrow hall leading to two doors. "Bathrooms. I'll be right back."

"I'll be right here."

Dare shook her head. "Go check me in so I don't lose my spot in the order, or we'll be waiting until the cows come home to get in."

"Meet you there, then."

It was only two doors farther down the main hall. Jesse slipped into the waiting room, a half-dozen bored magazine-reading people lifting their gazes to take him in. The men immediately went back to reading, one of them sniffing loudly. His body jerked every time he sucked in, a wet, disgusting noise. Jesse made a mental note to not sit anywhere near that section of the room, and not let Dare touch anything that might have been contaminated.

Hell, the magazines were probably toxic cesspools. He'd have to bring sanitizer the next trip.

"Can I help you?"

The young man behind the desk was waiting expectantly, drawing Jesse's attention from the women in the room looking his way. The guy wore a shiny plastic tag, with a *Hello, my name is* _____. *I'm here to help you.* He'd written in *Scott* with bright orange ink and added a half-dozen exclamation marks.

Jesse resisted making a smartass remark, choosing to answer softly. "Dare Hayes is here for her ten a.m. checkup."

Scott leaned to one side, grinning cheekily as he peeked around Jesse as if Dare were hiding behind his back.

For fuck's sake. So much for his resolve to be good.

"She's taking a piss," Jesse drawled. "She'll be here in a minute."

"Ah, yes." The receptionist lost his smile. He marked something off in his appointment book and moved a file from one side of the desk to the other.

Jesse glanced over his shoulder to discover an older woman watching closely while other gazes darted away to pretend interest in their germ-laden magazines.

Scott spoke up again, and it seemed he'd recovered some of his enthusiasm. "Ah-hah. I see this is Ms. Hayes's first prenatal checkup."

Jesse swore he heard the heads behind him swivel toward their neighbour. Shit — this *was* the first time anyone was picking up that Dare was pregnant, and now the small-town theatrics could begin.

Scott made more notes, speaking without looking at him. "You are?"

"Jesse Coleman."

The man raised a brow. "What relationship are you to Ms. Hayes? I need to know if I should put you on the file, or not."

His name on the file. *God.*

Screw them. He focused on the eager fellow with his bright orange pen. "I'm the father."

Scott tried again. "*Relationship* to Ms. Hayes?"

"Fiancé."

The word came out a whole lot louder than the previous bits of conversation, and the silence behind him grew deeper. Like an inhale before the rapid-fire questions and speculating began.

Verbal wild fire igniting in three-two-one...

The now stone-faced receptionist nodded then pointed toward the chairs. "I'll get the rest of your contact information in a moment, Mr. Coleman. If you'll take a seat."

Jesse strategically dropped into the second chair from the end. He stared straight at the door and ignored the speculative glances visible in his peripheral vision, rising to his feet when Dare finally joined him.

She glanced at the counter, but the receptionist was disappearing around the corner into the back rooms, called by a low-toned buzzer.

Jesse sat her in the corner seat then twisted his body to guard her from the peering eyes best he could. "You good?"

"Peachy." Her gaze darted past his shoulder, and her lips twisted before she eased back to meet his eyes. "Do you plan on looming over me the entire time we're here?"

"Pretty much. You know anyone?" He indicated behind him with a head flick.

"Yup." Dare rubbed her temples for a second. "Maybe they'll think I've got the flu."

He wouldn't mention his earlier announcement yet. "You want me to wait out here when they call you in?"

Dare frowned. "Why the hell did you drive out if — "

He laid a finger over her lips. "Shhh, darling. Inside voice."

A glare scalded him before she batted her lashes and linked her fingers together. "But my sweetheart of sweethearts, you must hold my hand."

"Now I'm the one who feels nauseated."

Dare wasn't even listening. She fidgeted on the spot, a mass of nerves. She finally stopped bouncing in her chair enough to reach past him to the pile of magazines.

Jesse caught her wrist. "Nope. You're not touching those things."

"You're kidding me." Her face folded into a frown, but fortunately whatever rampage she was about to go on was cut short by the nursing attendant calling her name.

Jesse rose with her, and the nurse looked puzzled for

a moment before her face lit with understanding. "Oh, you can stay there. I'm just weighing her."

Dare pointed a finger at Jesse and back at the seat. "Sit."

He grinned. "I already know how much you weigh."

Her eyes narrowed. "*Stay.*"

An idea popped into his head that was too good to resist. Besides, from the looks of things, she needed the distraction. Jesse pulled out his wallet and found a piece of scrap paper before settling in place, jotting down a number and leaving the folded note on her seat. He crossed his arms and leaned back in his chair, eyes closed.

She was back in under thirty seconds.

He waited.

Something bumped softly into his biceps, and he peeked one eye open to discover Dare's face inches away.

She fluttered the paper scrap. "Ha, ha. Funny man. How'd you do that?"

"Was I right?"

Dare narrowed her gaze. "Plus or minus five pounds. Do you have a side gig at the Stampede fairgrounds guessing people's weights?"

"Nope, but I've picked you up more than once." He let his grin widen as he thought back to one of those times, holding her against the wall as they screwed themselves silly.

His dirty thoughts must have shown because her cheeks darkened. "Stop it. Answer the question."

"I did. I picked you up. I pick up animals all the time, and it's easy to estimate weight after you've — "

He stopped. Maybe continuing with — *after you've hauled a few heifers around* wasn't the right thing to say to a woman he hoped to get into bed with again in the near future.

Dare raised a brow, goading him to continue.

" — after you've gained enough experience." Jesse pointed behind her. "The nurse is waving at you."

This time he got pulled along into an examination room. The nurse ordered him to sit in the chair in the corner, then got Dare up on the table and wrapped a black elastic band around her arm, cord leading off to a tall machine on wheels.

"I'm going to take some tests before the doctor arrives. Blood pressure and temperature — basic information so we have a guideline to compare to down the road. Relax, Darilyn. You'll feel a little pressure on your arm for a moment, but that's all. It works automatically."

"Are you going to take blood too?"

"And make you pee in a cup," the nurse announced cheerfully.

"Damn, you should have waited," Jesse teased.

Dare tilted her face toward him. "Trust me, I can pee anytime, anywhere."

He snorted. "I don't know that's a ringing endorsement for pregnancy."

"Still true."

The nurse clicked a button on the machine, and a low hum filled the room. "After your appointment you can get the blood work done. Have your fiancé drop you off at — "

"Fianc — ?" Dare's lips slammed shut, and she glanced at Jesse before rolling her eyes. "Sorry. Go on?"

The nurse finished explaining, then checked the blood-pressure machine, frowning as she read the data. "I think I'll run that again. It seems a little higher than it should be."

"I think my *fiancé* distracted me," Dare deadpanned.

If she was looking for an apology, she wasn't going to get one. Not for that. "You need to learn to relax more, *sweetheart.*"

If looks could kill — Still, Dare angry at him was better than her shaking in her boots.

Though he hated to admit it, even to himself, distracting her was distracting him from all the unknowns that were rising up and flapping in his face.

He needed to do this, but that didn't mean his heart wasn't in his throat at the mere idea of becoming a dad. Of having to be there for Dare not just for the next five months, but all the years after that.

— and he wasn't sure which was worse. The thought she might not need him, or that she would and his best wouldn't be enough.

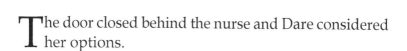

The door closed behind the nurse and Dare considered her options.

Jesse rolled himself to a spot directly in front of her, catching hold of her knees to pull himself in close. "I already looked, and unless you want to try to throttle me with the blood-pressure cuff, there's nothing in here more dangerous than a tongue depressor."

"You're such a pain in the ass," Dare declared.

"Guilty, but I'm now officially your pain in the ass. Congrats."

God. Annoying, devastatingly gorgeous *asshole* of a man. "Everyone in town now knows we're supposedly engaged and pregnant."

"Officially pregnant *and* officially engaged. Did you not get the announcement?"

He caught her hand as she swung at him, standing between her thighs, the rolling chair rattling off behind him. He cautiously pinned her arm behind her as he pressed their bodies together.

"Manhandling the pregnant woman again. You are consistent, Jesse Coleman."

"What can I say? I like handling you."

She was going to tell him to put his handling where the sun don't shine, but the words were cut off as he brought their lips together. Forceful, yes, yet careful. He held her so she couldn't easily escape, but the touch of his tongue was a seduction. Stealing her senses as he dipped in again and tasted her deeper. Wiping away her logic and turning her into a mass of quivering need.

A soft cough broke through the sexual haze. "Ready for your checkup when you are."

Jesse outright grinned as he stepped back then offered his hand to the doctor. "Jesse Coleman."

"Leslie Martins. I take it you're the father?"

"Yes, ma'am."

Dr. Martins turned to Dare, the older woman's familiar smile completely nonjudgmental. This was the same doctor who'd treated all her childhood illnesses, and helped pull Dare out of the dark days that followed losing her family. Dare didn't think she could have taken seeing judgment or disappointment on the woman's face.

Dr. Martins pulled the rolling chair under her as she pointed Jesse back to the corner chair. "Dare, I think we have a typo on the date of your last period. As in blank-space typo."

"Not sure when it was," Dare admitted.

The doctor frowned. "But you have February eighth as a conception date. You sure?"

"Yes," she and Jesse said at the same time, prompting a small laugh from Dr. Martins before she turned on them both with a lecturing tone.

"You conceived in February, and this is your first prenatal visit? You're already in your second trimester, which means I'm not happy with either of you. Prenatal care is important, and I expect you both to take these visits more seriously in the future, is that clear?"

"Yes, ma'am. I'll make sure of it from now on," Jesse said firmly.

Dare avoided his eyes. "We'll be here."

Dr. Martins took a deep breath. "One other thing. I'm in the process of sending out letters to all my patients, but I need to let you know that while I'm happy to be your doctor right now, we'll have to make alternative plans for down the road. I'm retiring the end of August."

Disappointment rushed in.

"You can't." Dare snapped her mouth shut guiltily. "I'm sorry, that was rude. I'm excited for you, but really?"

"I know it's a bit of a shock, but you can see one of the other doctors here in Heart Falls. You'll have to go to Black Diamond for delivery, anyway." The doctor laid a hand on her arm. "We'll talk about it more over the next months. You'll be fine."

"I'm going to miss you," Dare said honestly.

"I'll miss you as well, but it's good to see you moving on with life. New fiancé, baby on the way — life does go on." She nodded approvingly at Jesse before turning back to all business. "I need to finish the last couple tests and measurements." Dr. Martins flipped a few pages on her chart. "Is Jesse staying in the room or no?"

"I'm staying."

The doctor twisted to glare at him. "I was asking Dare."

"He can stay. I bet it'll be his first time seeing someone in stirrups and no horse within a country mile."

Jesse's face twisted.

"Good practice for down the road," Dr. Martins deadpanned. "I'll give you a minute to slip out of your things from the waist down and put on the robe. Opening to the front this time." She paused at the door. "Oh, and I will only be a minute, so don't go getting distracted again, or anything," she warned them.

Dare pulled on the robe before slipping off her jeans and panties, mind wandering to the news that Dr. Martins was leaving.

Jesse accepted her clothes like they were the crown jewels, folding them and placing them on the seat before turning back and distracting her from her memories. "Stirrups?"

She hopped back up on the examination table before patting his cheek and focusing on the matter at hand. "You poor, innocent soul."

"As bad as that?"

"You ever had your prostate checked, Jesse?"

His eyes widened.

"There's a reason women like lady doctors, and it's not just that they're female. Small hands. Enough said."

Dr. Martins returned. The dreaded stirrups were employed, and Dare's belly was measured in rapid order, and there was barely time for discussion. Jesse had worked his way to her side and somehow her fingers had slipped into his, linked together kind of over her head as she pretended she wasn't being poked and prodded in a most inglorious manner in front of a man she barely knew.

Good practice for down the road, indeed.

Jesse watched protectively as the doctor laid an actual tape measure over her belly and made notes. "You felt the baby move yet?"

Panic struck instantly because Dare had to shake her head. "Is that bad?"

"Nope, pretty common, actually. You've got a long torso, and this is your first. I bet Buckaroo is moving like crazy, but at this point you're not recognizing the sensation." Dr. Martins picked up a small device and turned back with a grin. "One benefit of you two being lazy about appointments. Ready to hear the baby's heartbeat?"

"Seriously?" Jesse's grip on Dare's fingers tightened.

"Of course. Dare's nearly twenty weeks along. The baby's heartbeat is loud and clear already."

Dare couldn't speak, but she nodded her approval.

She lay still as possible as the doctor placed the instrument on bare skin, the cool metal warming rapidly as Dr. Martins tilted it.

Thump.

Thump.

Thump.

At first Dare wasn't positive what they were listening to. It could have been any of a dozen machines in the room suddenly emitting sounds into the hushed moment, only it wasn't.

It was her baby.

The situation sank in further than before. There really was another little being in her belly, not just random germs demanding her body's attention, but a person being built one bit at a time. Reality kicked up a notch.

Heartbeats were real.

She remembered lying in a circle with her family, heads resting on each other's stomachs. Laughter would burst free as gurgles and rumbles echoed in their ears. But there were the times they'd quiet enough to hear other things. The rush of blood through veins. Air whispering into lungs. Hearts pumping as they powered life.

After fooling around with her boyfriend, she'd dropped her head on his chest and felt the unsteady pulse as they came down off the drugging high.

She thought back to Jesse and being held by him that first time after they'd reconnected. His strong arms had enfolded her against his body — his pulse a steady metronome under her palms.

Life.

Jesse collapsed into the chair with a lot less grace than usual, his grin frozen in place as he listened intently.

"That's the baby?" He glanced at the doctor. "It's not Dare's?"

"One hundred percent baby," Dr. Martins assured him. "There's a faint echo of Dare's heart if we change the angle, but what we've got right now is one healthy baby's heartbeat."

"One." Dare breathed a sigh of relief. "Thank you, Lord, for small mercies."

She expected Jesse to make some crack about twins being awesome, but he was motionless, his expression gone unreadable.

Dr. Martins was smiling, but she glanced at the clock as her face turned serious again. "I hate to rush this moment, but I have to keep moving. I need you to stop at the front desk and set up an appointment for an ultrasound and a few more tests. We'll need to discuss which you want to take, and which you don't. Before you leave, Scott will give you a package of information to read through."

Dare nodded, soaking in the last couple *thumps* before the doctor put her things away and headed to the door.

"Prenatal vitamins, as much rest as you can. Take care of yourself, and if you have any questions, let me know. Congratulations, and let's work on making a healthy baby."

"Thanks."

"Wait." Jesse snapped out of his daze. "When's the baby done? I mean, due?"

Dr. Martins smiled. "October thirty-first according to the charts. First babies are often late, so a two-week window either side would be perfectly normal."

The door closed. Dare fumbled to get upright for a moment before Jesse was there, his strong hand steadying her as she swung her legs to the side of the table.

He blocked her way, staring down at her belly as if she might explode at any time.

"Jesse?"

He blinked then glanced up, smile returning. "Heck of a thing, growing babies."

He had that right. "Heck of a thing," she agreed.

Chapter Eight

Blog post: Babies Grow in Bellies

Yes, I know, not a new development, but it really is a pretty odd concept when you come right down to it. This extra person is taking up room alongside my heart, lungs and other internal organs. Buckaroo has a heart (heard it!) and lungs and all those internal organs as well, which means right now I have two hearts.

So to speak.

Logically, this means I also have two brains, but the effects of this are dismal. I found my missing phone in the fridge on the shelf next to the milk this morning. Baby brain does not mean Mama is suddenly twice as smart. I am twice as hungry, though. This concept bears consideration, yes?

What would you like to suddenly be twice as good at, if having two means 2x as good? Thinking, eating, loving?

Dare settled back into a routine for the next couple days. Jesse had left quickly after dropping her back off at the ranch, but he'd been texting on a regular basis, so she guessed the prenatal visit hadn't scared him off completely.

She went for an easy ride Monday morning, the fresh

summer breeze playing over her as she and Baby took their time rounding the lake.

Her phone buzzed, and she grabbed it.

Jesse: *the fridge, eh?*

Dare: *shut up*

Jesse: *told you you'd find it*

Dare: *you did. What're you doing today?*

Jesse: *moving herds. Roping, yeehaw-ing. Tough cowboy stuff*

Dare: *I bet Morgan's in his glory*

Jesse: *yup. Dog heaven, chasing cattle. What're you up to?*

Dare: *riding for a bit. Going to help Ginny with the CSA boxes today.*

Jesse: *you be careful riding*

Dare: *yes, mom*

Jesse: *I mean it. I don't know Baby. Does she spook easy?*

Dare: *she's bombproof. Relax. Ginny's the one you should warn to take it easy on me*

Jesse: *okay. What's her number?*

She laughed out loud before texting back: *I was kidding*

Jesse: *I'm not. I just realized I have no way to get hold of you if something happens. Send me Ginny's #. And Caleb's & Luke's. Hell, send me the broody kid's as well*

Dare: *you're being silly*

Jesse: *fiancés are allowed to be silly. Don't argue, woman*

Fiancé. It was still not real, or at less real than the baby, but then again, she'd had over four months to get used to the idea of Buckaroo, and not even a couple of weeks to adjust to the idea of Jesse being around.

Heck, it would probably take at least four months to finally come to terms with his presence, which was fine, especially if she didn't need to spend a month or two of it puking. No quivering stomach was a win. The getting-married thing? Still not happening.

He makes other parts of you quiver that dry snarky voice in her head reminded her.

That he did. He'd been patient about her no-sex decree, although technically, she supposed they *had* had sex. Anytime they were alone in a room sexual tension simmered, and he'd gotten her off again during the last time he'd visited.

She was so weak, damn her hormones anyway.

With no real rush to be anywhere, she rode lazily, a pleasant buzz of relaxation resting on her by the time she returned to the barn.

She was brushing down Baby when a familiar voice called her name.

"Dare, you got a minute?"

She glanced over her shoulder at Dustin, continuing to stroke the currying brush over Baby's flanks, the repetition soothing and peaceful. "You're heading out late."

"Not that late, but I wanted to talk to you."

She turned to examine him closer. The fine crop of blue, purple and green bruises he and Jesse had been sporting had nearly faded to nothing. "I'm listening."

"I don't think you should get engaged to Jesse."

Unexpected topic. "Oh? Why is that?"

"Well, you don't need to. You can live here, on the ranch. You don't need him around."

She wasn't sure where this was going. "I'm having a baby, Dustin. Jesse's the dad. That kind of means he's got the right to be around."

"Yeah, well, but that doesn't mean *you* have to be with him."

The concern and outrage in his voice was too easy to read, and Dare sighed, leaning a hand against Baby's flank as she turned to focus on the youngest of the Stone family. "He's not a bad man. Spending time with him isn't a terrible thing."

"You should marry me."

The currying brush slipped from her fingers.

He darted down and grabbed it for her, holding onto the brush until she looked him in the eyes. "Okay, that was not the way I intended to do this, but I mean it. If you want to get married, you should marry me."

Wow. She'd had a fair number of surprises in the last while, but this one was really unexpected. "Dustin, you don't want to marry me.

"Sure I do."

She raised a brow.

"Honestly? I know we've never — But I've thought about — " His cheeks turned brilliant red. "Although not in a bad way, but I have thought about you as a woman. And you are. A woman, that is."

This conversation kept getting better and better. "I am a woman. Thank you for noticing."

He broke eye contact, scuffing the toe of his boot into the ground. "Yeah, I noticed. But not in a disrespectful way," he added.

Dare fought to keep from laughing straight out, because that was the last thing his youthful ego needed. "I'm honoured, but I'm not interested in marrying you."

"You should think about it. I mean we go way back. We know everything about each other, and I care about you an awful lot."

"Awww, I know you do. I care about you too, but Dustin, I don't care about you in *that* way."

He was the cutest thing with that enormous blush.
"You could learn."

Not in this lifetime. "I don't think — "

He moved in on her, scooping her up and planting
his lips on hers.

The only thing that kept her from raising a knee
and kicking him in the nuts was the fact he was Dustin.
Instead, she hung there like a limp strip of flypaper
until he made a disturbed sound and broke the contact
between them.

He wasn't a bad kisser, but he was...

Dusty.

Kissing him was the last thing she wanted, especially
in light of the sensual impact of Jesse's touch.

Dustin put her down, his embarrassment growing at
her lack of enthusiasm. "Yeah. Well, I guess that's...*that.*"

"That's that," she agreed. "Really, I'm honoured you
asked me, but I need you as a good *good* friend, and my
little brother. Just what you've always been. When the
baby arrives, you'll be a fantastic uncle, I know you will."

Dustin refused to meet her gaze. "I'd better get back
to work."

He vanished around the edge of the stalls, moving
as if his ass were on fire.

She went back to brushing her horse, something
inside trembling between amusement and sorrow.

Everything was changing. Nothing was ever going
to be the same because it couldn't. Time was moving
forward and the world was changing. This family that
had been her lifeline for so long would always be there,
but they were no longer teens.

Hope for the best and plan for the worst.

Still lost in thought, Dare made her way back to the

cottage. She was already walking up the stairs before she noticed Caleb rising to his feet from where he'd been waiting in the rocking chair.

Her first thought was the girls, then Ginny. "Everything okay?"

He nodded. "You're hard to track down these days. I thought this would be the best way to catch a minute."

Dare tossed herself into the second chair and motioned for him to sit again. "I hope you're not here to tell me you guys plan to beat up Jesse again."

"I didn't beat him up in the first place."

She rested her head on the back of the chair, closing her eyes as she rocked. "No, you're right. You'd never do such an undignified thing."

He ignored her and completely changed topics.

"I got something for you to think about." His voice changed timbre. He was always serious, but now he sounded...nervous?

Dare cracked an eye open to check him out. "What? I don't want to make decisions about the ranch right now."

"No, although that reminds me. You do know your shares in the ranch are secure. You've got income, such as it is."

"I know. We covered this already when I found out Buckaroo was on the way."

Caleb took a deep breath. "Yeah, that's what I want to talk about. Not regarding the financial stuff, but about Buckaroo."

An uneasy sensation crept in. "What?"

"I've been thinking about this a lot, and while I know Jesse has shown up, I think it would be better if you married me."

Shock and amusement struck at the same time,

making her snort in a very unladylike way. "You've got to be kidding."

Then damn if he didn't get out of the chair and go down on one knee in front of her.

Dare snapped her mouth shut to stop from swearing or laughing or shrieking, or any of those responses that would be inappropriate.

"It hit me the other day that this would be a smart idea for us. I'm a good father, and you'll never have to worry about being alone to take care of the baby."

There must've been some sort of hallucinogenic in her breakfast porridge. "I don't believe this."

He squeezed her fingers. "Will you marry me? We could set it up for this coming month."

She stared at him in horror. "Get off your knees. My God, has the whole world gone crazy? No. I can't marry you. You're my big brother."

"We both know we're not really related."

Somehow she got out from where she was trapped between him and her chair, stepping to the edge of the porch. "Caleb, I'm *not* marrying you. You don't think of me in that way, and I'm not marrying somebody just to get Buckaroo a daddy. Not you, not Jesse. No one. And I'm not having sex with you *ever* as that would be gross beyond belief. Holy hell, my skin is crawling."

His lips twitched. "Way to stroke a man's ego, Dare."

"Don't make me crazy. You don't want to have sex with me." She made a face.

"This isn't about sex, it's about raising a family."

"It's also about sex, because I'm twenty-six, and you're thirty-four. You can't tell me that you'd be satisfied never having sex for the rest of your life, because that's what would happen if we got married, because *ick*. Double *ick*."

126

This day was just too much.

She pulled open the door and glanced back at him, wiggling herself toward safety. "Okay, thank you. That was very sweet of you and I appreciate it, but don't *ever* think about doing that again. *Ever*."

She escaped into the house, all but running to her room where she threw herself on the mattress and buried her face in her pillow. Only then did she let loose all the frustration and horror and sheer twistedness of her morning. Laughter welled up from deep within her, rolling over again and again as she tried to bring her amusement under control.

Thank God Luke was already engaged. The only thing that would have made this day even more funky was a proposal from Walker.

Or, no, from *Ginny*.

It wasn't as funny as all that, but it was. If she was intent on doing the right thing by the baby, and *if* Caleb had asked her two months ago, she might have answered differently.

But now knowing Jesse was in the picture, and knowing he wanted to be involved, changed everything.

The fact that spending time with him made her heart pump and turned her insides to a quivering mess didn't weigh in her calculations. Not one teeny bit.

Liar.

But, hey, she had to give Caleb points for actually going down on one knee to propose. She didn't flunk out completely on inducing chivalrous gestures.

Yay, her.

By the time she'd pulled herself together and washed her face she had to hurry to make it to the gardens on time to meet Ginny.

She checked her mail en route and discovered another message from Jaxi.

Hey. Thanks for letting us know Jesse hasn't fallen off the face of the earth. He hasn't answered my email, but that's typical. Still love the jerk.

I've been reading your blog and...umm.

God — there is no way to ask this without being right in your face about it. You mentioned you've got Buckaroo on the way. I hope it's appropriate to offer you congrats.

This is really forward, but since I can't ask my stubborn jackass of a brother-in-law, I'll just take a risk and ask you. I haven't seen any mention on your blog of a man in your life. Other than that shot of my brother-in-law...

Is there a chance that Buckaroo is going to be a niece or nephew to me? Because if yes, I want you to know that if you need anything —

Heck, let me reword that. Even if you're not pregnant with a Coleman baby, honestly, I'm the kind who's enough of a busybody to want to help everyone out. You need anything, let me know. I've done the kid thing a few times. Checking the current baster button, I'm ready to pop in about a month, so things are pretty fresh in my memory.

You're not alone.

If it is Jesse's, he'd better be treating you right, or I'll tan his hide. Yes, I think I offered to do that before. Sometimes the old ways are the best.

I'll stop rambling, but I look forward to hearing from you.

Jaxi

She was still staring at her phone when she stumbled through the doors of the greenhouse.

128

Ginny glanced up from where she was kneeling in the dirt, a bandana over her hair and a smudge of dirt on her nose. "About time you showed, you slacker."

"Sorry, I was having a lazy morning," Dare deadpanned. Not for the world would she mention either of the proposals she'd received. If her brothers wanted to admit what they'd done, that was their business, but this was one bit of life history Ginny didn't need to know about.

The email from Jesse's sister-in-law, however...

Dare grabbed a hand trowel and joined her friend in the dirt, a row down but close enough they could speak without shouting. "Remember I told you I got an email from someone in Jesse's family?"

"Yep."

"And remember I didn't think he was too keen about me writing back, but last visit he said it was fine?"

"Yep."

"And remember — "

A clod of dirt hit her on the side of the head. She snapped her gaze to the left to discover Ginny kneeling upright with her arms folded over her chest. "Point. Get to it."

"I talked about being pregnant on my blog and his sister-in-law put two and two together and wants to know if Buckaroo is family."

Ginny whistled softly. "Well, I guess this is when we find out the skeletons in his closet."

Dare desperately needed more information, but she was also trying not to bug Jesse for more than he was willing to give. He hadn't wanted to talk about his family, so that was that.

Besides, she *had* family of her own. She had Ginny,

and the guys, and her nieces. And she had herself. That would be enough for Buckaroo.

But he could have a grandma and grandpa, and a bunch of aunts and uncles who all had children and knew something about raising them.

"You're sitting there with that faraway look in your eyes again. This part isn't that difficult, Dare." Ginny rested back on her heels, head tilting slightly as her expression softened. "You've been doing an amazing job figuring out how to take care Buckaroo on your own, and I know it's been tough. You keep having to make decisions, and I'm sorry I can't be more help, but what I can do is make you answer the questions you don't want to."

"A true friend."

"Forever," Ginny reminded her. "Do *you* want to meet his family?"

It was the question she'd been trying to avoid even thinking about. "I kind of hate you right now."

"I'll take that as a yes. Which means the next time you see Jesse, mention that since his family knows about the baby, maybe you guys should make a visit sometime this summer."

Dare blew out air in a long steady stream in the hopes it would keep her head from spinning. "I feel like hell dragging him into all this."

"Don't you dare do that," Ginny snapped, "or friend or no friend, I will come over there and shove a handful of dirt down your pants. He got into bed with you willingly enough, and it's not *your* fault you guys made a baby. He's done what's right by coming and spending time with you, but this isn't some dirty little secret. You're having a baby, and Jesse's the father, and if his family has an issue with that — "

"I don't think they do," Dare said quickly. "You're right, and I know it, and I love you so much, but this is too much to handle sometimes. Jesse's been great, but it feels like he's still adjusting. I don't blame him for that, but I also don't want to expect more of him than he's willing to give."

She held back the words on the tip of her tongue. *I'm scared to start relying on him.*

Ginny abandoned her weeding and shuffled over to wrap her arms around Dare, holding her close and patted her back firmly. "You are so strong, my friend. I'd be a quivering mess in your boots, so don't kick yourself for having moments when you don't know what to do. Don't give up on Jesse too quick — I read somewhere that guys are typically at least three months behind the program, even when they were involved in trying to make a kid happen."

That was reassuring. Dare kissed Ginny's cheek. "I'm glad you're my friend."

Ginny grinned then motioned to the long rows in front of them. "I'm so glad you're my friend because it means I don't have to deal with all these weeds on my own."

"I knew there was an ulterior motive to your pep talk."

They exchanged knowing smiles then got to work, and in the midst of the repetitive labour, Dare considered her options.

Chapter Nine

He'd limited himself to one cup of scalding hot coffee after crawling out from under the covers, but hours later Jesse's heart rate still hadn't dropped to normal, proving it wasn't the caffeine that had sent his pulse racing.

Sweet old doctors with grey hair and kind eyes could just go to hell.

He bet that evil Dr. Martins had done it on purpose. Between the damn stirrups and the inch-thick package of reading material on what disasters could happen during pregnancy, Jesse's usual rock-solid sleeps had vanished into a series of midnight apocalypses all populated by ghostly versions of Dare screaming as she begged him to help her, and he could do nothing but stand by helplessly.

To top it off, he was stuck here in the south, and she was there at Silver Stone ranch, and how the *hell* was he supposed to protect her when they were in different counties?

Yes, he knew his sisters-in-law had safely delivered kids, one of them on a regular basis, but hell, that was Jaxi. She was ballsy enough that if the Grim Reaper ever did come for her, she'd probably slap the scythe from his bony hand and demand he sharpen it before crossing the threshold of her house.

Dare was kickass too, but she'd never done this baby thing before. She didn't have a mom, or older sisters — *Fuck*. There went his heart racing again.

Sweat dripped from his brow, and he wiped it away angrily. He'd decided he couldn't let things carry on the way they were. He and Dare hadn't even discussed it, so quitting his job and making the move closer to Silver Stone ranch seemed to be jumping the gun. But if he meant to do everything possible to be there for her, something had to change.

The sleepless nights had contributed to one good thing. He gathered up the paperwork he'd completed for Bar M and headed to the foreman's office. He checked his phone for messages, but Dare hadn't contacted him since the previous night.

Damn it all, now he was being needy and clingy, but he couldn't shove away the concerns that reared over and over.

Damn Dr. Martins and her faux cheerful paperwork of doom and gloom. Even though he'd been back to visit only a few days after that first doctor's visit, and Dare had insisted everything was fine, Jesse couldn't stop worrying.

What if something happened? What if she needed him and he was somewhere out of reach, *and* a three-hour drive away on top of it?

This was bullshit, and there was only one thing he could do that would make things better. He should have done it in the first place.

The foreman rose to his feet as Jesse walked into the office. "Just the man I wanted to see."

Jesse somehow didn't think so, not after Tony found out what he had to say.

Jesse dropped the pile of papers onto the desk. "I've got about six months worth of projections ready for you, and I've added the data to the ranch computer."

Tony frowned. "How the hell did you get that much done so quickly? We only needed two months."

"I've been working late the past few nights. I figured it was only right because I need to give my two-week notice, and this way I'm not leaving you in the lurch as badly."

The foreman leaned his hip against the desk, arms folded across his chest, disapproval in every line of his body. "You're leaving already?"

Jesse didn't care what the man thought of him at this point. Maybe he could've made an excuse to make himself look better, but it was time to stop making excuses and face facts. "I'm moving closer to my girl. She's expecting."

Disapproval turned to disappointment. "Sorry to see you go."

"You've been good to work for, and if the next man you hire wants to talk, I don't mind getting him up to speed on what I was doing."

"Appreciate that." Tony looked him over. "You have a job lined up already?"

Jesse shook his head. He hoped — but he'd been reluctant to ask Caleb straight-up the last time he was there.

Tony grunted. "Well, you're welcome to stay on as long as you like. Just let me know when you're officially off the clock, and if you need it, I'll give you a letter of recommendation."

The schedule said Jesse was off until the following afternoon, so he hightailed it out, making it to Silver

Stone ranch shortly after lunch. He and Dare had a lot to talk about.

Not to mention the paperwork she'd demanded was burning a hole in his pocket.

Only when he parked by the cottage, her truck wasn't there. A quick peek around the small house proved she wasn't hiding in the woodwork anywhere.

He pinned his medical report to the refrigerator with brightly coloured magnets then went looking for her.

What he found instead was a group gathered by the large arena. Cowboys stood in small groups talking easily as they waited by the railing. Luke Stone appeared along with another couple of familiar faces — people he'd seen around the ranch when he'd been walking with Dare. One was a woman with dark hair that hung in long braids down her chest, and the other an older man with a grizzled grey beard.

Jesse made his way toward the head of the arena, stopping as Luke and his horse exploded out the box, chasing after a steer. Luke's arm moved in an easy sweep that sent the lariat over his head spinning in deceptively lazy circles before he cast it out. The loop wrapped around the animal's head like magic.

His horse had already stopped, keeping the rope tight as Luke slid off into a run, catching the steer and bringing it to the ground. He had one of the beast's feet looped with a smaller rope, and then three, before shooting his hands into the air to stop the timer on the clock.

It was a pretty piece of roping, and Jesse cheered with the rest of the crew, continuing his way to where he'd finally located the other Stone brothers.

Dustin spotted him first, his face falling into a scowl. He elbowed Caleb who barely moved, just angled his head and spoke sharply to his younger brother. "I'm not a punching bag."

Jesse joined them, looking for a way to smooth the situation. These men would be in his life from now on, and damn if he wasn't having the devil of a time reading them.

Well, Dustin was easy — he hated Jesse's guts.

"Afternoon. Nice bit of riding," he said to Luke who was dusting his hands on his thighs as he joined the group.

Luke shrugged. "Good horse."

"Bet you can't do it," Dustin taunted, all piss and vinegar.

"Since I don't have a horse, you're probably right," Jesse agreed, forcing himself to not take up the punk's implicit challenge. "Any of you know where I might find Dare?"

"She and Ginny took the girls to Calgary," Caleb informed him.

"You're stuck with us." Luke offered a grin. "Want a go? I can lend you a ride — that's no problem."

Out in the arena the old-timer swung and missed, the rope skittering on the ground as the steer escaped. The crowd jeered wildly.

"Poor Ashton. He's going to get razzed all night." Caleb lifted his stony gaze to Jesse's. "Our foreman. He doesn't often miss."

"We all have bad moments."

"Not me," Dustin snapped.

Luke gave his brother a slap on the shoulder. "Sure, you do. We just don't rub it in because we don't want you crying all over us."

"Fuck off."

Luke chuckled. "Grow up, Dusty. Or put your money where your mouth is."

"Bet I can out rope him." Dustin turned on Jesse. "Best two out of three, if you're not chicken."

Jesse took the coil of rope from Luke, testing the weight. "I'd love to accept your invitation, *Luke*." He glanced at Dustin. "I haven't taken on a challenge because someone called me a chicken since I was twelve years old. When you grow up a little, we can talk."

Maybe it was pushing it a bit — he was a stranger, they were family, but being a part of his own big family growing up had taught him a few lessons, and he wasn't about to ignore them all.

A momentary flash of his father hit. Mike speaking firmly to him and his brother after he'd caught them egging each other on into trouble. Or more accurately, if he was honest, Jesse egging Joel into trouble.

You want to test your limits, you go right ahead, but do it to prove to yourself it can be done, not to prove anything to others.

Jesse forced away the memories as Luke led him into the barn where a number of horses waited in clean, fresh stalls. "Dusty's not quite sure what to make of you."

"He's got time to figure it out because I'm not going anywhere. Dare and I are in this together, and unless she tells me to get the hell out, I'm not about to be scared off by some teenager."

"I'm not quite sure what to make of you, myself," Luke admitted. "If Dare did tell you to get the hell out, would you?"

"No."

Luke nodded approvingly, then he changed the subject altogether, pointing to the animals. "Samson here is a bit taller and broader than the rest, but he's good with a rope. Or you can try Thunder. She's been on the circuit."

Ha. That was a good warning to get. "Three swings before she shuts it down?"

Luke's grin said it all.

Interesting. "I'd love to try her sometime, but today I'll stick with Samson."

He went in and said hello to the horse, patting the solid neck and letting Samson take a good sniff of him before leading him out of the stall to be saddled.

"I've got to get back out there, but I'll get Kelli to come help you find things."

Luke took off one direction, and moments later the cowgirl with long braids appeared, carrying a massive saddle.

Jesse hurried over to take it from her.

"I got it," she insisted, placing the heavy leather on the rail made for that purpose. She held out a hand. "Hey. I'm Kelli. Luke sent me to help get you set up."

She showed him where the tack room was, grabbing a horse blanket and the rest of the gear they needed to saddle Samson.

Jesse took over, and she watched, curiosity in her expression. He waited for her to break down and ask who he was, but she surprised him and kept pretty close-mouthed.

"Come out this side." Kelli coaxed Samson forward, swinging open a door onto an empty arena. It was on the opposite side of the barn, the noises from the crowd watching the roping muted by distance and the solid wooden structure between them.

Kelli climbed on the railing, out of the way but

sticking close at hand if she was needed. Jesse ignored her and concentrated on learning the feel of Samson.

Every horse had a different personality, and riding another man's horse was never as comfortable as using his own, but if the skills were there, any duo could accomplish a day-to-day task like roping.

Jesse put Samson through the paces around the arena a time or two before riding up to Kelli's spot on the rail.

She held out a coiled rope. "He pulls softer than you'd expect, considering he's a big brute."

Jesse nodded. "I know his type. He's a soft marshmallow inside for all he tries to look like a bully."

Kelli smiled from ear to ear, like sunshine beaming down on him. "*Exactly*. That's exactly what I told Luke."

"You obviously know your horses."

She sniffed. "Feel free to tell that to Luke anytime. I'd appreciate the backup confirmation."

Jesse wasn't looking to get in the middle of what seemed to be a long-standing feud. Besides he had a challenge to face. He took a couple practice swings, getting used to the horse under him.

Then he followed Kelli around to the opposite side where Dustin was waiting on a red gelding.

"Ready to fall on your face, loser?"

Jesse resisted rolling his eyes. "You need to work on your insults."

Dustin pulled his horse into position in the box. Jesse had to admit the kid had the moves when it came to roping. From the moment he broke the timer and started the clock, to when the calf was lying on its back, trussed up neat and clean, only seconds had passed.

Dustin glanced back at Jesse cockily before mounting his horse and riding out of the arena.

It was a potentially embarrassing moment, but if there was one thing Jesse could do in his sleep, it was rope. Dustin was good.

Jesse was better.

He moved Samson into position as the familiar edge of anticipation and excitement bubbled in his blood. He took a deep breath, focus narrowing. The sound of voices and laughter becoming fainter as he gripped the rope, positioned Sampson and gave the signal to open the chute.

Samson moved forward the instant Jesse shifted his weight, man and beast working together, chasing after the steer as Jesse twisted his raised wrist once, twice, three times —

He barely remembered getting off the horse, the motion familiar and smooth as he tied the calf and stepped back.

Appreciative cheers reached him as Jesse returned to Samson, giving him a firm pat as a thank-you.

They returned to the gate, watching as others took their turns, setting up and going for it another few times. In the end, Jesse wiped the sweat off his brow with the back of his sleeve then didn't bother to hide his grin as he tied Samson to the railing, patting him happily. "We might have to do that again, sometime."

Samson seemed pleased with the idea as well.

When Jesse caught up with the Stone brothers, Luke was grinning, Dustin frowning and Caleb somewhere in the middle.

"You do know which end of the horse is which." Luke hit him on the back. Jesse held himself vertical with great difficulty, hiding a grimace.

Dustin grudgingly offered a nod. "You did okay."

Jesse hadn't expected vows of eternal friendship, so he took it. "Thanks."

Caleb was the one who threw everything into the air. His expression unreadable, he was eyeing Jesse a lot closer than he had to date.

He sighed. "Were you planning on staying the night?"

Jesse nodded. "You know when the girls will be back?"

"Late." The gathering of hands was breaking up, horses and men disappearing into the barn and far corners of the paddock. "Join us at the house for dinner."

Wonderful. Caleb appeared less than delighted while issuing the invite, and Dustin looked as if he'd swallowed a frog.

Which was reason enough for Jesse to grin and pretend he was thrilled. "Appreciate it."

Jesse took Samson back into the barn, removed the horse's saddle and put everything away. Kelli joined him, moving comfortably around the big horse.

"You like working at Silver Stone?"

Kelli shrugged. "It's my home. I've been here for nearly eight years."

She didn't seem old enough to make that claim, but Jesse put aside his curiosity and headed back toward Dare's cottage. He took a shortcut through the paddocks, lost in thought.

Dinner with Dare's brothers wasn't what he'd planned. He and Dare needed time together, and he was more than ready to put their physical relationship back on track. But since he had no choice in the matter, he'd put on a good face and hope it might —

Between one moment and the next Jesse found himself airborne, strong arms lifting him from the ground. He struck out in an attempt to free himself, a sharp curse escaping his lips.

"Let me go." He caught a glimpse of hats flying, and dark hair as he struggled, then suddenly he was free and headed for the ground.

Or maybe not, as cold wetness wrapped itself around him. He landed with a splash, barely closing his mouth in time as water washed over his head. He scrambled to sit up, catching hold of the solid edges of the watering trough he'd been unceremoniously dumped into.

Two highly amused faces peered back at him. Dustin laughed as he scooped up his fallen hat and jammed it on his head, walking away without a second glance.

Jesse sat there for a moment, shocked, angry and yet somewhat amused. Everything he wore was soaking wet, from head to toe, including his boots. He hadn't seen it coming.

It was better than a shotgun. Or a fist, for that matter.

Luke stepped forward and held out his hand.

Jesse eyed it with suspicion. "You have a buzzer on your palm that's going to shock me?"

The other man chuckled. "No such luck."

Jesse gripped Luke's wrist, pulling hard to make it to vertical. He stepped out of the metal tank, dripping over the hay-strewn ground. "You plan on baptizing me on a regular basis?"

"Nah. You just looked like you needed a little cooling off before dinner, since Dare's not here and all." Luke straightened his hat. "Consider it my *welcome to the family* gift."

"And what's Dustin going to give me? A shotgun in the back?"

"Ah, he's all talk. He'll settle down." Luke slapped

Jesse on the shoulder and walked him toward the cottage. "See, the thing you need to understand is she's been ours to take care of for a long time, and in some ways, we feel as if we screwed up."

"You don't need to protect her from me," Jesse promised.

"Well, glad to hear you say it, but you see, I don't know that for sure. You mean well, offering to marry her and all, but she's our sister. We want what's best for her, and..." Luke shrugged. "Go on. Get changed. I didn't mean to talk your ear off. We'll take it as it comes."

Jesse wasn't sure what that meant. Not then, and not when, after he'd retreated to Dare's place and showered up, he made his way to the main homestead.

The barbecue was going, smoke rising from the back deck of the house. Jesse rounded the corner cautiously, checking to be sure Dustin wasn't preparing another surprise.

It looked safe enough. Caleb was turning over thick steaks, and Luke grinned as he walked out the door with long necks dangling between his fingers.

"Look who's here, boys."

Which was when Jesse noticed there were no longer three of them, but four.

***

A day of herding her nieces through more than a dozen stores had left Dare exhausted. Heck, forget Emma and Sasha — Ginny was worse than both of them, constantly wandering off in a new direction, distracted by window displays.

What Dare wanted was to go home and crawl into

the tub for a long soak. She'd stopped at the main house to help Ginny get the girls headed to bed, only to find music blaring and lights on everywhere.

Her friend rolled her eyes then ushered Sasha toward the back of the house, Emma draped over her shoulder, fast asleep. "I'll take care of these guys. You go convince the wild animals to turn the music down."

"If they don't agree fast enough, I'm shutting off the power to the house," Dare warned.

"Works for me. I'm tossing the girls in bed then I'll be asleep the instant my head hits the pillow."

"Me too. No more marathon shopping trips." Although it had been necessary — Dare's expanding waistline wasn't going to put up with her regular jeans for much longer.

Ginny was already out of sight, so Dare made her way to the sliding doors off the kitchen, flipping off light switches as she went.

What the heck had Caleb been doing? This wasn't like him — the entire place was lit up like a Christmas display.

She paused in the doorway wondering if she was hallucinating.

Hallucinations would explain so much.

But no, in spite of a second harder glance, the scene didn't change. Her brothers were all gathered around the outdoor picnic table on the deck, a mess of bottles lining the edges of the table's surface as Luke dealt the cards. All of the guys looked a little rough around the edges, and bags of chips and empty plates were piled haphazardly on the counter beside the barbecue.

It was a classic men's-poker-night setting, but the guys themselves —

Caleb had a glittering tiara on his head, the sparkling

silver princess gear looted from his daughters' dress-up trunk. Luke wore a matching gold one, a purple robe draped over his shoulders.

Dustin wore a set of rabbit ears, a red cowboy bandanna pulled over his nose as if he were in the middle of a stickup.

Dare stepped onto the deck, squinting to see if the weirdness vanished. "I swear I haven't had a drink in months."

Five faces turned toward her, Walker and Jesse both rising to their feet.

Walker was on the same side of the table as her so he made it to her side first, scooping her up and giving her a tight hug. "Good to see you, baby girl."

"I didn't think you'd be home for a while yet." She offered a quick squeeze in return, but pushed him away rapidly so she could stare up in horror. "Can you even see me through that monstrosity?"

He'd had a gorilla mask shoved up on his forehead, and now he pulled it into place before lifting his arms and pounding on his chest as he made obnoxious noises.

Dare snickered. She was too tired for this. Any moment now she might start laughing hysterically.

Jesse stepped around Walker and pulled Dare into his arms. "Glad you made it home safe."

Then right there in front of her brothers he kissed her. Not a simple peck, either, but with a whole lot of heat and possessiveness. At this point she wasn't sure what was going on, but who was she to tell him no?

The man obviously had a death wish.

Then again, as she kissed him back enthusiastically, she realized Jesse was the only one of the lot of them not wearing something out of the girls' dress-up stash.

She gave a tug on the back of his shirt, and he slowed and let her up for air, full-fledged Coleman grin in place.

She looked him over carefully. "How come you're the only normal one?"

"I object," Luke spouted from the table.

"You're wearing a tiara," Dare pointed out, leaning into Jesse's body as she took another peek around the table. "Oh, you're right, there's absolutely nothing unusual about you."

Luke cracked a grin briefly before picking up his cards and staring at them.

"Not that I want to interrupt what looks to be a scintillating evening, but can we turn down the volume? Ginny's putting the girls to bed."

Caleb stood, nodding slowly. "I'll go tuck them in. You have a good day shopping?"

"Not as much fun as I think you've had," Dare offered to his retreating back before turning her confusion on Jesse. "Explain."

Inside the house, Caleb hit the master volume and the music went down to normal levels. Dustin had laid his head on the table, and one of his ears had gotten twisted, the long pink-and-white faux fur standing upright like a broken TV antenna.

Walker was finishing his beer, drinking from the bottle through the opening in the monkey mask and looking like a King Kong wannabe. Luke was looking at the cards Caleb had left on the table in front of him...

She raised a brow at Jesse.

He lifted his hands innocently. "Just getting to know your brothers."

He had another cut on his face, and she brushed her fingers over it. "Dustin?"

"Walker."

"He had it coming," her brother announced hotly.

It was too late for this type of conversation. Dare planted her fists on her hips and glared at the only two Stone boys within earshot sober enough to bitch to. "I would like all of you to stop beating on my boyfriend. He seems a decent guy, but I'm never going to find out for sure if you keep damaging him."

Walker peeled off the mask so he could exchange a confused glance with Luke.

Exactly how drunk were they? "You do understand *boyfriend*, yes?"

"Fiancé," Jesse whispered. "Remember?"

"Right. Fiancé," Luke agreed with a flourish.

"Jeez, Dare, I didn't hit him because of what he did with you." Walker made a face. "You already told us to mind our own business about that."

"Then why were you two fighting?"

Jesse caught her fingers in his and pulled her toward the table. "He didn't like the first forfeit he had to pay. I think you looked good with the pig snout," he offered casually to Walker.

Walker flashed him the finger. "Are we playing anymore?"

"I'm done for the night. Time to make sure Dare gets her rest." Jesse folded his cards and tossed them in the middle of the table. One of them landed on the side of Dustin's face.

A loud snore shook the table, the upright bunny ear quivering as Dustin's head rolled.

Enough. Dare kept a tight grip on Jesse and guided him down the steps, ignoring the good-natured bickering in the background between Luke and Walker.

Jesse's grip on her fingers was warm, and damn if he didn't start whistling happily as they approached the cottage.

Dare fought a yawn, her curiosity getting the better of her. "I hate to ask for an explanation, but if you can tell me in a minute or less what was going on, I might not have nightmares."

"Like I said, a bit of brotherly bonding. It was mostly Dustin's fault. He was getting cocky, and after the steaks were done, one thing led to another, and instead of playing poker for money, winner got to pick a costume for the others to wear."

He opened the door for her, following close on her heels as Dare attempted to get her sleepy brain to work through his words.

"Dress-up. You seriously convinced my brothers to use dress-up costumes instead of gambling."

He shrugged, taking her coat and hanging it on the hook by the front door. "I'm cheap. What can I say?"

It suddenly registered that he had really been there, with all four of her male family members, and other than some out-of-sight scuffling, none of her brothers had offered death or dismemberment when he kissed her. "Does this mean they've accepted you?"

"Oh, I'm sure they'll find reasons to not like me in the future, and I'm never turning my back on Dustin, but so far, so good."

Yeah, Dustin wasn't going to be an easy case. But the others? She was surprised it had gone as well as it had. "Far too charming for your own good."

He pulled her back into his arms. "Enough about your brothers. I take it you're pretty tired."

"Riding herd on three overexcited shoppers is

148

exhausting, even when I'm not pregnant."

He hummed in sympathy, rubbing a hand up her arms and over her shoulders, the gentle motion pulling their bodies into tighter contact. "I guess that's my cue to get you into bed."

Chapter Ten

As tired as she was, the words were enough to send a jolt of adrenaline through her system. "Jesse…"

He pressed a kiss to the side of her neck as he slipped a hand under her shirt. "I brought you my paperwork, but to prove what a gentleman I am, you don't have to look at it tonight."

His fingers were warm as he caressed and teased, and if she weren't so damn tired, it would've been exactly what she'd craved. "I want to…"

"…fuck. I know. But you can hold out until tomorrow for my cock."

A noise escaped Dare, somewhere between a laugh and a grunt. "Such an ass."

He patted her on the butt. "Bed, darlin'. Don't tempt me to do wicked things when you're asleep on your feet."

"Still be fun." Her words were slurring, and she was thankful for his guidance as he walked her into her bedroom and helped her get ready.

He didn't take advantage. Not when he stripped off her clothes, or when he knelt beside her, letting her balance with a hand on his shoulder as he wiggled off her pants and socks.

When she would have reached for her pyjamas, she found a warm Jesse-scented T-shirt being pulled over her head.

She nuzzled against his suddenly bare chest. "I like wearing your clothes."

"Hmm, I like you wearing my clothes too, although naked is even better. Now hit the can. Can you find your way?"

"If you didn't leave the seat up. Hate falling in."

Jesse laughed. "Common complaint of the fairer sex. I swear I will do my damnedest to keep you from falling in."

She took care of business and brushed her teeth, stumbling back to the bedroom in that half-asleep/half-awake state. That she was still vertical was a testament to the invigorating impact of Jesse's presence.

Damn hormones.

He'd already pulled back the sheets, and she collapsed, punching her pillow into position as she sank into the mattress.

"Good night, darlin'."

A gentle, chaste kiss landed on her cheek, shocking her enough she opened her eyes to peek into a slice of heaven, his blue eyes only inches away.

She stared for a moment before remembering what she was going to say. "You're really putting me to bed alone?"

"I really am." He stood and backed away, his deep voice wrapping her in a warm cocoon. "I know where to find you come morning. Now, hush. Rest."

Dare was about to protest when she woke, sheets toasty around her, the room dark.

Seemed she'd ended up catching a few zzzs in spite of herself.

She leaned up on an elbow to check the clock. It

blinked at her, pale blue digits in a dark background. Two a.m. and she was wide-awake.

Dare lay back, slowly stretching a hand toward the far side of the mattress, surprised and somewhat disappointed to discover she was alone in the big bed.

Disappointed. Huh. Maybe she should do something about that.

She poked her head out the door, not sure what she expected to find at this time of the morning, but the house was quiet, the ranch as well, and she made her way to the sink to get a drink.

Her gaze skittered to a stop on the medical report Jesse had pinned to her fridge. She bit her lip to stop from laughing out loud.

Over the years she'd gathered an eclectic collection of fridge magnets, and he'd strategically gone through them, using the ones with happy faces to hold the paper in place. But the starring role had been given to an oversized yellow arrow that proclaimed TO DO in bold black.

He'd strategically lined it up to his name.

The turkey was trying to be funny, but she totally understood where he was coming from. With so many things to figure out, and an entire relationship to build, she was sure there was something wrong with her that sex was the only thing currently on her mind.

His voice echoed in her brain. *This part was simple,* and she had to agree with the sentiment. Maybe they shouldn't base a long-term relationship on sex alone, but it seemed like cutting off her nose to spite her face to deny that she wanted him.

So? What was she waiting for?

Dare headed to the office, pushing the door open

carefully. Moonlight shone in the window like a pale blue spotlight. Jesse took up most of the surface of the small, single mattress, blankets kicked off to reveal his muscular torso, the edge of his boxers barely covering more interesting territory. She stepped toward the bed, the merest brush of guilt washing past for waking him up.

Considering what she was about to offer, she didn't think he'd mind.

She sat on the edge of the bed, and his eyes popped open, searching the room quickly before fixing on her face.

"You okay? What's wrong?"

Dare hurried to reassure him. "Nothing's wrong only..."

Suddenly awkward for no good reason, she hesitated.

Jesse sat upright, reaching for her. "You have a nightmare?"

She ignored the question and instead curled herself up on the mattress next to him. "It was lonely in my bed."

He wrapped an arm around her, laughing softly. "Here I thought I was being a gentleman and letting you sleep with no one making you twitch."

"Maybe I don't want to sleep."

He tensed. "Really?"

Dare went for the gusto, rolling as rapidly as the tiny space allowed until they were face to face. "Is it morning yet?"

His grin brightened. "You're one of *those* kids. On Christmas morning they had to lock you in your room to stop you from waking the entire household, right?"

Dare drifted a hand over his shoulder and down his

back, fingertips teasing along the elastic of his boxers. "You know this from experience?"

She found herself flat on her back with him stretched out full-length over her. "I told you we had a lot in common."

He brought their lips together and kissed her, soft for a brief instant before he took full control. The heavy weight of his torso pressed her down so she had nowhere to go except around him. She opened her legs to let his hips settle more firmly against her, dragging her nails over his skin as a blanket of warmth accelerated to high heat between one breath and the next.

Jesse shifted far enough he could kiss his way down her neck. "You need to lose my shirt."

He caught the bottom edge, bunched it up and slid it over her breasts. The next second he had her nipple in his mouth, the impact sending an explosive shot directly between her legs.

For all that he complained about her shirt, he didn't seem too worried about stopping to get rid of it. He just shoved the material out of the way so he could cup his hands on the outside of both breasts, pressing them together to work from side to side. Dare threaded her fingers through his hair, letting him give her pleasure as he took what he wanted.

"If I'm dreaming, this is the best dream I've had my entire life," Jesse teased, laying a row of kisses down her belly to finish between her thighs. "Look, here's a sweet little pussy, all ready to be petted."

Dare snickered. "Where do you get these lines?"

He answered by stroking a finger through her curls, followed by covering her with his mouth.

Cheesy pickup lines or not, damn, the man's tongue

should be offered awards. He teased her clit slow and steady, then faster until he damn near growled. "So fucking sweet."

He covered her completely. Licking and sucking greedily until she was gasping for air, her body quivering and ready to go.

"Now," she demanded, "get in me *now*."

He didn't take orders very well. Instead of listening he doubled down, increasing that magic touch with his tongue, slipping his fingers into her sex and thrusting deep.

The result was instantaneous. Her body exploded with pleasure, sex pulsing, thighs quivering, and she moaned involuntarily.

Jesse laughed softly, working his hand as he slid against her body until he could look into her eyes. "There it is, that delicious sound. You need to make it again."

She'd gone off so quickly, but she wasn't sure if it was a testament to his talents or to the fact that she'd been pretty much a born-again virgin since February.

Or maybe it was the combination of them, because he looked on the edge as well. Her body tightened around his fingers, attempting to hold on as he pulled free and levered himself over her.

How the realization made it through her pleasure-soaked brain, she had no idea, but an instant after it hit, the words snuck out. "Oh my God, I've never done this before."

He looked amused for a spilt second until he caught her meaning. "Hell. Me neither."

No condoms. Oh, boy.

Dare took a deep breath, cupping his face in her

hands. "Another thing we have in common. We should totally fuck."

Jesse laughed, gaze connecting with hers as something more serious drifted over his face. He placed his cock to her sex. "Ready?"

She answered by lifting her hips and surrounding the tip of his cock. His lashes fluttered closed with pleasure.

The next second he'd slid all the way in, and this time they both groaned happily. There was no pause, no chance to find control as he pulled back then thrust, the intimacy of being connected powerful and perfect. Hard motions, softer ones, teasing all her senses as he filled her. Over. And again.

Dare closed her eyes and soaked in the sensations. Her body tingled from head to toe, and every good memory she'd had of their one night together was more than matched as he fucked her. The mattress swayed under them even as he kept his power held in check.

After every hard drive the bedsprings creaked, and Dare dug her fingertips into his shoulders. "*Yes.*"

"More," Jesse growled. "I want more."

Oh, God, yes.

He leaned up on one elbow then caught her right leg, dragging her thigh over his hip. The new angle sent him deeper, and they moved together in a pounding rhythm as another peak built.

His lips connected with hers and he kissed her. Once, twice, grinding their hips together. That final brush over her clit closed the deal, and she came, sighing her pleasure into his mouth.

Jesse swore softly, driving his cock fully into her as his body shook with his release. Muscles taut, heavy gasps escaping.

Stillness washed over them. When he finally rested his head on the bed beside her, he held himself braced just far enough away to keep from crushing her into the mattress. They were sweaty, breaths mingling as they balanced on the limited space of her childhood bed, but she was content.

Confused, overwhelmed, but also sated, and for now? They'd found a connection in the simplest thing in the world.

It was enough.

Jesse whistled happily, sitting at the kitchen table.

"Stop smirking," Dare ordered, but there was a smile on her lips as she threw a muffin at him.

He raised his arm, and her missile bounced off his wrist harmlessly. He leaned over to pick it up off the floor then blew at the surface before removing the wrapper. "That wasn't a smirk. "

She folded her arms over her chest.

"*This* is a smirk." He leered, leaning forward as he took a big bite of the muffin.

Dare rolled her eyes as she got up from the table and carried her empty plate to the counter. "Could you at least attempt to hide that we've been making the beast with two backs the next time you see my brothers?"

Jesse pretended to consider as he hurried to swallow his mouthful. "You plan on not telling Ginny we had sex?"

Dare sighed mightily. "I won't outright tell her, but she's like some insane mind reader, or she's got a crystal ball. She probably woke up in the middle of the night the instant we started fooling around and made a note of it so she could tease me today."

They had another topic to discuss. Jesse went for it. "Just so you know, I gave my notice at Bar M."

Her face scrunched with confusion.

"I'll be working out my final weeks, then I'll find a job in the Heart Falls area," he explained. Understanding lit her eyes, then something closer to protest. He spoke before she could complain about his actions. "Hey, I promised to be there for you and Buckaroo. Can't do that from a couple hundred kilometres away, so you'd better get used to the idea. I'm sticking around, got it?"

She nodded slowly. "I hear you — although I still feel guilty. But...thanks."

His phone buzzed with a message. She brushed a kiss against his cheek before leaving him to it and disappearing into the washroom.

The water turned on, and Jesse considered ignoring his message and heading into the shower to join her, but he supposed that might be pushing it.

He glanced at the screen to discover a far too familiar message from his cousin.

Rafe: *Come home, you jerk*

Jesse chuckled before texting back: *are you really going with that as a permanent greeting?*

Rafe: *you like this better? Come home, you jerk, I'm getting married*

A sudden rush of adrenaline struck Jesse. The last time he'd talked to Rafe in person was when his cousin had been making a stupid mistake, and Jesse had called him on it.

Although, to be fair, Rafe had also called Jesse stupid

that day, so maybe it wasn't a contest. Still some gloating was necessary.

Jesse: *I told you Laurel was perfect for you*

Rafe: *I'm not marrying Laurel*

What the fuck? Jesse texted the message and stabbed the send key violently.

Rafe: *kidding. Of course I'm marrying her, idiot. Get your ass home so you can tell me* I told you so *in person*

His cousin had been sending him prods for the last four months, but this was the first time Jesse considered giving in. He wasn't about to explain everything though, so he sent a final message.

Jesse: *congratulations on getting the girl. I'll let you know if it works to come visit. Gotta run*

Then he turned his phone off so he wasn't tempted to answer any more questions. Instead, he gathered his stuff and got ready to head back south.

Morgan dashed back and forth between them as Dare walked him to the truck, looking pink-cheeked and fresh from her shower. Or maybe it was from the fooling around they'd done.

She tucked a loose strand of hair behind her ear. "I'm glad you stopped by."

Jesse grinned. "Me too. I'll be back when I can."

She nodded, stepping back before he was done. No way he was leaving without a kiss goodbye, and he told her so as he tugged her against his body.

Her face brightened further as she draped her hands around his neck. "I'm glad you like kissing."

"See? Another thing we have in common."

The kiss was over far too soon, but it was either stop now and head home, or he'd turn around and take her back to bed, and he'd never make it to work on time.

He dropped the tailgate, and Morgan jumped up into the back. Dare ruffled the dog's ears before stepping aside.

Jesse gave her a smack on the butt.

Dare swatted him playfully. "Drive safe."

She stepped toward the cottage. Jesse found himself grinning as he headed down the long private road leading to the highway.

Caleb was waiting outside the main ranch house, and waved him down.

Jesse lowered his window, grin turning to a smirk as he took in Caleb's appearance. The man looked a little worse for wear.

"How are you this fine morning?" Jesse asked on the verge of a shout.

Caleb cringed. "Asshole.

"I get that a lot."

"I forgot heavy drinking when there are kids in the house is never a good idea. They have no concept of sleeping in, or privacy. Rocking beds and hangovers don't go well."

"Got jumped, did you?" Jesse made sure not to mention that he'd gotten jumped in a lot more fun manner, probably earlier than Caleb.

The bed rocking had been much appreciated.

Caleb waved the comment off. "I'll live. Glad I caught you, though. I've been thinking…maybe you should move closer."

Jesse hesitated. He hated to get his hopes up, but that sounded like good news delivered with perfect timing, considering he was soon to be unemployed. "Was that a job offer?"

Dare's brother nodded slowly. "We'll have to figure

out where you can fit into the operation, but if you plan to stick around, you may as well work here."

Jesse buzzed with sincere gratitude as he pumped Caleb's hand enthusiastically. "Appreciate it."

Caleb stepped away without another word, headed back to the house. His powerful strides eating up the distance as if in denial of his hangover.

Over the next week, Jesse's life got calmer, and it didn't. With his notice given, the job in the south was slowly drawing to an end. Knowing he'd soon be permanently closer to Silver Stone ranch helped ease some of his nightmares, and he made the drive to see Dare the couple chances he got.

Still seemed like a bit of a dream world, and he was exhausted from the extra travel, but it couldn't be helped.

He and Dare were sitting on her porch in the evening one of the last days in June. He'd driven out that morning after finishing a night watch, and he'd need to leave soon, but the trip was the last time he could get away until his contract finished.

Not being around for five days in a row seemed outrageously long.

"You plan to be here for Canada Day?" Dare asked.

"Can't. They're doing a big push to move to the summer grazing lands, and need all hands on deck."

She changed the topic, or more accurately, brought it back to the same one. "Jaxi emailed again. Invited us up for the Coleman Canada Day party — said you could tell me about it. But I guess that's out."

"Sorry, but it is. I wouldn't do that to you your first shot out of the gate. That's the entire Coleman family, with all four clans, *and* friends, *and* anyone else brave enough to drop in, gathered in one place."

Dare shuddered. "Okay, I'm thankful we can't go. I'm more comfortable in smaller groups."

He didn't bother to answer that one because small groups were not likely at *any* Coleman event.

She glanced at him, mischief in her smile. "You're going to miss our Canada Day tradition, as well. I'll tell you the dirty details after you're back, though, so you have ammunition to tease my brothers."

Jesse raised a brow. "Sounds intriguing."

"Heart Falls annual charity auction is held on Canada Day. It used to be pies and quilts and a parade, but a couple years ago someone added a bachelor auction. It's now the bane of the boys' existence — and it'll be Dustin's first year. Luke's been gloating because being engaged to Penny gets him out of the danger zone."

Jesse had to laugh. "Since you and I are together, I'm safe as well. But seriously, maybe I should pull some strings to be here. I want to see what woman in their right mind would bid on Dustin."

"Don't put down the Duster-dude. I bet he gets the cute votes like you wouldn't believe."

Jesse looked out over the land, that sense of being moved forward against his will was back. Maybe it had never gone away.

"You realize Jaxi's not going to give up until we make an appearance." He caught Dare's eye, wondering at her stony expression. "Unless you really don't want to go, we should probably give in sooner rather than later."

She picked a bit of lint off her pants, pulling her gaze from his. "Is there a reason you don't want to go? Because we don't need to if they're trouble, and you're trying to avoid it."

"God, it's nothing like that." Jesse rested his elbows

on his knees and fought to explain what he could. "My family is great. I was just looking for some space from them is all, so it's been rough to wrap my head around going back. I'm sorry if I gave the impression that they're terrible people."

She shrugged. "I was trying not to make crazy assumptions. I know you said you missed them, so they couldn't be all bad."

"They're great," he answered firmly, kicking himself for yet another stupid decision gone wrong. "Let's set a date. I'm done work at Bar M July fourth, so we could go the week after, if that works for you. Before I get set into the schedule here on the ranch."

"I'm sure it's okay." Dare twisted her fingers together over and over. "I'm a little nervous to meet them."

Jesse laughed. "They're likely to never want you to leave. I'll have to peel you from Jaxi's clutches when it's time to go."

Her face folded into a grimace briefly before she pulled herself together and smiled weakly. "A week, or a weekend?"

"Three days at least," he suggested. He was proud the words sounded cheerful in spite of the churning in his gut.

She nodded. "You want to email them?"

He should, but damn if he could face that task after having up and left without any warning last February. "You go ahead and tell Jaxi to expect us on the seventh. She'll be in her glory organizing things."

Dare agreed, and Jesse leaned back and rocked in the silence that fell.

He was going home.

Going back with a fiancée and with a baby on the

way. His brain was still trying to wrap itself around that idea, and now he had another irritating voice inside his head he was desperately trying to ignore. The one drily pointing out that no matter how tough this was going to be, he was glad he'd been forced into it.

Admitting that?

Never.

Chapter Eleven

Blog post: Packing Problems
Stupid thing to admit, but I don't have a suitcase. Never seemed to need one, which says something about my usual happily homebound status. But I'm heading out for a few days and thus you get to enjoy Packing Adventures With A Newbie.

As options we have saddlebags, a backpack and a big-ass purse that my sister bought as a gag gift one Christmas, and by big-ass I mean of extraordinary *bootie nature. It's all about the bass, my friends…*

I was tempted to use the saddlebags at first before I realized there's a reason I store them in the tack room. (Ahem, use your aromatic imagination, and make it really horse-y.)

The backpack makes me feel as if I should be climbing mountains and fording streams, not stopping in for a coffee. It's also awkward because inevitably the item I want the most works its way to the bottom, and I have to dump the entire contents to get at it.

So — big-ass purse it is. Good thing I don't need much… stuff…oh, lordy.

ten-minute break. I know you didn't see me leave, but I did

Okay, I'm back and no longer hyperventilating. It hit me I'm going to need to haul baby stuff around in a while, not to mention the baby when it's no longer in my belly — and my heart just about pounded out of my chest. At some point this will become old hat, right?

glibbers with panic

I'm excited about the baby, don't get me wrong, but maybe a few of you out there who have a little more experience Buckaroo-wrangling can reassure me that, at some point, I too will nonchalantly deal.

It had been the longest car trip ever. Dare fought to keep from squirming, but the three hours seemed like twice that long, and the more distance they put between them and Heart Falls, the more she wondered what the heck she was doing.

Only the echo of Ginny's plainspoken questions kept Dare from ordering Jesse to turn the truck around and cancel the entire trip.

They'd left Morgan behind at Silver Stone. Jesse had suggested it, since he wasn't sure where they would end up staying during their time.

It felt wrong to Dare for Morgan to *not* be with them, although the dog was happy enough — he and one of Dusty's border collies had become fast friends, much to her little brother's disgust.

But no dog meant no distractions, which meant she had to face her fears straight on.

Did she want to meet his family?

She was iffy on her personal answer, but it was clear what Buckaroo's opinion would be. He or she deserved to have all the family possible — *if* they were good people. It was way easier to figure that out in person, and now rather than later.

She and Jesse would visit, and Dare would hopefully have the angelic choirs burst into song to let her know yes or no regarding spending more time with the Colemans in the future. This was an exploratory trip, nothing else.

Not a time to madly fall in love with his parents, or with the intensely nosy but caring Jaxi or…or anyone. Dare did not need these people for her own sake.

This was about Buckaroo. Period.

If she repeated that often enough she might even remember it.

The terror rushing through her at the thought of meeting his parents had left a terrible taste on her tongue.

"You okay?" Jesse didn't take his eyes off the road.

"Fine."

She stared straight ahead as well. This was the worst interaction the two of them had shared since reconnecting a month ago. Normally he was annoying, charming, flirtatious, infuriating —

Jesse, as she'd come to understand him, was a simple man. He could deal with pretty much anything if he could take control or take action. Right now, with the extended periods of silence and his grim determination to put as many miles under their wheels as possible, as quickly as possible…

He was out of his comfort zone with this trip, and gee whiz, didn't that make her concerns even more intense.

Squirming in her seat helped with the jitters, but did nothing to ease the increasing pressure on her bladder. Stupid when the discomfort was preferable to dealing with her fears.

She was about to give up and ask him to pull off onto the nearest convenient gravel road when she spotted a large green sign at the side of the highway.

Rocky Mountain House.

"It is far to the ranch?" Because she knew a mailing address in a town didn't always have much to do with where the ranch was located.

Thank goodness, this time it wasn't one of those we'll-be-there-in-an-hour situations. "Ten minutes to Blake and Jaxi's, if I take the back roads," Jesse offered.

"Okay." Ten minutes she could do.

She used as much Zen concentration as possible, staring out the windows as if she were memorizing the landscape. Ranch lands and farms whizzed by, with signs of familiar rural activities everywhere, and it wasn't that different from home, but it *was* different because this was where Jesse had grown up.

This was where Buckaroo's Gramma and Grampa lived.

The thought distracted her from the fact she had to pee badly enough that her back teeth were all but floating. Finally they pulled off the road at the top of a long driveway. The signpost at the entrance had an engraved wooden carving with *Colemans* in bold letters and *Make Yourself at Home* underneath.

If they had indoor plumbing, she'd be ecstatic. Heck, she'd take a conveniently located tree at this point of the game.

Jesse finally came to life. "Here we are."

He parked, then met her as she was already hopping out of the truck cab. She turned in a circle, trying to take it all in. The long, low ranch house, the mountains rising in the distance. It was…softer?…than the landscape at home, and she offered a comment as she followed him to the front door. "You have bigger foothills than I'm used to."

He snorted. "I'm not touching that one."

She offered him a groan at the cheesy joke. "Jerk."

That addictive grin of his appeared briefly as he hit the doorbell. "Usually I'd walk in, but I figure this might be — "

The door swung open and Jesse's face went white.

Dare snapped her attention to the house, but all she saw was a dark-haired woman, nothing to explain Jesse's reaction. Young, probably early twenties, the woman's gaze darted back and forth between Jesse and herself.

"Hey," Jesse rumbled.

Then he stood there like a lump after spouting the one word. A tall, silent, lumpy sentinel.

As opening lines, that one sucked. It told Dare nothing about who this woman was, or if they were in the right place, and more critically, ignored the plumbing issue.

Dare shifted uncomfortably from side to side, wondering how rude it would be to push forward and find a bathroom on her own.

The woman glanced at Dare, glanced back at Jesse, then shook her head. "Come with me," she ordered.

Dare followed, not caring at this point if she were about to be led to the lip of a volcano. Although the bathroom she was gestured into was a welcome alternative.

Once she could think again, she ventured back into the hallway to discover Jesse leaning on the wall waiting for her.

"Feeling better?"

"Much."

Jesse grimaced. "Sorry about that. I should have found out if you needed to stop."

"I could have asked," Dare told him.

"I know, but I should have thought of it."

A cough sounded from the room to their left. Jesse

169

guided her forward with a hand on her lower back, and Dare found herself standing before the woman again, only this time she was offered a glass of orange juice.

She sucked it back like it was the elixir of life. The glass was empty before she knew it.

Dare offered the woman a grateful smile. "Thanks. I didn't realize how much I needed that."

"No problem. I'm Vicki, by the way. Engaged to Joel."

"Jesse's twin?" She'd heard all the names before, but putting faces with them took extra effort.

Vicki nodded. "Jaxi said to tell you she's sorry she's not here, but she's kind of busy at the hospital having the baby."

Oh my God. "Seriously?"

"Her water broke last night. Marion came over — Mrs. Coleman — and got the older girls off to day camp then took the little ones home with her. I'm off work today, so I said I'd wait to meet you."

Jesse was checking his watch, of all things. "Damn. If it's twins, I win the baby pool."

"Jesse," Dare scolded him. "Really? That's what you're focusing on right now?"

He flashed her a grin, his gaze drifting to Vicki before snapping back to Dare.

Seemingly content to ignore each other, Vicki checked her own watch. "We need to do a little juggling. I expect we'll hear from the hospital anytime, but in the meanwhile, we can get you settled."

"We can't stay here if they'll be bringing home a new baby," Dare protested. Lordy, Dare didn't even know how long that would be. One day? Two? She hadn't been paying that much attention back when Caleb's girls arrived.

170

Maybe Dare could arrange to stay in the hospital until she got the swing of the parenthood thing. Just for a bit, like a few weeks — or months.

"You're right. Jaxi hoped you wouldn't mind — "

"We'll go to my old place," Jesse interrupted.

"You can't. Ashley's moms are living in the rental."

Dare glanced at him and raised a brow, but she didn't say anything right then. Ashley she recognized as one of the threesome, but *moms*?

The boy had some explaining to do.

Vicki shook her head. "Rental's full. Marion and Mike don't have extra room after changing their spare room to take care of the kids better — neither of you will fit in the triple bunk or the crib. The bunkhouses are full as well. It's been the best season yet, and well... I'll let Joel tell you the rest, but *we* have space. I cleaned up the second room in the trailer. There's a double bed in there, and you're welcome to it."

The orange juice in Dare's stomach went a little sour to match the expression on Jesse's face. Okay — she could be adaptable. "Thank you for sharing with us."

"No problem." Vicki glanced back and forth between them for a minute before coughing slightly. "Well, I imagine you'll want to look around a bit on the drive, so I'll just meet you there when you're ready."

"Awesome," Jesse finally spoke, taking Dare by the elbow and guiding her toward the door. "Thanks."

They were in the truck and on the road in seconds, as if the entire thing were a dream. A very brief, vivid and confusing dream.

"If there's no room for us, maybe we should go home," Dare suggested.

"No."

He snapped the word so quickly she pushed back in her seat and bit her tongue. Whatever was going on that had rubbed him the wrong way, she didn't want to add to his burdens, but he'd better not plan to keep her in the dark for too much longer.

Had he even said hi to Vicki? She'd been in the bathroom, so maybe she'd missed it, but the two of them had tension that could be cut with a knife.

Not what she'd been looking for, but then again, even bad answers were answers. This was a fact-finding mission, nothing more,

Wait for the Gramma factor, her brain reminded her.

Stupid brain.

She looked out the window as she sorted through the words to say. Something to let him know she wasn't trying to push an agenda, but he needed to keep her informed.

She was about to open her mouth when he spoke first. "Are you tired?"

Now he was going to be considerate and ask how she was doing? Dare shoved aside her frustration and answered the question. "A little. Nerves don't help."

Jesse made a soothing noise. "Everyone will love you. And I bet we'll be seeing the baby by this evening, so you'll meet Jaxi soon as well. She's an annoying pain in the ass, but she's pretty much the type people fall in love with the minute they meet her."

Which was one of Dare's worries, so she focused on other parts of his comment. "We'll see the baby tonight? It hasn't even been born."

He laughed. "By now, Blake and Jaxi are probably holding him or her, and Jaxi's bossing around all the nurses and making suggestions to help them run the ward more efficiently."

"You know I have very little idea how the baby thing works," Dare informed him, suddenly worried she needed to live up to his sister-in-law who seemed a paragon of motherhood. "Like, way closer to zero than one hundred. So please don't expect me to be a super mama like Jaxi — "

"Oh God, no," Jesse said quickly, his grin real as he looked her over. "I don't expect anything from you except you loving the kid for all you're worth. Jaxi's just...*Jaxi*. She'd tan my hide if she thought I was spooking you off."

"She's mentioned that phrase a time or two," Dare admitted. She took a deep breath. "*Moms?*"

Jesse groaned. "Caught that, did you? I'll give you the details later, but how about we get you settled in? You can put your feet up for a few minutes."

They were pulling into a parking space in front of a double-wide trailer, so there wasn't much she could offer other than "okay".

He dropped their bags on the porch just as a second truck pulled into the yard, Vicki frowning at them over the wheel.

Jesse coughed, then turned to face Dare. "Going to track down my brothers."

It was Dare's turn to frown. "You're not even going inside?"

She was talking to air. Jesse was behind the wheel, truck engine revving. He backed up rapidly, tires spinning as he raced for the exit, and the truck vanished down the driveway.

Dare and Vicki glanced at each other simultaneously. Silence hung on the air.

"He's eager to catch up with his brothers," Dare offered as an excuse.

The other woman didn't answer, just turned to the door and carried in the bags, heading down a narrow hallway. She pushed open a door with her shoulder then placed the bags on a small but neat bed that was covered with a gorgeous quilt.

"It's pretty. Thanks," Dare said.

The other woman nodded. "You ready for lunch?"

Dare was all but empty inside. Jesse had to be starving, but it was his own fault for leaving her so suddenly. She offered Vicki the brightest smile she could muster. "Please."

Vicki paused in the doorway before smiling softly. "Hey, I know this is a lot, but I *am* happy to meet you."

Dare nodded. "Thanks."

"I'll get lunch started." The other woman shuffled her feet for a moment before gesturing down the hall. "Washroom is that way if you need it, and there are towels on top of the dresser."

The door closed softly. Dare let herself collapse back onto the bed, staring at the ceiling as if the answers to life, the universe and everything would be found there.

No such luck.

She splashed water on her face, sucked in a deep breath for courage then wandered to the kitchen.

Vicki had the fixings for sandwiches out and was hard at work, the scent of tomato soup floating on the air.

"Smells great," Dare offered.

"Thanks." Vicki stared at the sandwich she was making as if getting mayonnaise to the edges of the bread was of vital importance. "By the way, congratulations on your engagement."

"Thanks."

Polite platitudes again. Ugh.

Silence returned until Dare couldn't take it any longer. She peeked around the room, desperately looking for some safe topic to break the awkwardness.

Her eyes fell on the oversized pickle jar on the counter that was covered with several stickers proclaiming *Swear Jar*.

It was over half full of coins.

A real smile came to Dare as she pointed it out to Vicki. "I haven't seen one of those for ages."

"It's a good idea that got out of hand." Vicki glanced up, amusement in her eyes. "I have a slight problem speaking my mind too bluntly. It helps remind me to watch my tongue."

Dare eyed the coin level. "You must have pirates in your family tree."

A laugh burst from the other woman. "Or whores — and you'll find out I'm kind of not kidding about that — but all those coins aren't my fault alone."

"Joel?" Dare thought back. "I've heard Jesse swear, but no more than the average guy."

"Joel's the same, but he got cocky one day and talked to the people I work with. They counted while we were cooking for a catered event, and everything that could go wrong, did. I owed a shit-ton when he found out the count. Oh, *drat*…"

She sighed, then reached into her pocket, dropping a quarter into the jar.

"That's kind of dirty," Dare agreed.

"Oh, it backfired on him." Vicki's eyes flashed as she continued the story. "Joel doesn't swear much around me, but after he pulled that trick I talked to Blake, and all the guys kept track one day."

Dare could picture how well that had gone over. "The boys can get raunchy in the fields."

"Hey, if I wasn't allowed to swear at work, neither was he." Vicki grinned. "He owed double what I'd paid. We've agreed work is off limits, although I am trying to watch my tongue there as well."

Dare joined in and laughed. "Good for you. Changing a habit is hard."

"A little at a time, I figure." Vicki handed her a plate, then gestured to the door. "Let's sit outside. It's nice enough out, and I didn't get a chance to clean up in here yet."

"Outside is fine, but the place looks great." God, Dare felt horrible for making more work for the other woman. "If you clean up more than this I'm going to feel woefully inadequate because my place gets less than a flicker of housekeeping, especially lately."

They settled into comfy chairs that faced the sun and continued to chat, soups and recipes a nice easy conversation topic.

Dare was glad for the food in her belly and the reduced tension. In fact, she found herself wholly relaxed for the first time that day. The sandwich went down easy, and Vicki was no longer frightening.

Once the meal was done, Vicki stole the empty plate from under her fingers, stacking their dishes and rising to her feet as she waved Dare off. "Stay here. I'll be back in a minute."

"I don't expect to be waited on," Dare protested.

"You can help with the dishes tonight," Vicki promised. "Or better yet, you can volunteer Jesse, and we'll get the guys to do the hard labour."

"Deal."

Vicki stepped away, and Dare leaned back in her chair and let the sun hit her full in the face. She was tempted to close her eyes and take a nap.

Instead, she made a mental list. A successful arrival in Rocky had been achieved. While Jesse was acting weird, Vicki had turned out to be nice enough. The sun was shining, and no one here was too scary —

She could do this. Dare laid a hand on her belly and soaked in the warmth of the day.

A gentle nudge pressed her shoulder, and Dare realized she *had* fallen asleep. "Shit. I'm sorry."

Vicki grinned. "Don't sweat it. You've had your eyes closed for not even ten minutes. I hear sleepiness is par for the course when you're pregnant."

"It's better than the nausea stage, that's for sure."

The other woman opened her mouth then closed it rapidly, a real smile curling her lips. "Come on. I've got an idea."

Chapter Twelve

Jesse hungrily took in the fresh sight of the fields and buildings that had been his backyard for most of his life. He drove the perimeter of the Six Pack land, staring out the window with a sense of wonder. Crops were up, and cattle grazed, and there was nothing out of the ordinary, but the taste of home was in his soul, and it was sweet.

At least until the realization he wasn't staying sank in. His gut churned. All the sweetness turned sharp. Bitter, like a cake that had been let cook a little too long. Chocolatey and rich inside, but with a layer of charred darkness on the surface.

It wasn't a thing anyone would want to eat.

Caleb's offer to find him a place at Silver Stone had put some of his worries to rest. Dare would want to be near Ginny, close to her brothers and the familiarity of her home. Jesse needed to be close to her and Buckaroo.

Visiting the Six Pack ranch was a good idea, though. He could put on a happy face and make it clear he was moving on, and that would be that.

He refrained from calling himself a lying bastard, no matter how truthful the description.

Jesse drove the back roads until he knew it was stupid to avoid tracking down his brothers. At this time of day they'd usually be scattered over the far reaches of the ranch, but with Blake and Jaxi headed to the hospital, custom said routine would have given way to an impromptu gathering.

He congratulated himself on calling it right when he spotted familiar vehicles gathered outside the main barn. Parking in the middle of his brother's trucks, Jesse paused for a moment until he'd gathered up enough *don't give a damn* to face them.

Only stepping into his childhood playground stripped away his bravado. The scents and sounds were echoes of the past, and he held onto the doorframe and waited for his heart to stop pounding.

Stupid fucking heart. Between worrying about Dare, and the baby, and getting riled up over his damn past, it was a wonder he didn't fall over from a heart attack.

He headed toward the corner where his brothers' voices rose clearly.

"We going to finish the north fields this week?"

"We'll get them done twice as fast without Blake checking his phone every five minutes to see what Jaxi's doing."

Laughter filled Jesse's ears, and he rounded the corner and walked into the middle of it.

Matt and Travis were there, lounging against wooden support posts of stalls. Cassidy sat on a bale with one foot up as he leaned on the stall behind him. The kind of gathering Jesse had joined in a million times before.

Only this time when they spotted him, the laughter vanished. Cassidy straightened, and Matt's eyes widened.

Travis swore and stepped forward.

Jesse wasn't sure what to expect, but if it was fists, he wasn't even going to defend himself. He froze on the spot and waited for what came next.

"You sorry son of bitch," Travis muttered as he closed in on Jesse.

"Travis." Cassidy's voice held a warning.

Jesse braced for impact.

It was a good thing too, because the next second Travis connected with him full force, wrapping his arms around Jesse's torso and squeezing the hell out of him. "Fucking *ass*. Where the hell have you been? I should tie you behind the tractor and drag you around – "

"You want to let him go now that you've proven he's not a ghost?" Matt stepped up. "Although I agree with the ass bit. Jerk. Dickhead."

Jesse wasn't going to argue, not with the sense of relief flooding his system. This could have gone so differently. Insults were just fine. "Good to know you guys are still working on your vocabulary lists."

Matt smacked him on the shoulder – harder than a friendly pat. "Stupid little brother."

"Are you coming back?" Cassidy asked. "Also hi, I guess. I'm not sure if I'm supposed to hug you or hit you."

"We could do both," Travis offered, the fire in his expression making it clear his suggestion wasn't a joke. Anger was replacing his earlier shock. "The only reason I'm not beating the shit out of you right now is that Rafe gave us updates."

"Plus Jaxi put the fear of God into us over this visit." Matt shook his head. "I hope you know what you're doing, but I don't think it's likely. What the *fuck*, Jesse? What the hell were you thinking?"

Cassidy made a rude noise. "Umm, Matt? You might want to make a more specific list before asking that."

"True." Matt raised a hand and counted off fingers.

"You fucking up and left without a word of warning. You didn't send Mom and Dad more than one damn update. You're engaged to be married to some woman from who the hell knows where who we've never met, and you've got a kid on the way."

"She's from Heart Falls, which isn't that far from here," Jesse snapped, temper flaring. "Beat the shit out of me for being a jerk and taking off unannounced, but you leave Dare and the baby out of your rants."

A slow clap sounded from the doorway, and they all turned toward the sound.

Joel stood there, hands moving rhythmically in approval, but his expression was ice cold as he spoke. "He's right, guys. It's not her fault, or the baby's, that Jesse's an ass."

Matt looked sheepish. "Sorry. I didn't mean for it to come out like that. Of course it's not her fault, but *jeez*, Jesse, you've got shit for brains."

"Not about Dare or the baby," Jesse insisted. He wasn't about to give an inch on this. He swore that none of his family would suspect he was anything but thrilled about his current circumstances, which meant lying his ass off. "They're the best thing that's ever happened to me. I brought her to meet all of you, and if that's going to be an issue, tell me now so I can turn around and take her home."

Cassidy waved him down, sliding off the bale to vertical. "You know you don't worry about that. We're looking forward to meeting her, and we're glad you've found someone special."

He held out his hand, and Jesse took it cautiously. Cassidy shook once then used the grip to pull Jesse in close. He spoke quietly under the pretense of offering a quick pat on the back. "You might want to apologize for the leaving bit, though."

Which was what he'd intended to do before getting distracted, damn it all.

Jesse stepped back. He made eye contact with each man before clearing his throat. "I'm sorry I left like that. It was wrong to hightail it out of here without a word."

"It was," Travis agreed. "Stupid, selfish — "

"Travis, when a man apologizes and means it, you don't keep harping on his stupidity." Cassidy strode to his partner's side, laying a hand on his shoulder. "Want to try again?"

"Stop being reasonable. He's my little brother and he fucked up big time."

"He said he was sorry." Matt shrugged. "Okay, Jesse, fine. Thanks for apologizing. I'm still pissed."

He hadn't expected much else. "I get it. Hey, how's Hope and the kid?"

Matt's expression turned on a dime, the disappointed frown flipping into a beaming grin. "She's amazing, and he's trying to walk. Colt climbs like a monkey — almost as bad as you and Joel, according to Mom."

"Walking? Holy hell, that's quick."

"That's what happens when you're gone for five months," Joel drawled. "Things change. Life moves on."

Ouch. Okay, Joel wasn't accepting his apology that easily either, and Jesse didn't blame him. Leaving the family had been hard, but cutting himself off from Joel?

Like severing his own arm.

He'd been the one to cause the pain, and it had nearly crippled him. He had a lot more work to do to repair their relationship, and it wasn't going to happen this moment, so Jesse turned to Travis instead of his twin.

"I see Cassidy's keeping you on a short leash."

Travis laughed. "He wishes."

"Shh, don't talk about sex around your brothers," Cassidy said with a wink.

"Oh God, not this again." Matt pointed a finger at the two of them. "We agreed you're not allowed to gloat."

Jesse didn't know what they were talking about, and the realization hurt. "Why would they gloat?"

Cassidy shrugged innocently. "Matt seems to think we've got some kind of advantage over a regular couple because even though Ashley's eight months pregnant, there's still sex happening."

That pile of papers from the evil doctor hadn't mentioned that detail. He'd read them through a million times, and he would have noticed anything to do with sex. "We can't have sex when they're pregnant?"

Travis, Cassidy and Matt exchanged glances before Cassidy spoke again, concern on his face. "Wow, okay, it's a good thing you came for a visit. Yeah, no sex after she's...what was it, guys, six months pregnant?"

"Five," Matt said, blinking harder than usual. "I mean, you can get her off, but no sex."

Jesse eyed them all, sudden suspicion hitting. "You're pulling my leg."

Travis shook head. "No, really. Ask her doctor."

Only Matt snickered, trying to turn the sound into a cough.

"You're all a bunch of sick jerks," Jesse declared.

"As much fun as this is," Joel interrupted, "I should get going. Who's dropping me off?"

Matt checked his watch. "Not me. I'm heading over to the bunkhouse with information for the crew."

Travis groaned. "Fine, I can get you home, but I don't

know why you keep arguing about taking an advance so you can buy a second vehicle for Vicki instead of making us drive you in circles."

"We've spent enough money this year. I'm not dipping into the funds for something we only need occasionally."

"I can drive you home," Jesse offered. "I left Dare at your place to get rested up. She's waiting for me."

"There, all settled," Matt said quickly, turning to Jesse. "Hope and I will be around tomorrow night if you want to stop by. She's teaching a quilting class tonight."

"Jaxi had planned to have everyone over three nights from now," Cassidy pointed out. "I guess that's off, with the baby arriving and all."

"Ha." Four voices, simultaneous. All the Coleman brothers eyed each other with amusement because there was no mistaking their commonly held opinion of their sister-in-law.

Travis slipped an arm around Cassidy and led him toward the barn door. "After all this time as a member of the Coleman family, and you still think Jaxi's going to cancel an event because of a minor detail like she gave birth a few days earlier? Cassidy, Cassidy, Cassidy. You disappoint me."

"See you there," Joel said, heading out the door without waiting to find out if Jesse was following him.

The silence as they climbed into the truck was deafening. Jesse waited until he'd backed the vehicle up before attempting to make conversation. "You're sharing your truck with Vicki?"

"Her car gave up the ghost in April."

"There's the old truck we learned — "

"It's okay. We've got it figured out." Joel stared

straight ahead, eyes fixed on the road.

This was hell. It was worse than it had been before Jesse had left. Back then he'd finally managed to put in a full day's work with his twin without any awkwardness. It was only when he'd bump into Vicki that things would go sideways.

Now to have Joel sit without a word when they were together...

So many things Jesse wanted to share. The new experiences he'd tried, the people he'd met — not all of going out into the world and being a part of a new operation had been bad, and Jesse had grown to appreciate the lessons learned by being a hand instead of one of the family.

He was itching to talk about the shock of finding out he was going to be a father, and he wanted to talk about Dare, and...

...and none of those were things he could share, not even with Joel.

The truth etched another deep scar in his soul.

They were closing in on the turn to the trailer when Jesse impulsively drove past, pulling in next to Whiskey Creek, the river that meandered through the Coleman land. There'd been a barn here at one point — it had burnt to the ground a few years earlier, and Jesse hopped out of the cab to discover the spot had been cleaned up and cleared out. Instead of the mess, a six-foot fence surrounded a garden area with growing green things stood in its place.

Behind him the truck door slammed shut, and he turned to discover Joel marching back up the road toward the trailer.

"Where're you going?" Jesse called.

Joel stopped dead in the road for five seconds, his back a rigid wall, then stomped on without a word.

Jesse sighed, and went after him. "Fuck it all, Joel, *stop*."

His brother whirled, fists clenched by his hips. "Why?"

"Because I want to…"

What he wanted was impossible. He fell silent under his brother's intense stare.

Joel spat out the words. "Questions like 'where're you going' don't sit well right now, bro. That implies you give a shit about the other person, and since that's not true, don't — "

"Of course it's true. Fuck it all." Jesse laid his hand on Joel's shoulder. "You're my brother."

His arm was brushed away by an angry motion on his twin's part. "Don't do this."

Pain struck again. "I apologized for leaving. What more do you want?"

Joel laughed, a bitter sound. "Seriously? You have to ask?"

He caught Jesse by the shirtfront and dragged him close, face only inches away as Joel stared daggers. "You apologized for leaving the family. How about you try apologizing for ripping out *my* fucking guts? You left, you — *You* — "

Joel's expression twisted, and he threw Jesse from him, turning his body to the side and staring over the Coleman land.

It would have been confusing if it weren't crystal clear to Jesse exactly what his brother was talking about.

He took a deep breath and fought for control. "You're right. You're so right. I made a mistake with the family, but I did something worse with you, and I'm so damn sorry, Joel."

No matter that he'd felt he had to leave, hurting Joel had never been his intention. It didn't change the issue at the root of the trouble, but this part of it, his sorrow at the consequences, was real.

"I'm sorry," he repeated again. "For hurting you."

Joel didn't move. "Asshole."

"Jerk," Jesse responded instinctively, and a hint of smile crossed Joel's face.

Joel turned and walked back toward the river at a much more reasonable pace. Feet moving as they talked for the first time in ages. "You've been lucky. Vicki and I take turns being the reasonable one. When I'm mad enough to spit at the mention of your name, she calms me down and stops me from lighting effigies."

Inside, Jesse's guts twisted again. "Vicki stands up for me? What the hell does she say?"

"That someday I'd miss your sorry ass if I track you down to kill you and that she doesn't want to have to resort to conjugal visits for the next twenty-five years of our lives when I get jailed for knocking your head off your shoulders."

Jesse snorted.

"Hey, when she gets ranting, it's all about poisoning you slowly. So you inspire bloodthirsty thoughts in us both."

"Vicki would get along great with Dare's sister. She's keen on poison as well."

Joel stopped beside a short section of split rail fence, placing a boot on the bottom rung. "Seems weird to think you've been gone long enough to have a new crowd of people willing to put you six feet under."

"We all need a talent," Jesse attempted to joke, but his brother didn't crack a smile, so he sighed and went for serious. "She and Dare's brothers were making the customary *welcome to the family* death threats."

Joel's face twisted for a moment before he brought it under control. "New family, huh?"

God. Jesse's stomach ached from every bit of sharing he did without telling it all. "I mean, they're great. They're hundred percent there for Dare."

This wasn't how it was supposed to be between him and Joel. They'd done everything together. Played, and laughed, and learned about life. They'd shared long talks late into the night, and they'd planned their futures, and now when he needed his twin the most, the walls between them seemed insurmountable.

A long, sad sigh escaped Joel. "Enough. I agree with Matt. I'm still mad, but I'm not going to hold this over your head, as long as you don't ever fucking do it again."

"Leave without a word? Not likely. Jaxi's got the bloodhound scent now. I'll never shake her."

Joel turned slowly to lean on the fence as he folded his arms and looked Jesse over. "Don't expect things to go back to the way they were."

This entire trip was shaping up to be worse than he'd ever imagined. "You hate me that much?"

"I hurt that much," Joel snapped. "And being mad at you hurts even more because I want to tell you it's all fine, but it's fucking not. But I guess we have to try and put it in the past and move on."

What was Jesse supposed to say? *Well, it's mostly over except for one great big huge thing hanging over my head. The same thing that made me leave in the first place.*

Like that would go over well.

"It's in the past," Jesse agreed with as much enthusiasm as he could muster.

Thankfully Joel changed the topic, gesturing to the garden area. "Like the changes?"

Jesse nodded. "Seems funny to have the old barn gone."

"Travis didn't want it around at all anymore. No lingering reminders for Ashley of the fire, so when we had the excavator out, they stopped off here to clean it up."

Excavators. "You digging a hole somewhere?"

Joel paused. "On Sunset Ridge. We got our house started."

A sudden shock went through Jesse for a brand-new reason. Sunset Ridge, where they used to ride as teens and young men, admiring the view and planning where they'd build their homes. Joel to the north and Jesse slightly to the south, next door to each other because they couldn't imagine being farther away than a stone's throw at any point in their lives.

They were going to end up a hell of lot farther than that, and the screw inside tightened again.

"Good for you," he forced out.

Building a home beside Joel was another thing he wouldn't be doing. Another step away from his family... and he couldn't complain. He'd taken the first steps down this path all on his own, and it's not as if he could go back in time.

The truth hurt, and the familiar sensation of being alone enveloped him.

He gritted his teeth and set his resolve. He had to make it through this damn visit with Dare, and then they could go back to Heart Falls.

Her home would have to become his.

Chapter Thirteen

It was her own fault for not asking more questions before getting into the big truck that Vicki herded her in. Dare was already in the passenger seat and they were headed down the highway before details regarding this "great idea" of Vicki's were shared.

"There's not much use in hanging around here until Jesse gets back. We may as well go say hi to Marion, and I can help with the kids." Vicki made a noise. "Not that she's ever complained about having anything or anyone thrust upon her at the last minute."

Dare nodded her agreement in a bit of a haze. At that point it was too late to escape unless she wanted to throw herself out the door of a moving vehicle. Although the comment about Marion dealing effortlessly with all the grandkids did register.

Gramma score: +25

Vicki took a quick peek at Dare before focusing back on the road. "I don't want to be too snoopy, because you're bound to have a ton of questions thrown at you. So don't feel as if you have to give out your life story, or anything." She paused to manoeuver the big truck onto the secondary road before continuing. "Although I think you're a brave woman to agree to visit for more than a day right off the bat."

"It didn't seem that dangerous when Jaxi mentioned

it, but I'm reconsidering," Dare confessed. "I hate to put you and Joel out."

Vicki waved a hand. "It's not a bother. We've got the room, and it's not as if you'll be there all the time. We'll be lucky to have a quiet evening to ourselves — everyone in the family will want you to come over, and that probably means everyone *else* who is free will drop in that night as well."

Dare fought to keep her shudder of dismay from being too obvious. "Did I mention I'm more comfortable in small groups?"

The other woman hummed in sympathy. "Close your eyes and pretend some of them aren't there? That's all I've got to offer. Sorry."

"I'll deal."

"You will." Vicki chuckled. "If it makes you feel any better, I did Thanksgiving dinner for my first 'meet the Colemans' event. It turned out fine, once my knees stopped knocking."

God, that would have been worse. "But did you swear?" Dare managed to tease.

Vicki snorted. "Definitely. At Jesse, if I recall right."

Ha. "Good thing he's charming most of the time," Dare offered in return.

Vicki didn't respond, her eyes fixed on the road in front of them.

Dare's nerves were still there, but in a way, Vicki's story had reassured her. She wasn't the first person to have to deal with *meet the family* pressure — heck, Jesse had already survived her brothers. This was just a short-term visit. It's not as if she had to convince all these people they wanted her around twenty-four/seven forever.

Fields and barns passed by, and as unfamiliar as the area was, Dare swore they were retracing their steps. The trip seemed to take them in a circle back to where they'd started.

"Where do Jesse's parents live?"

"Across the road from Jaxi and Blake's. Everyone in the Coleman family plays musical houses. There are five houses and the bunkhouses, and no one stays put for long, although that might change now that everyone's settling in a bit more. The trailer we're in has been lived in by Matt, Daniel, Travis and now us. I don't even know the history before Matt."

"Silver Stone ranch has got my place, and the main homestead, and everyone else lives in bunkhouses. Although Luke has been building a new place off and on for the last year."

Vicki offered a smile. "Joel and I are doing that. Well, the building a new place, not the off and on."

"Really?"

The other woman answered with a lot more enthusiasm, as if glad to have a safe topic again. "We started this spring. The foundation is in, and we hope to get everything on the exterior done by the fall so we can spend the winter finishing the inside."

"That's exciting."

"It is. It's also nerve-racking, because part of me doesn't want to take on too much debt, but Joel insisted building is a commitment for the future, and there's no reason to hold off when we can enjoy it now."

Dare nodded. "I understand the nervous bit. Sometimes it's easier to keep on with the familiar, although change can be good."

Look at her being all philosophical and positive and

shit. The only change she wanted right now was to not
be headed toward a meet-and-greet with Jesse's mom
and dad when he was nowhere in sight.

There was no getting out of it, though. Vicki drove
to the house where they'd originally met, then turned
east instead of west. The home was old but tidy, and an
older woman was coming out the door before the truck
engine was even off. She held a child in her arms with
a small girl following at her heels.

Vicki offered a sympathetic pat on the shoulder.
"Marion is okay. You'll do fine."

"I'm still going to kill Jesse," Dare muttered.

A snicker escaped Vicki. "You fit right into the family."

Dare didn't even get to open her door. An older man,
obviously Jesse's dad, appeared out of nowhere, and
suddenly there were two people with big smiles and
two little people with enormous staring eyes, all waiting
for her to climb to the ground.

Like the last time she'd stepped to the end of a high
diving board, a full flock of butterflies were doing loops
in her belly. Dare took a deep breath, mentally called
down curses on Jesse, then took the hand his dad offered
to balance herself as her feet hit the dirt.

"Welcome." His parents said it kind of in unison as
Vicki joined the gathering, winking secretly at Dare as
she took the squirming little boy from her mother-in-
law-to-be.

The silent gesture was reassuring, and enough to free
Dare from her momentary panic. She lifted a hand to
waggle her fingers. "Hi. You must be Mike and Marion."

"And you're Dare. You're exactly like I pictured,"
Marion offered with a happy smile, enfolding Dare in
a quick hug before stepping back and giving her space.

Marion rubbed her hands on her arms as if she itched to extend the embrace, but was resisting. "It's good to finally meet you."

"You too," Dare returned, holding her expression as positive yet neutral as possible.

Mike held out his hand then shook hers gently, the power behind his grip tempered. "Not everyone is a hugger, but you let me know if you ever need one — my grandkids say I'm pretty good at them. Even the teenagers, if you can believe it."

Dare nodded, unable to speak for a moment as the couple flipped in her brain from being the slightly intimidating "parents of the guy she'd slept with more than a few times and *oops*, now we're sort of related" into simply Buckaroo's *Gramma* and *Grampa*.

Which was why she and Jesse were here in the first place.

Marion laid a hand on the blond-haired little girl clinging to her leg. "This is Lana, and Vicki's got a hold of PJ. Their big sisters Rebecca and Rachel are at summer day camp for another hour."

Dare smiled down at the little girl. "Wow. You're pretty lucky to get to stay and help take care of your little brother."

"Gamma and me made cookies," Lana informed her, the importance of which beat out taking care of her little brother by a landslide.

PJ had no opinions on the matter, just kept squirming until Vicki put him on the ground so he could run over to a dump truck that had been waiting on the grass.

"Do you need to go inside for a moment, or would you like to come sit on the porch?" Marion asked.

"Porch is great," Dare assured her.

"Did you have a good drive up?" Mike asked, once they were settled around a picnic table behind the house with the kids installed in a sandbox on the porch where they were within sight and confined from running free.

Vicki snickered for the briefest second before turning it into a cough as she reached for a glass of lemonade.

Dare bit her lip to stop from laughing as well, instead offering the safest answer. "Roads were fine."

"I hope you have a wonderful visit, even with this little mix-up at the start. I thought maybe tomorrow I could take you around town for a while." Marion beamed at her before getting slightly flustered and focusing down at her glass. "If that's okay."

"I don't think we have any set plans, so if it works for Jesse, sounds great to me." Dare gripped her lemonade tighter and sternly warned herself against enjoying her time too much.

"If you'd like to come out to the barns while you're here, we have some new horses," Mike offered. "We could all go for a ride."

"We can take her down by Whiskey Creek — "

" — and along the ridge — "

" — and there's the lookout point — "

"It all sounds wonderful, and I'd love to go for a ride." Their enthusiasm was making her exhausted *and* thrilling her to death.

Jesse's mom opened her mouth, and Dare was sure it was to issue more invitations to more activities when an old-fashioned phone tone sounded, and both Mike and Marion jerked upright.

Marion scrambled in her pocket and pulled out a cell phone, answering it excitedly. "Blake?"

The baby.

195

Marion listened for a moment as happiness bloomed over her face. "Congratulations to you both. I'm glad to hear Jaxi's doing well."

Marion continued to speak quietly with Blake, with Mike leaning in to listen.

Vicki nudged Dare in the side to get her attention. "Told you we'd get the news soon," she gloated.

"You did," Dare agreed before teasing back. "Gee, you're like an all-seeing mystic."

Vicki snorted, then placed her fingers against her temples and *hmmm*ed as if she were communing with unseen forces. "I see…I see *you* about to be invited to visit the baby at the hospital."

Damn. "Not funny," Dare muttered, tempted to poke the other woman back.

Vicki arched one brow. "You doubt the all-seeing mystic?"

Before Dare could respond, Marion interrupted. "Vicki, could we ask a favour?"

She and Dare both faced the older woman whose smile seemed set to full brightness.

"I take it there's news?" Vicki eased her chair back as PJ laid his hands on her thigh and demanded to be lifted up.

Marion nodded. "Justin Michael has safely arrived, and they'd like us to come to meet him. I thought we'd take Darilyn now, then once the girls get home from day camp, we'll bring all the children to meet their baby brother when it's gotten a little quieter. If you could stay with them until we're back?"

"Of course." Vicki flicked a glance at Dare that said a blunt *I told you so*, hands steadying PJ's as he stole a sip of lemonade from her glass.

"We're going to go see them already? Didn't she just have the baby?" Dare felt a little like a football in the middle of the game of pickup. Or was it rugby? One way, then the other, as if she had no choice in the matter.

"The baby arrived over an hour ago, and everything was straightforward, so Jaxi insists people come soon as they're ready."

"Of course, she does," Mike said, offering a dry smile. "I bet Blake's just as eager to show off his son."

"I can stay with Vicki to help take care of the kids," Dare tossed out, not even thinking what she was saying.

"Nice try, but not going to work," Vicki muttered softly.

"Nonsense," Marion said. "Vicki is more than capable of handling the children on her own, and I know Jaxi's been looking forward to meeting you."

Marion was waiting so expectedly, how on earth could Dare say no?

This time it was her phone that rang.

Thank God, a reprise. "One sec, that's Jesse."

She got up from the table and stepped away to answer as Mike said quietly in the background, "So he does still know how to work one of those things."

Jesse's voice rang bright cheery. "Hey, darlin'. Miss seeing your smiling face here at the trailer."

Dare struggled for words. It wasn't as if she could scold with his parents right there, but she was tempted. "Gee, *darlin'*," she echoed his drawl. "You took off in such a high-tailed hurry, I didn't catch the bit about sitting and waiting for you."

Which totally wasn't the *what the hell am I supposed to do?* that she'd intended to demand.

"Since you're not sitting at my brother's, mind spelling out a little clearer where you are?"

No mercy at this point. She was dragging him under the bus with her. "Just getting to know your mom and dad. I've been invited to join in the party visiting the hospital. Your newest nephew has arrived."

Please, please, *please* let him read the terror in her voice and offer to come and rescue her.

No such luck.

"Nephew? That's great. Tell you what. I can meet you all at the hospital."

Dare took a deep breath. So — no rescue from that quarter. "Okay."

"Miss you, darlin'."

He'd obviously said it for the benefit of whoever he was near, and she wasn't in the mood. "Don't push it, *sweetheart.*"

She adjusted her expression firmly before turning back to his parents. While she'd been talking with Jesse, Vicki and Marion had carried their lemonade glasses inside and returned with prepackaged gift baskets in hand.

It seemed a trip to the hospital was taking place.

Dare offered the best smile she could. "Jesse says he'll meet us there."

Marion's eyes lit up before she twisted away, fussing with the package she held. "Well, that's good."

Mike laid a hand on his wife's shoulder before gesturing toward the door. "Let's get rolling."

Dare took the second basket from Vicki, thankful for something to do with her hands.

Vicki adjusted PJ and glanced over her shoulder to check on Lana who was making a sandcastle with cars on the turrets. "I've got the kids under control. Tell Blake not to rush home."

Marion kissed Vicki's cheek then hurried to the parking area.

It was tough for Dare to keep her feet moving, let alone the fake happy expression on her face. She was trying though, so it surprised her when Vicki laid a hand on her arm, pulling her to stop. The other woman struggled for a moment before grabbing Dare in for a one-armed hug.

Dare didn't breathe for a second before realizing she was so far out of her comfort zone she might as well walk blindly into the abyss. She squeezed back, PJ eyeing her inquisitively from only a few inches away.

"You've got this," Vicki offered quietly. "Really, how scary can it be now that you've met the parents?"

"Scary," Dare whispered.

Vicki smiled sympathetically. "I've been there. You can do this."

The vote of confidence was appreciated. "Thanks."

She hurried to catch up with Mike and Marion who were getting into a small Honda, Marion behind the wheel.

Dare would've climbed into the back seat, but Mike was holding the front passenger door for her.

"Ladies ride up front," he insisted.

Take the path of least resistance. "Thanks."

Blessed silence hung in the air until they hit the highway. Then it was a relief to have the questions they tossed her way be things she could easily answer.

"You have some great recipes on your blog," Marion started with, erasing all questions and doubts about whether they knew about the baby. Only she didn't delve into that topic, sticking to safer areas. "Do you find them online, or are they from a family cookbook?"

Dare didn't question her luck in avoiding the *other* topic while Jesse wasn't around. "A bit of both? My mom and her best friend liked to cook, and between them they collected a ton of recipes. My friend Ginny and I started sorting them out a few years ago, but there's a lot of work to be done."

"I'll have to pick your brain about that. I wanted to make a formal family cookbook some time, but organizing it is beyond me."

"I can take a look." Dare hesitated to offer more. They were only there for a few days, and she wasn't about to get inexorably tangled up with the Colemans.

She was not allowed to fall in love with the family, remember?

Mike shifted position in the back seat. "I was looking online at the Silver Stone operation. You've got a lot of quality bloodlines."

Another area she could speak on with confidence. "Caleb and Luke have been trying hard, and they've been lucky, but it's a work in progress."

"Always is."

For a few moments things were comfortable, and Dare forgot a little about being on show and having to make a good impression.

That moment of peace vanished when they pulled into the hospital parking lot to find Jesse waiting for them, leaning nonchalantly against his truck, immobile until his mom parked.

Mike spoke up as Marion pulled to a stop beside his truck. "Now don't you go crying all over him, woman."

Marion hurried to undo her seatbelt before shoving open her door. "You worry about your own tears, Mr. Coleman, and I'll worry about mine."

200

Dare was getting out of the car, so she missed the actual moment Jesse was enveloped by his mom, if a five-foot-three woman could envelop a man six foot plus.

Jesse wrapped his arms around his mom and hugged her back, his eyes closed, face twisted with emotion.

A moment later Marion had released him and Jesse held out a hand to his father.

Mike ignored it completely, pulling Jesse against his chest and patting him firmly on the back. "Good to see you again, son."

They were clearly emotionally wrought over the reunion, and Dare promised herself to give Jesse another firm *thunk* upside the head for not warning her more about his family dynamics.

She was so focused on their interaction she was caught by surprise when Jesse slipped an arm around her and turned to face his parents.

"It's not quite the introduction I had planned," Jesse began.

"We should get inside," Dare interrupted. She didn't want him to make some cocky, dramatic announcement at this point, and her discomfort was enough to give her the drive to be outright rude. "I need to make a stop."

The awkward moment passed as her unspoken demand was understood quickly — these people were used to dealing with pregnant women in a hurry.

Jesse kept hold of her hand, walking at her side silently as they headed into the hospital, Marion one step short of a dead run. Mike had a basket in one hand, and Jesse carried the other as the four of them made their way rapidly toward the elevator.

"We'll be right up," Jesse offered as he paused on the main floor outside the public washroom.

His parents waved as the elevator doors closed, and Jesse turned on her but she was already escaping into the washroom.

Maybe she could hide there for the remainder of their trip.

Dare didn't even have to go, but she took advantage of the opportunity to wash her face, wondering how it was possible her reluctance and uncertainty weren't etched into every line of her expression. She looked — normal. Far too normal for the riot of emotion in her gut.

The door opened partway and a masculine voice taunted her. "You need a hand? Because I will come in there."

"Stop stalking me," she ordered.

Then damn if he didn't follow through, stepping right in and closing the door behind him, one muscular wall of interfering S.O.B.

"What's wrong?" he demanded.

Really? Dare offered him the dirtiest glare possible. "You have to ask?"

He had the grace to look sheepish. "I didn't expect Vicki to haul you over to my parents without me."

"Gee, me neither." She rubbed her temples in the hopes the stress would ease before she ended up with a headache.

She found herself tucked against his chest, his strong arms pinning her in place, and for one brief second her throat tightened and she could barely breathe. Screw it. She laid her head against him and let herself soak in his strength.

"It's been a hell of a day for both of us," Jesse offered.

"It's not even three o'clock," Dare pointed out in a mocking tone of voice, not quite sure what he had to complain about, but hey, at least they were both suffering. "Gee, Wilkins, I can hardly wait for the next big adventure."

His arms tightened around her and a slow rumble shook his chest as he laughed softly. "Potty mouth."

Tension made her snicker. "Don't tempt me."

His arms were rocks, his body warm as they stood there, finding a moment of peace. It took a little while before her breathing settled, Jesse's deep inhalations synchronized with hers.

She'd finally found a balancing point when Jesse tilted her head back to examine her face, his blue eyes moving slowly, his expression filled with concern. "You ready for this?"

Dare managed a hesitant nod.

They separated, slipping out of the bathroom before anyone noticed. The elevator doors were closing before she realized she was clutching his fingers like a lifeline.

Screw it — right now, she wasn't letting go.

Chapter Fourteen

The elevator seemed to take an extraordinarily long time to reach the second floor.

"How will we know where to go?" Dare wasn't sure why she was whispering, other than it seemed the right thing to do.

"You're kidding, right?" Jesse's lips twisted. "Babies show up, we stop in. It's not just family, either. All my schoolmates that got hitched already have started having kids in the last while. I could walk you to maternity with my eyes shut."

I don't even know where to park at the Black Diamond Hospital.

The thought nudged her hard, and she ordered herself to stop obsessing over details, or she'd end up running the halls screaming in terror.

He squeezed her hand as the doors opened, and she instinctively stepped closer.

Here be monsters…

White walls with ribbons of colour splashed against them. Lines of bright lights, doors with *Private, Staff Only*. Wheelchairs, IV poles, laughing nurses —

It all flashed by so quickly, but she swore if anyone had asked she could have recited it down to the last detail. As if a super awareness had come over her, Dare let Jesse guide her as she stumbled down the hall, overwhelmed by the realization she'd be in a place like this eventually.

Not eventually...*soon.*

Sounds echoed off the pristine walls, and she tugged at the collar of her shirt, her mouth suddenly dry.

It wasn't memories making her heart pound. Her family hadn't made it to a hospital. There'd been no sorrow-filled treks to say goodbye. But goose bumps were rising on her skin, and a sense of foreboding made her cling harder to Jesse's fingers.

It didn't help that the next door was their destination. With no time to dig for courage, she was confronted with a sea of Coleman faces, a bevy of them gathered around a recliner.

A slightly older version of Jesse sat in the chair with a bundle of blue resting on his chest — that had to be Blake.

Marion caught sight of her before there was time to feel too awkward at invading a private moment. "He's falling asleep. You need to come and say hello."

Jesse's mom took her by the hand and before she knew what was going on, Dare ended up next to the chair, having been pulled past the gathered crowd to Blake's side.

She was torn between stealing glances at the baby and meeting the steady grey gaze of the man holding the child.

"Who's going to sleep, the baby or the daddy?" The words snuck out before she could stop them.

Blake smiled gently, curling up to a sitting position. "I'm too excited to sleep, so Ma has to be talking about Justin." He was on his feet, standing over her, the baby cradled comfortably in one arm as he offered his hand. "I take it you're Darilyn?"

She shook his fingers briefly, panic sneaking in. "I am. Don't you need two hands right now?"

Someone in the room chuckled, but Dare didn't know who because she was watching the baby so she could catch him if Blake's grip accidentally slipped. She'd been around Sasha and Emma as babies, but frankly had never been comfortable until they hit the sturdy-enough-to-crawl stage.

"I think we're okay," Blake assured her.

The baby opened his eyes, and all Dare's panicked warnings vanished. "Oh my God, he's so perfect."

Blake laughed. "You have good taste in babies. Yes, he's a particularly fine model."

Then he shocked her to pieces, wrapping an arm around her shoulders and pulling her close so he could press a kiss to her forehead. "Welcome, Darilyn."

Dare was too surprised to say anything, then the scent of new baby hit her, and whatever operating brain cells she had vanished into thin air.

She tilted her head down and fell into out-of-focus big blue eyes. Justin couldn't be watching her — she knew that — but it seemed as if he were peering into her soul, and even farther. Maybe communing on some cosmic level with Buckaroo.

Whoa. Unexpected and mind blowing.

So much so she finally realized she hadn't responded to Blake's sweet greeting. She peeled her gaze off the baby's face and offered a hesitant smile. "Thank you."

Blake adjusted the baby expertly, offering the bundle toward her. "Go on, you can hold him."

She quickly took a half step back before Blake could transfer the baby to her arms. "I'll just wait until later."

No way was she about to explain that she had limited

experience with newborns, and while she wanted to... *Hell, no.*

Fortunately, there were other eager arms to take her place.

Blake was still smiling. "Sorry we weren't there to greet you."

"Babies don't run on a schedule. It's no problem."

Blake had kind eyes. Not identical to Jesse's, but the family resemblance was there, through and through. Blake was thicker through the torso than Jesse's lean muscles, but like their father, they both had the look of men built by hard labour and endless chores.

Dare glanced over her shoulder to find Jesse standing in the doorway, gazing into the room as if he wasn't sure he should take that final step. Then she couldn't see him because a tall, blonde woman stepped out of what had to be a bathroom and enveloped Jesse in an enormous hug.

Jesse hugged the woman back, patting her shoulder gently. His gaze met Dare's, and the first real smile she'd seen since they'd arrived in Rocky lit his face. He mouthed the word *Jaxi*, but Dare had assumed as much.

"What a surprise to find you here." Jesse pulled back from the woman in his arms before glancing down at her briefly. "I thought you'd be out wrangling cattle already."

"Tomorrow morning," Jaxi joked. "Now, where is she? I'm so pissed I messed up our meeting."

The woman whirled far quicker than Dare imagined someone who'd recently pushed out a kid the size of a watermelon should move.

"Incoming, Dare," Jesse warned. "My sister-in-law, otherwise known as Jaxi the iron-grip."

"Oh, hush," Jaxi tossed over her shoulder as she

narrowed in on Dare, but instead of hugging her tight she stopped and looked Dare over from top to bottom, a smile blooming quickly. "I'm so glad to finally meet you."

Then she opened her arms and offered Dare the opportunity for a hug. It seemed deliberate, and a bit of a knot formed in Dare's throat.

Blake's welcome had been wonderful, but this seemed even more intimate. It wasn't just an offering of a momentary embrace, it was a gesture that let Dare decide if she wanted to step into the family circle, or not. Her own choice.

Or…maybe she was reading too much into it, which was entirely possible.

Don't fall in love with them, she warned herself again.

She stepped forward and let firm arms tug her in tight. Jaxi was no older than her, but she'd had so many different experiences that lent her an aura of confidence.

Or maybe it was that other bit of information that Jesse had shared. About how Jaxi had grown up with the Coleman family and basically bossed them all around — because there was a bit of that going on during the next moments as some people left and Jaxi offered plans for the next few days.

She probably would've gone out to the car with a group of them to continue giving instructions, but Blake closed in and scooped her off her feet.

"You need to take a rest," he told her sternly, carrying her to the bed and settling her on the surface.

Jaxi sighed heavily, but she wiggled until she was leaning against the lifted back support. "I feel great."

"I know you do, but you deserve to be off your feet for a little while." He pulled the blanket over her before pressing a kiss to her lips. Then he turned his gaze around the room in search of their son. "I'd like to claim him if you don't mind."

A dark-haired woman brought Justin forward and passed him back to Jaxi who did that one arm thing as well — far too confident for Dare's peace of mind.

Dare found an arm slipping around her waist as Jesse stepped beside her.

"He's one fine-looking kid," Jesse said.

Jaxi beamed. "Thanks." She glanced at Dare with a smile. "You just wait. Colemans make pretty babies."

Dare's face heated to supernova. Everybody had to have heard about the baby, but it seemed unreal to have it accepted like this.

For *her* to be accepted like this.

Jesse cleared his throat and turned to his brother. "Congrats."

"Thanks." Politely said, but without the warmth that had been in Blake's earlier words for her.

"Hey, we're going to be around for a few days, so let me know if you'd like me to help out," Jesse suggested. "I don't mind taking your shifts, especially for the early hours."

It seemed a generous offer to Dare, and she thought for sure it would be accepted.

But Blake simply shook his head and responded quietly, "No need. You enjoy your visit and show Dare around."

Between one breath and the next, tension in the room thickened. Jaxi was tossing disapproving glances at Blake as if trying to get him to read her mind and say something different. Marion fussed with the flowers by the window as she spoke rapidly in a low tone with Mike, also throwing telling glances at their oldest son.

The other visitors in the room exchanged looks then focused on offering final congratulations before leaving the room.

While their visit ended shortly after that as Justin began to fuss for his supper, and Dare was ready to make her escape, something seemed extraordinarily wrong.

Jesse? The happy, cocky, never-at-a-loss-for-words guy she'd been getting to know — and if she was brutally honest, beginning to care about — sat in icy silence as they got back in his truck and headed who knew where.

Suddenly it wasn't discomfort at being out of her home territory that was making Dare uneasy. She wasn't tied up in knots because she was wondering if there was something for her and Buckaroo in Rocky Mountain House.

Jesse's offer to help his family had been bluntly turned down, and maybe she needed to blame it on pregnancy hormones, but Dare was feeling supremely feisty on his behalf.

Screw this. It was bullshit — pure and utter *bullshit*. On top of the rest of the day, every nerve in her body vibrated with tension.

There seemed only one solution to both their problems, at least in the short term, and the moment they were out of the confines of the truck, Dare intended to make it happen.

Silence filled the cab, the pounding in his temples drowning out the road noise and the music on the stereo. Jesse felt entombed behind a thick wall.

He'd known coming home was going to hurt, but he'd underestimated the extent of the pain. The warm-up with his brothers, especially the discussion with Joel, made the reunion with his parents feel as if he were punching a bruise. Putting on a smile and making himself cheery instead of clinging to them as if he was a toddler had left him raw.

And then Blake —

Fuck.

Angry words swirled in his head, and with every one the salt that had been poured over the cut rubbed in deeper.

He knew damn well it was his own fault. He'd walked away last winter and left them all in the lurch, but he'd made the offer today in good faith. To have that tossed back so pointedly…

Jesse pulled into the parking space outside Joel's place and turned off the engine. Staring straight ahead without seeing a thing.

How the hell was he going to fix this?

Was it fixable?

The passenger door slammed, jerking him from his moody contemplation as Dare stomped away from the truck, her back rigid.

Jesus Christ, he'd screwed up. *Again.*

Jesse shoved his door open and raced after her. "*Dare.*"

She was fast enough she'd nearly made it to the trees before he caught her by the shoulder, whirling her to face him.

"Wait. What's — ?"

She fisted the front of his shirt and jerked them together, her lighter frame driving toward his. She wrapped a hand around the back of his neck and pulled hard until he bent toward her. Then her mouth was on his and all he could taste was her fiery passion.

Like a trigger had been pulled, lust shot sky high. He wasn't sure what had brought this on, but he couldn't deny her a thing when she was moving against him as if they were caught in a maelstrom.

Jesse wrapped his arms around her and picked her up, bringing her with him down the path that led to the fire pit. Out of sight of the trailer and anyone pulling into the yard.

It had been a long time since he'd been here, sitting with family and casually shooting the breeze after a long day's work. He noted the changes through a haze as he settled onto a wide concrete bench. Dare's thighs draped over his as he worked to get a little distance between their lips so they could talk.

They needed to talk, right?

She didn't want to back away, and he wasn't keen on the idea either, but somehow he tore them apart.

Dare's eyes were huge as she stared intently, cupping his face in her hands as she took a deep breath then spoke, clear and resolute. "Despite this being a day from hell — No, *because* it's been a hell of a day, I need you to do something for me."

"Anything," he promised, rash as it was to offer without more information.

Did she want to go home?

Her fingers fell to the bottom of his shirt and she jerked hard, ripping the cotton free from his jeans. "Fuck me. I need to not think for a while."

Jesse swore softly as she worked the buttons on his shirt. Mindless sex sounded just about perfect to him as well. He considered the logistics, though. Taking her into Joel and Vicki's house — what if they came home? The last thing he wanted was...

The absurdity of the situation struck, along with an inkling of understanding. He and Joel used to fuck around with the same woman all the time, and now the thought of anyone overhearing Dare, delicious noises slipping from her lips as she came, was enough to set Jesse's teeth on edge.

Maybe that was the way Joel had felt when he'd started seeing Vicki.

Dare sank her teeth into the muscle of Jesse's shoulder, fingernails scraping down his back as she growled. "Pay attention."

His brainpower was fading rapidly. "Dammit, Dare. I'm not fucking you here."

"No?" She shifted position, rising on her knees so her sex rubbed the ridge of his solid cock. "Then I'll fuck *you*."

Goddammit.

Joel's bitter comments, Blake's all-too-understandable rejection of his offer, his parents' obvious pain — with those sins on his tally, it was the anger pouring off her that rocked him the hardest.

"I was a shit — " he began.

"Don't talk, fuck," she ordered. She pressed their lips together, nearly consuming him. That edge of lust he always felt around her, the one that kept him on a hair-trigger, flipped the sexual energy between them past high to extreme.

She wanted him, here and now?

Hell, yeah. No way was he turning that down.

She had his shirt undone, shoving the material off so frantically somewhere a seam ripped, and he was glad.

The destructive action suited his mood, and with total disregard for everything except getting her naked as fast as possible, he caught hold of the front of her blouse and jerked his hands apart. He reached around to unclip her bra so he could slip the straps off her shoulders and abandon it to the ground with her now button-less blouse, leaving her naked from the waist up as she sat in his lap.

He caught her by the hips and lifted her skyward, breasts to his mouth, using his teeth on her nipple briefly before sucking it into his mouth. Dare tightened in his grip, butt cheeks clenching, body arched to meet him, and he soaked it in. Gloated even, in the way she fisted his hair between her fingers, pain jolting against his nerve endings.

Loud gasps of pleasure escaped her lips as he rocked her over his erection until she started undulating with him.

Enough.

No — it wasn't nearly enough, and that was the fucking problem. Jesse stumbled to his feet with her in his arms, frantically glancing around. He staggered the five feet it took to get to the gazebo, a small white archway covered with thick tangled vines. Little white lights had been woven around the entire thing. When he pressed her against the solid wood, one arm between her back and the rough surface, he hit a switch, and the lights twinkled around them as if they were a bloody Christmas tree decked out in full glory.

He didn't care. She caught him by the ears, damn near using them like reins to drag his mouth back to hers.

Jesse growled then took control of the kiss, suspending her in place with his hips pinning her tight. She squeezed her thighs around him, holding on as if he were a wild stallion she was about to ride.

Once more, *hell, yeah.*

He pulled back far enough to press their foreheads together. "If we do this here, I'm liable to fuck you through the damn wall."

A warning? Or a promise?

Dare dug her fingers into his shoulders. "God, yes," she begged.

He shook her loose. Her feet hit the ground for the moment it took to rip her jeans open and shove them past her hips far enough to free one leg. That was all he could wait before lifting her again, hand under her naked ass, her sex open to him. He slid his fingers through her curls, pressing his thumb over her clit. Satisfaction struck as another of those addictive moans escaped her lips.

He rubbed until her head fell back, the lights glowing against her auburn hair like a halo.

An angel and a demon, fucking in the Garden of Eden.

He knew which one he was, because there wasn't a single thing about what he had planned to do next that would get him past the pearly gates.

Jesse opened his jeans, his erection leaping upright to freedom. He aimed directly into her warmth. She sucked in a quick breath as he slipped the head of his cock between her folds, then he drove the air from her lungs, thrusting forward as he buried himself deep.

He should've slowed down. He should've stopped taking like an inconsiderate ass and gentle his actions, but when he glanced into her face, all he saw was encouragement.

Jesse let the raw emotions inside him take over. He pulled back and thrust again, the warmth of her wrapped around him and the tight pressure of her hands on his shoulders anchoring him in place. He repeated the motion, and again, aching need dragged up his spine as he clutched her close and tilted his hips at the end of each drive.

Dare cursed softly, egging him on. Tightening her legs around him and grinding her clit against his groin every time they connected. Her breasts bounced as they rubbed him, and while he wished his undershirt wasn't in the way so he could fully enjoy the sensation, there was no way he was slowing down. No fucking way was he stopping, not even to get naked.

"*Jesse.*" Dare arched, her face tightening as her body clenched around him, the gazebo arch creaking in protest as he fucked her wildly.

Her orgasm took him by surprise, and took him over the edge. He rocked into her one final time before losing it, pleasure rushing in, pressure exploding like the cap off a bottle of well-shaken soda.

He leaned into her, gasping as he clutched the wood of the gazebo to keep from falling over. The arm behind her back — he swore he had slivers from rubbing against the rough-hewn wood.

Dare released her death grip on his shoulders, stroking down the muscles of his back and returning to drag her fingers through his hair as she pressed kisses to his lips and along his neck.

They were both sucking for air as if they'd finished a marathon.

One perfect moment before reality kicked back in, and Jesse held on tight and enjoyed the sensation.

Chapter Fifteen

For the first time that day her muscles unclenched. Dare rested her head on Jesse's shoulder and took a deep, albeit unsteady breath as she let the sexual bliss in her veins trickle through her system.

"God, I needed that." Jesse sounded like Dare felt. Buzzed out on endorphins.

She let her fingers drift over his shoulders, slowly tracing the rock-firm muscles as he held her supported in midair. "Yeah, me too."

Dare would've been happy with the day magically coming to a close right then. To be instantly whisked back to her place for some peace and alone time.

Unfortunately, she was all out of magic.

"Sorry I missed your meeting with my folks." Jesse murmured the words against her neck, his tone sincere and a little sad.

"I'm still a bit pissed at you," she admitted.

His chest moved against hers as he let out a huge sigh. "Yeah, there's a lot of that going around." She attempted to straighten up so she could examine his face, but he leaned against her harder. "Stay put for ten seconds, woman. We don't have anywhere to be for a while."

Time to recharge their batteries in private sounded great. But this position wasn't one they could keep for much longer. "Could we at least pull up our pants?"

He chuckled softly, but separated them.

She bit back a moan at the teasing sensation as his body left hers. Her legs were shaky, and she held the gazebo for support as Jesse helped get her pants back on. Her blouse was useless, so he gave her his shirt, his hands lingered on the soft swell of her belly before he pulled back abruptly, jerking his jeans back into position as if angry.

"What's wrong?" she demanded.

"I'm sorry." Jesse growled the words.

Dare stared at him, confusion rushing in. "You better not be apologizing for the sex, because that was the first good thing about this entire day." She paused. "Okay, I'm exaggerating, because Vicki turned out to be pretty nice, and your parents, and the baby, but...but what the *hell* are you talking about?"

He gestured toward her belly. "I shouldn't have been so rough. It can't be good for Buckaroo."

Oh. Well, his concern was kind of sweet, even though it was uncalled for. "We're okay. I think sex on a trampoline is on the banned list, but that was fine. That was *awesome*, in fact, and exactly what I needed."

He led her to the bench and left her to get comfortable as he moved to the side of the fire pit and opened a small box that held supplies. He piled wood high then lit the kindling, the flames flickering steadily stronger. Dare stared at the orange and yellow flames crawling up the edge of the wood as Jesse returned to her side. She leaned her shoulder against his and they sat in silence.

Her body thrummed with lingering pleasure.

She had a special kind of situation with her family at Silver Stone. They were always around if she needed

218

them, but with having her own place, she'd gotten used to being able to retreat and get away when she needed a moment of solitude. A moment to recharge and retreat from others' expectations and judgment.

Dare took a quick glance at Jesse's face.

He was watching the fire, but his expression had grown tight again. Dare debated coming right out and venting her displeasure with Blake's high-handed dismissal.

Confusion rolled in along with her irritation — the refusal of Jesse's generous offer had been clear, but Blake's greeting toward *her* had been kind and sincere.

How was she supposed to deal with such contradictory reactions?

Jesse slipped an arm around her, tugging her against his side. "You upset with me?" He sounded tired.

"Mixed up, annoyed, confused." Sitting side-by-side meant she couldn't easily see his face, and maybe that was better. She stared at the logs as the fire consumed the fuel an inch at a time. "This whole trip might've been easier if you told me ahead of time there was something wrong between you and your brother."

Jesse stiffened.

"I was one second away from punching him in the gut in the hospital," she admitted.

He relaxed like a balloon losing its air. "Oh, you mean Blake."

What the hell? Dare twisted on the spot, peering into his face as she demanded answers. "Which brother did you think I was talking about?"

He shrugged.

No way. Dare shot to her feet and planted her fists on her hips. "Look, buddy. I am one thin thread away from losing it. The only reason I came — "

She cut herself off. She didn't need to explain herself, *he* did.

Jesse caught her by the hips and pulled her back into his lap, curling an arm around her shoulders so he could press her against his chest. He enveloped her like a cocoon, and it was easier to give in than to stop him.

Being held gave her a probably unfounded sensation of stability in the middle of her current life chaos.

"Blake didn't do anything wrong." Jesse spoke softly, the crackling wood in the fire pit punctuating his words.

Dare pushed back, ready to protest when loud greetings rose from the arbour entrance — an unfamiliar male voice followed by a female one.

"Hey, awesome. Jesse's already got the fire going. Bring the hotdogs."

"Warning, incoming horde."

An extremely pregnant blonde made her way toward the benches. Behind her a couple of men marched, one of them obviously a Coleman, bags of food dangling from their hands.

In under thirty seconds, at least a dozen other people had joined her and Jesse, and her questions were lost as she scrambled to slip off his lap and make sure all her bits and pieces were in place and covered.

The blonde woman smiled invitingly. "Once I finish waddling my way over to you, you can decide if you want a hug or not. I'm Ashley."

"Is it possible to hug you without making you pop like a tube of toothpaste?" Jesse asked, rising to his feet with his arm around Dare.

Ashley lifted her middle finger toward him and kept moving toward Dare. "That's your one free comment about my baby belly, Jesse. Next one, you'll find yourself out moping in the backfield with the rest of the brand-new steers."

A low hiss escaped all the guys in the vicinity.

"Oh! I understood that one." An older woman with long dark hair turned excitedly to the lady settling next to her on the bench. "Steers are what you call a bull after you cut off their testicles."

Ashley rolled her eyes, but she smiled as she motioned toward the two women. "Dare, I'd like you to meet my mama, Tina, and my mom, Skyler. They're a little excited by all the country-isms we keep tossing their way."

"If you'd speak English, we wouldn't have a problem," the blonde-haired Skyler answered with a firm shake of her finger in Ashley's direction before waving a greeting to Dare.

"Nice to meet you both," Dare offered, glancing between the women. "Do you live in Rocky as well?"

Tina shook her head. "Just here until the baby arrives then we're headed back to Oregon."

"Or a month later," Skyler added innocently. "You know, after Ashley's back on her feet."

Dare found herself back on the bench beside Jesse, both of them being handed long roasting sticks with hotdogs already stuck on the end.

Ashley settled on Dare's other side. She ignored the crowd of people for a moment, leaning in closer to speak privately. "Sorry for interrupting your tête-à-tête."

"No problem." Dare refrained from sharing they'd probably prolonged Jesse's life by arriving when they did. "Should I expect more Colemans to turn up?"

"Not tonight. Let me put names to the faces for you." Ashley glanced around the circle, pointing as she spoke. "That blond one's mine, and so is the Coleman beside him — Cassidy and Travis. Next are Daniel and Beth. Their three boys will stop running wild and settle down in a minute to start eating everything that doesn't move, so guard your hotdog. I heard you met Mike, Marion earlier today, and those are the twins, Rebecca and Rachel. You know Vicki, and that's Joel, so that's the lot for now."

Dare turned toward Joel, fascinated to see a second Jesse watching her solemnly.

The Coleman resemblance was strong between all the men — Travis and Mike were cookie cutters from different generations, but the twins…

"*Whoa.*" Dare attempted to seem nonchalant, but it was tough.

Vicki snickered, holding out a plate with a loaded hotdog bun, chips and salad. "Eyes back in your head, chica," she warned softly. "You only get to keep the one you came with."

"Mores the pity." Ashley let out an exaggerated sigh. "Everyone should have two healthy males to keep the home fires burning, if you know what I mean."

Dare glanced around the fire pit, shocked at the comment considering there were parents and kids present.

Ashley laughed, instantly aware of what Dare was thinking. "They're not listening. So? Can you tell the twins apart?"

It was a little daunting to think she might not recognize the father of her baby, but a closer look was enough to reassure her it wasn't going to be a problem. The men were identical, but…*not.* The tension in Jesse's face was sharper than the cool analytical expression his twin wore, and their eyes — the *way* they looked at her was completely different.

Thank God. "I can tell."

"We need to mix them up then test you — "

"We're not playing shell games for your entertainment, Ashley," Joel drawled.

Dare caught Vicki's gaze, widening her eyes in astonishment. Okay, physically there were differences, but Joel's tone and inflection were so similar to Jesse's it was scary.

"We can put a bell on Jesse if you'd like," Vicki offered.

"It's okay," Dare said quickly, remembering her manners. She rose to her feet and held out a hand to Joel. "Good to meet you."

"And you." He shook her hand firmly. "If you need anything while you're here, let us know."

She chased away dirty images as rapidly as she could — damn Ashley for making mention of threesomes. "Thanks."

Conversation turned light. Jesse roasted her a hotdog, and she obediently ate the food on her plate, but well before the party was over, she was ready to call it a night.

She rested her head on Jesse's shoulder, and he looped his arm around her, pulling her against his strong body. The warmth from the fire and his internal furnace meshed together until she was in a comfortable, foggy haze, voices and laughter blurring together.

Soft lips pressed to hers, and Dare blinked.

Bright blue eyes stared down at her, familiar heat in their depths as Jesse traced her face with his gaze before his lips curled up. She was lying on their bed in the small room in the trailer with him stretched over her.

He nuzzled against her neck as he whispered toward her ear. "You fell asleep."

Damn. "That's twice today. Your family is going to

think I'm narcoleptic."

"Everyone thought it was cute," he insisted. "I'm ready to hit the sack too."

She stroked her hands up his body, palms skimming over the hard bands and stripes of his muscles. "Hmmm."

His smile twisted. "What's that mean?"

Dare slipped under his T-shirt so she could scratch him. "Just *hmmm*. What do you think it means?"

He reached over his head to grasp the back of his T-shirt and strip it forward off his body. He lowered into contact with her again, miles of naked skin right there ready for her fingers to enjoy.

"Definitely means you want me."

"I shouldn't," she murmured, lips coasting over his throat as he rocked against her. Pleasure rising like a heater slowly warming up. "I'm mad at you," she reminded him.

"I'm mad at me too," he returned. "See? Another thing we have in common. We definitely need to fuck."

Dare snickered, the sound turning into a moan as he slid to one side and brought a hand between her legs.

Jesse covered her lips with his, swallowing the sound even as he slipped his hand under her panties and made her squirm. Fingers firm and confident as he stripped away the fabric and proceeded to stroke and tease, pleasure drifting in slow waves instead of the crash of fire and heat they'd shared by the arbour.

This felt right, though. Yes, she was a little mad that the day hadn't turned out perfect from beginning to end like some fairy tale, but it was hardly his fault that people refused to follow the scripts she wrote in her mind...

He kissed his way along her jaw to her ear, murmuring

softly how much he wanted her, and she twisted to meet his lips. Dare reached down to capture his fine ass in her hand, gripping his butt cheek under his boxers for a split second before attempting to push the elastic downward. Trying to get him all the way naked so she could pull him over her like a sexy blanket.

This time Jesse read her mind and moved eagerly, shoving his briefs away and nestling over her again, their bodies lining up perfectly. The heat of his cock rubbed her sex as he canted his hips, elbows braced on either side of her body.

Dare stroked her fingers through his hair, eyes closed as she soaked in the sensation of being under him. Being surrounded.

Being filled, as he adjusted his angle and slid them together.

"Oh, God, *ye* — "

Her words were cut off as he laid a hand over her mouth, bright blue eyes sparkling at her. "Shhh."

Dare blinked then snickered as she figured out what he was warning her about. He was shy? The man who'd had her screaming his name until she was hoarse the first time they'd had sex didn't want anyone to know what they were doing?

Jesse pulled back an inch at a time, gaze locked on hers. "Shh, or no cock for you."

"Ha, right." As if he was going to stop. Still, why take a chance? "I'll be very, very quiet," she promised.

He rocked forward, cock sinking deep. The thick length touched everywhere she needed and forced the sound from her lips.

"*Ohhhh...*" She glanced at his face guiltily. "Oops?"

His grin twisted, and he did it again. Slow retreat,

deep press forward.

All thoughts of being worried, or mad, or…well, *any* thoughts, frankly, vanished as he worked his magic on her. Connected, surrounded, a team striving for the same goal.

Which in this case was the pleasure rapidly overwhelming her, the tingling sensation in her core making her sigh happily as her orgasm hit.

Jesse was the one to hum approvingly at that point, his muscles bunching under her fingers as he rocked forward a few more times, pace quickening, hand under her hip lifting her higher so he could connect every last inch.

She was still vibrating when he came, cock pulsing deep. Breath rushing past her ear in heavy pants.

Okay, so maybe the day hadn't gone exactly how she hoped, but overall, she was pretty content to be where she was right then. In Jesse's arms.

Perhaps that was the biggest realization of the day.

Dare didn't need all his family to approve of her, or him, or *them*. She would do this thing with Buckaroo, and only people she chose to have around would be in their lives.

Right now, Jesse was a part of that — if he wanted to be.

Chapter Sixteen

Blog post: Small Town 101 — Jobs
You know the lists that get tossed around on social media?
"Top ten things you didn't know about Brad Pitt's sex life" or
"She thought she was going to a birthday party. You'll never
guess what happened next..."
Clickbait, am I right?
Here's my clickbait version of:

Best Jobs in a Small Town — number three will make
you gasp...

5. The Canada Post Rural Delivery Person
The one with the key to the large box on the rural route
mailbox. Oh, yeah, they know exactly *who's getting regular*
deliveries from Victoria's Secret and Adam & Eve toys.
4. Florist
I tell you, those people know who's been naughty or who's
been nice by what's being ordered, and their advice soothes
over tough times more often than a marriage counselor. Forgot
her birthday? Fifty-dollar bouquet. Got caught flirting with
the new girl at the café? Hundred-dollar bouquet. (Not to
be confused with the hundred-dollar bouquet with wine
and chocolate, which means someone is getting reaaaaally
lucky tonight.)
3. Fitness Instructor (see what I did there? ;))

Okay, they're on the list because this is the only job other than sex worker where you get paid to make others grunt, groan and moan. Suitable occupation for sadists and people with a twisted sense of humour.

2. Waitress at the café

Better hours than working the bar, and you still get all the gossip. And some flirting, but the old timers know to keep their hands off, and the visitors usually tip well. Depending on the café, the food can be a plus.

1. Rancher

Hey, did you expect me to say anything different? Think about it. They're good with their hands. Can stay in the saddle all day and all night, ahem. They look damn good in their hats — or out of them.

Oh, wait. I just said what I appreciate about a rancher's job, and not what they get to do. Oops?

Tell me — what job would you like best? Do you do one of these top 5? I'd love to hear your stories.

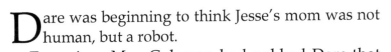

Dare was beginning to think Jesse's mom was not human, but a robot.

Ever since Mrs. Coleman had nabbed Dare that morning, Jesse waving them off as he headed to places unknown, Marion hadn't stopped. She seemed determined to haul Dare to every single store in town so she'd "know her way around in the future".

There'd been a lot of that as well. Those pointed moments where Marion made it clear she had no objections to Dare and Jesse becoming a permanent fixture in Rocky.

The woman knew everyone in town, which — okay, fine, small-town living and all, Dare understood that one.

But Marion didn't just know their names, she had something to share about every person they met that made the other person respond with a smile or a grin or a blush.

Unfortunately, the next move in this comedy routine was when they would turn to Dare for an introduction, and the smiles would tighten, or eyes would widen, an instant after Marion uttered those fateful words, "Jesse's fiancée."

There'd been a bit of this back in Heart Falls the couple times she and Jesse had gone out to do something together, but the response in Rocky Mountain House was spectacularly over the top. If she was to go by their expressions, she'd either hooked up with a mass murderer or the town's most eligible ruling elite.

In both cases, *she'd* been found wanting.

Dare found even her sense of humour being pushed to the limit by the time lunch rolled around and they stopped in at the café for a bite to eat.

Marion ordered the daily special then introduced Dare.

"Oh, *really?*" Their waitress, a pleasant enough looking young woman with dark raven hair slipped her pen behind her ear and cocked out a hip. "That's so nice."

Suddenly Dare understood everyone's aversion to the word "nice" because it meant a hell of a lot of things, none of them...well, *nice*.

The group at the table behind them caught Marion's attention, and she turned to speak with them, leaving Dare to the waitress's tender mercies.

"You and Jesse moving back to Rocky?" Laura hadn't yet perfected her casual-yet-digging-for-information tone.

"Just a visit for now," Dare slipped in with a pointed smile, handing back her menu. "Burger and fries, please. No onions."

Laura's gaze skipped over Dare as if assessing her curves. "You can get a salad instead of fries, if you want. No charge."

Oh, honey, you really don't want to go there. "Thanks, but fries are fine."

"Sure. So, you guys need to drop in at Traders while you're here," Laura informed her before smirking widely. "Tell Jesse that Heidi's working there again."

It wasn't worth the energy to react. "I'm sure he'll be thrilled," Dare drawled.

Laura sauntered off as Marion turned back to resume their conversation. Dare had to give it to the woman — Jesse's mom had perfected the art of small talk, and the entire meal whizzed past without another awkward moment.

But after lunch Dare was happy to be guided over to the Stitching Post, Hope Coleman's quilting store. The store was closed for the afternoon, and an impromptu gathering of a few Six Pack women had been arranged. Vicki wasn't there, but Beth and Hope were, as well as Jaxi with the baby, to Dare's surprise.

"You're already out of the hospital?" she asked, not sure if she were more shocked or terrified by this turn of events.

Jaxi shrugged. "If things go well, everybody is out pretty quick these days."

Oh boy.

Thank goodness distraction was at hand in the form of brightly coloured fabric.

"Do you sew?" Hope asked, balancing her son on her

hip. Colt held a stuffed horse that was made of a million different fabrics. He snuggled it tightly as he leaned his head on his mom's chest, thumb firmly inserted in his mouth.

"When I have to," Dare admitted. "They covered the basics in school, so I can deal with buttons and repairs. I'd like to make a few things for the baby, if you can suggest some simple projects."

Hope's face gleamed. "I knew I liked you."

A soft snort rose from Beth, and she glanced over her teacup at Dare. "Welcome to the Coleman clan. You just earned your first badge."

"Oh, come on," Hope protested. "She's engaged to Jesse. She's earned at least three others by now."

"Definitely." Jaxi grinned, holding up fingers as she made suggestions. "Knowing Jesse? She's a shoe-in for the extraordinary patience, a wicked sense of humour, and" — she glanced over her shoulder to check that Marion was out of earshot before turning back with a grin — "physical endurance."

A snicker escaped before Dare could stop it. "Sounds about right. Do I get a sash to put the badges on?"

Justin rooted against Jaxi, puckering his lips and making sounds of complaint. Without a pause the other woman lifted her shirt and offered her breast, and the baby went from protesting to gulping in contentment.

Jaxi glanced up. "A sash? No way. We tattoo them on your ass."

Dare didn't want to stare at Jaxi and the baby, but she was fascinated at how easy Jaxi made it look.

Which reminded her all over she had no idea what she would be doing in a few months. "Ah, branding iron, then," Dare quipped.

The other women laughed.

"Come with me. I'll show you a few beginner quilting options." Hope tried to put Colt down in the playpen beside where Marion had just settled, but he clung to her, sounds of protest rising. "It's okay, my little man. Mommy's going to be just over there with Auntie Dare."

A low thrill pulsed in Dare's chest at Hope's naming of her. It made no sense. She already *was* Auntie Dare, but for some reason, this felt different.

"Will he come to me?" Dare held her arms open, but Colt tightened his grip on his mom and buried his face against her with a cry of panic. "Or…maybe not."

Hope sighed then led Dare toward the back of the shop. "Don't take it personally. He's being a mama's boy lately, and *no* one but me will do. It's driving Matt crazy."

Dare tried to think back to when Sasha and Emma had been little, but not much about their babyhood had been normal. "No problem. My nieces cuddled with anyone, but I get that's not typical."

Hope adjusted Colt then pointed out a few different patterns on display. Dare tried to concentrate, but to be honest, she was distracted by secretly watching Colt, and the baby, and the other women in the room.

Beth and Marion were discussing something animatedly. Jaxi was listening to them without contributing, reclined back on the couch, one hand stroking Justin's head as she nursed him. Dare couldn't pull her eyes away.

A soft laugh rose from her side. "We're a bit overwhelming, aren't we?"

Dare met Hope's gaze. "A little, but not in a terrible way."

Hope nodded. "That's good. Being not terrible."

Dare laughed, and they rejoined the group.

"You know you're welcome to visit anytime," Marion offered sweetly.

"I'm sure we will," Dare said. "Everyone has been great."

She held her tongue regarding Blake's mixed-up contribution.

"You're family," Marion informed her. "You and Jesse belong here in Rocky. Why, if you feel like moving north, I'm sure we could do some house rearranging. We do that all the time."

"*Mom.*" Jaxi's tone held a world of warning.

Marion turned to her with an innocent expression. "What? You know we do."

Beth and Hope exchanged glances as Jaxi gave their mother-in-law a firm frown. "I wasn't talking about the houses. You *promised*. Don't push."

Marion sighed dramatically, winking on the sly at Dare. "See what I have to put up with?"

It was awkward, and yet not, because it was all done in the kindest of ways. Dare's phone rang, and she excused herself, stepping away to near the shop door to get some privacy. "I've been expecting you to text."

"Yeah, well it's been busy, and I can mind my own business," Ginny offered.

A very undainty snort escaped Dare at the idea of her sister-by-choice attempting to keep her nose out of any situation, let alone one as interesting as this. "Yeeeeeeah, *no.* I can't see that one."

Ginny hummed for a second then spoke again. "I'm trying to curb my curiosity?"

"That one I'll buy. How's everybody?" Dare turned on the spot to gaze back to where Marion was chatting with her daughter-in-law. Jaxi had finished burping the baby and now held him in that one-armed pose that scared the living daylights out of Dare every time she saw someone do it.

Ginny dove into her report. "The girls are driving Caleb mad. He's been interviewing babysitters, but so far every one of them Sasha has declared unfit for one reason or another."

"Then they probably were," Dare pointed out. "The kid's a pain in the bootie, but she's damn smart."

"I know, which is why Caleb hasn't hired anyone yet."

"Wait — why does he need a babysitter, and why is this the first I've heard of it?"

"Because you've had other things on your mind. The other *why* is because I gave him hell and told him he had to stop depending on me and you. Not that we don't love the girls, but he needs to plan ahead. You can't drop everything on a moment's notice forever. In other news — remember Dustin went on his date for the bachelor auction, and the woman sent him flowers afterwards?"

Ginny was changing the topic, but Dare let it go this time. "It was cute."

"He spilled the beans that she did it again — in fact it's been five days in a row, and he's a little freaked out."

Dare could picture Dustin's face, as well as the teasing he was probably getting from the other boys. It was all so familiar and predictable she felt as if she were there seeing the things that Ginny described.

She fit there. Heart Falls was home, and always had been.

"Tell me honestly," Ginny insisted. "On a scale of one to ten, how are the Colemans?"

Dare hesitated. "All over the place."

"Well, that was clear as mud." Ginny took a deep breath. "And Jesse?"

"Nine point five to a negative twenty-three."

Ginny swore. "He put his boot in it, did he?"

Yes, and no, and…

"We're good," Dare insisted, thinking back to the morning and being cuddled up in bed with his arms around her. She could hardly complain about his attentiveness then.

She also couldn't deny something was weird. Curiosity itched at the back of her brain. The man she'd met in February, and the man she'd spent time with in Heart Falls, were not the same man she'd been catching glimpses of over the past twenty-four hours.

Let it drop? Probably not, but she also wasn't going to try to describe her concerns over the —

"Hellllllooooo." Ginny's call was louder than polite, and Dare grimaced.

"Sorry, distracted," she offered in apology.

"I get it. I shouldn't keep you, but I miss you."

"Miss you too. We'll be home in a few days and I'll tell you everything."

Ginny offered her approval. "I've got stuff to tell you when you're home, as well."

"Did you change your mind about the bachelor dude you bought?"

"I refuse to answer on the grounds that…on the grounds that — well, that wasn't even close to the topic I have a secret about." Ginny cleared her throat. "Gotta run. Take care of yourself, and if you need me to text Jesse to remind him to behave, let me know."

"Love ya, Truth."

"Love ya, Dare," Ginny echoed before signing off.

Dare tucked her phone away slowly. Ginny had secrets? That was so...odd. They didn't have secrets from each other. Ever.

She thought back to the boys' proposals and grimaced. Okay, maybe a *few* secrets.

A strange sensation joined the rest in her belly. Things were changing, and there seemed to be no turning back the tide.

Was it even worth trying?

Jesse stared over the railing, itching to join in as a crew of hands took off, driving a herd from the barns and corrals where they'd been contained during a vet visit.

Getting to help with chores would've been a way to keep his hands busy and his mind off the chaos his life had become. A temporary distraction, but one that would help. Only two more days, then he and Dare would get back in his truck and head south, and he wouldn't have to play pretend anymore.

Another truck pulled into the yard and he paced toward it. His cousin Rafe gave a friendly wave as he parked.

Rafe climbed out of the cab then reached in to help lower Laurel to the ground. The delicate blonde gave Jesse a quick wave before hurrying to join Dare and Vicki at the other end of the corral railing.

Rafe watched after her for a moment then strode to Jesse's side.

No hesitation. His cousin hauled him in for a

backbreaking hug, smacking his hand between Jesse's shoulders as he growled a greeting.

"I'm glad you came home, you jerk."

Jesse laughed. "I see being married hasn't improved your sense of humour."

Rafe stepped back and eyed Jesse critically. "You don't look any stupider than before you left, but then again, you'd set a pretty high standard to beat."

"Shut up," Jesse muttered.

"Shutting, I guess." Rafe glanced toward the girls. "That her?"

"Dare? Yeah. You want to say hi?'

"Definitely." Rafe took off at a pace that covered the distance between the groups in an instant.

Jesse followed a little more reluctantly. His gaze met Vicki's, and she shifted awkwardly as he approached, her eyes averting and flitting over the landscape behind him.

It was all he could do to stop from turning around and letting Dare introduce herself.

Instead he focused on the face he figured was safest — Laurel wore the same sweet smile she'd always offered him. As if she wasn't quite sure he was harmless, but she was amused by him in spite of herself.

Somehow looking at the nonjudgmental acceptance Laurel offered brought everything back into perspective.

Fuck being a wimp. He moved in on the group and pulled Dare possessively against his side before offering Laurel the cockiest grin he could. "Mrs. Coleman."

Rafe's wife of all of a few weeks flushed prettily, and Jesse's grin deepened as he winked at his cousin. They were a good fit, those two.

Laurel's gaze flitted between him and Dare. "Congrats

on your engagement," she offered before speaking to Jesse. "I'd say the Colemans were falling like flies, but you were the last man standing."

Dare glanced at him. "Seriously? You're the last one?"

"Last *man*," Rafe clarified. "There are three Whiskey Creek Coleman cousins not hitched or engaged yet, but they're all girls."

"Women," Laurel corrected him.

"You're fighting a losing battle on that one," Vicki informed her. "I get my revenge by making sure to call them 'boys' whenever possible."

Laurel turned to Dare with a question about her family, and the three women chatted easily as they sauntered toward the arena where Joel and Matt were leading out the new horses.

Jesse and Rafe wandered behind them, distance widening until the two groups were far enough apart they couldn't hear the others' conversation.

"How's the visit been?" Rafe asked.

Jesse grunted, stepping toward the fence as if there was something vital to examine.

"That good? Damn," Rafe muttered, joining him at the rail.

Did he want to bitch? Jesse kicked at the ground and considered. Of course he did, but should he? It wasn't in line with his "keep a bold face and don't let anyone see the truth" line he'd been trying to pull off.

"It's been fun," Jesse lied, gesturing toward where the girls had stopped a good twenty feet from them. "She's having a great time."

Dare was examining the new breeding stock with interest, her face shining, and for a split second that knot in Jesse's belly eased a little. She *was* having fun — at least more fun than yesterday, and he was glad.

Then Vicki said something that made Dare laugh, the two women's faces bright as they stood next to each other, and tension spiraled upward in Jesse's belly as quickly as it had vanished earlier.

When it came to fucked-up situations, this was at the top of the list.

Rafe coughed, waiting until Jesse glanced his way to ask firmly, "You want to talk?"

Jesse faked it best he could. "Nothing to talk about."

"Course not." Rafe counted on his fingers. "You left here without much of a plan in February. It's now July and she's five months pregnant."

"Congrats, you can add."

"And you have a magic truck that lets you live in one town and work three hours away." Rafe examined him with deepening concern. "I had your address, remember? I know where you were, and she wasn't around for a lot of those months."

"She's around now."

"Clearly."

Jesse slapped his hands on his thighs. This was the only family member who had any idea why he'd left in the first place. As far as he knew, Rafe had never said a word to anyone else, or given anyone any explanations for his leaving beyond what Jesse had approved.

He also knew the kind of hell that Rafe had gone through without breaking, and he trusted the man.

Which was why he let his frustration rule and snapped back the truth that hopefully no one else in Rocky Mountain House would ever hear.

He spoke quietly, though. No way did he want this discussion overheard. "What do you want me to say,

Rafe? You want me to up and announce I got a total stranger pregnant, here, welcome her to the family…?"

Rafe's expression darkened. "No, because Dare doesn't deserve that bullshit. I get why you're doing what you're doing, but what I was trying to say — badly, I guess — is that you don't need to lie to *me*. If you need a safe place to talk, I'm here. But if you'd prefer to suffer in silence, at least have the decency to not piss on the tree you're trying to protect."

More cryptic bullshit. Jesse glared at his cousin. "What's that supposed to mean?"

Rafe folded his arms over his chest. "You're keeping quiet about your relationship with Dare, but it's pretty clear you've got issues with something or some*one* here in Rocky. The way you act every time Vicki is around, it's as if you want people to realize this isn't about you disapproving of the woman."

Dammit. Jesse caught himself staring at the group of women again, all three of them chatting animatedly. "Fuck. You're right.

His cousin snorted. "My God, did I really hear those words come out of your mouth?"

"It's just a visit," Jesse muttered. "You're right, though. I can pull my ass out of my head and pretend for a few more days that everything is great."

This time it was Rafe who grunted.

Jesse turned on him, not even trying to hide his exasperation. "*What?*"

Rafe hesitated for a moment then hit him with both barrels. "I've always looked up to you because you pretty much did whatever the hell you wanted to, and I didn't do enough of that for a long time. But right now, you're making a mistake, and I'm going to call you on it. You *do* need to get your head out of your ass, but you shouldn't have to pretend that everything's great. What happened was a long time ago and everyone else moved on. Do the same, and grow the fuck up."

If they'd been standing anywhere but in public Jesse would have responded to his cousin's cutting statement with his fists. "Gee, I'm so glad you're a safe person to talk to."

"I'm trying to help," Rafe snapped. "You left. I stayed, and since you'd told me what happened, I watched closer. Every time the Colemans gathered, I listened hard to see if there was any reason you needed to stay away. You know what? In all that damn time I didn't find a single one."

"Because it wasn't about you," Jesse growled.

"Wrong. *They* don't have an issue with you. It's always been about your feelings and guilt, and I'm telling you, it's time to move on."

Lectured by his youngest cousin. Great fucking day.

"I'm not telling you you're an idiot..." Rafe began again.

"Drop it," Jesse ordered, turning his back on Rafe. Two more bloody days and he could get the hell out of here.

"Not likely," Rafe offered. "This is what family does, you know."

"Kicks you in the balls when you're down?" Jesse demanded.

Rafe made a rude noise. "Oh, please. That's a little melodramatic, even for you."

Jesse whirled, catching hold of the front of Rafe's shirt in a fist. "You want a fight? You got one."

"*Jesse.*"

241

His name echoed in his ears at high volume, panic clear in the single word. He and Rafe turned toward the girls, expecting to see them making concerned gestures at the imminent fight.

Instead Vicki screamed again as she and Laurel struggled to hold up Dare, her body limp in their arms.

Chapter Seventeen

Situation normal — totally out of my control. Since when did chaos become my status quo? Seems like half of forever...

— Diary entry at eighteen, upon learning via email that her boyfriend had left Heart Falls and wasn't coming back —

A cloud blurred her vision, and Dare blinked hard as she struggled to put the last few minutes back into order. She'd been talking with Vicki and Laurel, and she'd been watching the horses, and then things got foggy.

She looked up into blue eyes and a stone-cold expression.

Dare laid her hand against Jesse's cheek. "Wow, you better hope the wind doesn't change direction because that would be one scary face to be stuck with forever."

If she'd expected his familiar grin to appear, she'd have been disappointed. What she got was zero change in expression as his gaze darted over her face. "How're you feeling?"

Two worried faces appeared over his shoulder, Vicki and Laurel, then Rafe was there as well, a furrow between his brows.

"I feel like the ball in the middle of a football huddle." Dare curled upright, or attempted to. Jesse's hand behind her back controlled the motion as he slowly allowed her to sit.

A flush of embarrassment hit when she realized she was in his lap and he was on the ground in front of a growing collection of his family. Her right cheek and eye stung.

She lifted her fingers to touch her face. "What happened?"

Laurel grimaced. "Um, that's my fault. I think I punched you."

"She was trying to catch you," Vicki offered quickly.

None of this made sense. "*Catch* me?"

Dare looked up at Jesse. He was wearing that unreadable expression.

"You passed out," he said.

"I didn't — " she protested, then stopped.

Had she?

That foggy blur in her head failed to offer up an answer immediately. She wiggled, testing to see if she had any unusual aches or pains, but everything seemed to be normal. "I did a systems check. I feel fine. Well, other than my…"

She stopped, hand dropping from where she'd been cradling her cheekbone. Laurel looked horribly upset.

Suddenly Dare was airborne. She grabbed at Jesse's shoulders as he rose to his feet with her in his arms then began striding at high speed toward his truck. "What're you doing?"

"Taking you to the hospital."

"Wait a minute." Dare pushed on his chest in an attempt to get him to lower her to the ground.

His arms didn't budge. It was like trying to move a brick building.

"Jesse, stop. I don't need to go to the hospital."

"You passed out, Dare. This isn't up for debate."

Confusion rushed in. "I don't think it's as bad as that."

Another voice joined in. "You're probably right." Mike Coleman arrived out of nowhere, his words laying a blanket of calm over her. "But going to the hospital is a smart idea, just to be sure everything's good. You're pregnant, after all."

How on earth was Dare supposed to deny that face? "Well, okay, but I'm sure I'm fine."

Mike pulled open the passenger door to Jesse's truck. "Just get checked up. No use in taking any chances."

"We'll come with you," Laurel offered.

Oh God, no. Dare should have seen this coming — it was like being around the Stone boys. Vicki was nodding and Rafe was digging out his keys, and the longer they stayed, the more people would want to join in.

"No, please, that's fine." Dare wasn't going to argue anymore about going, but she didn't need a crowd along for the ride. "Jesse will take me."

"I've got you." Jesse all but growled the words as he made sure she was completely settled, reaching over her to do up the seatbelt.

Dare sighed heavily. "My arms aren't broken. I mean, thanks for helping me out, but — "

"Don't argue," Jesse snapped.

He stepped back and closed the door, but even through the closed door Jesse's father's soft chuckle was audible.

She rolled down the window to speak to Mike as Jesse raced around to join her. "I'm sure it's nothing. Maybe it's from the travel. I am a little tired."

Mike patted her fingers where they lay on the window ledge. "My boy'll take good care of you. Call if you need anything."

They were off. Jesse kept from squealing tires in the yard, but once they hit the blacktop, he hit the gas and pushed the truck to high speed.

"I don't think we need to — "

The ice in his glare was enough to cut off her suggestion to take it easy.

Dare sat back and held her tongue. If he wanted to add a speeding ticket to his day, that was his business. Fine by her.

His rush meant they were back at the hospital where they'd been the afternoon before in no time flat, only at the opposite side of the building.

He abandoned the truck outside the emergency doors, pausing to snap up a finger. "Stay put."

Dare rolled her eyes, but a wave of dizziness hit, a rush of fear with it. "No arguments. I'll sit here like a good — "

Jesse wasn't there anymore. He was already racing around the truck to jerk open her door.

He lifted her out of the truck, refusing to let her climb down. Then they were through to the emergency desk. Her health card was processed followed by a flurry of questions before they were brought into a separate room behind a curtained-off area.

She lay there quietly, Jesse's fingers in hers as they waited.

Another wave of dizziness struck. Dare closed her eyes against the queasiness, and involuntarily tightened her grip on his fingers. Everything had happened so quickly she'd had no real time until now for anything to sink in. For fear to rub across her nerves like sandpaper leaving her raw and vulnerable.

"I'm scared," she admitted.

"It's going to be okay." Jesse brushed a loose hair behind her ear, his blue eyes fixed on hers. Dare locked onto his gaze even as her free hand slipped down to cover the swell of her belly.

A soft flutter greeted her, and some of the ice along her spine warmed. "I still feel Buckaroo," she whispered. "I just — "

They both jerked as the curtain slid back a foot and a bright-faced nurse glanced between them before her gaze settled on Jesse.

"Excuse me, but is that your truck outside the emergency doors? Because you're blocking the lane." The nurse tilted her head toward the front. "You've got time to go park before the doctor gets here."

"Screw the fucking truck," Jesse muttered, before Dare placed her fingers over his lips to silence him.

"Go. You've got time. That way we won't have to worry about hitching a ride to the impound lot when we're done here," she managed to tease.

He pressed a kiss to her forehead before leaving at a dead run.

The nurse slid up to the bedside the instant he left. She cleared her throat then spoke softly, gaze fixed on Dare's face. "Are you okay? Do you need me to help you?"

Confusion and Dare were having a heyday. "What?"

The nurse glanced over her shoulder before touching Dare's cheek gently. "Are you in a dangerous relationship? I can help."

Oh my God. "Oh, no, this isn't from Jesse. Someone bumped me when I fell."

The nurse waited as if considering.

"Honest to God." Dare felt terrible for sharing, but no way could she let anyone think Jesse was abusing her. "It was Laurel Coleman. She and Vicki were — "

Thank God for small towns where everyone knew everyone. The nurse's eyes widened and she interrupted with a gasp. "*Laurel* gave you a black eye?"

Dare made a face. "Is it going to be black?"

The woman nodded then let out a relieved breath. "Okay, as long as you're safe, we can move on. I'll need to take your blood pressure and information. You get to lie still and relax."

Utterly relieved, Dare obediently held out her arm for the cuff to be Velcro-ed into place, trying to figure out if she felt sick. "If you need me to pee in a cup, I can do that too. On command."

The nurse laughed. "We'll just wait for the doctor, if *you* can wait."

A list of questions later Dare was alone again, fears slowly spilling into the curtained area like an out-of-control magical vine. She debated grabbing her phone to call Ginny, but scrubbed that idea as soon as it hit. No good reason to scare her family until she knew what was going on.

Then Jesse was back, clutching the edge of the doorframe to stop from flying past her bed.

"You're a menace," Dare informed him.

"Where's the doctor? Why's he not here yet?" Jesse complained, turning around as if he was going to track down the man himself.

"Jesse," Dare warned. "Come here."

He was by her side in an instant. "How do you feel?"

She shrugged. "Physically? Okay. Still dizzy, but

everything else feels great."

His face was tight, and he found her fingers again. "I'll take care of you," he promised.

Dare closed her eyes. That tremor of fear was growing. She swallowed hard. "I'm scared," she repeated. "What if something's wrong with the baby?"

His arms went around her and Jesse pressed her head to his chest. His heart beat solidly under her ear. "Buckaroo is fine. Take a deep breath, and let's wait to see what the doctor says."

They stayed like that for a while, Dare holding back the protests she wanted to make to his calm assurances because he was right. There was nothing they could do at that moment but wait.

The curtain slid back like metal fingers on a chalkboard, and Dare tensed all over as an older man in white doctor's garb stepped into the space.

He offered a friendly smile. "So, I finally meet another part of the Coleman family." He shook Dare's hand then Jesse's. "Dr. Kincaid. I've delivered all Jaxi and Blake's babies, as well as other Colemans…"

His voice faded as he attempted to tug his arm free.

Jesse wasn't letting go. Instead he gripped the doctor by the wrist so he could rotate the man's palm toward the ceiling. Dare and Dr. Kincaid exchanged worried glances before Dare realized Jesse had laid *his* hand over the doctor's.

Jesse finally released the doctor, turning to Dare with a nod. "He's okay."

In spite of being scared to death, Dare felt amusement creeping in. Jesse had remembered her comment about small hands being important. "You're a nut."

Dr. Kincaid gestured for Jesse to move aside. "I'm

glad for the vote of confidence. Let's see if we can figure out what's happening with you."

Jesse slipped around to the other side of the bed, and she caught his fingers like an anchor as the doctor checked her, pushing and prodding gently.

Dr. Kincaid listened to her stomach, then pulled the stethoscope from his ears as he offered a gentle smile. "Heartbeat sounds strong."

Relief hit so hard Dare collapsed back onto the pillow. "Okay."

"I want to run a few more tests before I let you go," the doctor warned. "I don't like hearing that you passed out."

Dare nodded. "Whatever you think best."

He pulled a chart over and wrote down a list of items. "You're going to be here for a few hours." The doctor glanced at Jesse. "If you need to go — "

"I'm staying," Jesse cut in.

The doctor held up his hands. "Figured you would. You might need to grab some things for Dare if we have to keep her overnight, though."

Overnight? All the blood in her body seemed to be rushing past her ears at that moment. "I can't stay overnight."

"Of course you can." Jesse glared at her. "I'll grab your stuff."

"But we're supposed to — "

"You're *supposed* to listen to your doctor, and that's me," Dr. Kincaid lectured sternly before softening his gaze. "You Coleman women are all the same — stubborn as all get out. Now take it easy, cooperate with the nurses, and I'll be back in a couple hours to see how things are progressing."

Then he was gone and a new nurse was there, pushing

aside the curtains. Jesse helped Dare into the wheelchair the woman had brought, and the next couple hours were spent waiting for people to poke and prod her. An ultrasound was followed by another test with tabs connected to her belly.

Jesse stayed with her when he could, but there were times he was on the other side of the door and Dare stared at the wall, far too alone with her own thoughts.

Far too alone, *period*.

She was back in the curtained area, Jesse pacing the floor when Dr. Kincaid returned, his expression gloomy. "One bit of good news — the dizzy spells are caused by an inner ear infection, and we can clear that up pretty easy. But there are a couple tests I'd like the lab in Calgary to take a look at. We won't get results until Monday, and until we hear back from them, I want you to stay."

Dare took a deep breath. "Here in Rocky Mountain House?"

"Here in the hospital." The doctor held up a hand. "It's completely a precaution. I don't feel you or the baby are in danger, but there was something on one test I'd like to double-check. I want to be sure we're treating any issues before they become trouble."

Which made sense, and Dare got it, she really did, but the hollow ache inside just kept growing.

She nodded, not trusting her voice.

Dr. Kincaid patted the foot of the bed where Dare rested. "Stay here for now. I've asked one of the nurses to bring you to another room so we can free up the space in emergency. I'm on call for the rest of the afternoon, but the nurses will contact me if needed. I'll be in touch with your regular doctor as soon as I can."

Jesse shook the doctor's hand then the man was gone.

Quiet fell in their small little corner. Outside noises ebbed and peaked as a backdrop to the sound of Jesse's boots on the linoleum floor as he paced.

Dare worked to take slow, controlled breaths. "Well, so much for dancing at Traders tonight."

"Hey, you're going to be fine, that's the most important thing," he assured her. "Doctors like to be cautious, that's all." He kept pacing as he spoke, and Dare was jealous of his ability to burn off anxiety energy.

It was true what he'd said — she didn't have to like it.

Now that she knew she was stuck for a few days, she really needed to contact her family. She glanced around the room, shocked that in so small a space she couldn't find anything easily.

"Where's my phone?" She leaned toward the side table where her purse had been shoved.

He was there in an instant, all but growling as he placed the bag on the bed beside her. "Don't overdo it."

Dare raised a brow, nerves making her speak sharper than she'd intended. "If picking up my phone is going to be the straw that pushes me over the edge, then everything is *not* fine, Jesse. Don't baby me."

"I'm trying to take of you," he snapped.

God. He was right, but she wasn't capable of nuance right now. She was about to apologize when a new voice sang out cheerfully.

"Hello, behind the curtain." The pale fabric slid aside again, this time quieter than before. A dark-haired nurse with stylish dark-framed glasses stood on the other side, wheelchair beside her. "Your chariot awaits."

"Tamara?" Jesse grabbed the bag the woman offered before turning to Dare. "Another cousin, if you can't tell. Whiskey Creek."

Tamara dipped her chin. "The best part of the clan, you'll discover. Hey. You must be Dare."

"I recognize you," Dare said. "You were in the room when we visited Justin yesterday."

"Good eye." Tamara pushed Jesse aside without blinking, moving to the bedside. "Be useful and put her things in that bag, J-man. My turn to help your lady."

Tamara got Dare seated in the wheelchair, all the while ordering Jesse around. Her nurse's scrubs were a pale blue with little bears dancing over the surface. She was bossy and friendly, and even Jesse relaxed a little as Tamara cracked another joke.

Dare actually caught herself smiling as she was pushed into the elevator.

"You get one of the finest views in the hospital." Tamara stepped to one side until Dare could see her face. "It'll be quiet too. There's a second bed, but no one's using it at the moment, so you get the room all to yourself."

"Are you going to be my nurse?"

Tamara nodded. "Hope that's okay."

"I thought you were on the delivery ward," Jesse asked abruptly.

She turned toward him, one brow arched high. "You're so out of date, cuz. One of the joys of small-town hospital practice is I get to do it all. Delivery was before Emergency which was before Rehab. I switched to general Maternity six months ago."

"So I'm still considered maternity?" Dare asked, her hand rubbing her belly like a touchstone.

"Of course. You've got a bun in the oven, and we're going to do what we can to make sure everyone gets baked for as long as necessary — or something like that."

Tamara winked. "Analogies always fall apart if you push them too far."

"Pretty much," Dare agreed. "If there's internet, I'll be fine. I can get ahead of things on my blog."

"Basic internet is doable. No porn, though."

Jesse rolled his eyes. "You are a killjoy, aren't you?"

"Yeah, that's me. Stick in the mud, no sense of ha-ha whatsoever."

They'd arrived on the second floor. Dare was rolled down the hall and into a neat but very hospital-looking space. Light yellow walls, furniture made of shiny metal and pale particle board. The blue blanket-covered beds were separated by a green curtain until Tamara pushed it back to the wall.

Jesse placed the bag with her clothes on the chair beside a small closet before slipping up to the wheelchair and laying a hand on Dare's shoulder. "Back in a few."

"Okay."

He pressed a kiss to her cheek then was out the door before she could say anything more.

Tamara helped Dare get as comfy as possible with just her T-shirt and undies because even her maternity jeans were too uncomfortable to consider wearing while sitting around for a couple days.

"If you've got them, a pair of sweats will be the most comfortable. If you didn't bring any, I can loan you a pair. Make a list of the things you need to make your stay more comfortable, and I'll make sure you get any approved items."

"Approved?"

Tamara slid a tall, moveable tray into easy reach at the edge of the bed, adding a glass and a pitcher of water.

"No tuba practicing allowed, I'm sorry to say," Tamara informed her brightly.

"Well, damn. There go my aspirations to win the world tuba championship." Dare made an attempt to smile, which probably failed miserably. "Cell phones...?"

Tamara lost a bit of her shine. "Rotten reception most places except in a few corners and right outside the main doors, and the internet isn't fast enough for Skype. I'm sorry. If everything goes well tonight, I'll break you out for a while tomorrow morning. Okay?"

"Sure." She tried to keep her disappointment out of her voice. No phone was shitty news. If she didn't have a phone, she couldn't chat with Ginny. "Jesse and I will figure it out."

Tamara frowned, then glanced around the room. Dare realized she was looking for Jesse who hadn't returned yet.

The woman marched to the door and poked her head out the door. She glanced back then shrugged. "Guys have the worst timing. He probably got lost in the cafeteria. I'll grab you a few things."

Tamara was back within a minute with some magazines and a pad of paper, and she piled them on the bedside table.

"I have to make my rounds now." Tamara adjusted the backrest of the bed one notch higher without Dare having to say anything. "Buzzer is there on the right side of the bed. Sorry, but for now you'll have to call when you need to pee so I can be on hand if you get dizzy. Otherwise, relax best you can. I'll be back for the list in a bit and to give you the medication for your inner ear infection. If you want to chat."

"Thanks," Dare said sincerely.

Tamara left the room at full stride, the door closing with a soft *swoosh* behind her.

Silence.

The next second Buckaroo nudged her, and Dare's soul clung to the sensation. She slid her hands under the sheets to caress the little rounded spot under which who-knows-what was going on. A miracle? A tragedy?

Another soft flutter teased her from the inside — the sensation that had barely begun to be familiar over the past couple weeks. A touch of reassurance from her baby — and it was perfect and exactly what she needed...

Yet not nearly enough because the room was empty except for her and shadows and unanswered questions.

The soft buzz of hospital life drifted from behind the closed door, itching in Dare's ears. That and the sound of her breath, slightly ragged, echoed in the quiet. The longer she sat there, the more tension increased until her chest ached and her throat felt raw. The sheets were cold against her bare legs. In spite of the sunshine outside the window, in spite of the cheerful yellow stream of it falling across the bed where she lay...

She wanted it all to be a bad dream.

Coldness struck deep, dragging her into memories full of bitter loss and loneliness, and Dare closed her eyes against the stinging hurt striking her heart.

And yet...she wasn't a teenager anymore, torn from her family and stung by shock. She was a grown-ass woman with the ability to survive and save herself.

Another deliberate breath brought air burning into her lungs. Then slowly, determinedly, Dare opened her eyes and focused on the bright blue sky outside the window.

She'd get through this. One moment after another,

she'd make it to the other side, whatever the other side looked like.

If she didn't completely acknowledge that faint voice inside whispering *Jesse will help*, an unexpected warmth in her heart budded from a seed into a tiny green hope.

She didn't have to face this alone.

Chapter Eighteen

Jesse paused down the hall from Dare's room to get himself under control. He'd been moving like a madman since he'd left because he didn't want her alone for too long, but the last thing she needed was for him to barrel in as if pursued by a horde of demons.

He put his back to the wall so he could close his eyes for a moment and calm his breathing. As he waited, he went through his mental list in the hopes he'd remembered everything.

"You holding up that wall for a particular reason?"

Jesse turned on the spot to find himself being accosted by Tamara. Accosted was the right word, because there was fire in her eyes and her tone was pure trouble.

He didn't have the time or energy for bullshit right now.

"What'd you want, Tamara?" he demanded. He should have gone straight in to see Dare. "It's been a hell of a day already, and I'm not looking for any Coleman lecturing."

"Poor baby. Sometimes we just don't get what we want." She stepped forward to poke her finger against his chest. "I hope you're ready to get your head out of your ass."

"If you didn't read between the lines a moment ago, I was telling you to shut up and mind your own business," he warned.

"Who the hell do you think you're talking to?" Tamara didn't look at all impressed. "You want to scare me into shutting up, you'd need to be a whole lot more frightening. Besides, this is too important to scare me off."

Jesse sighed. He loved his family, really he did. His immediate family and the extended cousins, he loved them all, but sometimes they were more punishment than any man deserved.

He rubbed his temples. "Get it over with. I'll give you exactly thirty seconds, then I'm getting on with my day."

She lowered her voice, glancing down the hall before glaring sternly. "You don't seem to get it. I mean, you obviously care about Dare a little, but I wanted to make sure you know how serious this is."

His stomach dropped a mile, and he pulled up from his slouch, ready to run to Dare's side. "Did something happen while I was gone — ?"

Tamara had the grace to look sheepish as she held up a hand to stop him from racing off. "No, I didn't mean that. Dare's fine, but you were bitching at her pretty hard when I picked her up in Emerg."

For fuck's sake. Jesse pinched the bridge of his nose. Overprotective, snoopy cousins — although, Tamara meant well. He had to give her that much.

He met her gaze directly. "She was overdoing it, and I was trying to protect her. She's as stubborn as they come. Didn't even want to get checked out even after passing out."

Some of the implied violence in his cousin's eyes lessened. "Oh."

"Yeah, *oh*. I'm worried about her, okay? I might have snapped harder than I should have, but we're okay."

Tamara wrinkled her nose, her glasses shifting position. "I'm sorry. I thought you were flouncing around like you were making sacrifices. When you took off because you needed a hamburger, or whatever that was more important than being there for her — "

"You need to either curb your imagination or try minding your own business," Jesse drawled. Now he understood the lecture, but he didn't need to explain himself to Tamara. "Can I go see my fiancée, now? So I can tell her why I *flounced off*?"

"Brat. Don't rub it in," Tamara murmured. "I wa — "

"Are you holding a medical consultation in the middle of the hallway?" A good-looking doctor stared sternly down his nose at Tamara. "I'm sure you wouldn't be doing anything improper, now, would you, Miss Coleman?"

"Improper? Me?" Tamara laid a hand on her chest, her mouth gaping as if in shock. "Never."

"Don't give me attitude," he warned.

"Or what? You'll send me a scary email?" Tamara snapped back instantly.

The man's face went red, and he straightened up until he loomed over her. He took a step closer —

And found himself face to face with Jesse.

Jesse had no idea what was going on, but no one was going to mess with his cousin while he was around. That was his fucking job, thank you very much.

"You work here?" Jesse asked.

"I do." The man flicked his nametag importantly. "I was — "

"Good," Jesse interrupted. "The men's shitter on the first floor is jammed. You should go unstick it."

The doctor's face went white. Behind Jesse, a low

choking sound escaped Tamara as she attempted to hide her amusement and failed miserably.

The asshole, Dr. Tom, according to his nametag, drew himself to full height again. "I am *not* a janitor."

"Oh. Whatever." Jesse waved a hand and before biting his nail and ignoring the ass completely. He turned to his cousin. "So, Tam, what do you think? Extra bacon on the pizzas, or should we let the rest of the crew decide?"

Dr. Tom stood motionless for a second longer before growling in frustration and pointing a finger at Tamara. "You watch yourself. I'm keeping an eye on you."

"Yes, sir." She waited until he'd stepped out of earshot to mutter. "Only thing you can do is watch, *asshole*, because you're a nearly-dickless wonder."

Jesse snorted, his earlier anger and frustration washed away by her good intentions and his rising curiosity. "Gee, you know how to make friends and influence people everywhere, don't you?"

"He's a bastard," Tamara said, leaning on the wall beside Jesse as she checked her watch. "I went out with him a few times, and he seemed nice enough at the start. Decent dancer, and he gave great back rubs."

"Do I want to hear this?"

She shoved her glasses into place and pulled a face. "I should never have forgotten my rule to not fool around where I work."

"Bad breakup?"

She nodded. "He's been on my case ever since. He hassles me without cause, and I can't really tell him to fuck off."

He hesitated for all of a nano-second. "Dickless wonder?"

"*Nearly*-dickless." She held up her hand with thumb

261

and pointer finger spaced out two inches. "He drunk emailed me a shot of it."

Jesse lost it. It was partly her expression, partly the tension that held him in its grip, but once he started laughing it welled up from deep down and poured out of him. "Oh my God, was that the scary email?"

Tamara eyed him wryly. "Yeah, it was funny at the time, at least to me. *He* didn't appreciate the fact I couldn't stop laughing long enough to apologize for laughing."

"You know what they say, it's not the length but how you use it," Jesse offered between gasps.

"Said by the guys who have neither the length nor the moves, sadly." Tamara laid a hand on his shoulder. "I'm sorry for being a jerk and getting on your case, but I care about you and I want you to be happy. Dare seems like a great person. You've got a shot at something special here — I'd hate for it to get screwed up."

The one thing he truly understood was his family only got in his face because they cared. "I need to get back. Anything I need to watch out for or avoid?"

She gave him *the look*. "Don't go fooling around. I don't want to go blind if I walk into the room and interrupt you."

Jesse patted her on the shoulder and escaped, pushing through the door into Dare's room.

He'd expected to find her waiting impatiently, but she was sitting cross-legged on the mattress, eyes closed. Her palms were turned upward, wrists resting on her knees. Deep, even breaths lifted her chest before she let the air out slowly.

Like he'd attempted to do a few minutes ago, and he smiled as he crossed the floor. It took a moment to get his boots off, but once he was down to his socks, he hopped up on the foot of the bed and twisted to face her. Her eyes were closed, but she was smiling.

Jesse shifted awkwardly before giving up his attempt to cross his legs. Jeans weren't meant for yoga moves. Instead he let his legs open, feet draped off the edges of the bed, then he worked to match his breathing with hers.

Dare's smile widened.

He took advantage of the moment to examine her face. The shiner on her right eye was darkening rapidly, but the worry crease between her brows was gone, and she looked peaceful.

She looked beautiful.

Even more so when she opened her eyes to meet his, grey-green darkening to near hazel as she spoke. "Hey."

Jesse's heart did this weird kick-flip thing, and he had to work hard to keep from jolting upright. Suddenly the distance between them was way too much.

"Come here," he growled softly, opening his arms.

She shifted forward on her knees before turning and settling with her back against his chest, tugging his hands where she wanted them. One arm ended up around her body above her breasts, the other she deliberately adjusted until his palm rested on her belly.

Over the past month the gentle curve had been growing steadily, and as he rested his chin on her shoulder, she slid her fingers over his and held him there. Intimate — more intimate in some ways than the night before, slipping his body into hers.

"You doing okay?" he asked quietly, not willing to break what seemed to be a spell that had taken over the room.

"Shhh. Buckaroo is holding a hoe-down."

Jesse matched her breathing as he waited. She'd tried to get him to feel the baby move before, but so far, there'd been —

Her belly shifted under his thumb.

He held his breath.

Another fleeting touch, this time under his palm. "Is that you?"

"Nope." Dare let out a little happy sigh. "And it's not gas, if that was going to be your next question."

"Good to know, considering where you're sitting, and all."

She giggled. "Stop it. Don't make me laugh, or he'll stop moving."

"Our kid? Hell, now that he's started, I bet he doesn't give you more than a minute or two off. Get used to nonstop Buckaroo Love Taps."

She leaned back into him. "I needed this," she whispered.

Jesse waited. The heat between their bodies wasn't sexual, but a connection nonetheless. She stroked his knuckles softly as he kept his hand in place, thrilled at the continued sensation of bubbles percolating under her skin. "It's pretty damn cool."

Dare twisted her face toward him, and he couldn't resist. He brushed their lips together softly. A single kiss. Another.

The weight of her body against him increased, and he supported her as he took the kiss deeper. Tasting her lips, tongue teasing gently. Dare's even breathing picked up a notch, and his body came alive with something more than peaceful relaxation.

A cough echoed in the quiet of the room, and Dare broke away from him. Her gaze lingered on his face for a second before they turned toward the sound.

Dare was still buzzing with some weird combination of sexual desire and utter relief, but Vicki waited awkwardly near the door, examining the ceiling with great interest, and it wasn't right to leave her standing there.

Behind her, Jesse had stiffened. Silly man. Probably embarrassed to be caught cuddled up and smooching. Dare squeezed his fingers then escaped from his hold, sliding back to the head of the bed so he could hit the floor.

"It's safe," Dare informed Vicki.

The other woman smiled as she stepped toward the bed, a familiar bag in her hands. "You look good."

"I feel fine," Dare said, pointing at the bag. "You brought my stuff."

"Jesse called and asked me to bring it." Her gaze flicked to Jesse's for a split second then back to Dare's. "You hadn't unpacked much. I hope you don't mind I had to fold the things on the chair. I put your bathroom stuff in a plastic bag at the top so I didn't have to dig through anything."

"That's fine. Thank you for bringing it over." She was sure she had shorts in there.

The next thing she knew Jesse was standing in front of her, face folded into a frown. "Where do you think you're going?"

Drat. She'd automatically swung her legs around, intending to get changed. "Oops?"

"*Dare.*"

"I'm sorry. It's hard to remember to sit still when I don't feel sick, okay?" She tucked herself back under the covers and waited as patiently as possible, hands folded in her lap. "May I have my bag, pretty please?"

Vicki laughed, bringing it to the bed. "I'm glad you feel okay. Laurel said to apologize again for your face."

"She's not going to stop that, is she?"

Jesse raised a brow. "Apologizing? Probably not." Then he laughed. "Although it is pretty hysterical when you come down to it. Remember the shiner I had the night we met?"

"Yeah?"

He grinned. "Rafe gave me mine."

Ha. "Seriously? That was Rafe?"

"Yup." His smile tightened a little when his gaze slipped over Vicki, then he ignored her as he pulled a chair beside Dare's bed and sat down. "Here's the scoop. I know phone coverage is the shits in here, so I went out to the parking lot and made a few calls."

Dare dug through the bag as he spoke. "Obviously — Vicki." She glanced up at the other woman. "Which, thank you again."

"Oh, wait." Vicki stepped forward and unloaded a second bag that had been slung over her back. "I brought your computer too."

Hell, yeah. "I could kiss you. Perfect."

Vicki eyed the bed before bringing the bag to the table against the wall. "How about over here for now? You'll have more visitors soon, and you won't want this tossed around or dropped."

"Good idea."

Vicki glanced between them, hesitated then backed toward the door. "I'm going to head out for a bit. I'll be back later, okay?"

"Yes, please." Dare didn't want to keep the other

woman from whatever else she had planned, but the desire to spend more time with Vicki was real. "I'd like to visit some more."

Which was good and bad. *You're not supposed to fall in love with people, remember?* she scolded herself.

Maybe that was a flawed premise, the other side of her brain offered. *Buckaroo deserves awesome people in his life, and if you like them, they have to be awesome.*

Dare dragged herself back to alertness to discover Jesse staring after Vicki as she left.

She waved a hand to get his attention. "Sorry for the interruption. Phone calls?"

Jesse shook himself. "Right. Your stuff. Then I called Ginny — "

"Oh God, did she panic?"

"Sort of? That's what took so long. I was talking her off the edge. The minute I hung up with her, I'd made it nearly to the door when Caleb called wondering what Ginny was going off the handle about."

Dare considered collapsing back on her pillow like some melodramatic princess. "They'll be here in an hour, right?"

"Wrong." Jesse adjusted position, stretching his legs in front of him, all long and lean and far too sexy for her mental peace. "I convinced them to wait until tomorrow."

"Wow. You're good." Dare curled her legs up and wrapped her arms around them. "You should be a hostage negotiator or something, because getting Ginny to change her mind is like magic."

"That's me. Magical Jesse." He lifted his arms and folded them behind his head as he offered a grin. "No, that doesn't sound right. Jesse and his magic tongue?"

He winked and she let out a contented sigh, kind of shocked that she was able to feel this relaxed. "I hate that I'm sitting here when we had such plans to visit all your family and hit Traders, and the rest, but I'm happy they figured out why I was dizzy."

"Me too." He rose like a cat and stalked over up to the bed, leaning in with a flirty smile. "I'd suggest we pick up where we were before we were interrupted, but Vicki is right. There'll be more visitors soon, and you'd probably like to have some clothes on before they arrive, instead of less clothes, the way I'd like."

A shiver of desire rolled through her. "Didn't the doctor say something about not getting me excited?"

"I'm not getting you excited," Jesse said innocently.

Dare took the shorts she wanted out of the bag before offering him a deadpan expression. "Yeah, right. You get me excited just being in the same room."

His face — like she'd given him a gold star. "You weren't pissed when I left? Or that I called your family without talking to you first?"

It had to be a trick question. "Was I supposed to be?"

He shook his head.

Dare wiggled the shorts on, lying back to pull them over her hips. Jesse was there in an instant, helping smooth the fabric into place. "You told me you'd take care of me," Dare reminded him. "I figured that was what you were doing. And you were."

He stared at her with that unreadable expression for a beat, then leaned in to kiss her fiercely. One hand cupped the back of her neck, and the other found hers on the sheets, fingers tangling together.

Sweet, passionate. Needy and yet giving. She took it and soaked it in.

Then laughed against his lips as another cough echoed in the room.

———

After greeting his brother Matt and his wife Hope, and saying hello to his nephew Colt who was no longer a baby but a bright-eyed toddler, Jesse took off again.

Dare's words of praise were like a thermal sweater. Inside and out, he damn near glowed. She trusted him, and that feeling was pretty fucking glorious.

Only now he had work to do.

Tamara might have been off track when she lectured him about being thoughtless, but she'd hit the mark when it came to one thing. He'd been whining and moping inside — *face fucking facts, Coleman* — about how hard it had been to visit Rocky when there wasn't a place for him.

So fucking what?

This wasn't about *him*, not anymore. It never should have been. It was about what was best for the baby, and for Dare.

Considering when he'd proposed back a month ago it had been with the idea he was manning up, he hadn't done a very good job of it.

It was time he manned up for real.

The drive to Six Pack ranch was familiar enough he could do it in his sleep, but he eyed the passing scenery with a different eye now than the day before. Then he'd been looking for familiar sights. Now he looked for what was different.

He'd been gone for half a year, but his entire world

was no longer the same. Everything had changed — was it the same here?

The only signs of change, though, were good ones. Crops rising strong, herds grazing contentedly. There seemed to be more cowboys riding over the sloping foothills of their land than he could account for with only family, and Vicki's comment about the bunkhouses being full came back to mind.

Shit. He was more than a stupid idiot, he was a blind, stupid idiot. What if his brilliant idea turned out to be a fool's errand? No use in turning back. He'd be better off knowing, and maybe this would be a first step in rebuilding a connection to family.

Driving in circles, he realized, was a waste of his time. He hauled out his phone and sent a text to his brother.

Jesse: *you free? I'd like to talk*

It was only a moment later but it felt like an eternity before Blake responded: *I've got a few minutes. Come by the office in the barn*

The place was hopping as he parked in the yard and headed toward the room where his dad used to keep the old ranching records. Mike had done most of his office work in the house, but it seemed there'd been a change — another one — since Jesse had left.

He knocked on the door before pushing it open, whistling softly at the new setup. What used to be a dark room crowded with beat-up filing cabinets from the thrift shop was now a bright space with rows of neat shelves and two desks, edges touching opposite walls. They'd put in new windows and painted the walls white, and the whole place looked shiny and efficient.

"Place looks great." Jesse approached the desk Blake sat behind, dropping into one of the straight-backed wooden chairs opposite him.

"Thanks." His brother closed the ledger he was working on and gave Jesse his full attention. There was no judgment on his face, only concern. "How's Dare?"

"She's feeling good. Comfortable, at least."

"I bet she's scared."

Jesse hesitated. He was going to toss off something noncommittal, but from the expression on Blake's face, his brother was serious, Jesse let out a long slow breath. "I think she's a lot more scared than she's letting on, yeah, but the baby's moving lots. She was pretty upbeat when I left her with the girls."

"How are you doing?"

"Me?"

"You," Blake confirmed. He made a face. "Nothing I hate more than having to sit helplessly when Jaxi's hurtin'."

That unanswerable ache inside flickered up, but Jesse pushed it away, knowing somehow that his brother would let this one ride if he switched topics. "I know I was a bastard last February, and there's been a million times I wished I'd done that differently, because it was shitty to leave you a man short with no notice. I'm sorry."

He wasn't expecting Blake to outright forgive him or say that everything was fine, which was good because he got what he expected.

"You're right. You should've done things differently, but we can't change that now." Blake folded his arms across his chest. "What do you need, Jesse?"

"I need work," he said.

His brother raised a brow.

Jesse looked him in the eye. "I don't expect any

favours, but I don't know how long Dare will be in the hospital. It's only until Monday for sure, but what if it's longer? I don't want to sit on my ass and twiddle my thumbs. I need to work, not only because I need to take care of her. Because I'm going to go stir-crazy waiting until we know what's happening."

Blake eyed him, leaning back in his chair and staying silent.

"I mean it. You need me to clean stalls 24/7, I'll do it. I can't tell you how long I'll be around, so wherever you have tasks to be done. You know I can deal with just about anything, but put me where you need me the most."

Because whatever happened, he was going to make sure that Dare was taken care of. Right now that seemed to mean he needed to be here in Rocky Mountain House.

For the first time a crack appeared in Blake's iron-solid walls. "I can give you some jobs. Only between when you need to be with Dare, so before and after visiting hours."

"I want time with her, yes, but she doesn't need me there all day," Jesse pointed out. "You know Mom and Jaxi and the rest will want to visit."

Blake made a face. "True. But you need to stay within cell phone range."

"Starting tonight?"

His brother hesitated. "If you're ready. There's a crew headed out at eleven to the west grazing lands to pick up some cattle and move them to summer fields. They'll be back before seven." Blake stood and opened a thin cupboard with keys to the tractors and combines and all the rest lined up in neat rows. He pulled a set off the hook and tossed them to Jesse. "You can drive the trailer. Kent Parken is lead on the transfer."

The ache in his gut had spread until his chest and throat were tight. Before Jesse'd fucked up and left, he used to run lead, and Kent had been the hired hand.

Regret was the only emotion he felt — well, regret and gratitude that Blake was giving him a chance.

Jesse rose to his feet. "Thanks. I won't make you sorry."

Blake nodded tightly. "Jesse..."

Jesse paused in the doorway, turning back to wait while Blake considered his words.

"Tell Dare we're here for her. Anything she needs. She just has to ask."

God damn. The sincerity and the caring and the —

That hard knot in his chest was going to close off his throat one of these times. "I know she'll appreciate it."

I appreciate it. The words hung on the tip of his tongue. Why were they so damn hard to say?

Jesse gathered himself up, checking his watch. He had time to stop off at the trailer for a quick shower and to get changed before returning to the hospital.

If he was going to start burning the candle at both ends, he'd better get ready.

Chapter Nineteen

Blog post: Stuck in the Middle With You
Looks as if I'm in Pregnancy Prison for a few days. Just precautionary, but I have a confession — I'm not a very good patient.
Or maybe that should read I'm not very patient.
Either one…

Other than she wasn't sure what the mystery meat had been in the dinner offering, Dare's first evening in captivity went better than she'd expected. All sorts of visitors stopped by; a trickle in the beginning followed by more and more people until her room felt like a gathering place during one of Ginny's barbeques.

Hope Coleman waltzed in first with an entire box of flannel scraps and the other requirements for making squares for a baby quilt. Her husband Matt, one of Jesse's brothers, had come along, and to Dare's amusement he joined in the impromptu sewing lesson Hope gave, his thick fingers moving carefully over the soft material as he good-naturedly followed his wife's orders. Colt refused to let go of his mom, so Matt had acted as demonstrator.

The way Matt looked at Hope as she spoke, and the easy way he slipped a hand around her hip in a familiar caress spoke volumes about the connection between them. Dare ended up poking herself in the finger with her needle hard enough to draw blood, she was paying more attention to the simmering glances they kept giving each other.

Shortly after they'd arrived another set of Colemans marched through the door, and then another, and every one of them simply joined in the conversation, and there was no fuss and no awkwardness.

For which Dare was very grateful, considering she was sitting on a bed in her pyjamas for all intents and purposes.

By the time Jesse returned, damp hair curling at his neckline, the room had settled into small groups. The women all stitching together squares while the guys each cheerfully completed one before abandoning the task and pulling out a deck of cards. How they managed to play while holding babies and entertaining a couple of boys under the age of two, Dare had no idea.

Jesse stood beside the bed and offered her an amused smile along with a fresh glass of water. "What are you looking all bewildered about?"

She made a small gesture at the room and answered quietly, "It's like my room is Grand Central Station."

"There's no train arriving any time soon," he teased. "I hope you're ready to share your hospital food with the entire horde."

Dare pulled herself up regally. "Jell-O for all, my good man."

He leaned in close, forehead touching hers as he looked into her eyes. "You let me know when you've had enough, okay? They can come back tomorrow. In fact, unless you order them to stay away, it looks as if

Little Hospital Room on the Prairie is *the* happening place to be these days."

"I'm okay," she insisted, stealing a quick kiss before he stepped back. A dangerous smolder in his eyes promised her many things before he slid into a chair next to Matt and Daniel and joined in their card game.

The party broke up at eight o'clock when regular visiting hours were over, and she lay back on the bed surprisingly tired. "Considering I haven't done anything except lie here and talk, I'm pooped."

Jesse shrugged, settling in the chair beside her with a cup in his hands he'd appropriated from somewhere down the hall. The rich scent of coffee hung on the air. "No one's keeping track. If you want to hit the sack early, go for it."

"Maybe I will." She looked him over, wondering why he was drinking coffee at this time of the night. "You don't have to stay with me all night."

"I know. I'm going to do a pickup run for Blake tonight. I'm leaving in a couple of hours, but don't worry — if they need to get in touch with me, I'll be here pretty damn fast. I'll be back to see you first thing in the morning."

She thought it over for a moment, having to adjust her mental processes. "I thought Blake said he didn't need help."

Jesse put the coffee cup down, his expression going serious. "About that. I meant it last night when we were talking by the fire pit about this and got interrupted. Blake didn't do anything wrong, I did." He looked away for a moment before meeting her gaze again, his typical cocky teasing subdued until nothing but sincerity remained. "I was stupid when I left last February, and my stupidity put them in a tough situation. That's why Blake wasn't blowing sunshine up my ass, but I totally deserved it. I've talked to him. Apologized. It's okay now."

"That's good." His explanation didn't answer all her questions, but she was glad because some of the stress seemed to have leached out of him. When he finally kissed her good night an hour later, it was easy to give in to the siren call of her pillow.

The next thing Dare knew it was morning and the curtains were being pulled open to another blue-sky day.

She stretched a bit, happy that she felt so normal and rested — although considering she hadn't had to lift a finger for most of yesterday, her burst of energy made sense. She wasn't looking forward to two more days of limited mobility. AKA, sitting around on her butt.

"When you're done in the washroom, we've got some tests we need to put you through, as well as another dose of medicine," Tamara informed her.

By the time Jesse slipped into the room to say good morning, Dare's cheeks were sore from smiling. His cousin had helped pass the time by spilling the beans on some of his exploits when he was little, most of which were embarrassing.

Dare laughed at Jesse's expression when he realized what Tamara was talking about. "Your cousin knows all the good stories about you," she teased.

Tamara stood at the foot of the bed. Today she wore pale blue scrubs decorated with floating clouds, and the frames of her glasses were rainbow-hued. She gloated as she eyed Jesse who had folded his arms over his chest and was pretending to glare at them.

"Lies," he insisted. "Damn lies."

"Damn entertaining lies," Dare insisted.

"Truth is always stranger than fiction," Tamara taunted.

About an hour later, Tamara had just helped Dare back into the bed after a pit stop when the door opened, and Ginny and Caleb stepped in.

Dare's throat tightened at the sight of them. "I didn't expect you to come this soon."

Ginny raced across the room to offer a hug. "Are you kidding? After Jesse called they had to sit on me to stop me from driving up last night."

Caleb moved slower, his gaze taking in Dare before a curse escaped his lips. He fixed his gaze on Jesse, murder in his eyes. "You *bastard*."

Jesse rose to his feet as Caleb stormed forward, but Tamara moved the fastest, sliding in front of Caleb and slapping her hand against his chest. "Stop right there, cowboy. You want to tell me what's got you itching for a fight?"

"How the hell did she get a black eye, Coleman?" Caleb demanded at high volume, ignoring Tamara.

"Stop, Caleb," Dare ordered.

"Did you hit her?" Caleb pushed Tamara aside to get at Jesse.

Or he tried to push her aside. Even though Dare was watching, it was hard to see exactly how it happened. One minute Caleb was moving forward, and the next he was flying through the air then slamming into the floor with a body-aching crash.

Tamara stood over him, foot planted perilously close to his groin. Her rainbow and floaty-cloud outfit a stark contrast to her apparent danger-level. "I said back down, cowboy. No fights in this room, you got it?"

Caleb groaned, hand going to his head before he

collapsed and lay there, winded.

"Fuck." The strangled word barely made it past his lips.

Ginny stood at Dare's bedside, staring down at the strange vignette in front of them. "Um, you got a bodyguard, Dare?"

"Looks that way. Caleb, nobody punched me. Well, not on purpose. My face got in the way when they were stopping me from hitting the ground. I don't think you should go beat up the pastor's daughter, so stop being a macho-jerk."

Caleb made a noise. It might have been an apology, but Dare couldn't be sure.

She sighed heavily. "Tamara, you want to let my brother up?"

"Your *brother*?" Tamara swore softly. "Jeez, I'm sorry." She held out a hand to help him up.

Caleb gave her a dirty look and ignored her fingers, rocking up to his feet. He glanced at Jesse. "Sorry for assuming."

"I get it. Protective big brother. You did tell me you'd kill me if I hurt her." Jesse was smirking, though.

Tamara elbowed him in the side. "Don't be a jerk."

Jesse turned on her, his amusement fading. "Don't you step into the middle of a situation like that again. You could've gotten hurt."

His cousin rolled her eyes. "Yeah, right. Did you see him bounce?"

Caleb made another noise, this one decisively rude, but he moved cautiously as he passed Tamara en route to the bed. He slid his gaze over Dare and examined her closely. "Accidentally punched in the face? *Really?*"

"Yup," she said. "Just like the time you and Luke

went out after the strays and ended up — "

" — okay. That's enough of that." He held up a hand to cut her off before hugging her tight. "You scared us. You good?"

"I feel fine," Dare insisted. "Buckaroo is moving like crazy. I was just tired, or something."

"We're taking good care of her." Tamara had come up to the bedside and pushed past Caleb. "With that in mind, if I could get everyone to step back a little. It's a big room. Dare gets her share of the space and then the rest of you."

She was glaring specifically at Caleb, fists resting on her hips.

He didn't move.

Tamara made a feint toward his groin, and Caleb twisted in defense.

She was gloating far too hard as she reached for the rolling side table, swinging it around and forcing him to back up another couple steps.

Dare watched the interaction with amusement. Caleb's sense of humour needed a kick in the butt at times, but she was glad they were there. "Come and talk. Where're the girls?"

Jesse interrupted to say goodbye. "I'll give you a chance to visit. Regular visiting hours start at eleven, and I'm pretty sure my mom plans on stopping by, plus I don't know who else."

He covered up a yawn best he could, but Dare caught his fingers and gave them a squeeze. "Go get some shuteye. I'm not going anywhere."

He nodded. "I'll be back around five. You need anything?"

"Burger and fries? Or pizza — with the works."

He glanced at Caleb and Ginny before deliberately leaning in and giving her another one of those addictive kisses. It was far too natural to let her arms rise up and wrap around his shoulders, fingers stroking through his hair, soft against her palms.

He pulled back, cocky grin firmly in place. "Be good."

"Why should I start now?" she teased.

Ginny and Caleb settled into chairs as Jesse took his leave. Ginny twisted to watch him exit the room. "That was hot."

Caleb's face stiffened. "Ginny."

"Well, it was," she insisted, lifting her gaze to meet Dare's. "So, your hot-cowboy visit is turning out to be an adventure."

Caleb twisted in his chair, arms crossed at his chest. "Do you want me to leave the room so you can talk about *hot cowboys*?"

Ginny waved a hand. "You don't have to leave."

Dare snickered as Caleb let out a frustrated growl, but she was glad everything was normal.

Or as normal as it was able to get as Ginny turned thoughtful then placed a finger on her lips. "Okay, I'll be nice, and we won't talk about Dare's sexy cowboy."

"Thank you," Caleb drawled.

Ginny clapped her hands together and rubbed them. "So, Dare. Tell me more about your *bodyguard*. Was that not an awesome move she pulled on Caleb?"

It was no use. The small bundle of warmth inside her grew and grew and now it bubbled up into laughter. The long-suffering expression on Caleb's face just made it worse, and Dare let herself go, protected and surrounded by the lingering sensation of Jesse's caring and her family's presence.

Jesse picked up a few groceries before heading back to the trailer and stripping down. He took a quick shower and tossed himself into bed to grab a few hours' sleep before heading back to the hospital.

His rumbling stomach woke him. He pulled on sweatpants before stumbling to the kitchen and tossing bread into all four of the toaster slots.

He had the frying pan hot and was cracking eggs when the door opened and ice skidded up his spine. What the hell had he been thinking, walking around half naked in his brother's place?

"You making enough for two?"

Instant relief struck as Joel stepped to the counter beside him, eyeing the pan hungrily.

"That depends. Are you starving or ravenous?"

Joel reached in the fridge and pulled out another carton of eggs. "Definitely ravenous. I'll butter this batch of toast and start another."

They worked together in companionable silence for a few minutes. Jesse split the first set of eggs onto two plates before getting the second batch cooking and settling at the table. Joel popped down two enormous glasses of juice and turned on the coffeemaker for after.

It didn't bother Jesse that they didn't talk while eating — they'd always agreed in the past it was pretty much a waste of energy.

But by the time the second servings were on their plate Jesse paused for long enough to offer Joel a grin. "I'm still a better cook than you."

Joel looked at him, one brow rising slowly. "Do you really want to start this battle again?"

Being obnoxious about each other's cooking skills and teasing the hell out of each other was exactly where Jesse wanted to be instead of the awkward chasm and distance he'd pushed them to.

Jesse leaned back in his chair and pretended to plot. "Chili cook-off?"

A snort escaped his brother. "You did not win that one."

Jesse displayed his best shocked expression. "I could have sworn Dad and Blake said my chili was miles better than yours."

"Because you stole a batch of frozen chili out of Jaxi's and Mom's freezers and mixed them together." But Joel was smiling. "It was damn tasty."

"Way better than the stomped chicken."

Joel had just put a mouthful of egg and toast in his mouth, and he barely stopped in time from spewing it over the table. He gave Jesse a dirty look as he licked egg off his fingers. "We promised to never talk about that."

"No. We promised to not tease each other in public." Jesse looked around. "It's just you, me and the *chickens* here now."

His brother laughed as he demolished the rest of the food on his plate. "I never did hear Mom complain that she'd found a giant snowball in her freezer."

Sixteen-year-old hellions. In the dead of winter, they'd had the brilliant idea to save a massive chunk of snow in the freezer so that on some hot summer day they could haul it out and surprise their brothers with well-timed snowballs.

Only the specially packaged *do not touch* wrapped-up paper they'd hauled out of the freezer on the hottest day of the summer and then jumped on to get at the snow turned out to be not what they expected.

A soft chuckle escaped Joel.

Jesse could tell he was picturing that moment when the two of them realized that under their boots they'd been crushing not a firmly packed bundle of snow from the previous winter but one of his mom's frozen chickens.

"Do you remember how much hell that was to buy a new chicken and sneak it back into the freezer?"

"Didn't we have to bribe Mrs. Larsen at the Mercantile? So she didn't spill the beans to Mom?"

Joel nodded. "I still feel guilty every time I see her. I make Vicki do the shopping there."

Jesse didn't answer for a moment.

It was funny how much things had changed. Oh, he felt weird around Vicki, but the last couple days with Dare at his side had been pointing out to him that life should be a whole lot more about looking forward than looking back. It was as if he was awkward because he'd felt that way for a long time, not because he had any real reason now for it.

He glanced up and caught Joel smiling. "Am I in trouble? You usually looked like that when I was finally going to get in shit for something I did."

"Really? Huh." Joel shook his head. "You know, you're right. There were times it was a relief when the hammer fell on whatever nonsense we pulled, but I'm sorry if you felt like I was happy for you to take the blame. I was just thinking it feels good to have you back. Even with the lingering moments where I want to haul you up behind the barn and burn off some frustration."

Jesse nodded. "It's weird. There are moments when I feel as if I never left. There are times when I know

I fucked up so bad it's going to be a long hard road."

Joel reached over and grabbed Jesse's plate. "One good thing," he offered, stuffing the dirty dishes into the machine. "If you're on the right road and walking, you'll eventually get where you want to go."

There wasn't much Jesse needed to say to that. Instead, he glanced at the clock. "I've got to get dressed and head to the hospital for a while."

"I was going to pick up Vicki from work and take her over. You want a ride?"

Jesse shook his head. "Thanks, but Blake's got me in the barns tonight. I should take my truck so I can go straight over after visiting hours."

His brother nodded and headed out without another word, but as Jesse dressed and got in the truck, it was the closest to normal they'd been since Vicki had come on the scene and Jesse had lost his mind.

As long as he was on the right road — he just needed to keep walking.

Chapter Twenty

Blog post: Look Deeper
Sometimes I wonder what I'm not seeing that's right under my nose. When you live on a ranch in Alberta you get a reminder of this every spring as the crocuses come up, and a field that was barren and brown is suddenly dotted with purple.

Teasing us with a fresh reminder that what we see on the surface is not always all that's there.

The weekend passed in a blur. Jesse made sure he was at the hospital first thing in the morning before official visiting hours, and he stayed late as he could in the evening before taking off to complete the tasks Blake left for him.

In fact, once enough visitors had shown up that Dare was entertained, he'd slip away and head back to the ranch and do whatever he could to keep himself busy for a few hours.

Somewhere in there he slept.

He was in the middle of scrubbing all the milking equipment when Travis stuck his head in the door. "Hey, asshole."

Jesse pushed the brush against the inside of the bucket harder, but his lips curled into a smile. "What, buttface?"

A soft snicker escaped his brother. "I heard Blake gave you some jobs. I wanted to see if you remembered how to do this thing called work."

His brother's jerk-ish behaviour made Jesse feel a hell of a lot more welcome than if he'd tiptoed around. Jesse gestured to the chair beside the sink. "Go ahead, you lazy ass. Best seat in the house if you want to watch."

"Actually, I wanted to ask if you've got time to go for a ride?"

God, yes. The temptation was strong, but Jesse glanced at his watch. If he indulged, he wouldn't make it to the hospital on time to have dinner with Dare.

He shook his head reluctantly. "I'd love to, but I need to finish this before stopping today. Sorry."

Travis marched in, pulling a second scrub brush from behind his back as he reached for the next set of buckets. "Right answer. I'll give you a hand so you'll have time for a short break before you go see Dare."

Jesse stopped, slightly shocked as his brother began scrubbing. "You don't need to do that."

"I know, but I want to go for a ride, and Cassidy is taking care of Ashley, and you're the only other person I know who's willing to do the gully with me."

Jesus. "Do you have a death wish? The rains last year made that impassable."

Travis offered a huge grin. "Chicken?"

Oh, for fuck's sake. It wasn't only Dare's eighteen-year-old brother who had an issue. "Really? Did you revert to childhood while I've been gone?"

"I'm kidding." His brother laughed. "Runoff this

spring changed the landscape all over. There's a new route you need to see. You game?"

"Hell, yeah." It was a bizarre sensation to be back here where his life had been for so many years, scrubbing down equipment with Travis, fingers getting wrinkly as they worked together. Plans for trouble pushing them forward. "But I need to be back on time."

His brother chuckled. "Good to see you've lost your mind over a girl. I didn't think this day would ever come."

Jesse aimed the water a little off angle so a spray *accidentally* splashed Travis in the face. His brother ducked but kept working. "I guess I saw you lose your mind, and it didn't seem to make your balls shrivel up *too* much."

"Oh, my balls are just fine these days, thank you." Travis hesitated. "My balls are fine, but my heart's ready to jump out of my chest, especially when I get thinking too hard about the baby."

"I try *not* to think too hard about the baby," Jesse admitted before hurrying on. "Not because the kid's a bad thing, but it's like my brain can only handle so much."

Travis didn't answer for a minute. Instead there was a quiet scratch of the stiff bristles against metal bouncing off the wooden walls to accompany the country music playing from the overhead speakers.

"It's weird getting to this stage." Trevor spoke slowly, a lot less brash than Jesse remembered him. "Before Ashley and Cassidy came into my life, it was about getting the job done and moving to the next thing that would bring me pleasure. Now I find getting the job done is a kind of pleasure all in itself. It's like I don't have to go to the extreme to be happy anymore."

"Which is why you want to run the gully with me. Because that's nothing extreme," Jesse teased.

"It's a challenge," Travis corrected him. "You'll see what I mean when we get there, but seriously, I don't think less of you for being freaked out about having a kid on the way. But maybe you're going to be okay once he comes along. If you've got being an asshole out of your system."

"I don't know. Does being an asshole ever really leave someone's system completely? I mean, look at you."

Jesse stumbled against the counter with a laugh as Travis smacked him with his shoulder, walking past to hang up clean equipment on the wall.

They worked quickly, discussion moving to the things that had changed on the ranch while Jesse had been gone. He listened most of the time and let Travis talk.

It seemed there'd been a lot of changes to the Six Pack ranch, including combining efforts with the rest of the clan. A movement toward taking the four separate ranches and recombining them into the best use of resources.

It sounded complicated, but as Travis described it, Jesse could see the benefit. The increased ability to improve stock lines would make any geneticist drool.

By the time they had the horses saddled and were heading out down the coulee, Jesse was itching to reconnect with the land in a whole new way. It was late enough in the day that the summer sun had baked the earth, and the rich scent of grass and seeds and new growing things filled his nostrils.

On every exhale he let out some of his tension and confusion, restoring himself with the familiarity of home.

Travis led the way and Jesse let his borrowed horse follow, missing Danger but enjoying the ride anyway. When they broke into the open space that marked the start of the usual wild race forward, Jesse took off before Travis could get his horse ready. Blasting past him to enjoy the full-out sprint toward the edge of the cliffs and the rough-and-tumble trail heading into the more extreme section of Coleman land.

They raced through a rock-bottomed gulch, the horse's hooves clattering, the sound ringing off the rock walls on either side of them. The wind rushed past, refreshing and cool.

Travis managed to pull up even, an enormous grin on his face as they cut through the final section of the gully and let the horses slow to cool themselves as they walked back up to the top of the flatlands.

Where there used to be hard stone and sharp edges, the land suddenly changed, and Travis pulled to a stop. Jesse looked down into one of his childhood play areas and felt as if he were staring at an ancient temple.

"God, that's beautiful."

His brother grinned. "Surprised you, didn't I?"

In front of them lay a piece of geological history. Ages ago the Whiskey Creek River used to run through the gulch, before time and man had diverted its flow. For all the years of Jesse's youth, the dry, flat creek bed had been a mess of boulders and dust, the steep banks cutting away with erosion every spring. Dead trees and leaves blown in by the fall winds and winter snows had accumulated in heaps like broken cages.

Walking the horses through the riverbed used to be like taking a trip into Mordor.

"Spring runoff? Seriously, that's all that happened

here?" Jesse was looking into something closer to Paradise. The sharp embankments were smooth curves. Entire chunks of the landscape had crashed into the valley bottom and the sharp change lifted the floor and spread dirt from the top of the embankment.

Everywhere he looked wildflowers bloomed. The dry riverbed flowed with colour, splashes of red, purple and yellow creating a mosaic. A Technicolor *Wizard of Oz* backdrop.

Travis leaned forward on the saddle horn, absently brushing the neck of his horse as they looked into the changed landscape. "Springtime, and a few forces of nature of the female variety."

Jesse glanced at Travis in confusion.

His brother pointed to the side where a well-worn path led down into the river valley. "When we had all that rain, the canyon walls collapsed, and most of us wrote off this area as a lost cause. That's when the Coleman girls started riding here on a regular basis. Blake checked it out — we all did — and we figured it was safe enough. They always stuck to the one path down and up. Ashley and Jaxi stopped riding a few months ago, but the others kept coming."

The horses had taken their own lead and were following the path without being guided, and suddenly Jesse and Travis were surrounded by what could only be described as the scent of happiness. Blue sky. Sunshine. Heat shimmering off the riot of flowers as they lifted little faces toward the sun.

Jesse looked around him in astonishment. "It's not possible, though. How could they make this big of a change in such a short time?"

"They didn't." Travis glanced over, expression gone

291

thoughtful. "Turns out they started a couple years ago. Allison ordered wildflower seed in bulk, and she and Karen have been gathering seeds from around the Coleman fields for years. Every time they came to this area, the girls would toss down handfuls. Some blew away, some got caught in the rocks. All of it was lying dormant until the growing conditions got right."

The horse swayed under Jesse in a gentle rocking motion. Travis and he sat in silence as the horses carried them forward through an entirely new section of the land — or at least that's what it felt like. It was a place he'd seen a million times and still a place Jesse had never been before…

They were brushing down the horses when Travis made an interesting comment. His brother wasn't even really talking about a specific thing, but the words echoed in Jesse's head the entire trip back to the trailer where he grabbed a quick shower and got into clean clothes.

"Sometimes things change and we don't even know it, but the result can be pretty spectacular."

Jesse headed to the hospital, his thoughts running in circles. Talk about changes — Travis had always been someone Jesse could count on when he wanted to make mischief and raise hell.

When had his brother grown up?

He stopped off at A&W and grabbed burgers and fries, slipping up the back staircase and dodging nurses as he worked his way toward Dare's room.

He'd almost made it when a hand landed on his shoulder, fingers digging in and stopping him in his tracks.

"Where do you think you're going?" Tamara demanded.

Jesse employed his best sweet-talking voice. "Have

a heart, cuz. There's no way either of us can survive on the food around here."

She glanced down the hallway, then held out her hand. "Give me a burger, and I'll let you pass."

He clicked his tongue disapprovingly. "Blackmail, Tamara?"

She didn't budge. Neither did her hand. "Such a nasty word. I'd rather call it *supper*."

Jesse separated out one of the bags and handed it to her. "A Mama Burger and onion rings. Can I go now?"

Tamara was peeking into the bag, a wide grin on her face. "I'm impressed. I should've known you'd come prepared. Don't worry, I won't tell anyone that you're smuggling food into the hospital. Especially since there's nothing wrong with that — Dare can eat anything she wants."

Ah, shit. "Then why the hell did I have to pay your bribe?"

"You didn't. I *told* you I called it supper. Thank you."

Jesse chuckled. "No prob."

He turned to go join Dare when Tamara interrupted him. "By the way. Do Dare's brothers all work the ranch?"

Interesting. Jesse paused and examined her face.

His cousin was attempting to offer an innocent expression, but it wasn't working. She was blinking in a strange rhythm. "Yes. Why?"

"Oh, no reason. Just making a few notes on her chart."

At that she vanished, taking her ill-gotten goods with her.

Jesse walked into the room, a sudden streak of guilt hitting as he found Dare all alone. "Shit. Where is everybody?"

Dare looked at him over the top of her computer.

"Hey." She took a long sniff as she closed the laptop and put it away in its carry bag. "Good, you brought food. I'm starving."

He tucked away her computer stuff and slid the tray in front of her. "You could've called Tamara and got her to bring you dinner."

She made a face. "I wanted *real* food. I knew my hunter warrior would arrive soon to feed me."

Jesse laughed as he settled on the bed so he could put the burgers on the tray between them. "How come nobody's with you?"

Dare brought out all four burgers and examined each carefully before picking one with bacon and happily sinking her teeth into it. She closed her eyes and made a contented sound as she chewed and swallowed, wiping at her mouth before answering. "Because I'm a big girl and capable of being in a room all by myself without crying. Aren't you proud of me?"

"Dare," he warned.

"Don't get your panties in a twist. I sent everybody home. I took a nap, which is like a miracle all by itself, and I just got caught up on my next week of blog posts. It's been a mini-retreat."

He was glad to know she'd had a say in the matter and not just been abandoned. Although, he didn't really think anyone in this family would leave unless she insisted.

"Want to know a secret?" she whispered softly.

He nodded because his mouth was full of burger.

"I think Tamara is interested in Caleb."

Jesse barely managed to swallow before letting out a loud *ha*. "She was just pumping me for information about your brothers," he shared.

"Which she shouldn't have had to do because she'd already found out from me how old everyone was. Plus their names, and I think their boot size — the conversation got really random, but I think that was to try and throw me off the scent."

Jesse stole a couple of fries from the package on Dare's side of the table. "It makes sense, I guess. By the time you hit your late twenties, the dating pool in a small town is only about an inch deep."

"Tell me about it," she said. "I had to leave town, drive to the boonies and tie one on to find a guy."

They exchanged a grin before Jesse went back to the food and the topic at hand. "I suppose Caleb is decent enough, but I don't think he and Tamara would get along very well."

He tried for another fry, but Dare slapped his fingers away, laughing as he pretended to be in deadly pain. "Caleb is a catch," she insisted.

"Oh, really? Does that mean you're marrying him instead of me?" Jesse teased. She'd told him about Caleb's proposal.

Dare sat upright and folded her arms over her chest. "I didn't actually agree that *we're* getting married. In case you didn't notice."

A small detail that Jesse had been ignoring, which probably wasn't a wise idea.

He changed topics. "How's Buckaroo? He line-dancing or doing the two-step?"

Dare shifted her head from side to side. "He's pretty quiet during the day, usually, unless I'm really still."

"Which means never."

She tucked the last bit of a burger into her mouth and chewed sassily. Jesse hopped off the bed and got them glasses of water, and when they were done, he cleaned up the whole mess and moved the table aside.

"Scoot over," he ordered. "I want to take care of my fiancée."

She shifted toward the foot of the bed and he crawled up so he could place his hands on her shoulders, massaging her neck and back. Digging in his thumbs until her head was lolling to the side, and she was making delicious noises.

"You're killing me," he whispered, attempting to adjust so he had enough room his erection wasn't cut in two by his zipper. "Those are sex noises. Those are not allowed to be made outside of sex time."

"Oops? Sorry, but *ohhhh...*"

She did it again, the sound melting into his ears and along his spine as if she'd placed her lips to his body. Or her tongue, slipping over his skin. Licking along the edge of his six pack and headed south.

Jesse skimmed his hand lower, somehow massaging instead of feeling her up.

Okay, that was bullshit — he was totally feeling her up *as* he massaged, hands cupping her ass briefly before sliding along the side of her body until he brushed the heavy weight of her breasts.

"Tease," she whispered.

"I was told I'd be skinned if anyone caught us fooling around. I don't want to cause any troubles. You're in the hospital for a reason." He let out a heavy sigh then reined himself in. "Come on, baby. Lie down and let me cuddle you for a bit."

The bed wasn't big enough for the two of them, but with some wiggling they ended up stretched out together. Dare had tried to roll her back toward him, but Jesse resisted. Tugging her until she was flat on her back and he was on his side, halfway over her. Legs and torso touching all the way up.

"You had an okay day?" Jesse settled in and got comfortable. It took a moment before it registered that he had instinctively slid his hand over her belly, but once the fact sank in, he deliberately spread his fingers over her shirt and let his palm cradle the small round spot.

"I did. You have a very big family," she informed him.

A soft chuckle escaped him as he let his fingers stroke back and forth. "I might've noticed that a time or two. Who dropped in today?"

Dare lifted a hand and counted off on her fingers while she called out names. "That was the morning."

"Popular girl."

"In the afternoon there was Anna — let me get this right — she's the RCMP. She came in with her baby girl Kasey who they're calling Kay, and the vet who's married to another cousin..."

"Melody? Married to Steve."

"That's the one. Melody and Anna came in at the same time, and Melody had her little boy with her. His name is Jason and they're calling him Jay, which is kind of hysterical because they told me they ended up in the hospital the same time. Neither of them had any idea that they were planning on using those names."

Huh. "The kids can't be very old. I don't even know that it had registered they were expecting before I left."

"A month and a half old, so yeah, you probably hadn't even clued in." Dare looked thoughtful. "They were really cute. Even more cute than Justin, but not quite as cute as Colt."

Jesse laughed, running his palm in a circle in the hopes

that he'd convince Buckaroo to make an appearance. "You're rating my nieces and nephews?"

She twisted toward him, those expressive eyes catching hold and keeping him fixed upon her. "More like I'm working through my own thought processes. I really don't know very much about kids, Jesse. I helped out a little when Sasha and Emma were small, but things were weird back at the beginning with Wendy, so I didn't spend a lot of time around them when they were babies. I feel a lot more comfortable with kids once they're toddlers."

"You're going to do great," Jesse insisted, before reaching down and tangling his fingers with hers. He tugged them upward to his lips and kissed them gently. "Confession. I don't know much about babies either. I figure we'll make it up as we go along."

"We'll have to." That crease returned between her brows. "Well, if everything's okay."

"Shhhh." He kissed her fingers again and curled an arm around her. "Let's look on the bright side here. You've been feeling good, and you look great. You haven't had any more dizzy spells. Hopefully tomorrow morning the word is that you get to go home."

Dare tipped her chin slowly. "You're right."

The next second Jesse was tugged into different directions. The idea of home — if she got the all clear tomorrow they'd be able to pack up their bags and head to Heart Falls. The trip had gone well enough they could return at any time for a visit. Jesse could see his family without it being a horrible, earth-shattering situation.

This was good. No, this was great.

Why did it feel like the pit of his stomach had just dropped a foot?

He shoved the thoughts away, focusing back on Dare. "I hope you got enough quiet time, because the next few minutes we're bound to have another crowd of visitors."

"I don't mind. Everyone's been pretty neat, and while I wouldn't suggest bed rest as the best way to meet a family, in some ways it's been good because, hey, they know where to find me."

"Bonus points, because you can't run away," he teased. "You just kick the lot of them out of the room."

"It's okay that I was alone earlier," she insisted, stroking her fingers over his jaw as she examined his face. "I spend a lot of time by myself at Silver Stone. This having-somebody-around-all-the-time is a little overwhelming. Don't get me wrong, I appreciate it, but I needed time to breathe."

Words leapt to his tongue, and for an instant he considered tossing them away.

Something made him change his mind. Forced him to consider how much she'd dealt with over the past couple of days. She'd done it like a trooper too, and it was stupid to not share a personal secret when she'd been basically on display for his family.

Still, he spoke slowly, wondering if she'd get it. "It's going to sound stupid, especially considering how many of us are always around, but there are times even in the middle of a Coleman gathering I feel as if I'm alone."

Jesse stretched out and cradled his head on his arm. He expected she'd reiterate something along the lines of "being alone isn't always a terrible thing", but she didn't say anything for a minute or so.

When she spoke, it was enough to smack him hard.

"Just because someone is physically there, it doesn't mean they're really there for you. Or that they see you.

I think that might be worse than having them not around at all." Her eyes had gone dark again, her face tight.

"Lonely in the middle of a crowd?" Jesse shook his head. "It sounds pathetic."

"It sounds real," she chastised him. She ran her fingers into his hair, damn near petting him into a submissive pile of relaxation despite the serious topic. "I even think you can be lonely with another person, if you're not connected. If they're not really *there*."

He was one hundred percent sure she wasn't talking about them. "Who made you lonely like that, Dare?" he asked quietly.

She hesitated then shrugged. "Maybe my memories are overly dramatic. I dated someone in high school. I thought we were closer than it turned out we really were."

Jesse didn't have a good feeling about this. "I hate the bastard already."

Dare's gaze followed her fingers as she continued to slowly caress his jaw absently. "He didn't break up with me when the accident happened, if that's what you're wondering. It was our last year. Grade twelve, when you're making all sorts of big plans. I really liked him, and I thought we had something special, but anytime I tried to get closer, he'd have some good reason to pull back. And everyone else seemed okay with casual, as if it was just the thing to do — have a steady girl or boyfriend to go to all the school events."

Now this was starting to make sense. "So you were together physically, but not much more."

She nodded. "Until he wasn't even there physically." She stopped her daydreaming to look him in the eye. "A couple days after graduation he sent me an email saying he'd gotten the job in Calgary that he'd applied for, so wish him well and — that was it."

Jesse popped up on his elbow. "That was it, *what?*"

"The last email I got from him. He never came back to Heart Falls."

Stupid, rotten, miserable motherfucker of an asshole. "What's his name?"

Dare tapped him on the nose. "You are not tracking him down to peel off his skin, or any other of those oh-so-imaginative threats I've already heard from my brothers. We were both kids, and he acted childishly. Yes, it hurt my feelings enormously, but I should have seen it coming, and it was a long time ago."

But it meant she knew what it was like to be alone on a level that Jesse had never had to face except because of his own actions.

His own stupid behaviour reared up to smack him in the side of the head all over. "Well, he was an ass. Anyone who would treat you like that doesn't deserve to get to be around you, anyway."

"Agreed. Which is what Ginny has told me numerous times."

Jesse rolled over her, bracing himself on his elbows as he pinned her into place for a moment. "Kiss me."

Her gaze darted toward the door and back. "Tamara's going to do you bodily harm if she catches you in that position."

Probably right. Jesse stole a quick kiss before continuing his roll, all the way to a standing position beside the bed.

A knock on the door sounded a second after his feet hit the floor, followed by a chorus of *hellos*.

He glanced back at Dare to find she was grinning.

"You've got horseshoes up your butt," she teased.

"God, I hope not." But he linked his fingers with hers as another portion of the family stopped in to say hello.

Chapter Twenty-One

~Text exchange. Grade Eleven science class, Heart Falls High School~

Ginny: *Tiffany said Marisa told her Brant said Tyson told Mike he liked me*

Dare: *well, that was a waste of words*

Ginny: *why?*

Dare: *d'uh. You can tell Tyson likes you because he's always watching you*

Ginny: *omg, really?*

Dare: *you're as observant as a brick wall*

Ginny: *shut up. Go back to where you said he likes me and tell me more…*

Dare had made a shocking discovery, and she wasn't quite sure what to do with it.

During the wonderful chaos that was time with the invading horde of Colemans, she'd slowly come to a few conclusions.

She liked these people. Jesse had returned to being the stand-up guy she'd known in Heart Falls. Quick to laugh or make a joke except when —

Well, Dare wasn't blind. It was clear the only time he

morphed back into awkwardness or being inconsiderate was when Vicki was there. He'd drift around the room, talking with his parents, joking with his brothers, all comfortable and steady until he turned and came face to face with her.

It was also clear that while Vicki wasn't one hundred percent comfortable with him, her unease was a whole different type. More like secondhand discomfort. She felt awkward because of the way he acted.

Any fool could see that Vicki and Joel were wildly, totally and completely in love. There was no faking their level of connection. The little glances, the touches. They probably weren't even aware of them most of the time, until they were. Joel pressed a hand over Vicki's hip, and she looked up and offered a smile that made Joel's eyes flash — Dare had to look away, it was too private a moment to intrude upon.

Which is why she found herself pondering the things that she knew, and dropping them into a logical order.

A) Jesse had left his family suddenly last February

B) he got the black eye from Rafe regarding some issue with "a woman"

and C) the only woman Jesse was mixed up and confused around was Vicki.

The logical conclusion was he had left to avoid being around her.

Only Dare also knew that Jesse wasn't faking it when it came to enjoying the time he spent with *her*. The sweet kisses and caring gestures were real. She had no illusions that he was in love, but he did care for her and Buckaroo.

Ergo…

Jesse had been in love with Vicki when he left last winter.

Maybe she was taking a bit of a leap, but it made sense, and it put her on a strange teeter-totter. After Jesse had admitted that he'd taken off without a word, she'd understood better Blake's reaction — if one of her brothers had up and left on a whim without warning, when he came back for a visit Caleb would've tied the offender behind a tractor and used them to dig furrows.

But if Jesse had left so he didn't come between his brother and Vicki —

Back to Dare's dilemma. What did she do with this suspicion?

If they were returning to Heart Falls in a day or two, it would be different. But that afternoon she'd got an email from Ginny that had sent her thoughts spiraling.

Hey Dare,

Wanted to talk to you about this when we stopped in, but Caleb never gave us two seconds alone.

It sounds as if Buckaroo and you are going to be fine. I've got all my fingers and toes crossed for one hundred percent positive news soon. That said — have you thought about moving to Rocky?

I know, weird comment, and I'm not coveting your cottage or anything. Thing is, I've got a line on a really great opportunity. Yes, this is the secret I never got to tell you about. There's a CSA association that does worldwide apprenticeships. One year of travelling to organic community gardens in France, Germany — heck there's one in Thailand and a couple in South America. I didn't say anything when I applied because I figured it was a long shot, but I got word the other day that I've made the short list. I am so freaking excited.

Only trouble is, Caleb needs someone around to help with the girls. He's gotten pretty used to having you and me, but it's time for him to get a full-time nanny. I thought maybe if he realizes you won't be back permanently that might light a fire under his ass and he'll stop defaulting to us. I haven't told him yet about me going away because I wanted to tell you first.

You can work anywhere — you've said that a million times. You said Jesse's got work with the Colemans again. Just wanted to put the thought out there. I'll support you whatever you decide.

I should know within the next couple weeks if I got one of the positions. If I do, I'm on the road as of September 1. And...I've already decided if I don't get the position I'm going to travel anyway. Which means whether you're here or you're there, I'm going to miss you like hell, but it's time for me to do the next thing.

This is all probably a bit of a shock, and I'm sorry. I hope you know I love you with everything in me, and I don't want you to feel as if I've abandoned you. But you've got someone who cares about you. You've got a baby on the way. Between Jesse and Buckaroo, our world is going to change shortly, anyway.

I don't know, maybe this is me taking my step out into the big world in the hopes that I can find someone to be with and raise a family with. And yes, have a great big adventure in the meantime.

Still love me?

Ginny

The world was changing. Dare was excited for Ginny to have a neat opportunity, but should she stay in Rocky? It wasn't something she could decide in an instant, not with the flow of humanity through her hospital room.

Jesse stopped beside the bed, stretching an arm across the mattress to put himself directly in front of her. "That's a pretty neat trick. You look too damn serene for the level of chaos in here."

She examined his face, trying to read him. "The ability to daydream anywhere is both a gift and a curse."

He brushed his knuckles over her cheek then stepped back, barely covering a yawn.

"It's nearly eight. Why don't you head out with the rest of your family?" Dare suggested. "I'll probably hit the sack early. You can catch a couple of hours' sleep before you go back to work."

He nodded. "I might do that."

She glanced over and saw Marion examining them, face folded into a frown before she marched over to Blake and spoke firmly.

Jesse chuckled, and she turned her attention back to him. "What?"

"Sometimes your face is very expressive. Yes, my mother scares the living daylights out of me as well."

"She can be very intense," Dare agreed with a whisper. "I like her, don't get me wrong, but I wouldn't like to get on her bad side."

"You're carrying one of her grandbabies. You could commit murder and she'd go to bat for you."

Dare offered him an evil grin. "Good to know. Now, make sure you don't do anything that makes me want to murder you."

He snorted. "Too late. I seem to have that effect on just about everyone eventually."

Across the room what was a low conversation grew in volume, and Jesse and Dare's attention fell on Marion who had pulled Mike into the argument.

"But it's not right," Marion insisted. "Mike, you tell him."

Mr. Coleman shifted his feet, but he looked serious as he shook his head. "This isn't up to me, Marion. I gave control of the schedule to Blake, and I stand by his decision. I trust him, and you need to do the same."

"But Jesse is a part of this family too." Her volume rose again, indignation in her tone.

"*Jesus Christ*," Jesse muttered under his breath, squeezing Dare's hand before giving her a quick kiss on the cheek. "I need to do some damage control. I'll see you in the morning?"

"I'll be here."

"I never thought I'd see the day when one of my sons would — "

"Is there a problem?" Jesse interrupted as he slid into position next to his mother.

Marion put an arm around him. "I just heard that Blake has you working all sorts of terrible shifts. He can't do that. I want him to treat you better."

"Ma, it's fine. Blake has been more than generous in giving me some work while Dare and I have been stopped here in Rocky."

"He doesn't have to be generous. You're his *brother*," she protested.

"And he's in charge of making smart business decisions, and I stand by him completely," Jesse offered, a little more sharply than before. "You know damn well I haven't been an angel, but this isn't Blake punishing me. I'm thankful for what he's done, and I don't want any more of this in here. You want to complain, you can give me hell for being stupid later, but this conversation is over. I don't want Dare upset. It's time to go."

Marion whirled, hand rising to her mouth, worry in her eyes. "Oh my word, I'm sorry, Dare. I didn't mean to worry you."

Dare wanted to kick Jesse's butt for giving his mom hell, but at the same time, he was right. Marion had gone too far. "It's fine. I'm great, and honestly, you've all been wonderful. I know Jesse's been pleased he could help out."

"But now it's time to call it a night," Jesse said bluntly. "Come on, Ma. I'll walk you and Dad to the truck."

Marion insisted on stopping by the bed and offering another apology before they left, Jesse watching over her shoulder to ensure Dare was okay.

Jaxi lingered, motioning for Blake to go ahead. "I'll be down in a few minutes."

Blake nodded, then examined Dare's face before speaking in his deep, rich voice, so much like Jesse's and yet enough different to have his own unique timbre. A little slower, a little more measured. "You're a strong one. I think you've been good for Jesse."

"He's been pretty good for me too," she admitted with complete honesty.

Blake dipped his chin then headed out, leaving them alone in the room. Well, alone except for the baby in Jaxi's arms who was snuggled against her chest, his body moving with every breath.

"That was a little bit awkward," Jaxi said.

Dare shrugged. "She's a mama bear, right? If she thought somebody had done Blake wrong, she'd do the same for him. But to be clear, I don't think Blake did anything wrong."

Not anymore. Strange how quickly her opinion had changed.

"Yeah, Marion is like that. And family is like that. I wanted you to know that even when we disagree, or things go sideways, we *are* family. It felt like for a while Jesse forgot that, but I hope he's remembering. We're family, and we care about each other through thick or thin."

Something went *pop* inside Dare's heart. As if a seal had broken and now there was no way to hold back the emotions slipping out.

No matter what, Dare decided, she was keeping the Colemans. Whatever she and Jesse were was still to be decided, but the Colemans? They were people she wanted to be with. They were people she wanted Buckaroo to grow up around.

"Dare, I hope tomorrow we get news that you're all clear to get out of here. I was wondering what you're planning."

That made two of them. Dare offered a smile. "We were supposed to head home on Tuesday."

Jaxi settled into the chair beside the bed, adjusting the baby so he lay with his little face turned to the side. "You haven't had a chance to look around much," she started, before rolling her eyes and making a face. "Jeez, what's wrong with me? I never beat around the bush like this. I must be suffering from wishy-washy pregnancy hormones."

"Oh goody," Dare said. "I have more things to look forward to?"

A small laugh escaped the woman. "You have so many things to look forward to, wishy-washy hormones are at the bottom of your list. Listen, what I want to say is, straight up, Blake and I and the rest of the family would be thrilled if you guys decided you wanted to move to Rocky Mountain House."

Wow, this was moving forward at lightning speed.

ROCKY MOUNTAIN HOME

"Like next year? Or after Buckaroo arrives?"

"Next week? Heck, we can send the crew down and bring up your stuff, and you could be moved in — " Jaxi made a face. "Okay, that part will take a little longer until we can juggle you into a house, but yes, as soon as possible. I mean, whenever it works for you guys."

It was an incredible offer. If she hadn't had Ginny's letter that afternoon to push her brain in this direction, Dare would've been floored. As it was, she wasn't as shocked as she might otherwise have been.

Considering all sorts of *other* issues, the proposition wasn't something she was going to give any kind of answer to until she and Jesse had a long talk.

"That is an amazing offer, and I'm glad you feel comfortable welcoming me into your family. Thank you."

Jaxi gave her a considered look. "We love him. You know that, right?"

Dare nodded. That was the strange thing. She had zero doubts how the Colemans felt. She just didn't know what was best for Jesse's heart and soul.

"Is that enough reason to move here?"

Jaxi's eyes widened in shock. "*What* — ? Of course it is."

"It's a good enough reason to visit, and keep in touch, but we don't have to live in the same place to be family." Dare fidgeted with a quilt square that had been left on the tray beside the bed. She smoothed it under her fingertips, thinking hard. "Isn't the biggest thing we want is for everyone to be happy? If that's here — "

"It is," Jaxi insisted.

The woman was so full of enthusiasm she might overwhelm others, but Dare had years of experience dealing with the hyper energy that was her best friend

311

Ginny. She responded firmly. "Maybe you're right, but I don't think we get to decide that for others."

Jaxi settled back into the chair, an expression of sheepishness spreading. "I was pushing."

"You were," Dare agreed, "but I know it's *because* you love him, and your in-laws, and the rest of the bunch. But this has to be up to Jesse."

"And you." Jaxi raised a brow. "Hey, if you're going to rightly give me hell for trying to push my agenda, don't let anyone push you around either, not even my rather tenacious brother-in-law. You deserve to be happy too. In a relationship there are times you have to compromise, not cave."

"Bend, not break?" Dare smiled now. "You really care about the whole family."

"I really do."

"Does that mean what you're doing with your life is what you really want?" The question came out more judgmental than she'd expected.

Jaxi's lips twisted. "You mean the fact we're the same age and I'm a mom five times over?"

Justin's arms flailed for a second before he curled up tight again. Dare couldn't look away. "I'm not saying it's wrong, I was just wondering if it's really what you signed up for."

Jaxi laughed, and pure delight filled the room like thousands of butterflies taking flight.

"Getting to be with the man I love more than I love my next breath? Getting to see him play shining knight to our children as he gives them rides and shows them what hands-on love looks like every day? Did I sign up to be surrounded by a family who'd lay down their lives for me? People who guard and love my little ones now, and would in the future if anything ever happened and I couldn't be there for them?"

Jaxi rose to her feet, adjusting Justin so she could come to the bedside and curl her hand around Dare's fingers. Jaxi leaned in until their heads nearly touched, and the truth shone in her eyes as she spoke firmly. "I have no idea why I've been so blessed, but I wouldn't change a thing about my life. It's perfect for me. It's my dream come true."

It felt as if the bed was surrounded by tangible joy. Dare nodded again. "I'm glad to know that."

Jaxi squeezed her hand then backed up half a step before her smile changed. "Now you need to figure out what would make *your* life perfect. So we can make it happen."

What would make Dare's life perfect? It was too big of an idea to wrap her brain around yet. But at least she knew where to start.

A talk with Jesse.

Jesse's mom had been surprisingly quiet during the trip to the parking lot. She gave him a fierce hug though before he helped her into the passenger side of his dad's truck.

He closed the door and turned to go bury his frustrations in a night's hard labour when his dad stepped in front of him. Jesse expected some kind of comment, but all Mike did was offer a slow nod of approval before walking away.

It was quiet in the barns. Jesse moved through his

tasks meticulously, falling into a routine that was familiar and comforting. He debated giving Blake a call to assure his brother of his full agreement, but he figured the point had been made, and if his brother wanted to see him, Blake knew where he was.

By the time morning rolled around Jesse was back to a mostly Zen-like state. Today was when they'd find out if it was safe for Dare to leave the hospital, and at that point they could make some decisions.

He used the bunkhouse showers so he wouldn't disturb Joel and Vicki. He'd put spare clothes in the truck so it meant he was at the hospital right smack on time to join Dare for breakfast.

He pulled out a second Egg McMuffin from the bag and made a second attempt at bribery. "Are you sure I can't convince you to trade?"

Dare paused in the middle of another one of those damn sex noises she insisted on making while eating. "Nothing doing, buster. You keep your grubby paws off my oatmeal."

Then she upended the small side serving of raisins over the surface and stirred them in quickly.

Jesse groaned. "Well, forget it now. You've gone and contaminated it."

She licked her spoon, and his entire body tightened in response.

Tamara poked her head in the door. "I have news."

Dare stiffened, and Jesse dropped his breakfast back on the tray so he could grab her fingers.

"Relax," Tamara said, walking into the room. "This isn't any big *shiny* news yet. That's got to come from the doctor, and he should be here by about ten o'clock. By that time the lab in Calgary will have reported in, and

I ran this morning's tests down to the lab myself. So if everything is good, you could be breaking out of here sometime after lunch."

Which was great, awesome and a complete relief...*if* everything was good.

Strangely Dare didn't look as excited as he thought she would. "Thanks for that, Tamara."

His cousin gave a quick wave and left the room at her usual rapid pace.

He let out a long slow breath. "Okay. Ten o'clock it is."

"No one's planning on stopping in this morning, are they?" Dare asked.

He shook his head. "It's Monday, and since I worked all night I told Blake I was going to sit with you. I figured the doctor would be in. Depending on what happens, we'll take it from there."

She swooped her spoon through her oatmeal in distracted circles. "If I do have to stay in the hospital for longer, I don't need nonstop visitors. I don't mean that in a negative way, because your family has been awesome."

"I get it, and I agree. But let's wait to see what the doctor says."

"Agreed."

She finished her breakfast quietly. Jesse tried to distract her with descriptions of the time he'd spent the previous night taking care of the family's horses. Like old friends, the character of each animal was tied up in his mind with different adventures, and they finished the meal peacefully.

But when the dishes were cleaned up, she patted the mattress beside her hip. "Come here. We need to talk about something."

He pushed aside the tray and hopped up. "You're

not upset about last night, are you? Honest, things are better than I expected with Blake. Mom was out of line."

"I wasn't upset at the time," she insisted. "I understand why she said something, but you're right, you screwed up. I would think less of Blake if he didn't make you toe the line for a while."

A soft snort escaped before he could stop it. "Oh yeah, I screwed up royally. It's what I do."

His comment didn't go over well. She leaned in so she could glare into his face. "Don't be a jackass and put yourself down like that. I think you've done a lot of good things just during the time I've known you."

Somehow she always managed to make him feel better about himself. "Okay, I can *sort* of agree with you. You're a good thing, and I've done you."

Dare didn't roll her eyes, but he could tell she was tempted. Then she took a deep breath and shoved him off the cliff.

"I'm going to go on the premise that everything is fine and I'll be set loose today. Which means we pretty much get to go forward and do the next thing. I've been giving it a lot of thought, and I wanted to know what you think of us moving to Rocky Mountain House."

Everything inside him froze. "When? Next year? Or after Buckaroo arrives?"

For some strange reason that made her laugh.

"Maybe sooner than that." He sat back a little and she hurried on. "I'm not even saying for sure this is what I want to do, but I'm putting it forward as an idea. I don't *need* to be in Heart Falls, and there might be good reasons for me to not be there."

Okay, this was a conversation he had not expected to have right now. He fought to keep his emotions from showing, but it was probably a lost cause considering the *hell yes* and the *oh my God, no* battling inside him. He wasn't sure what his face looked like.

Then his confident, always-together woman began rambling.

"Dr. Martins is leaving. So it's not as if I even get to have her around to deliver Buckaroo. There's no hospital in Heart Falls, just the clinic, which means I have to go to Black Diamond when it's time. I like Dr. Kincaid, and obviously Jaxi and Blake like him, *and* your multitude of cousins. You said you could walk to the maternity ward with your eyes closed — I hope you don't have to, but that's kind of reassuring, all things considered."

Now her reasoning made more sense, even though he was still confused. "So…you want to live here *until* Buckaroo is born?"

She was fidgeting with the edge of the blanket now. "I know Caleb offered you a job, and you would do awesome working at Silver Stone, and if that's what you want then that's what we should do, but…" Dare met his gaze again. "If you can work here with your family again, it seems like that's what you should be doing. Not starting all over somewhere else. Not unless it's what you absolutely need."

"I don't know that either job is better than the other. If we move here that means you'd be leaving your family. What about Ginny? What about the girls?"

Dare wrinkled her nose. "Okay, this is Ginny's secret not mine, but she's not planning on being around after September. Yes, I'll miss the girls, but I also don't want to be their mom. I'm afraid right now Caleb might take advantage of the fact that I would be home with the baby."

"Oh, like hell would he take advantage of you. It's one thing to help with the rug rats at times, it's another for him to *expect* it of you." There. Something he actually had a solid opinion on. Maybe he hadn't lost his mind completely.

She shook her head. "I don't think Caleb does it to take advantage of us. He's a really good daddy, actually, but he is kind of oblivious to how much we do to help him out. You're right, if we go back, I'll have a talk with him. It's another thing that makes coming here work, though. But if the idea is too hard to consider right now, I understand completely, and I'm just as happy to go back to Heart Falls. We'll figure out the stuff with Buckaroo."

Confusion returned. "You're not making any sense. Which is it, Dare? Do you want to move to Rocky, or do you want to go back to Heart Falls?"

She took a deep breath and let it out slowly before looking him in the eye again. "I *think* I would like to move to Rocky, but if that is too difficult for you, I have no objections to making Heart Falls work."

Better, but it was still not quite there. "Why in the hell do you think it would be so hard for me to move to Rocky? I told you everything was looking great with Blake and the family."

She broke eye contact. "I know why you left."

Chapter Twenty-Two

Jesse's stomach slid from somewhere in his belly all the way to the main floor. "What did you say?"

She folded her arms in front of her body, fingers rubbing softly on her upper arms. "Are you still in love with Vicki? Because if it's a problem, then that's our answer right there — "

Jesus fuck. "I'm not in love with Vicki. Who the hell told you that?"

It was Dare's turn to look as confused as he felt. "No one told me, but every time you're around her it's as if…" Her eyes widened. "Oh my God, do you not *know* you're in love with her? I mean, I hear that's possible, to not know — "

"Stop it," Jesse ordered. "I'm not in love with Vicki, and I never have been."

Dare tilted her head. "So…she has nothing to do with why you left?"

There was the kicker.

He knew his mouth was opening and closing, but no sound was coming out, and sure enough, Dare's jaw dropped open in shock as well.

Okay, *this* was the last conversation he'd wanted to have today, tomorrow or any fucking day. "She's part of the reason why I left, but it has nothing to do with me being in love with her, and goddamn, never say that again. Joel would jerk my intestines out through my nose."

Which was probably a fair description of reality, and something he should've thought of years ago *before* he'd acted like a stupid jackass.

Dare shook her head. "Okay, I'm not smart enough to make heads or tails of this unless you just pony up and tell me."

Jesse shot to his feet and paced to the window, staring into the beautiful blue sky as he wondered at the irony. It was a perfect day and his world had to fall apart. "You know that moment when you want to kill me? It's here."

"You're not telling me anything," she pointed out.

He really didn't want to do this, but he had to say something. "Because it's history, and it's stupid."

"Try starting at the beginning," she suggested.

The beginning. Fine. That he could do.

"I didn't like it much when Joel started seeing Vicki. She had a bad reputation back then, although to be honest, Joel and I weren't much better. It had only been a few months earlier that we stopped sharing girls. Joel didn't want to anymore, but — " He broke off and dragged his gaze to meet hers. "God, I don't want to tell you this."

"Why?"

The honest truth spilled from his lips. "I don't want you to hate me. I can't stand to think of you kicking me out of your life." The truth seared into his belly. When had Dare become this important? Although, it made sense. Buckaroo meant they had a connection that would tie them together for a long time. "I don't want to tell you that I did something terrible."

Her face had gone white, and she looked scared to death. "How long ago?"

"A couple of years."

"Would you do it again? Right now?"

"My God, of course not."

The tension in her shoulders relaxed and she sucked in a breath of air. "Okay. Is it terrible, or just moderately awful?"

What kind of question was that? "How the hell do I know? Bad enough I was willing to leave my family."

The expression in her eyes softened again, and she spoke in a soothing voice that stroked him even across the distance of the room. "I can't guarantee that I won't be shocked, but I can say that I won't hate you, or want to kill you. Jesse, we all make mistakes and I can tell from how you've been acting you honestly wish you'd never done whatever it is you did."

Her face — she was as nervous as he was, and that gave him the courage to go on.

"I'll start at the end. Nothing happened. Nothing bad."

Her lips twisted. "I will come over there and put you in a sleeper hold if you don't start *talking*."

Jesse paced to the side of the bed, dropping into the chair hard enough that he groaned. "Turned out, Vicki's nothing like her family, but at the time, none of us knew that. Or maybe Joel did, but when they started hanging out together, I just about flipped. I was sure she was using him to get herself out of a bad situation."

"So you were worried about Joel. Did you warn him off?"

"Yeah." Jesse had thought over those days so often it was if he was watching reruns of his most haunting dreams. "He told me she was fine, and to trust him. But

I didn't. I was so sure she was faking being good that I thought I would just hand her a chance to be bad on a silver platter."

Dare had curled her legs up and wrapped her arms around them, and now her fingers tightened until they turned white. "Oh, *Jesse*."

"It was stupid, and too far, but I was sure she was playing Joel. I picked a night I knew he'd be late, and I went to the place they were sharing."

"And she turned you down."

If he could walk out of the room right that moment, he would have. Hell, he'd run, but that would mean giving up on everything that he'd started to care about deeply.

"This is killing me, Dare," he admitted.

"Me too. Can you just tell me? Because my imagination is working overtime, and I'm far too creative. I *know* you, Jesse. I know you didn't do anything wrong to Vicki that night, but you're scaring me."

She was right. He had to get the words out quick, like pulling off a Band-Aid.

"She didn't get a chance to turn down my proposal because she was in bed already, sound sleep. I had the brilliant idea to crawl in with her."

"Oh, damn."

He ignored Dare's whisper and rushed on. "I thought the good-girl bullshit Vicki was pulling would fall away, and when Joel got home he could decide what to do about her lying ass. He wouldn't have been happy, but I figured after he beat the crap out of me, we'd eventually get over it."

"I think Joel would have killed you, but go on."

She was probably right.

"Instead, I crawled in, and hell on earth happened."

He took a deep breath then rushed forward. "I didn't touch her, I swear I didn't, but then she rolled over and pressed her face to my chest. She even fucking said my name. *Jesse*. Straight up said it, and I thought she was picking door number one."

He couldn't meet Dare's eyes. He stared at the clock on the wall beside the door to the hospital hallway and forced the words to come. "But then she started crying. Soft at first and then these body-shaking sobs. The whole time she's apologizing to Joel for coming between us. Saying how she'll go away, and things can go back to how they were before. How she hates that *Jesse* is miserable. That she loves Joel so much, but she wasn't worth tearing his family apart."

A soft rush of air escaped Dare from the bed, but she didn't speak.

Jesse looked at her face, searching for a clue of what she was feeling, but it was unreadable. "It broke me, Dare. All thoughts of… Hell, I don't know. Whatever childish ideas I arrived with vanished. I'd been so fucking jealous, and without even trying, that girl smacked me hard enough to beat some sense into my stupid brain."

Dare sat in silence for long enough Jesse's heart had time to crawl up into his throat. Her face went through a multitude of expressions until she nodded slowly then spoke quietly. "Vicki and Joel don't know, do they?"

He shook his head. "I don't think so. After she went off like that all I wanted to do was escape. I patted her on the back and whispered some nonsense to calm her down. The whole time it felt like boiling oil was dripping on my soul. She finally fell asleep, her fingers clutching my shirt." A shirt that was soaking wet from her tears. The memory of that night refused to fade. "I got the hell out of there before Joel came home, and I swore I'd change things."

"But things still aren't right, are they?"

"No. Because every time I planned to make a move to fix things, I'd take one look at Vicki and guilt would gut me. She was so ready to give up her own happiness for Joel, for *me*, and I was so fucking selfish — "

"You've spent two years going out of your mind every time you saw her."

Jesse shrugged. "I suppose. Last February I decided I couldn't take it anymore, and there was no use in even trying. That's when I left."

For the next sixty seconds Dare examined him, her gaze drifting over his face. It didn't feel as if she was judging him though, but as if she was truly trying to find the next step to take.

That's what came out when she spoke. "I'll ask the question again, since this whole conversation started when I brought up the idea of moving to Rocky. What do you want to do? Do you not want to come back? Because we don't have to. Not if it's going to hurt you to be around your family."

This was too incredulous to believe. They were calmly discussing what he'd done. She was talking to him. She hadn't thrown him out, she wasn't looking at him with disgust.

He couldn't speak above a whisper, too raw inside. "How can you do this? How can you take in what I told you and look at me without being sick?"

Dare actually rolled her eyes. "Jesse Coleman, put the drama queen away. I'm not an idiot, and I'm pretty sure you're not one either. Or at least not *most* of the time. You did a shitty thing, and you shouldn't have done it, but it's in the past. *Years* in the past, and you're still kicking yourself daily. It's time to be done and move on."

"But — "

She smacked a hand onto the mattress angrily before ordering him onto the bed next to her. Then she caught his fingers in hers and squeezed them tightly. "You're wrong about one thing. You said nothing happened, but something did. *You* got changed by what happened. You learned something about Vicki and Joel that should have made you happy for them. What happened was you chose to focus on what you did wrong, instead of what they had that's right. Move *on*, Jesse. It's time to move on."

Rafe had made some comment to that same effect, but it seemed impossible to believe. "Maybe I need to go talk to Joel."

She sat up straight and fire came into her eyes. She dropped his fingers and grabbed hold of his chin so she could shake his head firmly. "No. That's the one thing you can't do."

"But shouldn't I?"

"Why? Will it make him feel better? Or will it hurt him even more? A confession that hurts other people isn't you asking for forgiveness, it's you being more interested in yourself and what you need. That's not a confession, that's masturbation." She slapped his cheek lightly then let her hands fall back in her lap.

"Jeez, Dare."

"I mean it," she said sternly. "Don't do that. Don't be that guy."

"What if he finds out? Wouldn't it be even worse to find out from someone other than me?"

"Who else knows? I mean, I swear I'll never tell."

Jesse made a face. "Rafe knows."

"Right." Understanding dawned in her eyes. "That's why he gave you the black eye — I like him, by the way."

A tiny sliver of amusement managed to push past Jesse's frustration. "Of course you do. You should like all my cousins and brothers then. I'm pretty sure every one of them has given me a black eye at some point in my life."

Dare sighed in exasperation. "Here's a clue, Jesse. That's not something to boast about."

"Sorry."

Her lips twitched. "Regarding Rafe, he's the only one you need to go talk to. Tell him how much it means to keep this quiet and let it go. Don't let him dictate what comes next." She lifted her fingers to stroke over his cheek and around his ear, caressing softly. "It's up to you, but if I were Vicki, and what you've said she cared about? What I'd want most was for you and Joel to be tight again. I'd feel terrible if it seemed as if I was the one keeping you apart. You've got to put this behind you. Not only for your sake, but for theirs."

It was an awful lot to take in. Jesse sat quietly, running through every single one of her comments, and the hard truths that she'd smacked him with. When she leaned forward and curled her arms around his waist, nestling their bodies together, a shot of pure adrenaline raced through him.

She wasn't rejecting him. She totally should have, but she wasn't, and he wasn't going to be a fool and give that up.

"Still going to feel guilty," he confessed.

"If you can feel guilty without acting like an ass then you go right ahead. Consider it your penance." She spoke against his shoulder, her head twisted to the side. "I hope someday you'll forgive yourself. Until then, keep your damn mouth shut."

She fell quiet again, and the silence in the room deepened. Jesse concentrated on taking slow, controlled breaths. Her body moved gently against his, and it was like a warm blanket had been wrapped around them to form a cocoon.

He didn't want to leave. Didn't want to break the spell that she'd seemed to cast over him. He held her in his arms, fingers drifting up to stroke through her long hair. There was still so much to deal with, but right then, for the first time in a long time, that knot of pain he'd been carrying eased the slightest bit.

My God, her brain was near to exploding. Jesse had been dealing with the pain of this whole mess for years?

In her mind he'd already been suitably punished.

While it would take some time for the dust to settle, her opinion of Jesse hadn't gone down. The fact he'd struggled with this, and known he made a mistake made it possible for her to want the best for him.

But Vicki? Had gone way up in Dare's esteem. It was impossible not to admire that even in her unconscious state the woman had been willing to sacrifice her own happiness.

Dare didn't think she could be that giving.

Jesse's confession explained so many things on another entire level. She wasn't going to hold this over

Jesse's head, but it was clear he had a lot of bridges to rebuild with his family. Admiration grew higher for the Colemans as a whole. She bet Jesse had been an absolute bear to deal with over the past years, but here they were. Still willing to accept him back, and accept her into their midst.

Jaxi's comment about being family through thick and thin made much more sense now.

Dare stroked her fingers along the waistband of Jesse's jeans, curling against him tighter. She wanted to bring the conversation back to what they were going to do, but figured maybe it was time she let him take a breather.

Besides, until the doctor gave her official word, it wasn't as if they could make any decisions.

Jesse adjusted position and suddenly she found herself being lifted into his lap, one arm supporting her back as his other hand tucked under her chin and lifted her lips to his. He kissed her slowly. A tender connection as if he was afraid she was breakable.

No — as if he was afraid that *they* were breakable, and he had to be cautious.

Dare welcomed his caress. Turned it around and sent back as much sweet longing as she could into her touch. She lifted a hand to his face, stroking her palm past the rough growth on his chin as he deepened the connection. Taking control and reigniting the wick of desire inside her.

Of course, that's when someone knocked on the door.

They broke apart, but Jesse gave her cheek one final brush with his knuckles. "We're not done," he warned her in a soft whisper.

"Mr. Coleman, if you would be so kind as to find a

different place to sit," Dr. Kincaid offered sternly as he marched forward, but there was amusement in his voice.

Dare wiggled back on the mattress as Jesse hopped off the bed and straightened himself. The doctor stepped closer, chart in hands as he came to stand near the foot of the bed. He looked extremely happy, and everything else they'd been talking about that had been distracting her from her main fears vanished.

Yes, her hands were on top of her belly again. "I didn't expect you until later today," Dare said.

He waggled the clipboard in the air. "I happened to be in early, and Calgary got back to us with results, so I figured I would let you know the good news as soon as possible. Test results — I'll give you the specifics later, but to put it plainly, everything we wanted to come back negative, did. There are no ongoing concerns for the baby, or for you."

"*Thank God.*"

Jesse caught her hand in his and squeezed. "Okay. That's...good. *Very* good."

Dr. Kincaid smiled. "It *is* good. I'm going to send a note to your doctor in Heart Falls. She'll want to keep an eye on a couple things going forward, especially your blood pressure."

"What if we ended up staying in the area?" Jesse asked.

Wow. Dare hadn't expected that.

He wasn't looking at her, instead focused on the doctor. "We're not sure what we're doing yet, but if we move into the area, can you take Dare as a full-time patient?"

Dr. Kincaid nodded immediately. "Of course. Not only do we already have a relationship because of this past weekend, I'm certainly not going to turn down the opportunity to deliver a Coleman baby."

Dare listened to the rest of the doctor's comments in a bit of a daze, pulling out her calendar to add his office number so she could set up an appointment in a month's time.

Dr. Kincaid left a final prescription for a couple tests. As the door closed after him, she and Jesse stared at each other.

It was fast. Really fast. "Are we staying?" she asked.

Jesse dipped his head slowly. "Why not? We might have just come for a visit, but your point about having a good doctor makes this into a no-brainer for me. Rocky is the best place for you to have Buckaroo. I'm not messing with that, if you're okay staying."

Yes. Of course. Dare pulled her brain back into line. This *was* about Buckaroo. It always had been.

"So, what comes next?" she asked.

Jesse pointed to the paper Dr. Kincaid had left. "I'll grab Tamara or whoever is on the nursing roster this morning and let them help you finish up that final test. While you're busy, I'll take care of the other details."

Still buzzing from surprise and the emotion of the morning, Dare accepted Jesse's quick kiss before he vanished. She moved in a happy daze, getting a few final bits of vital information along the way.

Jesse returned just as she'd finished dressing, packing her things into her bag.

"You ready for this?" he asked.

"Are you?"

He nodded. "I think staying in Rocky for now is a great idea."

That sounded a lot more confident than not even an hour ago. Dare eyed him closely. "You sure? You're not going to have troubles dealing with...anyone?"

He shook his head. "I'm a grownup, and you're right — it's my bullshit, not theirs. Time to keep my mouth shut and move on."

Cautiously optimistic, Dare agreed. "This isn't a commitment on either of our parts to stay for good, right? Just to be clear."

"No, but we'll stay for now. Until you have the baby for sure. We'll take it from there, and see what's best for Buckaroo."

"You can work?"

Jesse offered a thumbs-up. "I got hold of Blake. He said no problem to putting me full-time on the schedule. I called Joel, and we're welcome to stay at the trailer with him and Vicki until the rental is free. And before you ask again, it's not going to be a problem for me. You might have to remind me every now and then to stop being an asshole, but I can do this."

A strange sense of wonder slipped over Dare. "Okay. That sounds great."

A familiar sound, one she hadn't heard very much that day slipped from him. A soft chuckle, full of mischief and teasing. "I'm a little bit worried about putting you with Vicki, the way the two of you get along like a house on fire."

"It's good to have backup to counteract you and your brothers. As in, there's an awful lot of testosterone around when the Six Pack clan gathers," Dare pointed out.

He stepped toward her, slipping his arms around her. "I hope you don't mind all of the testosterone."

She slid her arms up his chest until she could link her fingers behind his neck. "By the way, I got to chat with Dr. Kincaid one more time while you were gone."

His face folded into a frown. "*Okaaaaay…*"

"Just wanted to double-check that it was okay to enjoy some *testosterone*, if you know what I mean."

A slow, seductive grin teased back. "*Ahh*, you asked the good doctor about sex."

"I did. He said it was fine." There was a whole lot more snickering going on than Dare had expected in response to what she thought was a brilliant bit of research. "What's so funny?"

Jesse pulled her tightly against him. "I wondered why he was smirking when I tracked him down to ask him the same thing."

She dropped her head against Jesse's chest. "Great. So now my doctor knows that we're sex fiends."

A snort escaped him. "He's the doctor to my entire family. I think he's probably aware we've got healthy sex drives."

Dare slapped Jesse's chest lightly, but even as embarrassing as it was, she was glad.

They were doing the next thing, both she and Jesse. Like taking a step into the unknown. Buckaroo rolled, and she caught her breath at the sensation.

It was all pretty unknown, to be truthful. An adventure, Ginny had said.

Oh boy. Ginny...

Chapter Twenty-Three

Blog post: Home Is Where You Hang Your Hat
Great news to report. Buckaroo has been given the all clear along with yours truly, and we've decided to stay in the area. Yes. We're moving.

I know, all my home-loving creature-comfort blog followers are wondering if I've gone around the bend. Maybe a little, but I'm sure that's a side effect of pregnancy.

The funny thing is, as much as I love Silver Stone ranch, it's not so much the specific items on the shelf as the emotions they evoke that make the place home. I was making a list of what I had to have to be happy, and I found myself writing down things like walks beside a creek, the sun on the mountains, watching chickens in the coop after you throw them a handful of feed. A hug that wraps around me like a warm blanket. A crackling fire.

Neat thing, they have all those things here, and more.

Ready for a challenge? Make a list — don't think about it too hard, just write down the first things that come to mind. What makes you happy? What makes you smile? If you'd like, share the top three items on your list. Oh, and if any of them are <u>things</u> I'm not going to judge. It's your happy list.

They talked about the timing of the move on the drive back to Joel and Vicki's trailer.

Jesse laughed. "It won't take much for me to move. I never unpacked at your place."

"I wasn't planning on bringing everything. Not until we have more room," Dare told him. "I don't need too many clothes because my stuff isn't going to fit for much longer, and I've already been offered more loaner maternity stuff than I could wear during a dozen pregnancies."

He nodded. "Just tell me how much time you want and I'll arrange it with Blake. He knows we need to do this, so he won't expect me around regular-like until we're settled."

Dare considered. She didn't have that big of a list she wanted to bring. "Could we go back tomorrow? Between your truck and mine, and the two horse trailers, we can grab everything and return on Wednesday. Morgan is probably missing us like crazy."

Jesse made a face.

"Too soon?"

"Oh, it's not that. I just realized your brothers aren't going to like this much."

She leaned back in the seat and adjusted the seat belt higher over her belly. "Good thing I don't run my life by brother-led committee. They don't have to like it. Besides, it's not as if they can even be mad about losing my help around the place. Other than watching the girls for Caleb, I wasn't going to act as a ranch hand for much longer, anyway."

"You want to grab Baby?"

"Definitely." She reached across the space between them to bump her fist gently into his arm. "Another thing I asked the doctor about. Yes, I can ride for a few more months, and I'll be the safest on her. I know her, and she's not about to act up."

He captured her hand before she could pull it back, linking their fingers together. "That's pretty funny the two things you made sure you asked the doctor about were riding and sex."

"Nearly the same thing," she teased.

"Well, I am hung like a horse."

A laugh burst free. "Here I was expecting you to make some comment about wanting me in cowgirl position."

"That's a given." He lifted her hand to his mouth, nipping at her knuckles before using his tongue to outline the grooves between her fingers. Desire raced up her spine as he sucked her pinky into his mouth.

She shivered. "Don't start something we can't finish."

Jesse sighed heavily. He pressed a kiss to her knuckles before setting her free. "I hate to admit you're right, but I should go and let Blake know our plans. Rain check on this?"

"You know it."

He pulled into the parking space outside the trailer. He made it around to her door before she could hit the ground.

They pushed through the door into the cozy home. Dare put her computer on the kitchen table while Jesse deposited her clothes bag on a chair.

"You need anything?" he asked.

"I'll be fine. I'll give Vicki a call to find out what she's got planned for supper to see if I can get it started."

For a split second he tensed before giving his head a shake. "You've got her number?"

"She gave it to me when we first got here."

VIVIAN AREND

His grin reappeared. "Like I said, you two together are going to be so much trouble."

His tone of voice wasn't quite *normal* normal, but he was trying. She decided moving forward was the best option. "As if you and Joel are innocent babes. Don't worry about me. Go on. I'll see you later."

It was actually a treat to wander through the small space alone. She hadn't lied when she told Jesse she appreciated the company over the weekend. If she'd had too much time by herself she probably would've worked herself into a tizzy worrying about Buckaroo, but now that they were doing the next thing, this moment of quiet was much appreciated.

Quiet, and time to catch up on a few things, including getting in touch with Ginny.

When her call went to voicemail she sent a text.

Dare: *you around?*

Ginny: *delivering boxes. What's up? You okay?*

Dare: *just got sprung from the hospital. Buckaroo and me are 100%*

Ginny's message came a couple of minutes later: *thank God. When are you coming home?*

Well now, there was a loaded question. Dare decided that this wasn't something she wanted to do via text message or even over the phone. Because she bet even though Ginny had supported the idea of Dare going away, she probably wasn't expecting it to happen this soon.

Dare: *I'll see you tomorrow and tell you everything*

Ginny: *rock on. Love you Dare*

Dare: *Love you, Truth*

Dare enjoyed wandering around, examining the

pictures on the shelf. Trying to learn more about Jesse's twin and the woman closest to him by what things they felt were valuable.

There weren't a lot of knickknacks though. A vase on top of the bookshelf held an arrangement of dried flowers, and a collection of all sorts of rocks filled a glass bowl. Other than that there were pictures of Joel and Vicki, a picture of a woman in her midtwenties holding a puppy, and pictures of Jesse's family, including a number of shots with just the twins.

Dare took one down to examine it closer. It must've been from before Vicki had come on the scene because the two of them were shoulder to shoulder, like identical bookends. She could see the connection between them and how much they enjoyed being around each other.

Maybe she did have something in common with Vicki. The woman had been willing to do anything to get the brothers back to this state of laughing connection. While Dare had other reasons as well for wanting to be around the Coleman family, letting Jesse and Joel work past their differences so they could be like this again was just as important.

Their sheer joy and connection spilled out visibly from the picture. The fact that even while he had to have been angry with Jesse for running off, Joel kept the picture up — that meant something.

That meant a whole lot.

Dare made herself a sandwich and wrote up a blog post, careful to schedule it to go off after she and Jesse arrived back in Heart Falls. No use in freaking out her family before it was necessary.

Then she got out her phone and gave Vicki a call.

"I don't know if you heard, but I've already been let

out of the hospital, and I'm hanging out at your place. Did you have plans for supper? Because I can get started on them."

"Give me five minutes and we can talk in person," Vicki said. "Hanging up before someone catches me on the phone while I drive."

It was barely three minutes later when the truck pulled into the yard. Dare met her on the front porch and this time there was no hesitation. She wrapped her arms around Vicki and gave her a heartfelt hug.

When she let go, Vicki was grinning. "I'm so glad everything's good with the baby. Joel told me your plans, and I'm really excited you and Jesse are staying in Rocky."

"Thank you for agreeing to live in crowded quarters for a while."

Vicki waved off the comment. "Honestly, this isn't that crowded. But let's make sure you're as comfortable as possible while you're here. I know you guys are going to move into the rental once Ashley's moms are gone, but right now I doubt they'll leave until late September."

They settled in the living room to talk. "When's Ashley due?"

"Middle of August."

Dare considered. "Wow, is she gonna make it that long?"

A soft laugh escaped Vicki. "She really is all stomach, but she's crazy healthy. She's planning on a homebirth."

Dare groaned. "Good for her. That leaves more drugs for me."

"Right? Although I wonder if it'll be Travis and Cassidy who need to be doped up."

So many things that Dare wanted to ask about, but

some of them seemed borderline rude. Then again, she didn't need to know everything about everyone this instant. She could control her curiosity.

It suddenly struck. "Hey, how come you're home?"

"My schedule is usually all over the place, depending on catering jobs, but I asked for this afternoon off. I wanted to get you settled in."

"I saw you moved some stuff around in the bedroom. That's more than enough space."

Vicki rose to her feet and headed to a cabinet along the wall. "Good. I emptied this out so you can use it as your office."

It looked like a bookcase with open shelves at the top. The bottom two thirds had a corkboard attached to it, and Dare hadn't given it much notice until now.

Vicki unsnapped a couple of hooks then pulled a lever, and suddenly the entire wooden face lowered into a desktop, and the corkboard became a sturdy leg.

"Oh, that's cool." Dare joined the other woman. Built in along the edge of the cabinet was a plugin and USB port.

"Daniel made it. Brother number three," Vicki reminded Dare. "It's been handy to tuck things out of sight, but there's enough room you can store stuff if you want. If you have a good computer chair, there's room in the corner for when you're not using it."

Perfect. "I'll bring one back with me."

They got to talking about other things then, but the whole time Dare kept being brought back to one thought. Why was this so comfortable? Why did she feel as if she'd stepped into a familiar place?

When the topic finally looped back to dinner, Vicki had a suggestion. "I thought we could go over to Blake and Jaxi's and make a few big batches of food. Even Jaxi won't say no to a helping hand with a newborn in the house. You okay with that idea? We can give Joel and Jesse a call, and they can join us over there when they're done for the day."

It seemed they were jumping in with both feet. "I'm game if you are. I'm an awesome chef's assistant."

Vicki smiled tentatively. "More importantly, you're going to be an awesome friend."

———⟨∽⟩———

While he hadn't expected to end up working side by side with Joel so quickly, it was a happy surprise when Jesse led his borrowed horse out of the barn to discover his twin waiting for him.

Joel held his horse steady as he eyed Jesse. "Get a move on. Or do you need me to lengthen your stirrups for you?"

Jesse glanced back at the saddle and realized he hadn't checked the equipment as thoroughly as he should've. He adjusted the length quickly on both sides of the saddle so he wouldn't end up with his knees around his ears as he rode. "Who was the last one to use this saddle? They must be about three feet tall."

Joel laughed. "You're going to break our nephew's heart. Every time Nathan shows up he checks his height against the markers on the main support beam, but he hasn't started his growth spurt yet. Last time he looked, Robbie had passed him."

Jesse finished the adjustments and mounted smoothly, guiding the horse to Joel's side. "That's gotta be hell on his ego, to have his younger brother taller than him."

"I don't know, was it hell on yours when I grew taller than you?" Joel taunted.

Jesse elbowed Joel on his way past before clicking to his horse and heading down the path toward their task. "That must've happened in some alternative universe. Sorry, bro, but as far as I remember you and I sprouted the same time. Damn near to the minute, according to Mom."

"I don't know that we've had all of us in a lineup for a while," Joel mused. "Which one of us is actually the tallest? I don't mean between you and me. Didn't Daniel have about half an inch on the rest of us?"

It was a curious thing to ponder, but Joel was right. Jesse wasn't sure where they'd all settled out.

It wasn't just when it came to their height. "I haven't had a chance to catch up with Daniel yet. How's the workshop doing?"

"Making a living. He tied the shop back into the ranch finances. Said he wanted to give the boys a chance to ranch if that's what they wanted down the road. Who knows. With all of the kids starting to show up, by the time Daniel's ready to retire, there might be some other Colemans who want to work with their hands in a different way."

Jesse glanced over at his twin. "Is that something you're thinking about?"

"Hell, no."

"Hey, I didn't think so, but I thought I should ask." Jesse offered a chastising laugh. "I'm a little out of touch, and I don't like it."

Joel didn't say anything for a minute, and they rode in silence, until they reached the field and found a half-dozen hands working to separate out the calves from their moms, the veterinary truck standing outside the gate.

He offered Jesse a quick grin. "Just remember that I'm always right. There's not much else you need to know."

Jeez. Jesse stuck out his tongue and pretended to gag before focusing on more important things. "I know I can out rope you."

"Loser pays for drinks at Traders," Joel snapped back. "You're on."

In the end they decided it was a tie, although Joel argued long and hard that the one calf they both dropped a rope on should have counted as his.

They'd gotten the message from the girls, but still headed home to get washed up before making their way to the original Six Pack homestead.

"If you're willing to drive me to work most days," Joel said, "I'll be able to leave the truck for Vicki."

"We're heading to Heart Falls tomorrow, and when we come back, Dare will have a vehicle too. That means three vehicles between the four of us. We'll figure it out."

Walking in the door at Blake and Jaxi's was like walking into a memory. The house smelled amazing — like all those days when he'd been a teenager and his mom had ruled the roost. Rich barbecue sauce and apple-pie scents mixed in the air. Only instead of a mess of oversized men's boots on the shelves by the door, there were dozens of pink and purple shoes barely the size of his palm. Bright pastel-coloured rubber boots were lined up neatly outside the door, and a multitude of hooks had been added in a second row at little-people height.

Jesse hung up his coat over Dare's then stepped into the warmth of the dining room.

342

Even here things had changed. There was music playing in the attached living room, but it was some upbeat kid's song instead of country music. A high chair had been pulled up to the long pedestal-style table along with a strange clip-on contraption. The highchair wasn't too unusual — his mom had one in the storage room that got hauled out whenever it was needed. As little people moved in on him, Jesse found himself smiling.

He glanced at Blake who was stretched out in a recliner, rocking baby Justin. "Girls smell a lot better than boys," he commented. "But I don't think they make any less mess."

Blake rocked all the way forward until he hit his feet. "I hear it gets worse before it gets better."

"I ordered a boy," Jesse informed his oldest brother.

A soft laugh escaped Blake. "Good thing whoever arrives is exactly who we need."

"Blake. Can we get a hand in here?" Vicki called from the kitchen.

Blake untangled Justin from his arms and held the baby bundle toward Jesse. "Here. I'm being summoned."

It wasn't the first time Jesse had held a baby, but it wasn't high on his *want to do this instant* list. He carefully tucked his hand under the kid's head to support him properly. "I'll just bring him to Jaxi."

Blake was already walking away, but he tossed over his shoulder, "She's in the shower, so you'd better not. Oh, and he needs to be changed. There are diapers in the main bathroom."

Full-out laughter echoed from his right, and Jesse turned to find Joel being far too entertained by Blake's orders. "Laugh it up, but you're coming with me as backup."

343

Joel lost a lot of his delight. "I don't know how to change a diaper."

"Bullshit. You know just as well as me. Besides, you'd better get in some practice before my kid arrives, oh Babysitter Supreme."

"I'm nixing that name. Makes me sound like I'm a dessert at Dairy Queen," Joel complained, but he accompanied Jesse into the bathroom.

The counter ran the length of the room, the sink off-center to the right. In all his years of living in the house, Jesse had never realized what a great baby-changing station it made. He carefully placed Justin on the quilted pad to the left of the sink, then began to unwrap his nephew.

"Find the clean diapers," he ordered Joel.

Joel moved past him and hauled out a wicker basket from an open shelf. "Oh, look, wet wipes."

Jesse couldn't stop it. He snickered so hard he nearly made himself choke. "You sounded way too excited about that."

"Asshole," Joel muttered easily, sliding the plastic container toward him and dropping a miniature diaper beside it.

By now Jesse had managed to undo the first layers of the soft flannel. Justin flailed his arms, his face screwed up tight. His mouth opened, and a sound emerged that would've been suitable in a horror film.

"You need to change him fast," Joel said.

"Brilliant suggestion, Einstein." Jesse undid the diaper, cringing as he used a clean section of the inside to wipe away a little of the damage. "God, how can something the size of a loaf of bread produce this much shit? It's like stinky superglue."

344

Joel tugged out a wet wipe and handed it to him. "Ours is not to question why, ours is just to sniff and die."

It took three wet wipes to get rid of the evidence, and then just as Jesse slipped a clean diaper under Justin's hips, the kid peed.

Jesse and Joel shouted, quickly tamping down their volume when Justin's eyes widened and his protesting cries turned to fear. They were more worried about the stream of pee shooting skyward like an out-of-control fireman's hose, rapidly sweeping toward where they stood. Jesse barely folded up the bottom part of the diaper in time to contain the mess.

"Jesus Christ, nobody told me those things were loaded," Jesse complained, speaking loudly to be heard over Justin's wailing.

Joel started laughing, trying desperately to hold it back as he grabbed another diaper from the bin.

Jesse held it together long enough to wrangle a fresh diaper under his nephew and get it done up with no further mishaps. He stripped the now wet one-piece from his screaming nephew and used a couple wet wipes to wash him down. "Is there another straitjacket for the kid in one of those baskets?"

While his laughter faded to hiccupping gasps, Joel checked all of the baskets, finally handing over a pale-yellow bodysuit thing. "You're doing awesome. I'm taking notes."

"I should make you dress him," Jesse threatened. "But you're obviously nowhere near as skilled as I am. You'd end up giving the kid a complex."

Joel leaned his back on the nearest wall, put his face in his hands and started howling all over again.

Justin howled louder, shrieks echoing off the

bathroom walls.

It was like trying to stuff an octopus into a glove. Jesse moved cautiously, making sure to keep his touch feather-soft, but eventually he had all Justin's body parts in the appropriate arm and leg slots with the buttons done up. He got Joel to find him another flannel blanket, and this part he managed to do properly, thinking back to the times Jaxi and Blake's little girls had taught him how to swaddle their dolls.

He hadn't realized how much easier it was when the dolls didn't fight back.

Thankfully, as he tugged the flannel over his nephew and trapped the little guy's hands and legs snugly in place, Justin's crying faded to sad whimpers that grew steadily quieter until all that was left was a low complaining murmur.

Jesse got Joel to guard the kid so he could scrub his hands quickly at the sink before lifting Justin against his chest. He rocked on the spot, making soothing noises. "It's okay, kid. I promise that nasty Uncle Joel will be way better at helping next time."

"You're such a dweeb," Joel said, stopping to wash his hands as well.

"*I'm* a dweeb? What're you washing your hands for? You didn't do anything," Jesse demanded.

"Proximity contamination."

They made it back into the main room where Joel paused for a moment to answer a question from their niece. Jesse carried on all the way to the kitchen, cradling a now-quiet Justin against his chest.

Blake was helping Vicki with something in the pantry. Dare stood beside a sturdy island countertop, two-year-old PJ helping her cut out biscuits with a metal ring as she used one hand to stabilize him.

She glanced up, and her expression changed as her gaze hit Jesse. Her jaw dropped open before she offered a sexy, hungry hum. "Wow. I think my ovaries just exploded."

"What?" Vicki glanced out of the pantry. She did a double take as Joel walked through the door to stand beside him. "Oh, *my*."

Jesse whispered softly to his brother. "I didn't think making biscuits was that much like foreplay. You have any idea what they're talking about?"

"Not a clue," Joel admitted.

Chapter Twenty-Four

Dare was asleep the instant her head hit the pillow. When she woke, it was to an empty bed because Jesse had already gotten up. Neither a good night's rest or room to stretch out were terrible things, but they didn't put sex back on the table either, and frankly she was itching for Jesse in a bad way.

Last night —

Oh. My. God. If she hadn't already been pregnant, the sight of Jesse holding Justin would've caused her to spontaneously conceive. What was it that Jaxi had said? Colemans made pretty babies?

They made gorgeous, mouthwatering men, as well.

Now they were on the road, headed back to Heart Falls to grab what they needed.

She was confused by how much she was looking forward to seeing her family, yet how much she couldn't wait to return to Rocky. It felt as if she were tethered in the middle of an enormous, invisible game of tug-of-war. Uncertain which side would win.

Instead of worrying about what she couldn't control, she let her gaze drift over the man at her side. It was warm enough he'd left his jacket and overshirt off, and his strong forearms were eye candy she was very willing to enjoy. His hands rested lightly on the wheel — hands she knew could bring her pleasure in all sorts of wicked ways.

She wiggled in her seat.

"You need a pit stop?" Jesse asked instantly.

Oh God, did she ever. But not for the reason he was asking. "I need to put my hands on you," Dare informed him. "And you need to be naked."

The engine roared briefly before he glanced her way with a warning. "*Dare.*"

She blinked.

Jesse's eyes darkened in the second before he focused back on the road. "In this dream world of yours, are you naked as well?"

"Depends. I'm either naked, or wearing teeny panties and a silky bra. Whichever you prefer."

He reached down and adjusted himself, shifting his hips awkwardly. "I didn't know you had such a mean streak in you, Darilyn Hayes."

She laid a hand on his arm, stroking gently as she let out an appreciative hum. "I'm not being mean," she insisted. "*Mean* would be me doing something like putting my hand in your lap and curling my fingers around your cock."

Jesse's grip on the wheel tightened, but he kept his gaze fixed on the road as she put action to her words. "You're asking for trouble."

"We both like this kind of trouble," she reminded him. She pressed her palm against him, rubbing the thick length. "I want you in my mouth. I want to taste you and get you all wet before I climb on top and go for a ride."

Dare had been so intent on what she was doing she hadn't noticed the change in vehicle sounds. He must've hit the turn indicator and the brakes sometime in the last thirty seconds because he was taking a right-hand turn off the highway down a narrow country road that led to nowhere.

"Side trip?" she asked innocently.

"You are so getting fucked," he informed her in a cheerful voice.

He hit the brakes, positioning the truck in the middle of a thick batch of spruce trees. The next second he had her seatbelt undone and she was being hauled across the bench seat into his arms.

One hand dove into her hair, pulling her into position so he could ravish her lips. Hunger and need and fiery lust filled his touch. Poured over her in the way he took control and answered all of her teasing requests.

It wasn't mindless pleasure, it was something *more* because he'd already learned where her hotspots were. Even now he tugged her hair lightly until she let out a groan of pleasure, then he coasted his lips along her jaw to the bottom of her earlobe and sucked.

She shivered, dropping her hand between her legs to press where an aching need teased.

His fingers wrapped around her wrist then he pulled her hand away. "That's my job," he warned.

"Then touch me," she begged.

He pressed his knuckles under her chin until she was staring into his bright blue mesmerizing eyes. "I will. But first, I heard something about your mouth and my cock, and I really *really* like that dream-world idea."

So did she. Dare wiggled off the bench seat to the floor, pulling him to the passenger side, his legs open so she could rest between them. He was already working on the button of his jeans.

She slapped his fingers away. "Mine," she scolded.

A soft chuckle escaped him as he willingly lifted his hands and placed them behind his head, gazing down with an affectionate grin. There was no doubt that he planned to make her very happy, but she was equally sure he wasn't about to let her get off the hook for her tease.

She lowered the zipper carefully, fabric falling to the sides as his erection swelled hard against his briefs. When she pulled that fabric away, his cock sprang free. An instant later she'd placed her mouth over the head.

A curse exploded from Jesse's lips, and she smiled as much as she could with her lips stretched around his girth. Then she licked and sucked, holding him at the base with her fingers wrapped around him to keep him aimed in the right direction.

A soft caress drifted over her head. Jesse was stroking his fingers through her hair. "Gorgeous. You're so fucking gorgeous, Dare. You blow my fucking mind."

She lifted with a *pop*, tilting her head back to offer a cheeky grin. "And here I thought I was blowing your cock."

"Right now, same thing," Jesse admitted before growling, "take off your pants."

Dare pouted. "But I wasn't done."

"Take off your fucking pants and get up here, now," he ordered.

She hid her smile as she wiggled and squirmed to follow his directions. The instant her ass was bare he was hauling her over him, her knees resting on the cushioning on either side of his hips.

Jesse slipped a hand between her legs and stroked expertly. "Hmmm. Did sucking me off get you wet, darlin'?"

"*So* wet," she admitted. "Oh. *Yes*, right there."

He'd placed his thumb over her clit and rubbed. Hard enough that electric sparks shot from her core to… everywhere. Her toes tingled and her hands trembled. She clung to his shoulders as he used his other hand on her hip to pull her forward so he could line up his cock.

No hesitation. She sank slowly onto his length. He watched her the entire time, gaze pinned on her face. Clearly alert for any signs of trouble, which was sweet, but not necessary because all she felt was pleasure. When they were finally fully connected, satisfied moans sounded in stereo.

He tipped his head forward until their foreheads touched. "I missed you," he said.

Dare snickered. "It's only been a few days. Sex fiend."

"Tell me you don't feel the same so I can call bullshit."

There were more important things to do. "Why don't you fuck me instead?"

No further encouragement was needed. He caught hold of her hips with both hands and lifted. Dare levered herself over him, taking stock of every delicious sensation. Dropping over his thick shaft sent heat throughout her body, and pulling up was just as addictive. Over and over until pleasure rippled under her skin as if something momentous was about to happen. Explosions, tsunamis — earth-shattering.

He put his hand back over her clit and pressed, and that was the trigger.

"*Coming.*"

The hand on her hip tightened, but he kept going. Pumping up, rubbing her clit. She squeezed tight around him, the waves making her clutch him tightly as she let her head fall back. A second later he joined her, muscles tight under her hands, hips jammed together. It seemed a long time later they both let out satisfied sighs, coming back to reality. Dare pressed the palms of her hands to his cheeks then leaned in and kissed him deeply. The instant before pulling back, she felt his lips move into a smile.

They were both still grinning by the time they reached Silver Stone ranch.

Jesse whistled, and Morgan came running at full tilt, ears flapping like wings. The dog got a hug and a head scratch from Jesse, then turned to Dare as if to say she'd been missed.

"I'm glad to see you, too, but I bet you had more fun here than you would have in Rocky. You wouldn't have understood what was going on." She knelt to give him a hug, and he sat, tail thumping as he accepted her adoration like it was his due, wide doggy smile in place.

"Joel said he's looking forward to seeing Morgan again," Jesse shared as he helped her to her feet.

"Of course, he is. Morgan's a good boy, ain't cha, pupper?"

Morgan panted, waiting patiently for someone to do something more exciting than just talk.

Dare chuckled. She should have warned herself against falling in love with his dog, but it was too late. "Yes, you get to come with us the next time," she assured Morgan.

Jesse paused on the porch after dropping off the couple of bags they'd borrowed from the Colemans for her to transport her things. "You mind if I go track down Caleb? I don't want to steal your thunder, but I feel as if I should let him know what's going on in terms of work. I don't want to leave him in the lurch, either."

"Makes sense. You know where to find me if you need me." In the distance Ginny was making tracks toward them like a bat out of hell. "I'll be talking my sister off the ledge. And packing."

"Look at you, multitasking goddess and all."

He gave her a brief, intense kiss before taking off toward the barns, whistling as he walked, Morgan at his heels. Obviously happy, which was pretty much what the sensation in her gut said too.

Funny how a good bout of sex could do that to a person.

Ginny was on the steps an instant later, crowding after her into the cottage. "Start talking. I saw that smooch you just gave your baby daddy. I take it his ranking has moved up a notch or two out of the negatives."

Dare headed to her bedroom and pulled open drawers to start packing. "He's out of the hole, yes."

"The Colemans? Are they approved Buckaroo material?"

"Definitely." She turned to Ginny, T-shirt in her hand. "They're not perfect, but they honestly care about each other. They already care about me and Buckaroo, which is kind of mind-boggling."

"I don't see what's mind-boggling about it at all," Ginny said sternly. "You're very care-about-able."

Dare grinned and kept going. "I'm happy to report that I don't have to go on bed rest, which is a good thing because even with Jesse's millions of family members to distract me, I don't think I could handle four months in the same room."

"I've never felt so relieved as when you sent word you were okay." Ginny sat on the edge of the bed. "But I do admit I'm concerned about your mental clarity. You just got back. Why are you putting things *into* a bag instead of out of it?"

Dare took a deep breath. "We've decided to move to Rocky, at least until Buckaroo is born. We're heading back tomorrow."

One of Ginny's brows rose to her hairline. She just stared, and stared. Then she glanced over her shoulder to make sure they were alone before whispering, "Blink twice if you're being held against your will."

Dare snickered. "That's rich — this is partly your idea. You're the one who said that we should consider moving."

"I thought *consider* meant taking more than thirty seconds. You've got to admit this is fast. You just went to check them out."

"I did. And I like them."

Ginny hopped off the bed and paced the room. "You really going to marry Mr. Sexy?"

"This isn't about him. This is about doing what's best for Buckaroo, remember? I feel as if being in Rocky is going to be a good thing for me up until the time he's born, but especially the days after, because oh my God, Jaxi and Blake's baby was adorable, but the idea of bringing something that teeny home and having to take care of it all by myself? *Hell* no."

The pacing stopped. Ginny's concern deepened as she folded her arms over her chest. "I can be here for you. You don't need to move."

"Ginny. No, I don't want you to put your life on hold any longer. That's not fair to you, and I'll just end up hating myself." Dare tossed the packing to the bed so she could catch hold her friend's hands. "I love you, and I love that you would sacrifice your plans for me, but I won't let you do that. Plus, it's not necessary. The Colemans will be wonderful to Buckaroo."

Her friend tilted her head. "What about you? Because

all kidding aside, is there something between you and Jesse more than just this baby?"

"Of course, there is. We're friends, at least I think we are." She wasn't going to mention their sexual compatibility was off the charts.

She probably didn't have to considering the way Ginny was giving her that Spock impression again.

"Good *friends*. Okay. That's why you're packing your naughty underwear."

Dare glanced at the bed, cheeks flushing as she realized what she'd abandoned in her hurry to confront Ginny. She rushed back and shoved the telltale garments away. "They're comfortable."

An inelegant snort escaped her friend. "Hey, I have zero problems with you doing a hot guy if he's treating you well. Although anyone who can't see beyond sex to what an amazing person you are doesn't deserve slinky undies."

"If he ever takes me for granted, I will make sure that Jesse's not allowed to wear anything slinky," Dare retorted softly before ducking away from Ginny's fingers and the threat of death by tickling.

They ended up laughing the entire time Ginny helped her pack.

Ever since Jesse had found his mostly bare-assed picture slapped up on the side of the barn wall at work, it seemed forces had been conspiring to work out his future with or without his permission.

The forward rush of events had mostly been neutral

or positive, but in the last two days he'd found himself wondering if he had a fairy godmother keeping an eye on him, because he certainly didn't deserve the kind of good that was landing in his path.

Not only was he able to work with his family in Rocky again, he'd been assured by someone whose opinion meant a lot to him that he could let go of his long-held guilt.

Every time he looked at Dare he heard her words again, insisting it was time to move on.

Then today when he'd tracked Caleb down, the announcement that he and Dare would be moving to Rocky immediately was greeted with a short grunt, a quick nod and a distracted request for help reading some old breeding records.

After Caleb nodded he understood what the paper said, Jesse reached out. "I'm still on board to help Silver Stone going forward," Jesse "We'd have to keep everything online, but if that would work, let me know."

"Luke and I will talk about it," Caleb promised. "I'll go get Dare's riding stuff together. Come on up to the house for supper."

"Dare would love that."

He returned to the cottage, transferring the couple of bags he found stacked on the porch into the back of his truck before going inside.

Dare and Ginny were in the office, looking perplexed as they stared at the computer screens.

"Need a hand?"

Ginny bounded toward him. It took great mental strength to resist throwing his hands up as a precautionary measure.

He nearly fell over when she tackle-hugged him,

squeezing tight for a moment before letting go and stepping back, her chin raised high. "But just because you haven't screwed up until now that doesn't mean you're off the hook." Ginny lowered her voice and tried to look intimidating. "I'm watching you, Wazowski. Always watching."

Dare pushed past her sister. "Oh, please. By no stretch of the imagination is Jesse a big green eyeball monster."

"But I swear I heard you call him Pookie-Bear." Ginny ducked as Dare threatened her with a pillow. "I know, get back to packing. I just don't know what else you want."

"Is everything out front all you need?" Jesse asked.

Dare gestured toward the office. "I'm trying to figure out what I need out of here, but until we've got more room there's no use in me taking much more than my laptop."

Jesse shrugged. "It's not like we're getting on a ship and travelling for three months. If you decide you need something else we can come down for the weekend and grab it."

"Or I can bring it up," Ginny offered. "Jesse's right."

"See, Dare? Even your sister knows I'm always right."

Ginny glared at him, but her eyes flashed her amusement.

Jesse caught Dare by the hand and pulled her closer. "If you've pretty much got what you think you need, let's go for a ride. We can visit all your favourite spots before we head out tomorrow."

Dare slid next to him, her hand resting on his chest, a pleased smile on her lips. "That's a sweet idea. I'd love to."

Ginny made a few gagging sounds, but the two

of them ignored her, heading out to enjoy the rest of the afternoon.

He enjoyed the evening surprisingly well, too. Sasha spent every minute she didn't have food in her mouth asking Dare questions about the new ranch, and Emma —

Well, Emma just about melted his heart by insisting she wanted to sit with him. She didn't say anything, just crawled into his lap and refused to move until it was time for her to head off to bed.

That night as he held Dare in his arms, the two of them sleeping in her room for one last time, the image of Buckaroo drifted through his mind like it had begun to do on a regular basis. Only this time, instead of a sturdy little boy he saw a sweet little girl with lots of red hair and a sassy smile.

Maybe that wouldn't be so bad.

Jesse gave it more thought as they headed back to Rocky the next day, both driving their own trucks and pulling a horse trailer. The quiet hours it took to head north were awesome at first before turning strange.

He missed having Dare in the truck with him.

It didn't take long once they were back in Rocky to get everything tucked away at Joel and Vicki's. He and Dare shared the dresser and the closet, and he barely had to fight for space.

"Are you sure you're a girl?" Jesse teased, eyeing the half-dozen hangers she'd commandeered in the closet, which were less than he'd used by the time he was finished.

Dare played dirty, kicking the door shut behind her then stripping her top over her head. "One word." She gestured to her body. "Boobs."

"Hmmm." He caught her by the hand, backing up

until he was sitting on the mattress, Dare tucked between his open thighs. Happily, Joel and Vicki wouldn't be home for hours, so it was the perfect time to get carried away. "I don't know that I should accept those as the real McCoy without testing. Just to make sure."

"Of course. I'd hate to think you were fooled by an imitation."

He skimmed his hands up the sides of her body, pausing to rest his fingertips on the growing swell of her belly. The curves added to her sexiness, and he leaned in and kissed her right smack dab in the middle of her torso while his fingers slipped around to undo her bra.

Dare acted coy for a moment, holding the cups against herself. One shoulder strap slipped off, then the other. "It's very good for my ego."

Jesse damn near had to wipe the drool from his mouth as he waited anxiously for her hands to move. "What is?"

"The expression on your face right now."

She was taking too damn long, so he caught her by the wrists and guided her hands away. The lacy fabric fell, landing on his thighs before sliding off onto the floor, but he didn't care because, well, as she had so elegantly put it —

"Hello, boobs."

He cupped her, gently lifting while he made sure to keep the deep red circles of her nipples visible. That let him play with them, brushing in circles with his thumbs, pinching lightly between thumb and the side of his forefingers. The peaks hardened, crinkling in as he teased until he couldn't stop from leaning closer and licking. Once, then again. Tickling the tip of his tongue around the hard nub before switching to using the flat.

His favourite part of sex with her — if it was possible to pick a single thing he liked best — had already begun. The noises. The music of her pleasure. The fucking awesome sounds of fucking…

Dare moaned as he touched her, threading her fingers through his hair. She arched her back to press her breasts closer when he teasingly backed away.

"Don't stop," she begged breathlessly.

"I'm no damn fool," he murmured. "But right now, I'm hungry."

"How can you — ?"

Her complaint cut off as Jesse caught the edges of her sweats and ripped them off her hips along with her panties. He lifted her into his lap, hands tight on her bare ass as he squeezed. "Need more directions? Climb up here and give me something tasty."

Jesse rolled back on the mattress, tugging Dare into position over him.

She glanced down, gaze playing peekaboo past the curves of her breasts and belly. "Your eyes are on fire."

"I'm starving," he complained. "Get up here."

His grip on her ass was enough to move her the final inches he needed to center her pussy over his mouth. He licked softly at first, teasing. Small motions over and over as her sweetness filled his mouth and made him eager for more.

Dare leaned forward and pressed a hand to the wall for balance. "Your tongue is magic," she whispered.

"Your pussy is fucking delicious," he answered back. "Hold on tight, darlin', this is going to get wild."

He took control then, locking her in place with his hands so his tongue could explore. Leisurely at first, slipping through her folds as if he were on a casual exploration. Licking with tiny motions over her clit. Her hips quivered as he increased pressure, stabbing his tongue deeper. Fucking her with it as he caressed her ass and stroked her smooth skin.

His cock was hard, his balls buzzing, his mouth watering with the taste of her. Every time she moaned it encouraged him, and he fucked her harder. Licked more. Teased and taunted until her clit was all but vibrating under his tongue.

He stroked a finger between her ass cheeks and teased there as well. All of her. He wanted every fucking bit of her.

Dare threaded the fingers of her free hand through his hair then clenched them into a fist. "Oh, God. I'm so close."

Jesse hummed his encouragement, licking greedily. Needing to hear her go over the edge. Needing to send her there.

Another sharp tug at his head was joined by a low gasp, and she rocked over him, grinding down on his face as she came. He didn't slow, didn't ease off, and she swore, wiggling to get away from his relentless mouth.

He rolled her to the side, ripping open his jeans so he could haul his cock into his hand.

Dare relaxed into a puddle in front of him, legs open, wetness from his mouth and her orgasm painting the lips of her pussy. Her heavy breasts moved with every hard breath she panted out even as her satisfied smile turned her into an erotic statue before him.

"So freaking gorgeous." Inspiration hit, and he reached between her legs, rubbing as gently as possible when everything in him screamed to go hard and fast. Heat and wetness covered his palm as he stroked, and

Dare groaned again, her eyes widening as she realized what he was up to.

"You're a dirty bastard," she whispered. "You're going to make me hot all over again.

"Yup," he agreed. He stroked his fingers into her, shaking with need as he pulled back and covered his cock with her moisture.

"Much better." He pumped hard, stroking over the head and using his thumb on the most sensitive spot as he let his gaze drift over her. "Touch your tits for me. Hold them up. That's it. Now open your legs, darlin'. God damn. So fucking right. Every inch of you is perfect and so fucking delicious, and later I'm going to fuck you from one end to the other, but right now...?"

He was seconds away from losing control. The sight of her all sexy and sated made him sweat. A pretty flush coloured her cheeks, partly from her orgasm and the rest from watching him jerk himself off. Her gaze was fixed on his fist where the head of his cock appeared over and over.

She licked her lips, and lightning sizzled up his spine. Dare wiggled upright, her breasts shifting, and he let loose a long, needy moan. And when she reached for him, fingers dusting his thigh, that was it. That was all it took to shove him over the edge.

Semen exploded from his cock to land in stripes over her breasts and belly. He knelt on the bed, determined to mark her all over, like a fucking caveman, branding her with his come.

Asshole move, maybe, but Dare didn't seem to mind. Instead she hummed happily, dragging a finger through a streak of white, and another hard jolt hit.

"You've fucking killed me," Jesse complained as he

collapsed to the mattress beside her, happy but spent.

"Hmm. You're a messy creature," she teased, rubbing her palms over her naked curves and covering herself with his seed. "Since I'm all sticky and messy — what else can we do that's dirty? I'll have to go have a shower before bed, anyway."

She knew exactly how to bring a dead man back to life. His blood heated to boiling and his heart pounded. "I have a few ideas," he offered, crawling over her and taking her lips.

Round two, starting now.

Chapter Twenty-Five

Blog post: Dates and Time

When people warn that the older you get, the faster time flies, it scares me. I can't imagine the days disappearing any quicker than they already do.

It's the beginning of August. It's been just over two weeks since we moved to Rocky.

It's been less than a month since we showed up for our first visit.

We won't talk about how short a time on the calendar it's been since Buckaroo announced he was planning to impact my life, but I'm already twenty-seven weeks into this pregnancy gig. Just three months to go before the kid stops poking me from the inside. Although, don't get me wrong. I'm not complaining because that is one cool sensation.

But here I am, having new adventures and new challenges, and I swear every day disappears before I've had a chance to fully wake up... Did I mention I'm hanging around with a shit-ton of Colemans? Me, the person who barely recognizes my own face in the mirror in the morning, suddenly has a lot of faces to put names to. I apologize again, cousin Steve, for walking straight past you the other day. You were very gracious to accept "pregnancy brain" as an excuse for my forgetfulness.

To my reading audience, remember how I mentioned the Colemans are pretty much all cut from the same cloth? There

is no way I shouldn't have recognized him as a relative.
Maybe time is moving so fast he was blurry —

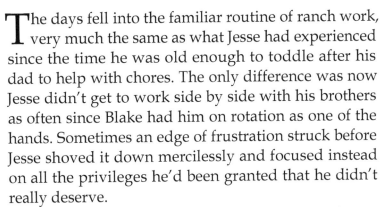

The days fell into the familiar routine of ranch work, very much the same as what Jesse had experienced since the time he was old enough to toddle after his dad to help with chores. The only difference was now Jesse didn't get to work side by side with his brothers as often since Blake had him on rotation as one of the hands. Sometimes an edge of frustration struck before Jesse shoved it down mercilessly and focused instead on all the privileges he'd been granted that he didn't really deserve.

Because they were living with Joel and Vicki, he got to spend more time with his twin than he had in the years before he left. That was a sweet enough reward to put up with the moments when he wanted to slap himself silly for his past sins.

And Dare was there. The woman was a bundle of positive energy, and every time he found himself slipping toward brooding, she would subtly, or sometimes not-so-subtly, remind him to mind his manners.

Like the time they were sitting around the bonfire in the evening, a couple more of the cousins and their partners joining the conversation.

Out of the blue Dare stood, stepping on his foot in the process before stumbling into his arms and clinging to him like a princess in need of rescuing.

"Oh, my hero," she declared dramatically before kissing him thoroughly. Appreciative wolf whistles exploded from the rest of his family.

"Not that I'm going to complain about you kissing me, but what was that about?" he asked as they made their way hand-in-hand back to the trailer a while later. "I didn't think you were into public displays of affection."

She shrugged. "You were glaring at Vicki. You weren't even aware of it, so I thought a little distraction all around might go a long way."

Jesse cursed. "I don't even know what I was thinking. Why would I be glaring at her?"

Dare tugged on his hand. "Old habits die hard. Do you still feel horrible inside when you look at her?"

"Guilty?" Jesse thought it through. "Yes, but it's different now. Less intense. Honestly, every time we're in the trailer and I feel it, I get up and clean something."

A burst of laughter escaped her lips. "I wondered what was up with your Mr. Clean imitation."

"You think it's stupid?" Jesse asked.

"Nope. I think it's a brilliant way to redirect your need for punishment into something that is good for everybody." She offered him a sweet smirk. "I like that there is less for me to tidy."

So daily he got up, reluctantly uncurled himself from the bundle of heat that was Dare, then headed into a full day of work followed by an evening spent doing something with her.

They visited with each of his brothers and their wives, and with Mike and Marion, but they also did more ordinary dating kinds of things, and those were the moments he'd catch himself forgetting the reason they were together was because of one hot night back in cold February.

Sitting in the movie theatre holding her hand felt right.

"Hey. Stop daydreaming and get moving," Matt

ordered, leaning on his shovel at the other end of the ditch they were digging by hand.

Jesse blinked himself back to the here and now, which was a distant field at the edge of Coleman property where they needed to fix a broken standpipe. "Shit. Sorry about that."

Matt glanced at his watch. "Coffee break. You and me are both foggy today."

"You skipping sleep to party?" Jesse teased.

"Colt's teething, and Hope has a summer cold. They're both miserable."

A moment later they'd both climbed out of the hole, sitting on the ground with cups of coffee. Jesse popped open his lunchbox to discover Dare had snuck in a pile of brownies, and he passed one over to his brother.

"Vicki makes the best brownies." An appreciative sound escaped Matt an instant after he bit into the chocolatey goodness. He took a sip of his coffee then gave Jesse a strange look.

"What's that about?" Jesse demanded. "I sacrifice one of my brownies, and you make a face?"

"How's it going, living with Joel and Vicki?"

That was a question to stop a man in his tracks. Ever cautious of Dare's warning in the back of his brain to keep his stupidity on the down low, Jesse considered what to say. He didn't want to flip off something nonchalant, but there was no way he could explain how earth-shatteringly monumental it was to slowly accept his mistakes and move on.

"Did you ever have something you spent a lot of time and energy on before realizing you were focusing on the wrong thing?"

A derisive snort escaped his brother.

Jesse eyed him in confusion.

"You're asking a man who wasted years trying to make someone happy when the one woman who means everything to me was right there under my nose." Matt leaned forward on an elbow. "Sometimes I kick myself for having been so stupid, and then Hope catches me and points out that we can't change the past, we can only enjoy the future. So that's what I do, every damn day."

A huge shot of guilt and regret washed over Jesse. He really was a sorry son of a gun.

"I'm an ass," Jesse said. "I've been so focused on me and *my* world that it didn't even hit until now what kind of hell you went through."

"Yet every day I get to spend time with the woman I love, and we've got a great if slightly cranky kid that we made — life's pretty damn good," Matt insisted. Then he grinned. "Look at you. You might actually be growing up."

"Shut up."

"No, I mean it, this is a good thing." Matt's grin got wider. "I can hardly wait to see you all thrown out of kilter down the road when you're trying to figure out how to convince your baby girl that she really does want to go to sleep because *you* can't keep your eyes open an instant longer."

Jesse smirked. "You think Dare's having a girl?"

"Got my bid in. Girl, November third."

"Dare is going to hate you for that," Jesse warned. "She's already insisting Buckaroo will arrive early."

Matt slapped him on the shoulder, and they finished their break before climbing back into the ditch and getting muddy. But Jesse was grateful that the entire conversation — other than the talking-about-babies bit — had been so completely normal.

He was back with his family, and this felt right too.

Friday night after supper, he and Joel washed up the dishes while the girls took off to get changed. A visit to Traders was on the agenda — finally. It was the first time they'd been able to make it since Dare got out of the hospital, and they were both looking forward to dancing and relaxing.

Jesse checked inside, shocked but grateful that the only thing he really felt about spending the evening with Joel and Vicki and the other Colemans who'd be there was anticipation.

He popped into their bedroom and found Dare standing in front of the closet in her underwear and bra.

He slipped behind her and pressed a kiss to the nape of her neck. "I don't mind the outfit one bit, but I'm not letting you go to Traders like that," he warned.

Dare turned, discontent written on her face. "I hate to be stereotypical, but I've got nothing to wear. Nothing I can go dancing in."

He let his gaze drop over her body, tempted to suggest they stay home to do some horizontal dancing. She was an eager partner between the sheets, but getting out was important too, he was coming to realize.

He stroked a hand over her belly. She'd noticeably popped in the last week. It wasn't something he'd expected, but in truth he thought the baby bump was damn sexy.

"Buckaroo making your favourite outfits not fit?" She didn't answer, but her lower lip stuck out in a pout. He leaned forward and nipped at it. "I thought you were going to borrow some things from Jaxi and the other girls."

"I did, but I skipped a size somewhere in the last two days."

He reached into the closet and grabbed one of his shirts. "Wear the jeans you've got with that stretchy bit in the front, and put this on. With your boots, you'll be the best-dressed cowgirl in the place."

She went to take the shirt from his hands, but he held it hostage for a moment. "I get a kiss in payment."

Dare give him a quick smooch before stepping away to get dressed. "I'm surprised you didn't demand a blow job."

He slapped his thigh. "Dammit, you're right. I'll remember that for next time."

The Traders Pub parking lot was packed with a typical Friday-night summer crowd. He caught Dare by the hand, Joel and Vicki following, as they headed straight to the dance side of the place since Dare wasn't drinking.

The Colemans had taken over the east corner of the standing tables off the dance floor. Couples slipped on and off the hardwood area, people shifting around enough that as the room warmed up, light coats were discarded and hung on the hooks attached to the vertical wooden posts.

They danced a little then visited. Dare only had to ask on the sly for name reminders a few times. Lee and Trevor were there from the Moonshine clan with Rachel and Becky, Rafe from Angel with Laurel. Tamara and Lisa from the Whiskey Creek side of things. Just him and Joel from Six Pack.

It was a far cry from the days when all fifteen of them had been single and out for a regular Friday-night whoop-up. Only seven cousins were out tonight, although five with partners. None of the couples with kids, though — maybe that's what made it feel so different.

Come November, he and Dare wouldn't be out on a regular basis either. Not without wrangling a babysitter.

The world was changing.

Dare took off toward the washroom, which gave Jesse his first opportunity to chat with Rafe about something that needed discussing. He motioned his cousin to the side, and they walked away, leaving the rest of the Colemans gathered at the edge of the dance floor.

Rafe ordered them a couple of beers and passed one to Jesse, a question in his eyes.

The place was noisy enough that where they were standing they were pretty much alone in a crowd. Jesse twisted toward the dance floor but spoke in Rafe's direction. "You know the thing that I told you was an issue before I left?"

Rafe grinned briefly before washing it away with a swallow of beer. "You mean the thing that I said you didn't need to worry about anymore? The thing I said wasn't really a thing?"

"Jackass," Jesse muttered.

"Jerk." Rafe just stood there like a Sphinx. "I *am* waiting for you to admit I was right. You know, about the thing that I don't even know what you're talking about anymore because it never happened."

So much for having to warn Rafe not to discuss what Jesse had confessed to last February.

Only something Dare had said stuck with him, hard, and it was important to share that bit. "Fine, you were right, but also wrong, because something did happen. I got my ass handed to me that night, and I hope I'm smarter because of it."

Rafe smacked his hand on Jesse's shoulder and squeezed tight. "I'm very glad that the King of Guilt has decided to abdicate his throne."

It was taking a while to disassemble the thing, but that was a pretty accurate image. Pulling down his past regrets one brick at a time and using them to build that road into the future.

"How are things going with Laurel?" Jesse asked.

Rafe eased his back to the bar, leaning side-by-side with Jesse. His gaze found Laurel in the midst of the family gathering. "I'm in love. That pretty much sums it up. My heart beats faster every time I see her. I wake up every damn morning wondering what I did to deserve her — you know, all of the typically cheesy *fallen head over heels in love* things."

"I'm glad. It's pretty clear you two were meant to be together. You know, like I told you before I left," he added.

"Jerk," Rafe returned happily.

While they talked, Jesse watched the rhythm of the dance before them, as family and friends slipped off and on the floor and into conversations. Laughter and smiles and deep connection. It's what had been there for so long, and yet so often Jesse had felt on the outskirts of it.

This time something seemed noticeably new, but he wasn't quite sure what had changed.

His favourite redhead reentered the room, heading toward the family. She'd pulled on a pale blue T-shirt that stretched over her belly before tying his shirt over top, and she looked pretty damn cute. With the extra weight in front, her hips swayed more than before, but her strut across the wooden boards was enough to make his body instantly go into high alert.

When she stepped up to Joel and slipped a hand around his hip, Jesse's spine straightened so fast it nearly snapped out of his skin.

He was moving toward them an instant later.

Joel hadn't even glanced at her, completely focused on his conversation with their cousin Trevor. Still, he automatically stretched a hand out to curl it around Dare's hip. Only his fingers brushed her belly, and just as Jesse arrived, Joel and Dare both realized their mistake and sprang apart as if jet-propelled.

For one second conversation fell quiet as everyone waited to see what would happen. Dance music pulsed, hot and heavy, but no one spoke. Vicki turned from where she'd been hidden behind a couple of the girls, concern in her eyes.

Jesse was utterly shocked to discover honest amusement bubbling up inside. He reached out and caught hold of Dare's fingers, tugging her against him and lifting her chin.

"Wrong Coleman," he teased before pressing a light kiss to her lips.

Her cheeks were bright red when he pulled away, but her eyes sparkled. "Maybe I should take Vicki up on that offer to put a bell on you."

"Maybe you should, but you better make it a big bell." He winked as she tapped him lightly on the chest. "An *enormous* bell, so it goes with all the other things about me that are bigger than life."

"Like your ego?" Joel tossed out.

Laughter rang from the group, a sense of relief on the air, but when it came down to it, Jesse was more focused on pulling Dare onto the dance floor and into his arms than worrying about a silly mistake.

She settled against him, the strange and yet familiar Buckaroo bump between them as he guided her around the dance floor.

"That was pretty impressive," she offered. "You know, you not going all caveman."

"Just let me know if Joel and I need to coordinate our clothing in the future."

"How about you and me coordinate our *un*-clothing in a couple of hours?"

He liked where this was going. "Are you trying to seduce me, Ms. Hayes?"

"I'm offering to fuck your brains out, Mr. Coleman."

He glanced at his watch. "Oh, look at that. It's time to go home already."

Jesse picked her up. Right there in the middle of the dance floor, he swung her into his arms and marched toward the door. Applause broke out from the Colemans and others in the bar.

Dare clung to his shoulders, laughter escaping her lips. "What are you doing, you crazy man?"

"Bullshit on hanging around for a couple of hours after you make an offer like that. I've decided to save the caveman behaviour for the moments that matter the most. This definitely counts."

Dare didn't argue as he settled her into his truck. "Take me back to your cave," she offered.

So he did.

Dare thought she would miss Heart Falls more, but the truth was she heard from Ginny nearly as often as before, just without the random drop-ins and thievery of chocolate from her pantry. She got text messages from the boys on a regular basis, and a phone call every week from Caleb, who refused to enter the technical revolution.

The girls Skyped her. Sasha chatted up a storm about everything they'd been doing. Emma made Dare teary-eyed as she held out her favourite stuffy like an offering then hugged it fiercely. They both whined about the babysitters Caleb seemed to be running through like sand, Sasha with loud, determined phrases like "mean and stubborn", Emma with all too evocative eye motions to back up her sister's complaints.

Her blog was going strong, and the new *Ranching with Buckaroo* section was a big hit. More than that, there'd been a special kind of joy getting to know the other Coleman women better, especially Vicki.

It wasn't as if Dare had been living in a cave. She'd had friends at school. She'd had all of the Stone family, but having to step into a new setting where everyone else seemed solidly connected had forced Dare to step out from behind the computer screen.

A screen which had to be located a little farther away on a weekly basis as Buckaroo took up more and more room.

Dare caught herself now and then staring at her belly in surprise. Not as if she could forget it was there, but still, sometimes she did. She went to roll over in bed one night, and it seemed easier to put a hand under her belly to help turn — it was weird having a body that wasn't quite hers alone anymore.

Suddenly they were two-and-a-half months out from Buckaroo Arrival Day, as Jesse had begun to put it. Somehow Dare refrained from stepping on his toes every time he made some comment about BAD to the bone.

When his phone rang during breakfast, Jesse checked the display then answered it, his expression more confused than anything. "Hey, Travis. Did I miss something on the schedule? Am I late?"

Dare and Vicki exchanged glances.

"Time?" Dare asked quietly.

Vicki shrugged. "Could be."

Jesse hung up, his expression complete puzzlement. "All he said was 'Ashley's in labour', then he hung up."

"It's time." Vicki popped to her feet and hurried to the fridge. "I have a basket ready for you to take."

Dare was eager to go *and* scared to death. She turned to Jesse who was sitting like a lump at the table in stunned silence. "Come on. We gotta get over there."

This time Jesse and Joel exchanged panicked glances before Jesse turned back. "Are you out of your ever-lovin' mind?"

"Nope. I told you this," Dare reminded him. "Remember? I said Ashley thought it would be a great idea for me to get a little more experience with what having a baby was like, since I have no idea. Well, other than cows and cats and ranch animals, but human babies are different."

She had him by the hand and was tugging him to his feet, the reluctant sack of bones that he was. "I thought that meant we were going to babysit sometime. With supervision."

"It means Ashley, who is having a homebirth, decided since she was already going to have a bunch of people around, she doesn't mind having us watch what goes on to deliver a people baby."

Dare guided Jesse toward the front door.

Behind them at the table Joel was laughing out loud.

VIVIAN AREND

"You really know how to have a good time, bro. You can keep Travis company after he faints."

"I don't know if this is a good idea," Jesse complained again.

She shoved him into a chair and pushed his boots at him. "Neither do I, but we're doing it. Get a move on, and I might let you hide out if you really feel squeamish."

Vicki handed him the basket, and they were in the truck and headed over to the house across the coulee from the homestead.

A veritable party boatload of trucks and vehicles were parked there, and when they went to the house, Ashley's mama Tina was waiting for them.

"They've got everything set up in the studio." She pointed to the building behind the house. "I'll be over in a little while. Just making some tea."

Jesse slowed his pace. "We don't need to rush. I'm sure this is going to take a long time."

Maybe he was right.

"If I slow down I might chicken out," Dare admitted, holding his hand tightly enough he couldn't get away. Tight enough she couldn't turn on her heel and escape.

They pulled to a stop outside the door, and he took a deep breath. "Okay, I first thought you were crazy, but considering there's no getting out of doing this with Buckaroo, you're right. I'm not looking forward to it, but knowing a little more what will happen will make it easier down the road."

They'd been taking prenatal classes, but that kind of knowledge wasn't the same.

Of course, what they found in the studio was nothing like the hospital birth that Dare planned on having. The large, open-air studio space at the top of the stairs had been given a few key additions. Like usual, the sun streaked in the windows creating golden rectangles that decorated the hardwood floor, but in one corner a king-size mattress had been added, covered with blankets towels and pillows. Beside that a group of upright wooden chairs, as if waiting for a musical ensemble to gather. Outside on the deck, though, was the star of the show. A wood-fired hot tub big enough to hold a half-dozen people.

Jesse grinned as he stepped forward. "You guys put a hot tub in Ashley's art studio?"

"We were told to decorate the place the way we wanted, and if you hadn't noticed, Ashley has a decidedly hedonistic mindset." Cassidy was in the hot tub, holding Ashley against him. Her head rested on his shoulder, bikini-covered breasts and the round of her belly bobbing against the surface of the water like three islands in the ocean. "It's not quite the proper temperature at the moment, but it works for today."

Ashley lifted a hand and waved. "Hey, guys. You made it on time."

Dare stepped toward the edge of the tub and slipped a hand in. "That feels comfy. Is it nice?"

The other woman nodded. "You really need to hit the swimming pool. All the support when you're ninety percent stomach is incredible. Makes it easier for the back rubs, because right now it feels as if I'm being squeezed into a tiny little space while a million knives stab into my lower back."

"But hey, Dare. Don't worry, this giving-birth thing is a breeze," Travis muttered from the other side of the hot tub.

Ashley held up her middle finger. "Love you too, asshole."

"Just saying." Travis came to the side of the tub and caught her fingers, pressing a kiss to her knuckles. "Maybe you should consider not freaking out the other pregnant lady."

Ashley's eyes brightened. "She'd rather know what to expect than have rainbows and sunshine lollipops tossed at her.

Dare wasn't sure. "Although, lollipops are nice."

Behind Ashley, Cassidy laughed, the sound turning into soothing encouragement. "Breathe, Ash. Breathe."

Ashley obeyed, a long, slow inhalation followed by a purse of her lips as she blew air at Travis. Staring into his eyes as she worked through the contraction.

Everyone got caught up in the rhythm, the whole room breathing in unison until Ashley let out a sigh and relaxed back into Cassidy's arms. "Whoa, that's one more done. They're getting stronger."

Skyler, Ashley's mom was there, reaching into the tub to brush a hand over her belly. "You comfy, sweetie?"

"Yup." Ashley motioned at her mother. "Mom is a midwife, so she gets to pull double duty."

"Your mama — Tina," Dare said. "She was making tea. She said she'd be out in a minute."

Skyler laughed. "No, she won't." Dare must've made a face because the woman took pity on her and explained more thoroughly. "Tina is not much into childbirth. That's why I had Ashley. When she was born, Tina went out drinking."

"I volunteered to follow that tradition," Travis offered, "but I was told in no uncertain terms I needed to be here. There were words like *cut off for life* and *cut off for real* bandied about."

He was joking, because as the contractions continue

to hit it was obvious Cassidy and Travis were the only support team Ashley really needed. Cassidy offered soothing words of comfort, and Travis acted as an anchor, occasionally bullying Ashley into doing the next thing.

"You're doing good cop/bad cop with her," Jesse pointed out quietly when Cassidy stepped aside to dry himself. Travis had taken Ashley from his arms and carried her to the side of the room to use the towels there.

Cassidy took a deep breath as he glanced across the room to where Ashley stood, the situation teetering at the point where the baby's arrival was imminent.

"It's what she needs right now. Although frankly, if Travis orders either of us to jump, we're pretty used to asking *how high*." He grinned at Dare. "Don't get me wrong, we like it."

Dare's cheeks flushed as Cassidy excused himself and headed across the room. He stopped and wrapped his arms around both Travis and Ashley, and it seemed as if Dare was watching something holy and intensely private. As if Travis and Cassidy were gathering an infusion of love and pouring it into Ashley to help her finish the important task before her.

Cassidy kissed both of them on the cheek, then headed across the room to help Skyler wrestle with a low, wide-seated chair.

Travis had an arm around Ashley, walking slowly in a circle with her. Dare was called forward to pace beside them, Ashley giving a running commentary of all the things she expected the guys to do in the future to make up for her current condition.

"Daily foot rubs?" Travis asked.

"I'd demand hourly, but the ranch might complain

if you had to stop that often." Ashley waved a hand magnanimously. "I don't want to put your family out."

Her joking lightened the tension, as did her comments about the artwork in the room and wanting to finish some projects. Toward the windows and open work area, a number of Ashley's pallets and easels stood, partially finished projects right there in the open.

"I thought artists were shy about people seeing their stuff," Jesse said.

Ashley waited until she was done panting through another set of contractions before offering a tired grin. "Jesse, what have I ever done to make you think I'm shy?"

She had a point. Travis had a hand on the towel wrapped around her waist, but other than a bikini top, she was without another stitch of clothing.

"Art is something different than seeing body parts," Jesse insisted. He had hold of Dare's hand, squeezing as he tried to appear calm even though it was clear to Dare he was as floored by all this as she was. "Speaking of body parts. I really hope Travis and Cassidy plan to let me live after today, right?"

Ashley rocked to a stop, air escaping through her teeth as she grimaced. When she could breathe again, she stuck out her tongue. "I'm wearing a bra for your sake. My hou-ha doesn't count. It's most definitely *not* a sexual organ at the moment." She tilted her head back to gasp at Travis. "Oh, my God. I think it's time."

He and Skyler led her to where Cassidy was lowering himself into the strange, low chair. She settled in his lap, between his thighs. Cassidy wrapped his arms around her then let Ashley get herself comfortable, gripping his arms as Travis moved into position in front of her and their gazes locked.

Dare and Jesse stood to the side, and he slipped his arm around her shoulder and pulled her close, murmuring in her ear. "You doing okay? It's not too much?"

"I'm going to have to do this. I don't know if I'm more scared now or less, but I *think* I'm happy I'm here."

And then with Jesse's arm holding her tight, Dare got to watch as Ashley got down to serious business. Her mom helped Travis catch the baby while both men encouraged Ashley with sweet words, and strong words, and exactly what she needed.

The expression on Cassidy's face was enough to make Dare's throat tighten — the sheer glow of pride and happiness as a little girl was laid in his and Ashley's arms.

Ashley stroked a finger over a teeny cheek, the baby's cries barely more than protests from a cooing dove. "Welcome to our family, sweet one."

Cassidy pressed a kiss to Ashley's temple as he carefully picked up one of the baby's hands. "She's beautiful."

Travis caught her other fingers in his, sliding up so he could put an arm around Ashley and Cassidy's shoulders. "Of course, she is. Love made her."

Dare was torn. It was impossible to look away, and yet after everything they'd witnessed during the birth, *this* was the moment when it felt as if she was intruding on something far too private.

She glanced up at Jesse to find his expression unreadable. Tension had taken root in his body as he watched the tableau before them.

Then he cleared his throat softly. "Congratulations. That was the most incredible thing I've ever seen."

Three sets of eyes turned toward them briefly, a smile on Ashley's face as if she'd completed a marathon — exhausted, yet satisfied. "It's the most incredible thing I've ever done."

Cassidy and Travis nodded briefly before turning their attention back on Ashley and the baby.

Dare had to know. "What's her name?"

Cassidy forced his gaze up. "Daisy. Daisy Joy Coleman."

She and Jesse took their leave, but Dare doubted that the three new parents even noticed, too wrapped up in each other. Sweet words of love drifting between them, three sets of arms cradling that tiny life as they officially welcomed Daisy into their hearts and lives.

They stopped at the house and let Tina know. She nodded, then picked up a thermos that sat waiting on the table and headed briskly toward the studio.

Dare and Jesse sat in silence on the ride back to the trailer. More mysteries of Buckaroo's imminent arrival had been answered, but there was a different, intensely powerful question that refused to let her alone.

A question that refused to be ignored.

Buckaroo would arrive when he was good and ready, and while she wasn't looking forward to it, she could handle the physical work of labour and delivery.

Jesse would be her support. He could be both good cop and bad cop for her, she was sure of that as well. He'd proven repeatedly he only wanted what was best for Buckaroo.

What she was trying to ignore was the part inside her that wondered if their friendship and his resolve to be there for Buckaroo could ever be more.

If she would ever have someone — *Jesse* — look at her the way Cassidy and Travis had looked at Ashley.

Chapter Twenty-Six

September arrived. Vicki started a countdown calendar for Buckaroo, much to Dare's amusement.

"I think you're more excited than I am," Dare said.

Vicki didn't deny it. "I *am* excited. All babies are special, but your belly is the one in my living room most evenings."

Dare laughed. "If my expanding belly is your biggest source of entertainment, we need to get you out more."

One of the biggest things about sharing a small living space was they had to get really good at minding their own business to provide privacy for the other couple. Yet in spite of how much time they spent bumping elbows with Joel and Vicki, Jesse's Mr. Clean imitations only flared every now and then, which Dare took as a good sign.

They were in the kitchen one morning, rushing to get ready for the day. Jesse was meeting up with a crew, and Dare and Vicki planned to tour the rental house to see what else was needed to make the place comfier for when Skyler and Tina moved out, and Jesse and Dare moved in.

Joel, who'd been on night shift, slid into the kitchen whistling too merrily for a man who should be ready to hit the sack, damn near bouncing on the balls of his feet as he helped set the table.

Vicki rolled in a few minutes later, offered a quick hello and then dropped into her chair. She made the most awful face after taking a sip of her coffee.

Shoot. "Did I forget the sugar?" Dare asked.

Vicki put the cup down on the table. "No, you made it perfect. I just... Umm..."

She glanced at Joel.

He nodded, smile widening as he gripped her fingers before she turned back to them. "We have news. We're expecting."

"Oh my God, that's *awesome*." Dare jumped to her feet — well, as much of a jump as the basketball in her belly would allow — and came around the table to offer Vicki a hug. "I'm so excited for you guys. When are you due?"

Jesse rose to his feet as well, offering a handshake and a back pat to Joel. If Jesse's enthusiasm was muted, neither Vicki nor Joel were aware of it because they were excited enough for all four people in the room.

"Early June," Joel said, tucking Vicki against his side and kissing her briefly. "It happened a little quicker than we expected."

"*Joel*." Vicki flushed. "Okay, you are not allowed to go around telling everybody this part."

He wouldn't stop grinning. "I won't, but you have to admit it's pretty funny that the first month we try, we score."

It was Dare's turn to hide her laughing expression. First month? Sounded fairly familiar.

Fortunately, Jesse managed to maintain enough control to not make some comment about the twins' super-powered-sperm or anything along those lines.

Then they were sworn to secrecy.

"I know it's early, but I figured with us spending so much time together, you were going to get suspicious sooner than later," Vicki explained.

"Um, you know what? I just realized that's a rotten excuse. They're moving out next week," Joel reminded her.

Vicki didn't look at all repentant. "Okay. I just wanted to tell Dare. Sue me."

In spite of having to keep the news secret, there were plenty of other opportunities to celebrate. Not even a week later, all the Coleman clans gathered for an after-dinner joint-family baby shower.

"This isn't typical," Jaxi pointed out, as they carried armloads of decorations into the banquet area at Traders Pub that had been rented for the night. "Usually the Coleman gatherings are Canada Day and Boxing Day, and we take turns hosting those. But it's been a busy year, so everyone agreed that a joint event would work the best rather than all the families trying to do something for each new arrival. Also it totally works as a farewell party for Ashley's moms."

Vicki put down her pile of things, a mischievous smile twisting her lips. "Go on, admit it. There've been too many new arrivals for even you to keep up."

"That too." Jaxi eyed Vicki with suspicion. "What you smirking about?"

Dare didn't say anything.

"You're imagining things," Vicki said dryly. "Let's get the decorating done so we can grab some supper before everyone arrives."

By seven p.m. the place was hopping with family and friends everywhere.

It was a good thing they had a large room because

they needed it. To make it easier, each of the couples and their new baby had their own dedicated table for people to drop off presents.

The two babies from the Moonshine clan were now three months old. Melody and Anna sat next to each other, chatting together animatedly. Steve, who was carefully cradling Jason, gave Mitch Thompson a bit of an evil eye. Mitch held Kasey draped over his arm with devil-may-care nonchalance.

"These kids were born the same day," Steve complained. "How come I feel as if I'm handling nitroglycerin, and you look like Mary Poppins?"

Mitch shrugged, his dark T-shirt moving over biceps covered with full sleeve-length tattoos. "You're the first in your family to have a baby. My little sister Katie has two, and my big brother Clay and his wife had a little girl a month before Kay arrived. By the time the next one arrives, we'll all be as comfortable as Blake."

Dare glanced across the room to discover Jesse's oldest brother surrounded by children. He held Justin while he consoled Lana over something, leaning over and patting the four-year-old on the back as she wept crocodile tears. The twins, Rebecca and Rachel, were holding PJ's hands, guiding him in a slow, careful circle near Blake's feet.

"This place is absolute chaos," Jesse muttered.

It was beautiful chaos in Dare's opinion. "I want to see Daisy. You coming?"

He followed at her side as she dropped off the presents they'd gotten for each of the families.

After the gifts were opened, everyone was herded toward chairs. Dare rubbernecked and could not fathom a better place to be. She pictured Buckaroo years from now in the middle of this kind of bedlam, with willing hands to pick him up when he fell, and older cousins available for games and mischief.

Vicki and Joel's coming baby a playmate in his life who would always be there.

The sound of a spoon clinking into the side of the glass slowly brought everyone's attention to where Mike Coleman had climbed the steps up to the stage at the head of the room.

Jesse's dad ignored the chair, putting a few pieces of paper down on the table beside him. He cleared his throat briefly before speaking, loud and clear. No microphone needed, just the big deep sound of a man of quiet confidence.

"I have the privilege of saying a few things on this special occasion. It's been a hard choice what to focus on. The most important thing, I decided, is this is the perfect time to tell my boys I'd sure appreciate it if you'd finish clearing that north field sooner than later. You're blocking the shortest route to my favourite fishing hole."

Laughter bloomed.

Jesse draped his arm over the back of Dare's chair, enclosing her in the circle of his embrace.

Mike went on. "I could talk to my daughters-in-law, and soon to be ones, and tell you I'm so proud to have you in our family. Plus, I'm more grateful than you can ever know for putting up with my sons. You're women, and a man" — he made eye contact with Cassidy — "of great patience, because I know my boys. They're too much like me to be easy to live with, so thanks for taking them off me and Marion's hands. Remember, the rule is 'you picked, it's yours'. You can't give them back now."

"Worst return policy in history," Beth Coleman

VIVIAN AREND

complained, her arm curled around Daniel's as she grinned at her husband.

"Oh, you have nothing to complain about," Marion Coleman teased back. "Mike insists the 'hundred percent satisfaction guarantee' made all other parts of a typical offer void and null."

"That's some pretty fancy tongue tangling. You sure you aren't a lawyer instead of a rancher?" Beth asked Mike.

"Just a man who knows what's good for him — no matter that it took a while to sink in." Mike sat on the edge of the table, legs stretched in front of him, arms folded over his chest. In that moment Dare could see Jesse in the future. Dark hair shot with silver, plenty of laugh lines and a few worry lines and a whole lot of life-lived worn on his face.

Mike was a handsome man, his eyes taking in the gathering thoughtfully. His face showed traces of emotion as his gaze lingered on the new babies. On his wife.

On Dare and Jesse.

Then he nodded. "But, ladies, I hope you'll indulge me for one moment, because I really do want to talk to my sons and my nephews, because you're mine just as surely as if I'd sired you. You're family, which means you're just as stubborn and as blind as my own — and just as able to see the trees in the forest when someone points them out."

Jesse wiggled in his seat

"You now know, or will know, the feeling of being floored that you're responsible for another human being. You handled your own life recklessly, then you fell in love, and there isn't anything you wouldn't do for that

390

lady. Then suddenly she's the one doing all the work, and all you can do is hold her hand, and it reduces you to nothing.

"Doesn't matter how strong you are, or how many bales you can toss. Your muscles are nothing, your smarts are nothing. You're *nothing* as they show more strength than we'll ever have, and in the end we get to meet an amazing new person who didn't even exist before.

"That's when you suddenly realize you're not there because you're the strong one. The provider or the protector. You're there because you need *them* to breathe. You didn't open your eyes and actually see the world around you until this moment."

Mike stopped and his grin widened. "I bet you all drove home from the hospital the way you drove the day you took your driver's test. Cautious. Overcareful. Hell, I bet most of you drove home and your wife sat in the back seat watching the baby to make sure they were okay. Because sitting up front while that bit that'd been in her belly for half of forever — two feet away was too much distance."

Heads were nodding.

Cassidy straight-up pointed at Travis who had their little girl out of her car seat and draped over his chest like an additional body part. "He sits in the back seat with Daisy."

More laughter. Dare twisted so she could offer a private smile to Jesse —

He was gone. The chair beside her was empty, and the door to the hall was closing silently.

Dare fixed her smile firmly in place and turned to face the front of the room.

She deliberately focused on other things as Mike kept

speaking. She thought about how much, at a moment like this, she missed her own dad. Or she missed what she imagined he would've been like — hopefully like this strong, kind man who was determined to be more than just a figurehead for a complicated group of people. An impact on all the lives he touched.

The empty seat beside her all but waved to get her attention.

Okay, fine. Dare would admit it. She was tempted to go after Jesse, but if he needed her help to work something out, he would ask. She had to believe that.

The man she'd met that wild, footloose February night had been energy and power and full of life in the midst of her sorrow. The Jesse she'd gotten to know better during their time together in Heart Falls had been determined and rock solid. Teasing and fun, yet there for her.

He hadn't once let her down. Not really. His determination to move forward as he stepped back into life in Rocky had impressed her and given her hope.

Whatever had made him walk out now was important — and she'd find out soon enough. But until then she would be patient.

And soak in the family around her.

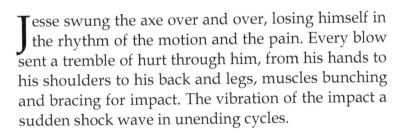

Jesse swung the axe over and over, losing himself in the rhythm of the motion and the pain. Every blow sent a tremble of hurt through him, from his hands to his shoulders to his back and legs, muscles bunching and bracing for impact. The vibration of the impact a sudden shock wave in unending cycles.

Laying waste to the woodpile at the rental house was a good pain. Pain that washed away the frustration and confusion and left him empty. Unthinking.

Or at least it used to. This time his attempt to hide in the work wasn't succeeding the same as usual. Now instead of a peaceful, thoughtless haze, the questions and accusations kept coming.

He was supposed to be helping Dare, but he felt as if he was failing her most of the time. She didn't *need* him, and the baby didn't *need* him — they needed someone, but hell if he deserved for it to be him.

"Son."

His father's deep voice broke through the internal noise, and Jesse blinked hard, the axehead dropping from his tired grip to the ground. "Hey."

Mike stepped to the right and visually measured the pile of split wood at their feet before lifting his gaze to examine Jesse's face. "Want to talk about it?"

Jesse's first response was to deny there was anything to talk about, but his father wasn't a stupid man. Straight-up lying was the wrong choice, and considering he'd hightailed it out of the baby shower without a word — even a fool would know something was wrong.

Mike Coleman? No fool.

Jesse swung the axe once more to set it into the chopping block. He wiped the sweat from his face with his shirtsleeve before grabbing his coat off the nail where he'd abandoned it thirty minutes ago.

"I keep screwing everything up," he admitted. "Even when I try to make things right, I just add fuel to the fire and make things worse."

"Then stop chopping wood, son. If the fuel pile gets empty, it's harder to keep stoking the flames."

It was his own fault for being cryptic in the first place. He deserved that convoluted bit of advice.

"Hell if I know what you just said," Jesse admitted.

Mike folded his arms, eerily reminiscent of his position earlier that night on the stage, sharing wisdom that had rocked Jesse to the core. "Why'd you run?"

Jesse paused. "You're not talking about tonight, are you?"

His father shook his head. "I think I know why you left tonight, but I'm shaky on last February."

There was pain in the words, and Jesse kicked himself all over again. "I'm sorry I left without telling anyone. It was wrong."

Mike nodded slowly.

He considered saying more. Dare's warning rang clear, though. The issues were and always had been his alone. He'd been so focused on himself back then —

Dare. Oh my God, he'd done it again.

"*Fuck.* I abandoned Dare at the damn shower." He snatched a piece of wood off the ground and hurled it at the woodshed. It bounced off, clattering downward with a crash. "God, I am so fucking *stupid*. This just confirms to everyone I'm an ass."

"No one knows." His dad cleared his throat. "Well, the part about you being an ass *tonight*. Dare told people you had something to take care of. Marion and I brought her home — they're doing some kind of womanly bonding ritual while I track you down."

Relief that she was okay warred with a twisted amusement at his father's carefully chosen words. "But people still think I'm *mostly* an ass, just not one tonight?"

"What do you usually act like, son? Can't blame people for calling a horse a horse."

Amusement bloomed into full-out derisive laughter. "You've never been shy to say it like it is."

His father's face tightened. "Wrong. I knew something was up with you for a long time before you left, and I didn't call you on it soon enough. I'm sorry for that."

Goddamn, his father was apologizing to him? "You didn't do anything."

"That was the trouble. I'm your father, and while I'm not responsible for you like I was when you were a little tyke, I'm always going to be your daddy. That means I should have kicked your ass and helped you fly straight a few years ago. Maybe it would have saved you a world of hurt."

"Don't you go blaming my behaviour on yourself," Jesse warned. "I'm responsible for me."

Mike nodded. "You are, but that's my point. I'm responsible for me, and family's the place where all of us connect. You need some help finding that place? Because we want you, son. We want you in this family, lock, stock and barrel."

"I'm not proud that I'm going to be a dad," Jesse confessed, the words rushing from him. "You were talking about that, and it made this sick lump stick in my belly because I'm *not* proud, and I couldn't stand another moment watching everyone else soak in your words and nod in agreement when that's not what I've got. Sitting and wishing things were different."

Wishing that he felt even a bit like what he saw in his brothers' and cousins' faces that night.

What he'd seen that morning a week ago in Joel's eyes as he looked at Vicki.

His father let out a heavy breath. "Well, now. I wondered, but I couldn't be certain. You and Dare — is

395

that not right, either?"

Jesse shook his head slowly. "I care about her. I'm going to look after her and the baby, but we're not in love."

Mike walked to the woodpile and worried a log piece with his foot before lifting his gaze to meet Jesse's "I can't make promises, but I don't see this as an impossible task. For you to fix what's wrong in your world. I do see it being something you're going to need to pull up your britches and put your ego aside to get the job done."

Jesse considered before offering a response. Was his ego getting in the way? Maybe, but hopefully less than before.

He *didn't* want to admit it had all been an accident. Dare. The baby.

"I want to be proud."

His father nodded. "You want to be in love?"

The question stopped him in his tracks. "I don't know how to answer that."

Mike took a deep breath. "Okay, leave that one for now. Son, I think you're getting ahead of yourself. I imagine being the youngest in a big family is a strange place to be. You get to see the journey those ahead of you took, and if you like where they're going, you just need to follow their lead, right?"

Jesse waited.

His dad stared off into the distance. "Only you need to follow your own path. Even if you like where they've ended up, chances are you'll walk a different road to get there."

"This sounds like a repeat of your *be your own man* spiel."

"Probably, because it's true." Mike grinned. "I like

to reuse my best material. Saves energy. Six boys, you know."

In spite of the frustrations Jesse felt inside, in spite of the worry he wasn't really needed, laughter rose. "Yeah, I might have noticed a time or two."

Mike slapped him on the shoulder.

"Let's focus on one issue. You're not proud because it's something you've accomplished. You're proud because it's something you're privileged to be a part of. Something greater than yourself, that you couldn't do alone."

Jesse considered the strength Ashley'd displayed the day Daisy arrived. "Couldn't give birth — damn straight."

His dad ignored his comment, reaching into his pocket and pulling out the long strip of paper he'd been peeking at during the baby shower.

He looked at it for a moment before holding it to Jesse.

"You missed the end of my speech. I worked hard on this, so I'd like to give it to you. Don't worry about it now, but I hope you read it later. I hope you think on it, and if you ever want to talk, my door is open." He glanced up at the twinkling stars that were blinking into existence as the sky darkened and night fell. "We should get back to the ladies. They're bound to have a late-night snack on the table — you probably could eat after chopping the equivalent of two men's work."

Then he refused to say anything more.

Jesse apologized to Dare when they entered the house, but she brushed it aside, curling up against him and offering a kiss in return. The swell of her stomach was there between them, Buckaroo moving in protest as their bodies connected briefly.

His mom and dad left not too much later. When he

came back in the house after walking them out, Dare had disappeared into the washroom, the shower running.

Jesse sat at the kitchen table and pulled out Mike's speech.

Words matter.

A man can buy a field and pay for cattle to live on it, but if that's all he does, he's not a rancher. A rancher — I'd make a list, but we all know how much work it takes to make the Coleman land our home. We know with every bone in our aching bodies, at times. Day after day, month after month, year after year. It's work that makes the difference.

A farmer's not someone who dumped a bucket of grain in a field then walked away. A man's not a husband because he said "I do" one fine Saturday afternoon then never saw his wife again.

A man is a father because he planted a seed. He's a daddy because of everything else he does.

Don't be a father to your children — be a daddy.

Jesse sat in the quiet darkness and let the words sink in. Or more like, he sat there, unable to move. He felt as if he'd been flattened with a heavy rock. His heart pounded and his ears rang, and if he moved too fast he might just fall over.

His dad was so fucking right — no surprise there.

Jesse shoved to his feet and marched into the bedroom in time to see one of his T-shirts fall into place over an otherwise naked woman.

Dare had a hand over her mouth, yawning, as she turned to face him. "Hey. I'm sorry I didn't wait. I'm so ready to crash, but I want to talk too."

Jesse pulled the edge of the quilt down and gestured

her in. "We can talk in here. I'll be one sec."

He hurried, stripping to his briefs and returning as quick as he could after getting ready for bed. Crawling between the covers and reaching for her.

Dare turned toward him, stroking a hand through his hair. "You okay?"

"Maybe." He took the time to breathe in her scent, all warm and soft and growing more familiar by the day. "Sorry for taking off on you."

"It's okay, really." Her eyes were huge. "Talk to me."

So much was going through his head at that moment, and some of it he was just starting to get a handle on himself. He wasn't sure he wanted to even try to voice what he was feeling.

But one thing he could admit. One thing that he wanted her to know. "I don't regret that we're here. It took a little while for everything to sink in, but I do want what's best for the baby."

"I know you do." She was all but petting him, fingers twirling in his hair. "I mean that. Maybe you can't see it, but I can."

He took a deep breath. "I want to feel proud when Buckaroo arrives."

Dare frowned.

"You know that expression Blake gets when his girls crowd around him? Or the way that Matt's face damn near glows when he holds Colt. Hell, I want to look at Buckaroo the way my dad looks at us, his grown-up sons, or at least the way he looks at us when we're not acting like asses. Like he's shocked and amused and astonished all at the same time."

"You don't think you're going to look like that?"

He hesitated. "I'm not sure. I don't think so."

She nodded slowly. "Okay."

Silence stretched between them for a moment before Dare spoke again.

"I don't think it's my place to tell you how you should feel, so I'm not going to. But can I suggest that maybe you're a little too close to the situation, and it's making it hard to see the truth?"

More cryptic comments. Jesse chuckled. "I need to pin a note to my chest that says, *Homegrown Cowboy: please use small words.*"

Dare pressed her lips against his and kissed him softly. "Small words? Here you go. Tomorrow is another day. Now, cuddle me."

She awkwardly rolled and curled herself up against him.

"See, *that* I understood," he teased, pulling her hips more firmly against him before resting a hand on where Buckaroo was hiding out.

He fell asleep with a million thoughts racing through his mind, and the baby's motions bumping his palm.

Chapter Twenty-Seven

Text messages, February 8th, ten plus years ago

Dare: *you guys on the road already?*
Mom: *heading out in five if your father and Walter can stop gossiping with the hotel owner*
Dare: *ha. Good luck on that*
Mom: *I know, but they're having too much fun to interrupt. Anyway, we should be back by lunch. Don't bother making anything in case we're late*
Dare: *okay. I'll see you when you get home*
Mom: *try to be dressed by then, k?*
Dare: *pyjamas are perfectly fine Saturday pants*
Mom: *lol. Sure they are. Love you, sweetie*
Dare: *love you too*
...
Dare: *you guys get lost or something?*
...
Dare: *Mom, where are you?*
...
Dare: *Mom?*

Jesse cursed his lousy timing. Of all the days for him to be on horseback out in one of the more remote sections of the ranch. He glanced over his shoulder at the thick black clouds roiling in the sky like some over-the-top special effects in an apocalyptic movie.

He guided Danger a little farther from the trees, trying to judge the correct distance so the forest would act as a wind block, yet they'd be out of reach of the branches being torn free and hurled toward the open field.

The wind had grown stiff enough it whipped through the crown land beside him. Eerie sounds whistled through the branches as if there were monsters hiding nearby, waiting for their opportunity to jump out. Bitter chill carried on the air, and another swear escaped as Jesse noticed a growing layer of white clinging to the ground.

It was fucking *snowing*. Barely the beginning of October — it wasn't supposed to snow yet.

He dragged his coat around him tighter, turning up the collar and hunching his shoulders to get out of the wind.

"Sorry, guys," he apologized to his horse and dog. "This was supposed to be a nice relaxing job."

Danger had his head down, tilted away from the wind as Jesse guided him on the safest route back to the horse trailer. Morgan wasn't very happy about the weather, either. Instead of running ahead with joyous glee like he had at the start of the day, he was tucked in close, moving strategically to use Danger as a wind block.

By the time they made it back to where his truck was parked, Jesse was chilled to the core. Danger went willingly into the trailer, eager to hide from the stormy weather.

Jesse rubbed Morgan down before letting him into the cab of the truck instead of ordering him into the back of the truck. "Just this once," he said. "It's not fit out there for man or beast."

With the heaters blasting, it still took thirty minutes for the inside of the cab to get warm enough that Jesse could take a deep breath, his gaze fixed on the road to make sure he didn't end up in a ditch. Every gust of wind picked up snow and flung it across his windshield, damn near creating a whiteout.

What had taken an hour to drive that morning took three to get home.

The instant he stopped in the yard and opened the truck door, Morgan took off at a run for the protection of the porch. Jesse led Danger into the horse shelter at the rental house, offering soothing words as the wind threw itself at the building hard enough to rattle the roof.

He had the saddle off and was reaching for the blanket when the door opened behind him. The wind grabbed it, slamming it against the solid wood of the barn.

Then Dare was there, rushing forward to grab hold of his shirt and shake him. "You..."

She was vibrating, eyes wild. Jesse wrapped his fingers around her wrists and attempted to pull her free, but she clutched him tighter, pressing her face against his chest and clinging as if she would never let go.

"Dare, what's wrong?" He laid a hand on the Buckaroo bump. "Everything okay?"

A second later she'd released him only to slide her icy cold hands up and link them around his neck. She pulled hard, jerking him toward her until she could catch his mouth with hers. Kissing him violently, fire and passion and fear in her movements.

She'd been scared — that much was clear.

Jesse reached down to pick her up, kissing her in return. Promising assurances even while stoking the fire that constantly burned between them. He walked to the side of the shelter where there were stacked hay bales, settling her on a blanket. Then he reached up and cupped her face in his hands, slowing the connection between them. Kissing deeper before pulling back to stare into her liquid-filled eyes. "Hey. I'm okay. Everything okay with you and Buckaroo?"

She nodded, then shook her head. "The baby's fine."

Her voice was ragged and pain-filled. He stroked her cheek. "But you're not fine."

Dare blinked, and a single tear rolled down her cheek. "The storm."

That's all she said, but her words were punctuated by a roar from nature, the walls of the barn shaking around them. She cringed, eyes closing tight as she hid herself against him again.

Something twisted inside Jesse. He pushed her knees apart so he could step in tighter, wrapping her in his arms until he could press their bodies together as close as possible with her belly.

He swore when he discovered she was nearly as icy as he was.

"What the hell have you been doing to get so cold?" he scolded, rubbing her back, trying to get heat into her torso.

Dare shook her head from side to side. "Waiting on the porch."

"Jeez. I'm sorry I'm late. The roads were a mess."

She shivered hard enough to nearly break them apart. Then instead of clinging to him, she was touching him more intimately. Hands slipping around so she could scratch her nails down his back. Feet hooked around his thighs. He didn't want to be getting turned on, but there was no way to resist the temptation of Dare in full seduction mode.

Because that's what she was doing. With her fingers driven into the back of his hair, she tugged him toward her neck. Pulling apart her shirt until her bare breasts were visible. Their heavy weight pressed against him briefly before she rocked back and jerked his shirt free from his jeans.

"Dammit, Dare. Let's go inside. You can ravish me there."

She wasn't listening. What she was doing was rubbing her palm over his dick with deliberate intention. He would've had to be dead to not react. When she popped open his zipper, he ignored the twinge of guilt that said they were fools for doing this in the cold air of the unheated barn. The rafters shook, wind whistling through the cracks as she all but ordered him to take her nipple into his mouth.

A sound escaped her, but this time it was sexual instead of fear, and that's when he decided to hell with it. This was what she wanted. For whatever reason, here and now, she needed him?

Not a fucking problem.

Only he took control. Shifting her hands behind her so that she leaned back enough he could reach both her breasts more easily. Gazing down at her, his mouth watering. "Right here?"

"*Yes.*"

No hesitation, so he gave none either. Instead he moved in and nipped lightly, and she cursed.

Jesse licked an apology before murmuring against her skin. "Sensitive?"

"Yes. Now, shut up and fuck me already."

He had his hands on the back of her pants, stripping the material away with great appreciation for the extra elastic in the waistline. Meant he didn't have to move her far to drag everything off her and leave her bare from the waist down, her shirt hanging open.

She wanted this, and he had no intention of taking his time. It was too damn cold out to linger.

He slipped his fingers over her sex, going straight to her clit. Circling with increasing pressure as he moved up and kissed her, her breasts and belly in contact with him as he got her ready.

She stretched against him, lifting her lips from his. "I need you inside me."

He tested her wetness, shocked to find she was ready. "I don't want to hurt you."

Dare shook her head as he backed off just far enough to release his cock. "*Please.*"

It was the work of a moment to line up with her opening and gently slide in. She'd replaced her hands on the blanket, leaning back so that the only connection between them was the intimate glide of his cock into her passage.

Jesse gripped her hips, watching as his length disappeared over and over. Slowly at first, but as she moaned her approval, something else took control from him. The storm mixed with their lovemaking to create another layer of sound and motion.

He glanced up at her face.

He'd expected to find her eyes closed as she concentrated on finding pleasure, but instead she was staring at him. Her lips were slightly in an O, but her eyes were fixed on his. The emotion written there — fear had been washed away by sexual pleasure leaving something less readable.

Whatever she felt, Jesse felt privileged to be a part of it. To witness it, and make it appear there. She was so damn beautiful.

He was turned on like crazy. Everything about this woman made him want more. He caressed her hips as he slowed the pace just enough to allow him room to touch her clit.

That's all it took.

"*Jesse.*" A whispered benediction.

A second later he joined her. Stilling his hips against hers so he could enjoy the tight squeeze of her body around him. Mind-blowing pleasure.

He could've stayed there for longer except it was damn cold. "We're going inside right now," he ordered, as he pulled free then helped put her pants back into place.

Jesse wrapped her up in the blanket and guided her across the yard and up the porch stairs to the house. As they passed him, tucked into his protected spot out of the wind, Morgan's tail thumped in greeting against the thick pillow that was his bed. He raised his head from the oversized bone he was gnawing on for long enough to bump his nose against Dare's leg, and she bent to caress his head.

She was clearly in love with his dog, Jesse realized. Before rushing out to the barn she'd taken the time to give Morgan a welcome-home treat.

Now it was Jesse's turn to take care of her. Inside the door he pointed down the hall. "Hot shower. I'll be back after I take care of Danger. We'll have a drink and talk."

Dare nodded, not meeting his eyes.

"Hey." He pressed his fingers over her cheek. "I'll be right back. I promise."

He worked quickly, needing to be with Dare, but refusing to leave his animal uncared for after the hellish ride Danger'd been through.

Soon as he could, though, Jesse was back in the house to discover Dare all wrapped up in an oversized robe, fuzzy slippers on her feet, making cups of tea for them.

The smile she offered this time was far more real. "I'm okay. Go have a shower and warm up yourself. Then we'll talk."

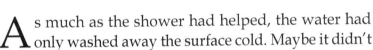

As much as the shower had helped, the water had only washed away the surface cold. Maybe it didn't make any sense, but Dare knew exactly what had driven the ice from inside her heart.

Making love with Jesse.

She grabbed the fixings for grilled cheese sandwiches and got them cooking while Jesse showered and dressed. Putting food on the table was a nice distraction from letting her mind linger on what had been haunting her since the early afternoon.

From the moment the first snowflakes began to fall and the sky clouded over, an inkling of fear had strolled in like it owned her ass. It'd been a long time since the nightmares had been so real, but she'd been attempting to nap on the couch when the storm started in earnest, and somehow the wind and blowing had just been enough to take her back in time.

In spite of being warm through and through, another shiver struck.

Jesse was there, rubbing his hands down her arms and pressing a kiss to the side of her neck. "Let me take over. You go wrap yourself up again."

She shook her head, "I'm okay, really I am. Get yourself a drink, and I'll have the sandwiches ready in a minute."

He kissed her again before taking off to follow her instructions, topping up her cup of tea before settling into a chair at the kitchen table.

She slid a full plate in front of him, then pulled her chair so she could sit beside him.

Jesse laughed softly. "Good thing I know how to eat one-handed."

He squeezed her fingers.

She hadn't even been aware she'd grabbed hold of him. Whatever. She wasn't going to apologize for it. "I'm glad you made it back safe."

"It wasn't that bad," he insisted. "I just didn't want to take any chances."

Oh boy. "That's good. No chances is goodness."

He leaned forward and looked up into her face. "What happened? I didn't know you were scared of storms."

"I'm not," she insisted. "It's stupid, because it's not even like there's any real connection..."

"Oh." He held her hand a little tighter, stroking his thumb against the back of her knuckles. "Your family."

A deep sigh escaped her.

Jesse hesitated. "You know, you never did tell me what happened. You don't have to, but if it would help, I'm here for you."

"I know. And I'm glad." She examined his face.

It truly wasn't the storm's fault. It was all about suddenly feeling very alone — and *that* sensation she wasn't strong enough to take.

"Ginny and I had a science fair in Calgary. Provincial finals, and everyone drove out to cheer us on. At the end of the day Ginny and I went home with our classmates on the school bus — legal liability and all that stuff. My family and her parents drove home together, but outside of Calgary a storm came rolling in, so they stopped in a motel. It was the responsible thing to do. Avoid winter driving conditions because who knows what could've happened, right?"

He didn't speak, just put his arm around her and pressed his lips to her temple.

"We got home on the bus fine. The next morning, they checked out of the hotel to head home and some asshole who'd been out all night drinking swerved into their lane. I waited and I waited, but they never came home."

"Jesus, Dare. I'm so fucking sorry." He pulled her body against him, holding the back of her neck. The two of them tangled together. "I'm sorry you were scared today. I'm sorry being late reminded you of what you lost."

She'd been more than scared, she'd been *terrified*, but she didn't want to admit that.

As time had passed, as she tried to contact him and got no response, the less she'd been able to control her fear. Yes, it was because she'd been reminded of what she'd lost — the people who she loved the most.

That's when it had hit her like a clap of thunder echoing against the roof. As she alternated between staring out the living room window and standing on the porch, peering in vain down the lane in the hopes she'd see his truck returning...

She *loved* him.

There was no denying it anymore. Yes, she admired him, and enjoyed his company. She loved how compatible they were when it came to sex, but all of those things together weren't just friendship, and weren't just because of Buckaroo.

When they came out to Rocky, she'd warned herself she wasn't supposed to fall in love with the Colemans. The truth was she'd probably been in love with *him* already back then.

Love. That was what had scared her so much. The thought of having lost the man she loved.

Now she faced a completely different dilemma. What did she do with this discovery? Was he ready for her to up and announce what she felt inside?

It was going to take a little more deliberation before she came to a conclusion. All she knew right now was that being together was exactly what she needed.

She let him read the sincerity there in her expression. "Sorry for jumping you in the barn, but totally not sorry."

"I get it." He leaned in closer, his voice a caress. "It's not my place to tell you how you should feel, but I think sometimes the best response to high emotion is high-test, wild sex."

His grin widened.

Dare had to fight to keep from grinning in return. "Only *some* times, though?"

Jesse nodded, his expression suddenly all respectable and correct. Like a professor delivering a lecture or a preacher from the pulpit — only a whole lot more irreverent. "Definitely. Other times call for blow jobs, doggie-style, or even anal."

A laugh burst from her that was more like a donkey bray than a genteel lady, and Jesse joined in.

They ended up in the living room, covered with blankets as they cuddled together and watched lighthearted movies until the storm blew over. Buckaroo went to town, the surface of her belly moving like some alien infestation, and she caught Jesse watching her stomach more than the TV screen.

It was cozy. It was comfortable, and it was exactly how Dare had imagined two people in love would spend an evening.

By the next morning the weather had returned to more typical October temperatures. The snow melted and left behind puddles in the yard. Jesse kissed her goodbye, and kissed her belly, and she leaned against the doorframe and watched him leave, and wondered how on earth she was going to manage to stop from letting her love burst free.

Because that's how she felt. As if she were bursting at the seams with the need to shout how much she loved him.

She did a little work on the blog, but it was no use. The itching drive to discuss her discovery wouldn't let her concentrate. She absolutely needed to talk to someone about this.

Her text to Ginny went unanswered. She wasn't about to talk to her brothers. Good thing she had somebody else she trusted who was a lot closer at hand.

Vicki was working that week at the golf course, putting together a long line of desserts for the upcoming Thanksgiving weekend. When she saw Dare come in, she stopped what she was doing, washed her hands and handed over a hot-from-the-oven cookie. "Perfect timing.

412

Next batch is already in the oven, and I need a break."

"Gingersnaps. Yummy." Dare took a big bite of the warm cookie, washing it down with some tea while she gathered her courage.

Vicki raised an eyebrow. "You look far too serious considering you're demolishing a cookie."

"I need some advice," Dare admitted.

Her friend smiled. "I'll give it a shot."

"How do I make Jesse happy?"

Vicki coughed, leaning forward as if the cookie piece she'd just swallowed went down the wrong tube. By the time she cleared her throat, her cheeks were bright and her eyes a little on the wild side. "Girl, if that's what you need advice on, I'm the last person you should talk to."

Dare paused. She wasn't going near Jesse's secret, but this one was hers to share. "When we got here, I thought he was in love with you."

Vicki's jaw dropped. "I'm pretty sure he hated my guts."

Dare shook her head. "It didn't look like hate to me." She paused. "You don't think that way now, do you?"

Vicki frowned. "No. Actually, I was telling Joel that the other day, how different it is now with Jesse. So much more comfortable..." She panicked for a moment. "Not in a way like I'm hot for him, or anything. You know I'm head over heels in love with Joel, right?"

"Of course you are." Dare sucked in her courage. "I don't know how to be head over heels. But I want to be."

"With Jesse?"

"It would be convenient, seeing as he'll be in my life, and all."

"Oh, honey, there's nothing convenient about Jesse

Coleman. Or about love, when it comes down to it."

Vicki shook her head. "But I don't get it. Why are you acting as if you just figured out you're in love?"

Dare fidgeted for a minute before confessing. "He offered to marry me because I was pregnant. He was doing the right thing."

The confusion on Vicki's face grew thicker. "Okay, you're not making any sense whatsoever. You think *Jesse* is just doing the right thing?"

"Of course he is."

Vicki flustered for a minute before waving a hand. "I mean, I agree he's doing the right thing by being there for you and the baby, but…"

Dare waited, impatience rising by the second.

Her friend stopped fussing and a look of complete satisfaction replaced the earlier frustration. "Oh, this is good. This is *really* good."

"*What?*" Dare didn't attempt to keep her irritation out of her voice. "I will do something evil to you if you don't stop looking at me like I'm the most interesting science experiment you've seen in a long time."

Vicki relented, a smile blooming across her face. "It's just that it's pretty clear to me that you're in love."

Dare swallowed hard. My God, she hoped wearing her heart on her sleeve didn't end up embarrassing Jesse. "You can tell?"

Her friend nodded. "Unless you're up for Academy-nominee-level acting awards, everything since you showed up on Jaxi and Blake's doorstep has said you were a couple. A *real* couple."

Dare did a double take. "Wait. You think *Jesse's* in love with me?"

"That's what I just said." Vicki raised a brow.

414

"You didn't know that part either? What have you two been doing? And that was a rhetorical question because obviously..."

She gestured toward Buckaroo.

"Hey, you're in the same condition," Dare pointed out.

"Well, it's pretty damn hard to say no to a Coleman when they're being all sexy and whatnot, but this isn't about the babies." She leaned back in her chair, a gloating expression on her face. "So. What do you do with this newfound knowledge? Or more specifically, how can I blackmail you with it?"

"I'm not too pregnant to put a hurt on you," Dare warned, but she was smiling because maybe it wasn't a terrible thing. Maybe if Vicki thought she and Jesse were already a real couple, then it wasn't too far of a stretch for it to *be* real.

Still, she was cognizant of the fact Jesse was still finding his way back home. He had enough things he was working on.

She met Vicki's gaze. "I think what I need is for you to just be happy for me, and let me figure out when and where it's right to let Jesse know how I feel."

Vicki caught her fingers in a squeeze. "I am happy for you. I'm actually *really* happy, because I didn't expect this."

"For me to fall in love with Jesse?"

Her friend shifted uncomfortably for a moment. "It's a little more selfish than that. I didn't expect Jesse to have such good taste when he fell in love. I always thought he'd pick someone who was a bit of an asshole, but you're not."

"I'm a lot of an asshole?" Dare teased, glowing inside from the phrase *Jesse falling in love.*

Vicki laughed. "What you are is a wonderful person, and I'm glad he brought you into my life."

"I'm glad too." It wasn't just family for Buckaroo that she'd discovered. It was family for her as well, and she shuffled out of the chair and offered Vicki a close hug, and it was nothing like that first day when they'd met, almost reluctant to discover they enjoyed each other's company.

It was real.

Dare shook a finger at Vicki. "Don't you say anything, and I mean not to Joel either."

Vicki made a face. "Really?"

Dammit, she couldn't make that kind of demand. "Okay, if you *have* to talk about what a fool I am, you have to make Joel promise not to tell Jesse. I swear I'll get around to it as quickly as I can."

Her friend drew an X over her chest. "I solemnly swear I will make sure Joel doesn't tell Jesse that you are already head-over-heels in love with him."

Dare snickered. "That will have to do, I guess."

Vicki loaded up a half-dozen cookies, and Dare headed home, holding tight to a bag that contained a warm gift of friendship.

It was nearly as sweet as the warm glow of love in her heart.

Chapter Twenty-Eight

Jesse somehow managed to step on Dare's last nerve before they'd even finished breakfast. She spent more time glaring than finishing her toast.

"What?" he demanded.

Her eyes narrowed. "If I have to explain why I'm mad, you're going to regret it."

"I just said I didn't think you needed to be hauling stuff all over the house. I can help you when I get home later."

"After I said decorating was something I was looking forward to doing? I'm *bored*, Jesse. There's not a lot on the approved list for me with this weight in front of me."

She picked up her toast and snapped off a piece, baring her teeth at him. Mad, but still able to tease.

He could handle that. "Okay. If it makes you happy, and it's on the approved list — "

"Asshole," she muttered, loud enough for him to hear, all the while picking an invisible speck off her sleeve.

He ignored her, but couldn't stop his smile from widening as he kept going. " — I hope you have a wonderful time decorating. If there's anything you need help with, I'll be home later."

Dare swallowed then offered a sheepish smile. "Sorry I'm a grump."

He grabbed their plates and carried them to the counter before returning to press a kiss to her temple.

"You're cute when you're a grump." He leaned over and spoke to her belly. "Be good for your mama. No elbowing her in the bladder, and keep those boots off her ribs."

He pressed a kiss to the swell, somewhat astonished Dare was able to continue to do as much as she was with Buckaroo taking up so much room.

His good mood followed him all the way over to Joel's.

His brother stepped out of the trailer, Vicki following. Joel turned back and gave Vicki a concentrated kiss, one hand sliding possessively over her waist. She wasn't showing yet, but it was clear they were both pretty hyped about the baby.

It was Joel who brought up the idea. "I want to go up to check out the house. Come with me? We can ride."

Ever since they'd returned to the Six Pack ranch, Jesse had been avoiding Sunset Ridge. The thought of it, though, had become this itch at the back of his brain. It seemed smarter to stay away than have to face the final truth — that his earlier decisions had changed part of his future irrevocably.

But now, with Joel asking, it seemed he just had to face the truth and deal.

"Sure," he agreed as cheerfully as possible.

Which was how they ended up stepping back in time, the horses carrying them on the familiar route to where the land hit the foothills, variations in height rising in waves and rounded hillocks as if the land itself were pregnant.

They approached from the east, which meant they

were nearly at the top of the rise before the building site became visible.

What the hell?

He looked over at Joel. "What's going on?"

His brother's lips curled into a smile. "Looking good, right?"

Without answering Jesse's question, he urged his horse ahead till there was too much distance to demand a response.

Because when they'd topped the ridge, there wasn't just one house in construction, there were two.

By the time Jesse caught up with Joel, his brother had dismounted and left his horse grazing. Jesse dropped his reins as well, and made his way to where activity was visible, a crew of men raising sheeting onto sidewalls and nailing it into place.

The building site made no sense. *Two* houses?

Oh. The Colemans were always doing house shuffles. Maybe Matt and Hope didn't want to live in town anymore.

The ache in Jesse's gut got deeper.

"The post-and-beam packages were up for sale," Joel shared. "Someone paid the first half of the deposit then went bankrupt, so the company offered a fire sale if we'd take the frames off their hands. All we had to pay were the outstanding second payments. It was too good a deal to turn down."

"Only paid half? Seriously?"

"We were in the right place at the right time." Joel lifted a hand and pointed to the nearest house, the one on the north. "Vicki and I decided to put a small porch on this side for when we want to catch the sunrise, but the bigger porch is on the west."

Jesse couldn't make heads or tails of it. In fact, all he could do was point at the second building.

His brother hesitated. "Blake said not to say anything yet, but fuck it. That's *your* house, Jesse. Yours and Dare's"

The words didn't make any sense. *"What?"*

For a second Joel didn't say anything then his lips curled into a smirk. "Damn your face right now is hysterical."

Screw what his face looked like, it felt as if his brains were dribbling out his ears. "What the hell are you talking about?"

Joel gestured at the second construction rising on the south lot. "When we brought in the guys to do the foundation, I convinced Blake it only made sense. Like taking down the old barn. There was no reason not to have them do the second basement while they were here. Plus, it *was* a sweet deal on the framing packages."

"You're building us a house." Jesse shook his head.

"The Colemans are building two houses," Joel corrected him. "Vicki and I get the house to the north, and if you want it, the one to the south is yours."

There was nothing real about this entire situation except when Jesse looked hard and blinked, the house was still there. Walls finished to vertical, the roof already shingled.

"I don't understand," he admitted.

"You always said you wanted the south site."

"It's a better site," Jesse said automatically. "That's why I bossed you around to make sure you knew I wanted it."

"It's a matter of opinion which is better," Joel said easily. "And I couldn't build there."

"Why not?"

Joel looked shocked. "It was yours."

Jesse stared at him, unable to move.

His brother took a deep breath. "When you left, it was a hell of a shock, but even when I was pissed off beyond belief, I always hoped you would come back. When you finally came to your senses, I wanted you to have what we'd always dreamed about. I didn't want you to feel like you'd been left out of something that was important to us both."

Something turned inside Jesse at that moment, like the final tumbler falling into place to undo a lock.

There are moments that define a life, he realized.

Leaving his family, even for what turned out to be childish and selfish reasons, had been one of those moments. His stupid decision to crawl into bed with Vicki had been another. Heck, he could argue it had been the catalyst for everything that had come after. Choosing to track down Dare, choosing to return to the ranch — those were all forks in the road where he'd decided which way to go.

Yet right now it hit hard that it was still a selfish way to live. To consider which path he'd felt led to take, and which turns had brought him to this moment.

In spite of being rightfully upset, Joel had made a deliberate choice to continue to love him. Even though Jesse had all but slammed the door in his face, his brother had left space in his life for Jesse's return.

It wasn't about considering which path was right for him, but which path was right for him *and* the people around him. Everyone he cared about.

The idea was humbling, and awe-inspiring, and more than a little like a very heavy two-by-four being expertly applied to Jesse's stubborn-ass ways.

The apology he'd offered months ago had been real, but nowhere near enough. He knew that now.

He also knew he was up a creek without a paddle, and the only way he was getting out of this was with a heck of a lot of help. Dare had that same kind of sacrificial giving heart. Since the moment he met her she'd been there for him, and believed in him —

But right now he needed to focus on Joel. On finally making everything between them right.

Jesse cleared his throat. "I need to tell you something. Back when you and Vicki started dating, and I got all judgmental. I didn't do it to be malicious. I thought I knew better than you what was going on. I was trying to protect you, and misjudging Vicki. And misjudging you, because I was the stupid one, not you. You were moving on, and I was trying to stay in control." He stepped in front of his brother. "There're no words that can change what I've done. I wish — "

Joel slapped a hand on his shoulder. "That's not the direction we're looking anymore, remember?"

Right, but still…he needed to actually fucking say it.

"Joel, I'm sorry. For the things I did that drove a wedge between us. You did nothing wrong. *Nothing*, this is all on me, and okay," he hurried to finish because Joel was lifting his fists as if to forcibly shut him up. "I'm looking forward now, and what I'm saying to you is — I'll be there for you. I don't know what that will look like, and hell, I expect I'll screw up again, but *never* again will I cut you off because at least I know better."

Joel's face twisted for a moment before he frowned. "You damn ass."

The words came out choked, and suddenly Jesse

wasn't breathing too easily either. His throat seemed to be closing up, and his eyes were watering.

He pinched the bridge of his nose. "Stupid dust."

Joel snorted — this kind of squeaking noise between amusement and tears, and fuck if it wasn't just enough to toss Jesse's control into the wind.

He caught his brother in a bear hug and squeezed him tight. It seemed the only way to stop from breaking down and crying like a baby.

Joel held him tightly, one hand patting him on the shoulder. It wasn't gentle — more as if his brother was trying to pound some sense into his feeble brain.

Jesse didn't care that it was borderline painful, because it was Joel — hell, if his brother wanted to run him over a few times with the John Deere, he'd willingly toss himself to the ground and wait.

When they broke apart Joel was grinning. "You want to check out your house?"

"Hell, yeah." He followed Joel on the well-worn path toward the front door. "I still can't believe you guys would start building this house when you didn't even know where I was."

"Rafe did tell us you were in Alberta and that he was keeping in touch with you. He didn't tell us much more, even when we threatened to mess up his pretty face."

Which was what Jesse had figured. "I'm glad you knew that much."

"Hey, as mad as I was about you taking off, you found Dare when you went AWOL. Can't complain about that."

"She's the best thing that's ever happened — "

Jesse stopped. One step away from entering the house that he hadn't deserved but had gotten anyway. "Fucking hell, I'm a fool."

423

She was another thing he hadn't deserved but had gotten anyway. Her, and Buckaroo.

"Jesse?"

He glanced up at Joel. "I'm in love with her."

Joel laughed. "You're just figuring that out now?"

"Yeah." He'd been clueless, but in this case he didn't mind so much. Something about having finally come to his senses created this wonderful sensation. He wasn't going to regret he had taken this long to figure it out, because holy fucking hell, he was in love.

There was nothing more to think about.

Wait, there *was* more to think about. How was he supposed to go about telling Dare?

He turned on the spot and slammed smack into Joel who was standing there with a stupid grin on his face.

"I need to go find her," Jesse insisted, attempting to push past his brother. "I need to tell her."

Joel didn't move. "It is *so* amusing to watch you turn into a love-struck fool."

"You're in my way," Jesse warned.

Joel raised a brow. "I thought you were going to look through the house."

Suddenly Jesse didn't know which way to turn. He wanted to look at the house, but he needed to tell Dare that he loved her. Hell, he wanted to go find Dare so he could tell her about the incredible, unbelievable house, *and* so he could tell her he loved her.

"Your feet stuck to the ground?" Joel teased.

Jesse whirled toward his voice and nearly tipped over, he was so out of control and discombobulated. His brother was a dozen paces away on the path leading back toward the horses.

"Where are you going?" An out-of-the-blue thought

424

struck. "Oh my God, what if Dare doesn't love me? Wait, that's stupid. Of course she loves me, but if she *doesn't*, I'm going to find a way and *make* her fall in love with me, because this is crazy, and there's no way that — "

A laugh escaped Joel. Soft at first, then with rising volume and enthusiasm until he was shaking his head and nearly crying. It was contagious, and Jesse caught himself grinning as well.

"So. You're in love, are you?" Joel patted him on the shoulder when they finally pulled themselves back under control.

"I think so. If wanting to act like the world's biggest dork, and do anything I can to make her smile means I'm in love. Also, I want to step in and protect her from anything that could remotely hurt her."

Joel nodded, walking at his side back to the horses, his arm strong and supportive around him. "Sounds like love to me. Now, what are you going to do about it?"

Jesse was ready to shout it to the mountains. "I'll make it up as I go along."

His twin laughed. "Now that sounds like the Jesse I've always known."

She spent the first ten minutes after Jesse left kicking her own butt for being cranky.

It had to be hormones. *Stupid freaking pregnancy hormones.*

Guilt slipped in, and she had to admit the truth.

She patted Buckaroo fondly, even though by this point the enormous bubble in front of her seemed more determined to get in her way than cooperate. "Mama is sorry she's in a bad mood. I need to tell your daddy something important, but I keep chickening out. You need to learn from my mistake. It's important to always be brave."

She wasn't the fastest home decorator at the moment, and she had wonderful plans Jesse had nearly spoiled by refusing to get out of her hair. But he was right, there were some things she just couldn't deal with on her own.

While she waited for her help to arrive, she pulled the pile of pictures and wall hangings out of the closet where Vicki had stashed them for her a couple of days earlier.

An hour later the bedsheets were in the dryer, the pictures were all hung, and she popped her feet up on the coffee table and closed her eyes for a few minutes.

The rest time was perfect because she had energy again when the doorbell rang. She awkwardly pulled herself to her feet, thrilled to see a delivery van outside.

"Right on time," she offered as she swung the door open.

Jesse's brother Daniel stood on the doorstep, workmen behind him carrying parts for a new bedframe and mattress.

Daniel offered an enormous hug, careful of her belly. "Show me which rooms you want set up, and I'll get the guys to make the switch."

Once they'd moved out of the way, the men took over. Daniel escorted her back to the kitchen where he insisted she sit down while he brought her a drink and slid a second chair closer so she could prop up her feet.

"You're just as bad as the rest of them," she complained. "I'm not breakable."

"No, you're not," he agreed. "But if you think I'm not

426

going to treat you extra careful right now, you haven't spent enough time around my ma and dad yet."

She would give him that much. "Mike and Marion have made quite an impression on me. They did a good job raising you boys."

Daniel was the brother she'd spent the least amount of time around, but she liked him. Dare admired that he'd picked his own path, even though his woodworking was different from what the rest of his family loved.

He offered a smile. "They're *still* doing a good job, even when they're not handing out advice. You wouldn't believe the number of times I've caught myself asking, *What would Mike do?* He's got big boots for us to try and fill."

"Well, from what I've seen whenever your sons have been around, you're doing a great job."

Jesse's brother grinned harder. "I hope so. Beth has a lot to do with it as well. She's pretty damn amazing."

They visited until the workmen announced everything was set up and then Daniel gave her a farewell hug. "Bring Jesse over on Saturday night. The boys want to teach him some new game, and Beth has some fun things put aside for you to peek at for your blog."

Then she was alone again, hurrying to get everything done before Jesse showed up. She cranked up the music and sang along as she settled into a comfortable groove, making beds and fluffing pillows.

She was even good and avoided dragging furniture around.

Well, she was *mostly* good, just wiggling one dresser until it rocked itself into the spot she needed it.

By the time Jesse returned, she'd had time to make up the bed and arrange some extra decorations. The guest room looked shiny as well, ready for when her family from Heart Falls stopped by.

Now she had other plans for the rest of this day.

Jesse shot into the room as if he were jet-propelled.

She looked him over carefully. "How many cups of coffee did you and Joel have today?" she asked with a laugh.

He turned his gaze on her, and like a predator with its game in sight, stalked closer. "Just one."

Whatever had come over him, she had zero objections. Jesse's fingers cradled the back of her head, his fingers tightened on her hair and he adjusted the tilt of her head until her mouth was within easy reach.

The kiss he laid on her was scalding hot.

His other hand dropped to her lower back, supporting her as he kissed her until she was breathless. Pulling away just far enough to stare into her eyes, the beautiful blue reflecting there mesmerizing her.

"Well, hello," she murmured happily, wondering what had put this kind of energy into his entire body.

"Did you have a good day while I was gone?"

He brought her to vertical and she nodded. "There's a surprise for you in the bedroom."

Instantaneous grin.

Dare rolled her eyes. "I'm not talking about *sex*. Well, I could be talking about sex, but that's not the surprise."

Jesse slipped his fingers through hers, walking slowly down the hall at her side. "Right. The decorating."

He stole a glance into the room that had been set up as a nursery, his mom and Jaxi and Vicki and all the girls coming over to get it ready a week ago. A flannel quilt made of dozens and dozens of squares hung over the edge of the crib — the one the family had started the day

Dare went into the hospital. His fingers squeezed hers for a moment before he moved on to the guest room.

He paused in the doorway. Dare looked at it with new eyes, smiling at the little things that had been brought from the cottage down at Silver Stone.

"It looks great, but where did you get the bed?" he asked.

"It's the old bed. I bought a new one for the master bedroom."

He looked damn impressed. "Nice."

Dare nodded. "You know, this is the first time in my life I've ever bought a bed. Is that stupid?"

Jesse shrugged. "I don't know. I've never bought a bed before, either."

Amusement returned. "Seriously? Jeez, what a slacker."

He pulled her into the guest room and took a leisurely stroll around, laughing as he glanced at the poster on the wall. "Cowboys are like guns. If you keep one around long enough, you're going to want to shoot it."

"Truth in advertising," she said.

He took his time and was properly appreciative, but she was eager for him to get to the main event.

His response entering the master bedroom was worth the effort. "Holy shit. This is gorgeous, Dare."

The bed was a four-poster, with solid wooden beams for corners. Queen-size, which meant she didn't have to be farther away from him than necessary. Not that she'd *told* him that yet, damn her ass.

"Daniel and his boys made the bed. The quilt is from Hope's stash." Dare stepped forward and pointed to a pair of pictures on the wall. "Your mom and dad gave me this, and I got Caleb to send me the other one."

Two pictures, aerial shots. Six Pack and Silver Stone, beautiful pastoral scenes with the mountains in the distance. Different, unique and yet distinctly home in her heart.

He examined them closely, happiness written all over his face. "I love them. Thank you for doing this up so beautifully."

His gaze fell on another poster that she'd placed on the wall opposite the bed. He didn't say anything, not for a few minutes before turning back to her, a smile on his lips. "Is that true?"

"The saying on the plaque? Definitely."

My heroes have always been cowboys.

She'd seen the phrase in a magazine, and now the bold proclamation hung there in a spot where she'd see it every day.

Jesse nodded firmly.

Then he took her hand as they continued the tour, moving to the bedside. He ran a hand over the quilt before pressing on the mattress, glancing back at her slyly. "Seems firm enough."

The next thing she knew she was seated on the bed, Jesse leaning over her, one hand planted on the mattress on either side of her hips. "Do you like it?" she asked.

"I like lots of things. You might need to be a little more specific."

She wiggled backward, thrilled when he joined her. "The bedroom."

"*Our* bedroom."

It wasn't a question. Plus, his entire intonation was different than the casual way he'd said that phrase before.

Dare's heart gave a little kick. "Ours?"

He nodded before reaching for her. "I've been

430

thinking about something you said once. Funny how it stuck in my mind, but there's a certain complaint I need to correct."

Totally distracted. That's what she was. He'd lifted her hand to his mouth and was nibbling on her fingertips. "You forgot to eat lunch? You need a snack..."

"You like peanut butter on celery but don't like raisins on top, which is really odd considering it's called ants on a log for a reason, and you like raisins in everything else. Including cookies, which I forgive you for because you add enough chocolate chips to hide them."

She couldn't help it. A giggle escaped as he kissed her little finger then moved to the next.

"You drink pop with ice, water without ice, and milk straight from the container — and don't say you never, because I've caught you. Twice."

"Guilty," she admitted, wondering what was going on, but happy to let it unfold as he gave her another kiss, this time sucking the tip of her ring finger into his mouth before pulling away.

Dare relaxed back on the bed as he moved intently through her next two fingers and thumb.

"You like wearing pale sunshine colours, or browns and blues, but your first pick for house stuff is all bright colours. When you're working on a blog entry that's not quite right you wander around in a daze. Sometimes you get thinking so hard you stop and don't move for ages. You're wickedly loyal to friends and family, but you don't put up with bullshit from them just because they're yours."

He paused to undo the row of buttons at the front of her blouse.

"Not that I'm complaining." Dare offered with a sigh

of pleasure as he stroked the skin he exposed, his big palm sliding along her ribs. "But what're you doing?"

"Fixing a mistake."

He lifted her up just far enough to undo her bra, and somehow a minute after that she was down to nothing but her undies. "Hmm. I would have called it *Stripping Dare*, but you go on and do your thing."

Jesse picked up her foot and rubbed along her arch, and she just about melted into a puddle. "Your sex noises — my god, you make them all the time. Every fucking time I get hard, which is a real pain when we're at the dinner table with my family and you're damn near orgasming over the dessert."

She laughed, then groaned as he kissed her toe. "Oops?"

"You smell like heaven — half the time it's because you've got on some herbal thing Ginny concocted, and half the time it's because you spent hours outdoors in spite of hauling this precious burden around with you."

He caressed a hand over her belly, the expression in his eyes one of adoration. He might think he didn't have *the look*, but he totally did.

Something inside her crumbled to a messy pile of love-struck mush. "*Jesse*."

One sweep of his hand later she was naked, and then he was too, pulling her into his lap and looking over her with awe on his face. "When we reconnected, you said what I knew about you I could list on one hand, and you were right."

Memory like a steel trap. "I guess."

Jesse laid her hand on his chest then covered it with his own. "I know lots more now. I know where your ticklish spots are, and where to rub to make you relax, or make you *really* turned on."

His hands slid over her in sweeping caresses. Brief touches that were heating her up and proving his point. Making her want him even more than she already did.

Dare let her head fall back as she closed her eyes and felt the caring in his touch. He caught her by the hips and pulled their bodies together. Buckaroo bump and all.

His face — his *eyes*. Dare cupped his cheek, and he took a deep breath.

"Sometimes in your sleep when you have a bad dream you'll tighten up, but you turn to me and tug my arm over you as if you're sure that I'll protect you, and I know…" he took a deep breath, rushing on with that cocky attitude turned into something far more precious, "…I know I'll fucking do it. I'll do *anything* to be there for you, because I love you."

The ball of joy inside Dare didn't just burst. It exploded like a firecracker, filling the room with light and energy until the walls glowed. "Really?"

His eyes sparkled, happiness shining out. "I can say it again, and again, until I use *all* your toes and fingers if you want."

"I love you too." She couldn't believe this was happening. "I mean, I've been trying to tell you for a couple days, but I didn't want you to think you needed to say it back, and now you — "

Jesse cut off her rambling with a kiss that turned molten. She was a very willing participant as he lifted her hips and guided them together.

Slowly. So very slow and careful, until she rested in his lap and they were totally connected.

She sighed, and he laughed, and then they looked into each other's eyes.

"I really do love you," Dare said. "And this

feels amazing."

Jesse helped her rock over his length, their bodies connected and touching as they moved. Intimacy wrapping them in a spiral of pleasure. The pretty surroundings a backdrop that faded away as he took her past the point of no return, the two of them shaking in each other's arms.

They lay back under the quilt for a while after that, arms and legs tangled together as much as they could with her belly between them, but he refused to let her roll over. Just stared into her eyes and stroked hair back behind her ear.

"I like your wall hanging," he told her.

Dare smiled. "I made it myself."

He nodded. "Can I be one of your heroes?"

She let out a happy sigh. "You're my first choice for hero, every time."

Chapter Twenty-Nine

Blog post: Plant a Seed

One of the things I admire the most about people is when I discover they've done something that has far-reaching consequences they may never get to enjoy.

The simplest example of this is people who plant a tree. You've seen it, driving through a new area of town where there's nothing but infrastructure in place. Roads, maybe, and the skeletons of houses rising in the middle of barren land. Once the houses are there, people put in lawns and plant trees, and in some ways it looks a little ridiculous because the trees are about the size of a pencil, but future-thinking people don't look and see what's there at that moment. They're imagining what it will look like tomorrow.

Then we drive across town to a community that's been there for years. The trees rise above the rooflines, green growing things everywhere.

In the country, we plant windrows. At the edge of a field we put in a line of trees that are nothing but hope and anticipation. Five or ten years down the road, they'll become a solid line of protection that keeps the soil in place and the crops from damage.

Sometimes we don't know what a difference we'll make in the future. Sometimes we do — a deliberate choice.

Either way, it's an interesting concept to consider that while we live in the present we're impacting the future.

Jesse knew exactly what he wanted, but getting to that point was proving to be far more difficult than he expected.

He'd been blessed far more than he'd deserved, and had a fair share of miracles, but the good things had come down to fate a lot of the time.

He and Dare had met by chance. He'd only tracked her down because of the meme. Even his first proposal had been spur of the moment, but now that he was no longer being stupid, and both he and Dare knew they were in love, he wanted to do it up right.

He wanted this proposal to be very deliberate. Something that she could look back on and know that he'd put thought and energy into it because she was worth it. A memorable experience for the rest of their lifetime. He was so ready to do this.

Dare was not cooperating.

Not that he expected her to willingly follow his lead when he wouldn't tell her what was going on, but fate was making it impossible to sneak her away without anyone else coming along. And by anyone, he meant Vicki.

Thick as thieves, the two of them. The fact it didn't make his mind hurt was another miracle he'd just accept.

That morning he'd made sure to find out when Vicki was busy at work. Then he'd rearranged *his* work schedule so he could sneak away to have an afternoon coffee with Dare, and finally put into play what he'd been setting up for a while.

Only when he drove into the yard, Vicki's truck was there.

Fine, he wasn't going to even try to be sneaky anymore.

Jesse took the stairs two at a time and pushed into the living room to discover them pouring over something on the computer screen. "Ladies."

Vicki straightened up, grabbed their empty glasses and headed to the kitchen. "Hey, Jesse. I'll be right back, Dare."

Dare attempted to rise to her feet and failed. She rolled her eyes and held out a hand. "Help the pregnant lady. I'm stuck."

He chuckled as he stepped forward and lifted her to her feet. "Hey, did the Buckaroo bump drop about a foot since this morning?"

"You're so observant." She patted him on the cheek a couple of times a little sharper than necessary before offering a real smile. "What are you doing home so early?"

He opened his mouth to tell her he was stealing her away when the sound of tires burning out in the parking area drew their attention to the front window.

Tamara was getting out of her old beater of a truck, marching toward the door as if she had an agenda.

So much for his and Dare's quiet get-together.

The front door opened, and both Jesse's and Dare's phones went off. By the time Tamara was through the door, Vicki's phone was ringing as well, vibrating on the table hard enough it wiggled toward the edge.

Tamara slipped off her boots and left them on the mat. "Twenty bucks says those are from Jaxi or Blake."

Jesse glanced at his phone. "Blake. He wants to know if I've seen you."

His cousin slipped across the room to give Dare a quick hug. "Now you have. Ignore them for a minute.

437

They're probably going ballistic over there trying to figure out what's true and what's rumour."

This didn't sound good. "Tamara, what's up?"

She let out an enormous sigh. "I got fired."

"Oh my God, why?" Dare caught Tamara by the arm as Vicki returned to the room to add her voice to the question.

Tamara opened her mouth and then closed it quickly. "Okay, this is a lot more awkward than I thought it was going to be. I have been accused of violating the patient/doctor confidentiality agreement. Because of that they can fine me, and or fire me, or both."

"Are you going to get a lawyer?" Vicki asked. "Someone to fight the charges?"

Tamara made a face then pushed her glasses firmly into position. "No. Because it's true."

Jesus. Jesse stepped forward. "Tamara, what the hell?"

"Look, it happened a long time ago. I knew what I was doing. I still believe I made the right decision, but they have every right to do this."

"Why did it come out now?" Dare had settled back in the chair, and the rest of them joined her so she didn't have to crane her neck.

"Yeah, that's the part that sucks. Dr. Tom didn't like me, and I'm guessing this is his final *fuck you* gesture, but that doesn't change the truth."

"Then why did you do it, if you knew this could happen?" Vicki asked.

"What happens now?" Jesse added.

Tamara paused before answering.

"Chances are once the rumour mill gets hold of this, and with everyone speculating exactly who I talked about, I'm about to become the town pariah." She shrugged. "Actions have consequences. I'm not about to go and tell everybody why I did it. If people don't know me well enough to assume it was for a good reason, then I don't care about their opinion. Yes, I could've been wrong, I'm not invincible, but I feel as if what I did was better than not doing it."

"So now you're unemployed, but your ego is intact?" Jesse asked.

"My soul — which is more important," she retorted, before making a face. "I need to leave, though."

"What?" All three of them.

"There's no way I can stay. I'm not too proud to get a job at a store in town, but I don't think I can hold my tongue and provide customer service to people who assume the worst."

"Can you get a nursing job somewhere else?" Dare asked.

Tamara hesitated again. "Terms of the agreement. The criminal charges would be dropped if I agreed to give up my license."

"Jesus, Tamara. *Criminal* charges?" This was more serious than a slap on the wrist.

"I know. I'd do it again in a heartbeat — what I did was legally wrong, but it was morally right." She turned to Dare. "The reason I'm here is to ask a favour. You think your brother would hire me as a nanny?"

Dare's eyes widened. "Seriously?"

Tamara nodded. "I can't actively nurse, and I don't want to go back to working on the ranch because that means I'd still be living here. But you were telling me about Emma and her speech issues, and maybe I could help in an unofficial capacity. I like kids, and I'm pretty easy to get along with."

"You'd be working for Caleb. Will that be a problem?"

She shook her head. "If he's not still pissed off at me for getting the jump on him in the hospital."

Vicki leaned forward, curiosity written all over her. "Wait. How come I didn't hear this story before?"

All three of them waved her off.

Dare didn't hesitate. "You'd be perfect. Ginny is already gone, and since I can't be with the girls, I would love to have you there. Caleb is not going to have a problem with it, because I will tell him he can stick his ego up his ass."

Like the air going out of a balloon, tension drained out of Tamara. She collapsed back in the chair, pulling off her glasses to wipe at her eyes before replacing them. "Okay. Now I can breathe again."

Dare was punching in a message on her phone. "How soon do you want to start?"

"I need a couple of days to pack, that's it."

She nodded, hitting send then looking up. "We'll have to wait to hear back from him to make it official, but thank you."

"God. I'm the one who needs to thank you. You're saving my life here," Tamara said.

Jesse hurried forward to help as Dare worked to get to her feet. "Hey, you're a mutual-admiration society."

Dare rested her hands on Tamara's shoulders. "You trusted us enough to come right away. That means a lot."

"You're family." It was all Tamara needed to say.

It was all it took to have tears forming in Dare's eyes. He slipped his arm around her shoulders and squeezed tight, waiting as her phone went off again.

"Message from Caleb?" he asked

She nodded, reading aloud. "If you think it's a good

idea, I trust you. I guess."

Tamara snorted. "It's not the most enthusiastic hiring I've ever had, but I'll take it." She stepped forward and offered Dare a hug. "I'm so glad you're part of this family, and not just because you saved my bacon right now."

Jesse and Vicki both gave Tamara a hug. She took off, leaving a whirl of energy in the room.

Before they got distracted with anything else, Jesse figured it was his chance to nail down Dare.

"There's something I want to show you," he said. "Can you get away for half an hour?"

"Sure." She finished texting Caleb back before offering a smile. "Let me hit the washroom so I don't have to find one wherever you're taking me."

He watched her walk away, his hand slipping into his pocket to reassure himself he still had everything he needed.

He was finally going to do this.

The silence stretched, and he suddenly became aware it was just them in the room — him and Vicki.

They were alone, and he wasn't being overwhelmed with guilt or frustration, and the realization was pretty spectacular.

They spoke at the same time.

"I wanted to — "

"There's something — "

They both stalled out.

Jesse gestured. "Go ahead."

Vicki nodded and rushed onward. "I've wanted to say something for a long time, but kept chickening out. I wanted to tell you that I'm sorry we had a hard time in the beginning, and I'm honestly glad you're back."

He examined her face, but she was staring at him

441

seriously with just the faintest hint of a smile. "You didn't do anything wrong."

Vicki shook her head. "Yes, and no. I needed to grow up a little. I was so skittish when Joel and I started dating that I set us up for disaster with the things I imagined might happen. If I'd been more trusting maybe I could have avoided driving a wedge between you and Joel. So I'm sorry. I really do want what's best for you. And for Dare, and the baby."

Jesse's throat was tight, but he nodded briskly, fighting to swallow so he could speak semi-normally.

Dare had called it. It was time for him to take her advice on the other parts of this situation.

"We're good," he insisted, "if you can forgive me for being a jealous asshole and not treating you right. I'm glad I didn't mess things up between you and Joel — you guys are great together."

She nodded, head bobbing rapidly. "I love him to pieces. And yes, we're good."

Jesse glanced down the hall, but there was no sign of Dare yet. "I never got a chance to mention this before. I appreciate you making Dare feel so welcome right from the start. You didn't have to, especially considering she was with me. I figured if anything you'd have been warning her off."

"What makes you think I didn't?"

Jesse's head snapped back to find Vicki covering her mouth as she fought back laughter. "Did you just *tease* me?"

"Hard to believe, huh?"

It was impossible to describe the emotions swelling inside him. "I liked it. It's feels pretty normal — like family."

Vicki nodded. "Exactly like family."

They grinned at each other like fools, which is how Dare found them as she came to his side and took him by the hand.

He led her out to the truck, ready to make a memory.

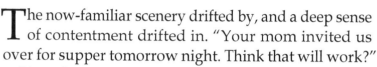

The now-familiar scenery drifted by, and a deep sense of contentment drifted in. "Your mom invited us over for supper tomorrow night. Think that will work?"

"Sure."

Dare tangled her fingers in his. "I think Tamara will be good for the girls. Emma will like her."

Jesse snickered. "Sasha will let us know."

Was it wrong to ask the question? She went for it anyway. "I didn't want to ask because I'm just curious, like Tamara said, I don't need to know the details. I trust her, but…"

"Do I know what she did?" Jesse hesitated. "She said it happened a while ago."

"Couple of years."

He shook his head. "I'm not sure. A few years ago I wasn't paying a lot of attention to the world around me."

Dare stroked his fingers. "I trust her, though."

"Me too. She'll be great for the girls. That Dr. Tom is an asshole," Jesse snarled. "The only reason he's dragging this up is because his ego got hurt."

"Sounds as if his ego is bigger than anything else."

A laugh burst from Jesse before he grew serious again. "Yeah. Still sucks for Tamara. Having to leave Rocky."

She knew what he was saying, but then, there was another side to consider as well. "I've left Heart Falls and Silver Stone, and it's turned out okay so far. Maybe this is the first step on Tamara's journey to a new home."

He nodded, then turned off the highway and took them down a dirt road that led into the depths of Six Pack land.

Dare looked around with interest as he pointed in different directions and named the landmarks. West toward Angel and Whiskey Creek land. Southwest to Moonshine, and beyond that to the mysterious Uncle Mark's section.

When he stopped beside a lone tree on the hilltop, she waited in the truck for him to come to her door.

"I'm a little pregnant for a hike in the snow," she warned as he helped her to the ground and took her by the arm.

"It's all melted," he promised. "Just need you to come round the corner here."

He led her to the base of the old tree. The thing was a behemoth, with gnarled branches and a sturdy base. A weatherworn heart was carved in the trunk, with Vicki's and Joel's names in it, and she had to smile. She traced a finger around the edges. "That's sweet."

Jesse looked thoughtful for a moment. "You were right, by the way. About Vicki and Joel. We're good, once I got my head out of my ass."

"I do like you un-assholed," Dare teased.

He arranged her so she could lean comfortably on the trunk before placing one hand on the tree beside her to turn himself into a wind block.

Then he stared at her face. His expression so clear and readable. He was baring himself to her — ready to give her nothing but the truth.

"For a lot of years I struggled with where I fit in. I

was never alone, yet I was too damn cocky to admit that I was lonely. Just because I was surrounded by people didn't mean I was connected to them." He stroked her cheek. "I know a lot of that had to do with how I was acting. I shouldn't have expected people to want to cuddle up with a hedgehog."

She didn't speak but she nodded.

"I don't feel alone anymore," he declared.

"I'm glad that you're back with your family. That you and Joel are good friends again." It was easy to be happy for him. A little as if she'd been waiting for the rain to stop falling, and their patience had been rewarded when a beautiful rainbow appeared.

He cupped her chin in his fingers. "It's not just them. I mean, I love them, and I'm glad to be back and accepted, and I'm never going to be so foolish to throw all that away again, but it's not enough."

She didn't understand. "How can it not be enough?"

Jesse took a deep breath "I can't do this without you."

"Do what?"

"*Anything*. I'm nothing without you, Dare. Even with all of my family's love and support, you made the biggest difference. You're the one who, in spite of everything I did wrong, kept seeing the good in me. The good things I could do if I stopped doubting *and* stopped thinking about myself, and started putting myself out for others."

Her throat grew tight at the emotion in his eyes, and the seriousness of what he was sharing.

"I wouldn't have seen it if it wasn't there," she insisted.

"Maybe." He leaned in and brushed his lips over hers. "Or maybe it's there, because like a seed with the potential, you're the one who helped it grow."

445

She was about to reassure him that he was a good man when he went down on one knee in front of her, and her heart leapt into her throat.

His grin was back. That one-hundred-percent cocky-bastard, sexy as sin, flirtatious, irritating and addictive Jesse who'd won her heart from the first moment he'd walked into the bar.

He caught her hand in his. "Darilyn Hayes, soon to become Buckaroo's mom. As much as I love that you're carrying my baby, that's *not* why I want to marry you. I want to marry you because you own my fucking heart. I want you in my life because I love you until I'm stupid with it, and I need you to say *yes* so that no matter where we are, I'll always be home."

Every part of her from her toes to the top of her head was ready to shout. "You love Buckaroo?"

He leaned in close, talking to her stomach. "She's talking about you, kid. I think she's avoiding the question, but to get this straight, yes. I love you. Boy or girl, I don't give a damn. I'm going to count your toes and fingers, and kiss every one of them, and tell you every day that I love you, even when you're driving me around the bend."

Dare fought back the tears that threatened to fall.

Jesse wasn't finished. He rubbed his hand over her in a gentle caress. "You just be quiet for a bit, though. Your mama is ignoring a very important question, and I need to give her my full attention."

As if in answer, Buckaroo shifted position, the motion rolling the surface of her belly.

Jesse laughed, kissing her bump before looking up at her with laughter in his eyes.

She dragged in a shaky breath. "If I wasn't already in

love with you, that would have sent me over the edge."

"Kissing your belly?"

"Talking to our baby like he understands every word you're saying."

"Buckaroo's smart. Like you said, *our* baby." Jesse rose to his feet and curled a hand behind her neck. "I mean it, Dare. I swear as long as I've got breath in my body, I'll be there for you. I'd wrestle death to keep you safe."

She was going to be a blubbering mess if he kept this up. "*Jesse...*"

He kissed her, lips so soft and tender against hers before pulling back just far enough to give her a saucy wink. "I didn't hear a *yes* yet from those sweet lips of yours. You gonna marry me for all the right reasons?"

"Where's the fun in that?" Dare teased.

Bright laughter rumbled up from deep in his chest. "You're trouble today."

"Today and every day, isn't that how you like me?"

He leaned closer. "Say *yes*."

"But I want to marry you for the sex."

Jesse laughed out loud then touched their foreheads together. "Tell me *yes*, woman."

Dare cupped his face in her hands. She spoke from the depths of her heart, and the only words she had to say, pretty much said it all. "I love you."

"I know." He winked at her indelicate snort. "*Dare*."

No more holding back. No more teasing, because the truth poured out of her heart and very soul. "Yes. Yes, I'll marry you. Not because Buckaroo needs a daddy, and not because your family is so damn awesome. Not because marrying you means I get to be around Vicki and Joel, who fit into my world and my heart very nicely, thank you."

He waited, love written all over his face.

She reached up on her tiptoes and whispered against his lips. "*Yes*, because you're home to me too."

Chapter Thirty

They didn't make it back to the rental.

They didn't even make it to the *truck* before Dare swore.

Jesse had a hand around her waist, and he didn't think she'd slipped. "Did you twist your ankle?"

"No." She glanced up, eyes wide. "I think you need to take me to the hospital."

"*Now?*"

Dare nodded, then made a terrible face. "Oh, *hell*. Okay, this is not going to be fun."

He didn't bother to try and change her mind. Just got her into the truck and drove at slightly slower speeds than their trip that summer.

Dare made a few calls then tucked her phone away. "Wait. Stop at Tim Hortons," she ordered.

"Seriously?"

"You can use the drive-through. I haven't had supper yet, and if this ends up being a marathon, I'm not eating that damn hospital food. We'll bring a box of Timbits for Dr. Kincaid."

Jesse laughed, glancing over in concern as she puffed through a contraction. "So this is really happening."

She linked her finger through his and offered a slightly scared smile. "It really is."

In spite of her worries about a marathon, everything

from that moment forward turned into a blur. He got them safely into town, grabbed Dare's requested sandwich and doughnuts, and they were pacing the halls outside the maternity room in a blink of an eye.

Fine, it took a lot longer than that in reality, but he couldn't pull the individual moments out. Just snapshots of time that registered hard enough Jesse knew he'd never forget them.

Like Dare focusing on his face as she relaxed through the last of the contractions. Her eyes fixed on his, anchoring herself in him.

The endless moment that passed between Buckaroo being a bump-maker and suddenly being *there*. A living, squirming, crying baby.

The light in Dare's eyes as the doctor laid their son in her arms — *a son* — and she blinked back tears. Hell, Jesse wasn't too dry-eyed himself at that moment.

In the moment of calm before the rest of the Colemans began to arrive, Jesse wrapped his arm around the woman he loved. He pressed a kiss to the baby's forehead. "Hey, Buckaroo. It's good to finally meet you."

"He's beautiful," Dare whispered.

"He is, but you're even more beautiful." He brushed a stray hair behind her ear. "Thank you for making our son."

Dare tilted her head, smile going watery. "Don't make me cry."

"I'm not," he protested. "I mean it. You did amazing."

She leaned into his side, and they stared at the baby's little scrunched-up face for a bit. Jesse traced a finger over the teeny brow and wondered how the sound of his own heart wasn't echoing off the walls, it was pumping so hard.

"He looks like a Coleman," Dare said.

Jesse chuckled. "I'll take your word on it."

Then he kissed her, one arm curled protectively around both her and the baby, because there was no way he could separate himself from them right then. He stared down at his family in amazed wonder and knew he was never going to feel alone again.

Joel and Vicki were the first to arrive, while Jesse was still reeling at the little bit of humanity in his arms.

Vicki hugged Dare then stood impatiently beside Jesse, waiting for her turn to hold the baby. "Sweet thing. What's his name?"

"Joseph Michael. After both our dads," Dare shared. "We plan on calling him Joey."

Jesse looked up into his brother's pleased expression. "That's as close as we could get without making you do double-takes every time we call his name."

Joel gave Jesse a hug then gazed down in approval. "I like it." He reached for Joey's hand, letting little fingers curl around his. "Hey, big guy. I'm your Uncle Joel. I'm the cool uncle, got it?"

"Take a picture of them, please?" Dare asked Vicki.

Vicki nodded, snapping a couple before bringing the phone over to show her. "Like them?"

Dare's eyes filled with tears. "They're perfect. Thank you." Then she motioned toward Jesse. "Go show him."

"I can email it to you," Vicki offered.

"No," Dare ordered. "Jesse, you've got to look, *now.*"

There wasn't much that Jesse wouldn't do for her any time, let alone after the past few hours. But when Vicki held the phone in front of him, Jesse's heart picked up a pace. Dare wasn't just being sentimental.

"You see it, don't you?" Dare's voice was filled

with love.

He cradled his son carefully as he made his way back to her side. "You're amazing."

"You've got *the look*," she insisted.

It was humbling for Jesse to realize how much this woman meant to him. Being with Dare was the best gift ever, and every day it kept getting better. Even tired as she was from bringing their son into the world, even now she was making sure *he* was happy and cared for.

To point out a fear he'd had could be wiped clear. He *was* proud to be a daddy. He didn't deserve either of them, but hell if he was ever going to give them up.

He looked down at the woman he loved, and the little bit of perfection they'd accidentally made and realized all the lonely, broken pieces inside were fixed and better than new. "I love you so damn much, Darilyn Hayes. You are my fucking world. You and Joey."

Then he kissed her. Right there, as the door opened and his parents and other family poured in, he kissed her with everything in him.

Jesse Coleman was home.

Epilogue

It would've been nice if as soon as they'd realized how much they loved each other everything was perfect from that moment on.

Everything hadn't been perfect.

This was her, after all, Dare thought. Stubborn and determined and not ready to be wrapped up and protected like she was made of spun glass.

And *him*. Cocky, arrogant, sexy-as-sin bastard that he was.

Between the two of them, they were both stubborn enough that they fought on a regular basis, sometimes about the stupidest things. But overall they got along great, and when they didn't, making up was always a lot of fun.

Because *that* they always did — made up. Talked. Just straight up were there for each other, and for the family, because this was who they were. Who Jesse had always been, even though he'd gotten a little twisted for a while there.

Dare got frequent updates from Ginny who was having the time of her life trucking all around Europe. A certain Frenchman was described in great detail in one letter before he'd been abandoned for a more charming Italian, although Dare wasn't sure if it was the man or his vineyard that had Ginny's heart pounding faster.

Dare missed her friend, but she was happily distracted with a whole lot of new joys to experience.

Like her first Christmas in Rocky. First Christmas as a *family*.

Coleman tradition said Christmas Eve was for the immediate family, and Christmas Day with the larger clan. Boxing Day was set aside for the entire horde together in the twice a year, no-holds-barred event.

It was incredibly special to spend their first Christmas Eve day with just their little family. Her, Jesse and Joey making the first of many memories as an intimate family.

But she and Vicki had conspired to make a certain change, and when Joel and Vicki showed up on their doorstep for supper, the joy in Jesse's eyes made the small modification to tradition worthwhile.

The next day at the Six Pack gathering, Blake and Jaxi's home was bursting to the seams as children played, babies were passed around, and packages were unwrapped. Dare counted — there was a total of twenty-six bodies for just the Six Pack gathering.

No, make that twenty-six plus *three* because added to Vicki's pregnancy both Ashley and Hope had announced they were expecting again, in August and September the coming year.

Blake casually left a card under the tree letting Jesse know he was back to full rights and responsibilities in the Coleman ranch.

Oh, and the deed to their house.

But her favourite gift was a picture frame that matched the others she'd admired. The cutout image of a tree had been filled with the picture of her, Jesse and Joey, and it was enough to make her want to burst with happiness.

That spring after the calves finished dropping and before seeding was done, she added another regular feature to her blog. *At Home on Sunset Ridge.*

They'd managed to finish all of the main floor living spaces in the two houses, more than enough room for them to move in. Between the two buildings, Jesse and Joel laid a brick patio large enough for children to play on while adults visited, a fire pit to one side. Joel moved the arbour from the trailer, and Dare held Joey in her arms as she watched the twins work together. She grinned mischievously at Jesse as he held the wooden structure in place while Joel leveled it.

"Make it solid," Dare teased. "I wouldn't want anyone to get hurt if it were to accidentally fall over."

"Someone would have to be pushing pretty hard to make this move," Joel said innocently, pulling a snicker from his brother. Joel rolled his eyes as he glanced between the two of them. "Jeez, you guys. Stop it. I don't want to know."

Springtime also brought wedding plans. Dare had discovered something of vital importance that was leading up to one of the biggest memories yet.

After Joey had been tucked into bed. Dare laid a hand on Jesse's knee to get his attention as they relaxed together on the couch. "I have an idea. Say yes."

Jesse smiled at her with amusement. "Yes."

Then he tumbled her into his lap and kissed her thoroughly until her cheeks were flushed and she was gasping for air when he finally let her up.

Or more correctly, let her breathe, because she'd somehow ended up lying flat on her back with him stretched over her. "I wasn't finished talking," she complained.

His grin widened, and his hands moved in wicked ways over her. Teasing. Stroking. "I already said yes."

"You don't even know what you just agreed to."

He shrugged, his gaze drifting down her body. "It's your idea. It's bound to be a good one."

"It's my and Vicki's idea."

Not a single flinch — his smile just got wider. "Even better, because that means Joel will be happy too. Go ahead, tell me what we're doing."

"Hosting two weddings. August fifteenth. Here at Sunset Ridge."

That made him sit up, still holding her fingers as he brought her back to vertical. "A double wedding?"

She nodded. "Turns out Vicki's been putting off their wedding because she didn't want to have their big day without you around. She hoped at some point you and Joel would be friends again so you could be his best man."

Jesse's face tightened for a moment and he swallowed hard. "I really don't deserve my family."

Dare shook her head. "I really think you do, but I agree they're pretty special people. So, what you think? You okay sharing our day with Joel and Vicki?"

He nodded. "That would make it extra special."

The rest of the family thought it was perfect as well. Plans were put in place for the wedding to be held long enough after Vicki's baby arrived for everyone to enjoy themselves.

June rolled around. They hit the middle of the month before Vicki grew exceedingly annoyed. "It's not fair. You were two weeks early. How come I couldn't have that?"

Dare shrugged, catching Joey in mid-wobble as he

made another attempt to walk. "You didn't throw up for three months straight."

Vicki grimaced as she attempted to adjust position, her belly far too big considering her petite size. "Okay, that's true, but at this point I'd be happy to exchange — "

She broke off, her mouth opening in shock.

The guys, who were usually attentive but not excessively so, cued in on the sound or lack thereof like magic.

An instant later Joel was beside Vicki, looking her over frantically. "Sweetheart?"

Her eyes were wide. "I feel funny."

"Funny how?" Joel demanded.

She met Dare's gaze. "I really want to push."

Joel shook his head. "Oh no you don't. We're going to get you up and get you to the hospital — "

Vicki caught his hand in hers and squeezed, teeth gritted together as her breathing increased in pace. "No. We're going to have this baby, *now*."

Which is how, in spite of Joel's demands that she wait for the hospital, Vicki ended up giving birth at home.

Dare acted as coach best she could. Joel caught the baby with Jesse encouraging him along. By the time the ambulance arrived, all the excitement was over.

Jessica Marie was lying in her mama's arms having a snooze while Joel stared in amazement. Joey had fallen asleep in the playpen kept in the living room for when little people visited.

Jesse? Well, he held on to Dare as they sat across the room from the new parents, and he whispered how astonished and proud and crazily-lucky he was to be there. To be with her and get to witness his brother and Vicki's joy.

Family — a growing, sharing experience like Dare had never imagined.

Now, a couple of months later, she put the final touches on today's blog post.

Blog post: Wedding Bell Blues
It's not what you think. You've been listening to me post about pre-wedding jitters for the past six months, and today is finally the day.

I'm not at all nervous anymore.

In fact, the blues *are what's outside the door. After two weeks of clouds, the sky cleared last night. An Alberta bluebird day. For those of you who have never seen it, consider the pictures you've drooled over of a Caribbean ocean, or a pristine glacier-fed lake.*

But most importantly, this blue is the colour I see every day when I look into the eyes of the man I love.

Oh, and about those bells...

The happiness inside was real. Dare glanced out the window of her new home, past the picture frames filled with shots of family from near and far, and offered up a prayer of thanks for all her blessings.

Then she hit publish and went to get ready to say *I do, forever* to the man she loved.

———————————————

Joel fidgeted with Jesse's tie then adjusted the bright blue handkerchief tucked into his suit pocket. They were waiting with their brothers out behind the garden shed. The one tucked away to the back of the open area where the wedding was about to take place.

Midway between their two homes, the sound of laughter rang on the air as family and friends gathered.

Jesse was ready for this. He was *more* than ready for this, which created a happy sensation in his gut.

Dare had done the old-fashioned "refused to be seen" in her wedding get-up route, and he wanted a peek.

After a year together she just got more damn beautiful every day, and he couldn't wait to make her officially his.

Joel, on the other hand, was nowhere near as collected. "Then after the vows we have to sign something. Then we have to — "

"Why're you trying to memorize this?" Jesse demanded. "The justice of the peace will tell us where to go next, and if he doesn't move fast enough, Jaxi will jump in. Poof — instant wedding organization."

His twin nodded. "I know. I'm just... I want to get on with it."

"You ain't the important ones today," Blake pointed out. Their oldest brother leaned against the wall beside the window.

Matt snickered. "Come to think of it, you've never been the important ones."

Jesse adjusted his cuffs, smoothing the sleeves. "Come on. Everyone knows that the farther down the birth order, the more important the kid. Because they were trying for perfection after dealing with you."

A snort escaped Travis. "You got that sideways, bro. The fact they went for it again means *we* were so awesome they were hoping for the same results. Notice they stopped after you two?"

Even Joel mustered a terse chuckle.

"Heads up." Daniel joined them. "Beth says

music starts in under five minutes — the ladies are finally moving.

For one lingering moment there were the six of them. Gathered in a semicircle, tall and solid, and most definitely family. Jesse skipped his gaze over his brothers in turn, solid respect and love for each one of them rising up. Blake — who'd proven he was a man of principle and a man of compassion. Willing to do what was hard to build the strongest family possible, just like their father.

Jesse gazed at Matt and Daniel, each who had settled into happiness in their own way. Travis who had become so much more than a rule-breaker and a wild card.

Then he let his gaze rest on Joel. His brother who was more than family — he was Jesse's best friend again. Better friends than before because Jesse had learned a thing or two regarding how to give a damn about someone other than himself.

Blake stepped forward and placed an arm around his and Joel's shoulders. "We Colemans ain't the prayin' type, but it seems right to say a word of thanks that we're all here. That we get to work together and play together and today — celebrate together. We've pulled through some tough moments, and dealt with our differences, and I think we've come out stronger on the other side. We're lucky we've each found the perfect partners willing to head into the future with us.

"I'm glad we're brothers. I'm glad we're *family*, and I look forward to every damn day from here on, even through the rough times, because you're all with me."

Jesse's throat tightened up, and Joel coughed. Even Travis looked touched.

Music started in the background, but Jesse had to say

it. "You're the best brothers ever. Thanks for putting up with my bullshit and making me grow up. Double thanks from the woman crazy enough to agree to get hitched to me permanently, and from my son, *and* my future kids. We couldn't do this without you."

"Jeez, you want me to be a blubbering fool?" Joel complained, wiping at his eyes before flashing a grin. "Stop procrastinating. It's time."

They accepted a firm pat on the shoulder from Blake then slipped around the corner to where they were expected to stand at the front of the gathering, waiting for Dare and Vicki to arrive.

Jesse caught Joel before they moved to their assigned positions. "That thanks goes extra for you, considering you've put up with more of me being an asshole than anyone else."

Joel shook his hand firmly. "Asshole or not, you're my other half. Love you, jerk."

They grinned at each other, then Jesse took those final steps.

There was no motion from the door of the house yet, so he let his gaze drift over the gathered crowd. Daniel and Beth's boys were seating the guests, Lance all gangly and teenage awkward in a dress shirt and tie, Nathan and Robbie only a little less so, but all of them proud as they guided the last arrivals to their places.

The entire Coleman horde was there, and at each face a memory or two flashed into Jesse's mind. Running wild with his cousins Steve and Trevor from the Moonshine clan. Trying to talk his way out of a speeding ticket or two from Anna. Chatting about horses with Karen from the Whiskey Creek. Time spent with Rafe and Laurel — too many good memories to put them all in a neat little package.

Then there was his family and Dare's.

Hope with a baby belly out to forever with Matt hovering protectively, Colt wiggling in his grasp. Beth and Daniel found their seats, and the boys settled next to them contentedly.

Travis had one arm around Ashley, the other holding bright-eyed, blonde-haired Daisy who happily sang a nonsense baby song while they waited. Cassidy sat beside them, cradling the newest arrival to the clan. Baby River had arrived only a week earlier, with a shocking amount of dark hair and a decidedly Coleman look to his features.

Blake and Jaxi. Mike and Marion. All Dare's brothers and Ginny — the lot of them were seated together in one giant mixed-up batch. Children had been passed around and were being contained on random laps. Emma Stone sat next to Rebecca, Sasha held Lana's hand.

Baby Jessie lay sleeping in Ginny's arms while Joey clung happily to Luke's shoulder. There'd been enough visits between the ranches that even the non-Coleman-looking person was family to their son.

Jesse's cup of happiness overflowed.

Something bumped him from behind, and he glanced down to discover Travis at his heels. "What's up?"

Travis tugged the bottom of Jesse's pant leg. "You had a smudge."

He sounded far too amused, but then the music swelled, and Jesse ignored everything except the vision leaving the house.

Dare and Vicki stopped just shy of the back row of seating, hugging each other fiercely.

There was another joy he might have missed if he

462

hadn't had the good luck to stumble into Dare all those months ago — that the girls loved each other as friends as deeply as they did only made his and Joel's lives better.

They broke apart, each moving to the top of the aisle that led to where he and Joel waited. While he supposed Vicki looked nice, Jesse only had eyes for Dare.

She'd picked a slim dress in a rich blue shade that matched the cloth in his pocket, the fabric clinging to her curves. Her hair was twisted up on top of her head, a few long strands curling down in a way that made him want to take her somewhere private to mess her up.

Neither of the girls had anyone to give them away, and Dare had sweetly but firmly turned down the offer from Caleb. Jesse realized how right this was. This was her, giving herself into his hands to care for, and love and protect.

Her choice, his privilege.

She walked slowly toward him, a smile growing on her lips that teased his senses. A sexy, trusting look meant for him alone.

A smile he was going to spend a lifetime enjoying.

But when he finally took her hand in his, her sweet, sexy expression turned to pure mischief as she pressed something soft against his palm.

He glanced down at his hand in confusion.

A piece of plastic fruit?

"You stole my cherry, now you gotta marry me," Dare said softly.

That was all it took to push him over the edge. Screw protocol.

A low growl escaped as Jesse tugged her close so he could kiss her. Right then and there, as laughter rose from the gathering. Dare smiled against his lips before wrapping her arms around him and kissing back enthusiastically.

They'd get to the wedding eventually.

Another Epilogue

The vows were done, and they kissed again, this time with a little less laughter.

Then the justice of the peace motioned toward the table where there were forms waiting to be signed.

Jesse took a step forward, and something rattled. Bell-like.

He stepped again, and it grew louder, like a Santa at the mall at Christmas.

Dare snickered, glancing at Vicki. "You didn't."

"It wasn't me," Vicki protested, but she was laughing as well.

Jesse lifted a foot and music rang out. Around his boot was a collection of sleigh bells. He checked the other side — yup, another set.

He joined in the laughter, shaking a finger at Travis.

It would be the work of a moment to remove the bells, but when it came down to it, *what the hell*.

He took Dare by the hand and walked forward —

Happily ringing.

New York Times Bestselling Author
Vivian Arend

invites you to meet the Colemans. These contemporary cowboys ranch the foothills of the Alberta Rockies. Enjoy the ride as they each find their happily-ever-afters.

Six Pack Ranch
Rocky Mountain Heat
Rocky Mountain Haven
Rocky Mountain Desire
Rocky Mountain Angel
Rocky Mountain Rebel
Rocky Mountain Freedom
Rocky Mountain Romance
Rocky Mountain Retreat
Rocky Mountain Shelter
Rocky Mountain Devil
Rocky Mountain Home

About the Author

With over 2 million books sold, VIVIAN AREND is a New York Times and USA Today bestselling author of over 50 contemporary and paranormal romance books, including the Six Pack Ranch and Granite Lake Wolves.

Her books are all standalone reads with no cliffhangers. They're humorous yet emotional, with sexy-times and happily-ever-afters. Vivian pretty much thinks she's got the best job in the world, and she's looking forward to giving readers more HEAs. She lives in B.C. Canada with her husband of many years and a fluffy attack Shitzu named Luna who ignores everyone except when treats are deployed.

Made in the USA
San Bernardino, CA
17 July 2017